THE BETTY NEELS COLLECTION

Betty Neels's novels are loved by millions of readers around the world, and this very special *2-in-1 collection* offers a unique opportunity to relive the magic of some of her most popular stories.

We are proud to present these classic romances by the woman who could weave an irresistible tale of love like no other.

So sit back in your comfiest chair with your favorite cup of tea and enjoy these best of Betty Neels stories!

Romance readers around the world were sad to note the passing of **Betty Neels** in June 2001. Her career spanned thirty years, and she continued to write into her ninetieth year. To her millions of fans, Betty epitomized the romance writer, and yet she began writing almost by accident. She had retired from nursing, but her inquiring mind still sought stimulation. Her new career was born when she heard a lady in her local library bemoaning the lack of good romance novels. Betty's first book, *Sister Peters in Amsterdam,* was published in 1969, and she eventually completed 134 books. Her novels offer a reassuring warmth that was very much a part of her own personality, and her spirit and genuine talent live on in all her stories.

BETTY NEELS

Dearest Mary Jane

and

The Daughter of the Manor

H HARLEQUIN® BESTSELLERS

Recycling programs
for this product may
not exist in your area.

ISBN-13: 978-0-373-60596-5

DEAREST MARY JANE AND THE DAUGHTER OF THE MANOR
Copyright © 2014 by Harlequin Books S.A.

The publisher acknowledges the copyright holders
of the individual works as follows:

DEAREST MARY JANE
Copyright © 1994 by Betty Neels

THE DAUGHTER OF THE MANOR
Copyright © 1997 by Betty Neels

Printed in U.S.A.

CONTENTS

Dearest Mary Jane

CHAPTER ONE

IT WAS FIVE o'clock and the warm hazy sunshine of a September afternoon was dwindling into the evening's coolness. The Misses Potter, sitting at a table in the window of the tea-shop, put down their teacups reluctantly and prepared to leave. Miss Emily, the elder of the two ladies, rammed her sensible hat more firmly on her head and addressed the girl sitting behind the tiny counter at the back of the room.

'If we might have our bill, Mary Jane?'

The girl came to the table and the two ladies looked at her, wondering, as they frequently did, how whoever had chosen the girl's name could have guessed how aptly it fitted. She looked like a Mary Jane, not tall, a little too thin, with an unremarkable face and light brown hair, straight and long and pinned in an untidy swirl on top of her head. Only when she looked at you the violet eyes, fringed with long curling lashes, made one forget her prosaic person.

She said now in her quiet voice, 'I hope you enjoyed your tea. In another week or two I'll start making teacakes.'

Her customers nodded in unison. 'We shall look forward to that.' Miss Emily opened her purse. 'We mustn't keep you, it's closing time.' She put money on the table and Mary Jane opened the door and waited until they were across the village street before closing it.

She cleared the table, carried everything into the small kitchen behind the tea-room and went to turn the notice to 'Closed' on the door just as a car drew up outside. The door was thrust open before she had time to turn the key and a man came in. He was massively built and tall, so that the small room became even smaller.

'Good,' he said briskly. 'You're not closed. My companion would like tea…'

'But I am closed,' said Mary Jane in a reasonable voice. 'I'm just locking the door, only you pushed it open. You are not very far from Stow-on-the-Wold—there are several hotels there, you'll get tea quite easily.'

The man spoke evenly, rather as though he were addressing a child or someone hard of hearing. 'My companion doesn't wish to wait any longer. A pot of tea is all I am asking for; surely that isn't too much?'

He sounded like a man who liked his own way and got it, but Mary Jane had a lot to do before she could go to her bed; besides, she disliked being browbeaten. 'I'm sorry…'

She was interrupted by the girl who swept into the tea-room. No, not a girl, decided Mary Jane, a woman in her thirties and beautiful, although her looks were marred by her frown and tight mouth.

'Where's my tea?' she demanded. 'Good lord, Thomas, all I want is a cup of tea. Is that too much to ask for? What is this dump, anyway?' She flung herself gracefully into one of the little cane chairs. 'I suppose it will be undrinkable tea-bags, but if there's nothing else…'

Mary Jane gave the man an icy violet stare. 'I do have drinkable tea-bags,' she told him, 'but perhaps the lady would prefer Earl Grey or Orange Pekoe?'

'Earl Grey,' snapped the woman, 'and I hope I shan't have to wait too long.'

'Just while the kettle boils,' said Mary Jane in a dangerously gentle voice.

She went into the kitchen and laid a tray and made the tea and carried it to the table and was very surprised when the man got up and took the tray from her.

In the kitchen she started clearing up. There would be a batch of scones to make after she had had her supper and the sugar bowls to fill and the jam dishes to see to as well as the pastry to make ready for the sausage rolls she served during the lunch-hour. She was putting the last of the crockery away when the man came to the doorway. 'The bill?' he asked.

She went behind the counter and made it out and handed it silently to him, and the woman called across, 'I imagine there is no ladies' room here?'

Mary Jane paused in counting change. 'No.' She added deliberately, 'The public lavatories are on the other side of the village square on the road to Moreton.'

The man bit off a laugh and then said with cool politeness, 'Thank you for giving us tea.' He ushered his companion out of the door, turning as he did so to turn the notice to 'Closed'.

Mary Jane watched him drive away. It was a nice car—a dark blue Rolls-Royce. There was a lonely stretch of road before they reached Stow-on-the-Wold, and she hoped they would run out of petrol. It was unlikely, though, he didn't strike her as that kind of man.

She locked the door, tidied the small room with its four tables and went through to the kitchen, where she washed the last of the tea things, put her supper in the oven and went up the narrow staircase tucked away behind a door by the dresser. Upstairs, she went first to her bedroom, a low-ceilinged room with a latticed window overlooking the back garden and furnished rather sparsely. The curtains were pretty, however, as was the bedspread and there were flowers in a bowl on the old-fashioned dressing-table. She tidied herself without wasting too much time about it, and crossed the tiny landing to the living-room at the front of the cottage. Quite a large room since it was over the tea-room, and furnished as sparsely as the bedroom. There were flowers here too, and a small gas fire in the tiled grate, which she lighted before switching on a reading lamp by the small armchair, so that the room looked welcoming. That done, she went downstairs again to open the kitchen door to allow Brimble, her cat, to come in—a handsome tabby who, despite his cat-flap, preferred to come in and out like anyone else. He wreathed himself round her legs now, wanting his supper and, when she had fed him, went upstairs to lie before the gas fire.

Mary Jane took the shepherd's pie out of the oven, laid the table under the kitchen window and sat down to eat her supper, listening with half an ear to the last of the six o'clock news while she planned her baking for the next day. The bus went into Stow-on-the-Wold on Fridays, returning around four o'clock, and those passengers who lived on the outskirts of the village frequently came in for a pot of tea before they set off for home.

She finished the pie and ate an apple, cleared the table and got out her pastry board and rolling pin. Scones were easy to make and were always popular. She did two batches and then saw to the sausage rolls before going into the tea-room to count the day's takings. Hardly a fortune; she just about paid her way but there was nothing over for holidays or new clothes, though the cottage was hers...

Uncle Matthew had left it to her when he had died two years previously. He had been her guardian ever since her own parents had been killed in their car. She and Felicity, who was older than she was, had been schoolgirls and their uncle and aunt had given them a home and educated them. Felicity, with more than her fair share of good looks, had taken herself off to London as soon as she had left school and had become a successful model, while Mary Jane had stayed at home to run the house for an ailing aunt and an uncle who, although kind, didn't bother with her overmuch. When her aunt had died she had stayed on, looking after him and the house, trying not to think about the future and the years flying by. She had been almost twenty-three when her uncle died and, to her astonished delight, left her the cottage he had owned in the village and five hundred pounds. She had moved into it from his large house at the other end of the village as soon as she could, for Uncle Matthew's heir had disliked her on sight and so had his wife...

She had spent some of the money on second-hand furniture and then, since she had no skills other than that of a good cook, she had opened the tea-room. She was known and liked in the village, which was a help, and after a few uncertain months she was making just enough to live on and pay the bills. Felicity had been to see her, amused at the whole set-up but offering no help. 'You always were the domestic type,' she had observed laughingly. 'I'd die if I had to spend my days here, you know. I'm going to the Caribbean to do some modelling next week—don't you wish you were me?'

Mary Jane had considered the question. 'No, not really,' she said finally. 'I do hope you have a lovely time.'

'I intend to, though the moment I set eyes on a handsome rich man I shall marry him.' She gave Mary Jane a friendly pat on the shoulder. 'Not much hope of that happening to you, darling.'

Mary Jane had agreed pleasantly, reflecting that just to set eyes on a man who hadn't lived all his life in the village and was either married or about to be married would be nice.

She remembered that now as she took the last lot of sausage rolls out of the oven. She had certainly met a man that very afternoon and, unless he had borrowed that car, he was at least comfortably off and handsome to boot. A pity that they hadn't fallen in love with each other at first sight, the way characters did in books. Rather the reverse: he had shown no desire to meet her again and she hadn't liked him. She cleared up once more and went upstairs to sit with Brimble by the fire and presently she went to bed.

It was exactly a week later when Miss Emily Potter came into the shop at the unusual hour—for her—of eleven o'clock in the morning.

Beyond an elderly couple and a young man on a motorbike in a great hurry, Mary Jane had had no customers, which was a good thing, for Miss Emily was extremely agitated.

'I did not know which way to turn,' she began breathlessly, 'and then I thought of you, Mary Jane. Mrs Stokes is away, you know, and Miss Kemble over at the rectory has the young mothers' and toddlers' coffee-morning. The taxi is due in a short time and dear Mabel is quite overwrought.'

Mary Jane saw that she would have to get to the heart

of the matter quickly before Miss Emily became distraught as well. 'Why?'

Miss Potter gave her a startled look. 'She has to see this specialist—her hip, you know. Dr Fellows made the appointment but now she is most unwilling to go. So unfortunate, for this specialist comes very rarely to Cheltenham and the appointment is for two o'clock and I cannot possibly go with her, Didums is poorly and cannot be left...'

'You would like me to have Didums?' asked Mary Jane and sighed inwardly. Didums was a particularly awkward pug dog with a will of her own; Brimble wouldn't like her at all.

'No, no—dear Didums would never go with anyone but myself or my sister. If you would go with Mabel?' Miss Potter gazed rather wildly around the tea-room. 'There's no one here; you could close for an hour or two.'

Mary Jane forbore from pointing out that although there was no one there at the moment, any minute now the place might be filled with people demanding coffee and biscuits. It wasn't likely but there was always a chance. 'When would we get back?' she asked cautiously.

'Well, if the appointment is for two o'clock I don't suppose she will be very long, do you? I'm sure you should be back by four o'clock...'

Miss Potter wrung her hands. 'Oh, dear, I have no idea what to do.'

The taxi would take something over half an hour to get to the hospital. Mary Jane supposed that they would need to get there with half an hour to spare.

'I believe that there is a very good place in the hospital where you can get coffee—dear Mabel will need refreshment.'

Mary Jane thought that after a ride in the taxi with the overwrought Miss Mabel Potter she might be in need of refreshment herself. She said in her calm way, 'I'll be over in half an hour or so, Miss Potter. There's still plenty of time.'

A tearfully grateful Miss Potter went on her way. Mary Jane closed the tea-room, changed into a blouse and skirt and a cardigan, drank a cup of coffee and ate a scone, made sure that Brimble was cosily asleep on the end of her bed and walked across the village square and along the narrow country lane which led to the Misses Potter's cottage. It was called a cottage but, in fact, it was a rather nice house built of Cotswold stone and much too large for them. They had been born there and intended to live out their lives there, even though they were forced to do so as economically as possible. Mary Jane went up the garden path, rang the bell and was admitted by Miss Emily and led to the drawing-room, where Miss Mabel sat surrounded by furniture which had been there before she was born and which neither she nor her sister would dream of changing.

Mary Jane sat down on a nice little Victorian button-back chair and embarked on a cheerful conversation. It was rather like talking to someone condemned to the guillotine; Miss Mabel bore the appearance of someone whose last moment had come. It was a relief when the taxi arrived and the cheerful conversation was scrapped for urgent persuasions to get in.

They were half an hour too early for their appoint-ment, which was a mistake, for the orthopaedic clinic, although it had started punctually, was already run-ning late. It was going on for three o'clock by the time the severe-looking sister called Miss Potter's name and by then she was in such a nervous state that Mary Jane had a job getting her on to her feet and into the consulting-room.

The consultant sitting behind the desk got up and shook Miss Potter's nerveless hand—the man who had demanded tea for his tiresome companion. Mary Jane, never one to think before she spoke, said chattily, 'Oh, hello—it's you—fancy seeing you here.'

She received a look from icy blue eyes in which there was no hint of recollection, although his 'Good afternoon' was uttered with detached civility and she blushed, something she did far too easily however much she tried not to. The stern-faced sister took no notice. She said briskly, 'You had better stay with Miss Potter, she seems nervous.'

Mary Jane sat herself down in a corner of the room where Miss Potter could see her and watched the man wheedle that lady's complaints and symptoms out of her. He did it very kindly and without any sign of impatience, even when Miss Potter sidetracked to explain about the marmalade which hadn't jelled because she had felt poorly and hadn't given it her full attention. A nasty, arrogant man, Mary Jane decided, but he had his good points. She had thought about him once or twice of course, and with a touch of wistfulness, for handsome giants who drove Rolls-Royce motor cars weren't exactly thick on the ground in her part of the world, but she hadn't expected to see him again. She wondered about his beautiful companion and was roused from her thoughts by Sister leading Miss Mabel away to a curtained-off corner to be examined.

The man took no notice of Mary Jane but wrote

steadily and very fast until Sister came to tell him that his patient was ready.

He disappeared behind the curtain and Mary Jane, bored with sitting still and sure that he would be at least ten minutes, got up and went over to the desk and peered down at the notes he had been writing. She wasn't surprised that she could hardly make head or tail of it, for he had been writing fast, but presently she began to make sense of it. There were some rough diagrams too, with arrows pointing in all directions and what looked like Latin. It was a pity that no one had seen to it that he wrote a legible hand when he was a schoolboy.

His voice, gently enquiring as to whether she was interested in orthopaedics, sent her whirling round to bump into his waistcoat.

'Yes—no, that is…' She had gone scarlet again. 'Your writing is quite unreadable,' she finished.

'Yes? But as long as I can read it…you're a nosy young woman.'

'The patients' charter,' said Mary Jane, never at a loss for a word. He gave rather a nasty laugh.

'And a busybody as well,' he observed.

He sat down at his desk again and started to write once more and she went back to her chair and watched him. About thirty-five, she supposed, with brown hair already grizzled at the sides, and the kind of commanding nose he could look down. A firm mouth and a strong chin. She supposed that he could be quite nice when he smiled. He was dressed with understated elegance, the kind which cost a great deal of money, and she wondered what his name was. Not that it mattered, she reminded herself, as Miss Mabel came from behind the curtain, fully dressed even to her hat and gloves.

He got up as she came towards him and Mary Jane

liked him for that, and for the manner in which he broke the news to his patient that an operation on her hip would relieve her of pain and disability.

He turned to Mary Jane. 'You are a relation of Miss Potter?' His tone was politely impersonal.

'Me? No. Just someone in the village. Miss Potter's sister couldn't come because of Didums…' His raised eyebrows forced her to explain. 'Their dog—she's not very well, the vet said…' She stopped. It was obvious that he didn't want to know what the vet had said.

'Perhaps you could ask Miss Potter's sister to ring the hospital and she will be told what arrangements will be made to admit her sister.'

He addressed himself to Miss Mabel once more, got to his feet to bid her goodbye, nodding at Mary Jane and Sister ushered them out into the waiting-room again.

'What is his name?' asked Mary Jane.

Sister had her hand on the next case sheets. She gave Mary Jane a frosty look. 'If you mean the consultant you have just seen, his name is Sir Thomas Latimer. Miss Potter is extremely lucky that he will take her as a patient.' She added impressively, 'He is famous in his field.'

'Oh, good.' Mary Jane gave Sister a sunny smile and guided Miss Mabel out of the hospital and into the forecourt, where the taxi was parked.

The return journey was entirely taken up with Miss Mabel's rather muddled version of her examination, the driver's rather lurid account of his wife's varicose veins and their treatment and Mary Jane doing her best to guide the conversation into neutral topics.

It took some time to explain everything once they had reached the cottage. Mary Jane's sensible account interlarded with Miss Mabel's flights of fancy, but pres-

ently she was able to wish them goodbye and go home.
Brimble was waiting for her, wanting his tea and company. She fed him, made a pot of tea for herself and,
since it was almost five o'clock by now, she made no
attempt to open the tea-room. She locked up and went
upstairs and sat down by the gas fire with Brimble on
her lap, thinking of Sir Thomas Latimer.

Nothing happened for several days; the fine weather
held and Mary Jane reaped a better harvest than usual
from motorists making the best of the last of summer.
She had seen nothing of the Misses Potter but she hadn't
expected to; they came once a week, as regular as clock-
work, on a Thursday to draw their pensions and indulge
themselves with tea and scones, so she looked up in
surprise when they came into the tea-room at eleven
o'clock in the morning, two days early.

'We have had a letter,' observed Miss Emily, 'which
we should like you to read, Mary Jane, since it concerns
you. And since we are here, I think that we might indulge ourselves with a cup of your excellent coffee.'

Mary Jane poured the coffee and took the letter she
was offered. It was very clearly worded: Miss Mabel
was to present herself at the hospital in four days' time
so that the operation found necessary by Sir Thomas
Latimer might be carried out. Mary Jane skimmed over
the bit about bringing a nightgown and toiletries and
slowed at the next paragraph. It was considered advis-
able, in view of Miss Mabel's nervous disposition, that
the young lady who had accompanied her on her previous visit should do so again so that Miss Potter might
be reassured by her company.

'Well, I never,' said Mary Jane and gave the letter
back.

'You will do this?' asked Miss Emily in a voice

which expected Mary Jane to say yes. 'Most fortunately, you have few customers at this time of year, and an hour or so away will do you no great harm.'

Mary Jane forbore from pointing out that with the fine weather she could reasonably expect enough coffee and tea drinkers, not to mention scone eaters, to make it well worth her while to stay open from nine o'clock until five o'clock. The good weather wouldn't last and business was slack during the winter months. However, she liked the Misses Potter.

'Three o'clock,' she said. 'That means leaving here some time after two o'clock, doesn't it? Yes, of course I'll go and see Miss Mabel safely settled in.'

The ladies looked so relieved that she refilled their cups and didn't charge them for it. 'I hope,' commented Miss Emily, 'that Didums will be well enough for me to leave her so that I may visit Mabel. I do not know how long she will be in the hospital.'

'I'll try and find out for you.' The tea-room door opened and four people came in and she left them to their coffee while she attended to her new customers: two elderly couples who ate a gratifying number of scones and ordered a pot of coffee. Mary Jane took it as a sign that obliging the Misses Potter when she really hadn't wanted to would be rewarded by more customers than usual and more money in the till.

Indeed, it seemed that that was the case; she was kept nicely busy for the next few days so that she turned the 'Open' notice to 'Closed' with reluctance. It was another lovely day, and more people than usual had come in for coffee and if today was anything like yesterday she could have filled the little tea-room for most of the afternoon...

Miss Mabel wore an air of stunned resignation, getting into the taxi without needing to be coaxed, and Mary Jane's warm heart was wrung by the unhappiness on her companion's face. She strove to find cheerful topics of conversation, chattering away in a manner most unusual for her so that by the time they reached the hospital her tongue was cleaving to the roof of her mouth. At least there was no delay; they were taken at once to the ward and Miss Potter was invited to undress and get into bed while Mary Jane recited necessary information to the ward clerk, a jolly, friendly woman who gave her a leaflet about visiting and telephoning and information as to where the canteen was. 'Sister will be coming along in a minute; you might like a word with her.'

Mary Jane went back to Miss Potter's cubicle and found that lady was lying in bed, looking pale, although she mustered a smile.

'Sister's coming to see you in a minute,' said Mary Jane. 'I'll take your clothes back with me, shall I, and bring them again when you're getting up?' She cocked an ear at the sound of feet coming down the ward. 'Here's Sister.'

It was Sir Thomas Latimer as well, in a long white coat, his hands in his trouser pockets. He wished Miss Potter a cheerful good afternoon, gave Mary Jane a cool stare and addressed himself to his patient.

He had a lovely bedside manner, Mary Jane reflected, soothing and friendly and yet conveying the firm impression that whatever he said or did would be right. Mary Jane watched Miss Potter relax, even smile a little, and edged towards the curtains; if he was going to examine his patient he wouldn't want her there.

'Stay,' he told her without turning his head.

She very much wanted to say 'I shan't,' but Miss

Potter's precarious calm must not be disturbed. She gave the back of his head a look to pierce his skull and stayed where she was.

She had had a busy day and she was a little tired. She eased herself from one foot to the other and wished she could be like Sister, standing on the other side of the bed. A handsome woman, still young and obviously highly efficient. She and Sir Thomas exchanged brief remarks from time to time, none of which made sense to her, not that they were meant to. She stifled a yawn, smiled at Miss Potter and eased a foot out of a shoe.

Sister might be efficient, she was kind too; Miss Potter was getting more and more cheerful by the minute, and when Sir Thomas finally finished and sat down on her side of the bed she smiled, properly this time, and took the hand he offered her, listening to his reassuring voice. It was when he said, 'Now I think we might let Miss…?' that he turned to look at Mary Jane.

'Seymour,' she told him frostily, cramming her foot back into its shoe.

His eyes went from her face to her feet, his face expressionless.

'Miss Potter may be visited the day after tomorrow. Her sister is free to telephone whenever she wishes to. I shall operate tomorrow morning at eight o'clock. Miss Potter should be back in her bed well before noon.' He added, 'You are on the telephone?'

'Me? No. We use the post office and Miss Kemble at the rectory will take a message. Everyone knows the Misses Potter. I've given the ward clerk several numbers she can ring. But someone will phone at noon tomorrow.'

He nodded, smiled very kindly at his patient and went away with Sister as a young nurse took their place.

The promise of a cup of tea made Mary Jane's departure easier. She kissed the elderly cheek. 'We'll all be in to see you,' she promised, and took herself off to find the taxi and its patient driver.

By the time they were back in the village and she had explained everything to Miss Emily it was far too late to open the tea-room. She made herself a pot of tea, fed Brimble, and padded around in her stockinged feet getting everything ready for the batch of scones she still had to make ready for the next day. While she did it she thought about Sir Thomas.

The operation was a success; the entire village knew about it and, since they foregathered in Mary Jane's tea-room to discuss it, she was kept busy with pots of tea and coffee. Miss Kemble, being the rector's sister, offered to drive to the hospital on the following day. 'The car will take four—you will come of course, Miss Emily, and Mrs Stokes, how fortunate that she is back— and of course my brother.'

Miss Emily put down her cup. 'It would be nice if Mary Jane could come too....'

'Another day,' said Miss Kemble bossily. 'Besides, who is to look after Didums? You know she is good with Mary Jane.'

So it was agreed and the next day, encouraged by Sister's report that Miss Mabel had had a good night, they set off. Mary Jane watched them go holding a pee-vish Didums under one arm. She took the dog up to the sitting-room presently and closed the door, thankful that Brimble was taking a nap on her bed and hadn't noticed anything. She would have liked to have visited Miss Mabel and now she would have to wait until she could find someone who would give her a lift into Cheltenham.

As it turned out, she didn't have to wait long; Mrs Fellowes popped in for a cup of tea and wanted to know why Mary Jane hadn't gone with the others. 'That's too bad,' she declared, 'but not to worry. I'm driving the doctor to Cheltenham on Sunday—about three o'clock, we'll give you a lift in, only we shan't be coming back. Do you suppose you can get back here? There's a bus leaves Cheltenham for Stratford-upon-Avon, so you could get to Broadway...' She frowned. 'It's a long way round, but I'm sure there's an evening bus to Stow-on-the-Wold from there.'

Mary Jane said recklessly, 'Thank you very much, I'd like a lift. I'm sure I can get a bus home. I'll have a look at the timetable in the post office.'

It was going to be an awkward, roundabout journey home and it would depend on her getting on to the bus in Cheltenham. She would have to keep a sharp eye on the time; the bus depot was some way from the hospital. All the same she would go. She wrote a postcard telling Miss Mabel that she would see her on Sunday afternoon and put it in the letterbox before she could have second, more prudent thoughts.

Miss Emily, coming to collect Didums, had a great deal to say. Her sister was doing well, Sister had said, and she was to get out of bed on the following day. 'Modern surgery,' observed Miss Potter with a shake of the head. 'In my youth we stayed in bed for weeks. That nice man—he operated; Sir someone—came to see her while I was there and told me that the operation had been most successful and that dear Mabel would greatly benefit from it. Nice manners, too.'

Mary Jane muttered under her breath and offered Miss Potter a cup of tea.

She was quite busy for the rest of that week, so that

she felt justified on Sunday in taking enough money from the till to cover her journey back home. If the worst came to the worst she could have a taxi; it would mean going without new winter boots, but she liked Miss Mabel.

She usually stayed open for part of Sunday, for that was when motorists tended to stop for tea, but she locked up after lunch, made sure that Brimble was safely indoors and walked through the village to the doctor's house.

Miss Mabel was delighted to see her; she seemed to have taken on a new lease of life since her operation and she insisted on telling Mary Jane every single detail of the treatment. She had got to the momentous moment when she had been out of bed when there was a slight stir in the ward. Sir Thomas Latimer was coming towards them, indeed, he appeared to be about to pass them when he stopped at Miss Mabel's bed.

On his bi-weekly round he had seen Mary Jane's postcard on Miss Mabel's locker and, without quite knowing why, he had decided to be on the ward on Sunday afternoon. It had been easy enough to give a reason—he had operated the day before on an emergency case and what could be more normal than a visit from him to see how his patient progressed? His casual, 'Good afternoon,' was a masterpiece of surprise.

Mary Jane's polite response was quite drowned by Miss Mabel's voice. 'Is it not delightful?' she enquired of him. 'Mary Jane has come to visit me—Dr Fellowes gave her a lift here. She will have to return by bus, though. I'm not sure how she will manage that, it being a Sunday, but she tells me that she has everything arranged.' She beamed at Mary Jane, who wasn't looking.

'I have been telling her how excellent is the treatment here. I shall recommend it to my friends.'

Just as though it were an hotel, thought Mary Jane, carefully not looking at Sir Thomas.

He stayed only a few minutes, bidding them both goodbye with casual politeness, and Mary Jane settled down to hear the rest of Miss Mabel's experiences, until a glance at the clock told her that she would have to go at once if she were to catch the bus. Not easily done, however, for Miss Mabel suddenly thought of numerous messages for her sister so that Mary Jane fairly galloped out of the hospital to pause at the entrance to get her bearings. She wasn't quite sure where the bus depot was and Mrs Fellowes's kindly directions had been vague.

The Rolls-Royce whispered to a halt beside her and its door opened.

'Get in,' said Sir Thomas. 'I'm going through your village.'

'I'm catching a bus.'

'Very unlikely. The Sunday service leaves half an hour earlier—I have that from the head porter, who is never wrong about anything.' He added gently, 'Get in, Miss Seymour, before we are had up for loitering.'

'But I'm not...' she began, and caught his eye. 'All right.' She sounded ungracious. 'Thank you.'

She fastened the seatbelt and sat back in luxury and he drove off without saying anything. Indeed, he didn't speak at all for some time, and then only to observe that Miss Mabel would be returning home very shortly. Mary Jane replied suitably and lapsed into silence once more for the simple reason that she had no idea what to talk about, but as they neared the village she made an effort. 'Do you live near here?'

'No, in London. I have to live near my work.'

'Then why are you here?'

'I visit various hospitals whenever it is found necessary.'

A most unsatisfactory answer. She didn't say anything more until he drew up before the tea-room.

He got out before she could open her door and opened it for her, took the old-fashioned key from her and opened the cottage door.

It was dusk now and he found the switch and turned on the lights before standing aside to let her pass him.

'Thank you very much,' said Mary Jane once again, and bent to pick up Brimble, who had rushed to meet her.

Sir Thomas leaned against the half-open door in no hurry to go. 'Your cat?'

'Yes, Brimble. He's—he's company.'

'You live alone?'

'Yes.' She peered up at him. 'You'd better go, Sir Thomas, if you're going all the way to London.'

Sir Thomas agreed meekly. He had never, he reflected, been told to go by a girl. On the contrary, they made a point of asking him to stay. He wasn't a conceited man but now he was intrigued. He had wanted to meet her again, going deliberately to the hospital when he knew that she would be there, wanting to know more about her. The drive had hardly been successful. He bade her a pleasantly impersonal goodbye. They were unlikely to meet again. He dismissed her from his thoughts and drove back to London.

CHAPTER TWO

SEPTEMBER WAS ALMOST over and the weather was changing. Fewer and fewer tourists stopped for coffee or tea although Mary Jane still did a steady trade with the village dwellers—just enough to keep the bills paid. Miss Mabel made steady progress and Mary Jane, graciously offered a lift in the rectory car, visited her again. Sir Thomas had been again, she was told, and Miss Mabel was to return home in a week's time and see him when he came to the hospital in six weeks' time. 'Such a nice man,' sighed Miss Mabel, 'a true gentleman, if you know what I mean.'

Mary Jane wasn't too sure about that but she murmured obligingly.

Miss Mabel's homecoming was something of an event in a village where one day was very like another. The ambulance brought her, deposited her gently in her home, drained Mary Jane's teapots and ate almost all the scones, and departed to be replaced by Miss Kemble, Mrs Stokes and after an interval Dr Fellowes, who tactfully sent them all away and made sure that the Misses Potter were allowed peace and quiet. Mary Jane, slipping through the village with a plate of tea-cakes as a welcome home gift, was prevailed upon to stay for a few minutes while Miss Mabel reiterated her experiences. 'I am to walk each day,' she said proudly, 'but lead a quiet life.' She laughed and Miss Emily laughed too. 'Not that we do anything else, do we, Mary Jane?'

Mary Jane smilingly agreed; that she had dreams of lovely clothes, candlelit dinners for two, dancing night after night and always with someone who adored her, was something she kept strictly to herself. Even Felicity, on the rare occasions when she saw her, took it for granted that she was content.

The mornings were frosty now and the evenings drawing in. The village, after the excitement of Miss Mabel's operation, did settle down. Mary Jane baked fewer scones and some days customers were so few it was hardly worth keeping the tea-room open.

She was preparing to close after an unprofitable Monday when the door was thrust open and a man came in. Mary Jane, wiping down the already clean tables, looked up hopefully, saw who it was and said in a neutral voice, 'Good evening, Oliver.'

Her cousin, Uncle Matthew's heir.

She had known him since her schooldays and had disliked him from the start, just as he had disliked her. She had been given short shrift when her uncle had died and for her part she hadn't been able to leave fast enough, for not only did Oliver dislike her, his wife, a cold woman, pushing her way up the social ladder, disliked her too. She stood, the cloth in her hand, waiting for him to speak.

'Business pretty bad?' he asked.

'It's a quiet time of the year. I'm making a living, thank you, Oliver.'

She was surprised to see that he was trying to be friendly, but not for long.

'Hope you'll do something for me,' he went on. 'Margaret has to go to London to see some specialist or other

about her back. I have to go to America on business and
someone will have to drive her up and stay with her.' He
didn't quite meet her eyes. 'I wondered if you'd do that?'
He laughed. 'Blood's thicker than water and all that...'

'I hadn't noticed,' said Mary Jane coldly. 'Margaret
has family of her own, hasn't she? Surely there is someone with nothing better to do who could go with her?'

'We did ask around,' said Oliver airily, 'but you know
how it is, they lead busy social lives, they simply can't
spare the time.'

'And I can?' asked Mary Jane crisply.

'Well, you can't be making a fortune at this time of
year. It won't cost you a penny. Margaret will have to
stay the night in town—tests and so forth. She can't
drive herself because of this wretched back, and besides she's very nervous.' He added, 'She is in pain, too.'

Mary Jane had a tender heart. Very much against her
inclination she agreed, reluctantly, to go with Margaret. It would mean leaving Brimble alone for two days
but Mrs Adams next door would feed him and make
sure that he was safe. It would mean shutting the tea-
room too and, although Oliver made light of the pau-
city of customers at that time of year, all the same she
would be short of two days' takings, however sparse
they might be.

Oliver, having got what he wanted, lost no time in
going. 'Next Tuesday,' he told her. 'I'll drive Margaret here in the car and you can take over. I leave in the
afternoon.'

If he felt gratitude, he didn't show it. Mary Jane
watched him get into his car and pulled a face at his
back as he drove away.

Oliver returned on the Tuesday morning and Mary
Jane, having packed an overnight bag, got into her el-

derly tweed suit, consigned Brimble to Mrs Adams's kindly hands, and opened the door to him.

He didn't bother with a good morning, a nod seemed the best he could manage. 'Margaret's in the car. Drive carefully; you'll have to fill up with petrol, there's not enough to bring you back.'

Mary Jane gave him a limpid look. 'Margaret has the money for that? I haven't.'

'Good God, girl, surely a small matter of a few gallons of petrol...'

'Well, just as you like. I'm sure Jim at the garage will have a man who can drive Margaret—you pay by the mile I believe, and petrol extra.'

Oliver went a dangerous plum colour. 'No one would think that we were cousins...'

'Well, no, I don't think that they would, I quite often forget that too.' She smiled. 'If you go now you'll catch Jim—he'll be open by now.'

Oliver gave her a look to kill, with no effect whatsoever, and took out his wallet.

'I shall require a strict account of what you spend,' he told her crossly, and handed her some notes. 'Now come along, Margaret is nervous enough already.'

Margaret was tall and what she described to herself as elegantly thin. She had good features, marred by a downturned mouth and a frown; moreover she had a complaining voice. She moaned now, 'Oh, dear, whatever has kept you? Can't you see how ill I am? All this waiting about...'

Mary Jane got into the car. She said, 'Good morning, Margaret.' She turned to look at her. 'Before we go I must make it quite clear to you that I have no money with me—perhaps Oliver told you already?'

Margaret looked faintly surprised. 'No, he didn't,

he said…well, I've enough with me for both of us.' She added sourly, 'It will be a nice treat for you, a couple of days in town, all expenses paid.'

Mary Jane let this pass and, since Oliver did no more than raise a careless hand to his wife, drove away. Margaret was going to sulk, which left Mary Jane free to indulge her thoughts. She toyed with the idea of sending Oliver a bill for two days' average takings at the tea-rooms, plus the hourly wages she would earn as a waitress. He would probably choke himself to death on reading it but it was fun to think about.

'You're driving too fast,' complained Margaret.

Oliver had booked them in at a quiet hotel, near enough to Wigmore Street for them to be able to walk there for Margaret's appointment. He had thought of everything, thought Mary Jane, unpacking Margaret's bag for her since that lady declared herself to be exhausted; a hotel so quiet and respectable that there was nothing to do and no one under fifty staying there. Her room was on the floor above Margaret's, overlooking a blank wall, furnished with what she called Hotel Furniture. She unpacked her own bag and went back to escort Margaret to lunch.

The dining-room was solid Victorian, dimly lit, the tables laden with silverware and any number of wine glasses. She cheered up at the sight; breakfast had been a sketchy affair and she was hungry and the elaborate table settings augured well for a good meal.

Unfortunately, this didn't turn out to be the case; lunch was elaborately presented but not very filling: something fishy on a lettuce leaf, lamb chops with a small side-dish of vegetables and one potato, and trifle to follow. They drank water and Mary Jane defiantly ate two rolls.

'I cannot think,' grumbled Margaret picking at her chop, 'why Oliver booked us in at this place. When we come to town—the theatre, you know, or shopping—we always go to one of the best hotels.' She thought for a moment. 'Of course, I suppose he thought that, as you were coming with me, this would do.'

Mary Jane's eyes glowed with purple fire. 'Now, that was thoughtful of him. But you have no need to stay here, Margaret, you can get a room in any hotel, pay the bill here and I'll drive myself back this afternoon and get someone from Jim's garage to collect you tomorrow.'

'You wouldn't—how dare you suggest it? Oliver would never forgive you.'

'I don't suppose he would. I don't suppose he'd forgive you either for spending his money. I dare say it won't be so bad; you'll be home again tomorrow.'

'Oliver won't be back for at least a week.' Margaret paused. 'Why don't you come and stay with me until he is back? I shall need looking after— all the worry of this examination is really too much for me. I'm alone.'

'There's a housekeeper, isn't there? And two daily maids and the gardener?' She glanced at her watch. 'Since we have to walk to this place we had better go and get ready.'

'I feel quite ill at the very thought of being examined,' observed Margaret as they set out. She had felt well enough to make up her face very nicely and put on a fetching hat. She pushed past Mary Jane in a cloud of L'Air du Temps and told her sharply to hurry up.

Wigmore Street was quiet and dignified in the early afternoon sun and the specialist's rooms, according to the brass plate on the door, were in a tall red-brick house in the middle of a terrace of similar houses. Mary Jane rang the bell and they were ushered into a narrow hall.

'First floor,' the porter told them and went back to his cubbyhole, advising them that there was a lift if they preferred.

It was very quiet on the first-floor landing, doors on either side and one at the end. 'Ring the bell,' said Margaret and pointed to the door on the left.

It was as Mary Jane put her finger on it that she realised something. The little plate above it was inscribed Sir Thomas Latimer! She had seen it on the doorplate downstairs as well but it hadn't registered. She felt a little thrill of excitement at seeing him again. Not that she liked him in the least, she told herself, as the door was opened and Margaret swept past her, announcing her arrival in a condescending way which Mary Jane could see didn't go down well with the nurse.

They were a little early. The nurse offered chairs, made polite conversation for a few moments and went across to speak to the receptionist sitting at a desk in the corner of the room.

'I didn't expect to wait,' complained Margaret. 'I've come a long way and I'm in a good deal of pain.'

The nurse came back. 'Sir Thomas has many patients, Mrs Seymour, and some need more time than others.'

Five minutes later the door opened and an elderly lady, walking with sticks, came out accompanied by Sir Thomas, who shook her hand and handed her over to the nurse.

He went back into his consulting-room and closed the door and Mary Jane decided that he hadn't noticed her.

However, he had. He put the folder on his desk and went over to the window and looked out, surprised at the pleasure he had felt at the sight of her. He went back to his desk and opened the folder; this Mrs Seymour he

was to see must be a sister-in-law—she and Mary Jane
came from the same village.

He went and sat down and asked his nurse over the
intercom to send in Mrs Seymour.

He could find nothing wrong with her at all; she described endless symptoms in a rather whining voice,
none of which he could substantiate. Nevertheless, he
sent her to the X-ray unit on the floor above and listened
patiently to her renewed complaints when she returned.

'If you will return in the morning,' he told her, 'when
the X-ray results will be ready, I hope that I will be able
to reassure you. I can find nothing wrong with you, Mrs
Seymour, but we can discuss that tomorrow. Shall we
say ten o'clock?'

'He is no good,' declared Margaret as they walked
back. 'I shall find another specialist...'

'You could at least wait and see what the X-rays
show,' suggested Mary Jane sensibly. 'Why not have
a rest in your room and an early night after dinner?'

First, though, they had tea in the hotel lounge and
since it was, rather surprisingly, quite a substantial one,
Mary Jane made the most of it, a little surprised at
Margaret, despite her pain, eating a great many sandwiches and cream cakes. Left on her own, she poured
a last cup of tea and thought about Sir Thomas. She
hadn't expected him to recognise her and after all he
had had but the barest glimpse as he had stood in the
doorway. As he had ushered Margaret out of his consulting-room he hadn't looked in her direction. All the
same, it was interesting to have seen him again in his
own environment, as it were. Very remote and professional, thought Mary Jane, eating a last sandwich, not
a bit like the man who had pushed his way into her tea-
room, demanding tea for his friend. She sighed for no

reason at all, picked up a magazine and sat reading, a girl not worth a second glance, until it was time to go up to Margaret's room and warn her that dinner would be in half an hour.

Getting Margaret there by ten o'clock was rather an effort but she managed it, to be told by the nurse that Sir Thomas had been at one of the hospitals since the early hours of the morning operating on an emergency case. He would be with them as soon as possible and in the meantime perhaps they would like coffee?

'Well, this is really too bad,' grumbled Margaret. 'I am a private patient...'

'This was an emergency, Mrs Seymour,' said the nurse smoothly and went to get the coffee.

Mary Jane sat, allowing Margaret's indignant whine to pass over her head. Like him or not, she felt sorry for Sir Thomas, up half the night and then having to cope with someone like Margaret instead of having a nap. She hoped he wouldn't be too tired...

When he came presently he looked exactly like a man who had enjoyed a good night's sleep, with time to dress with his usual elegance and eat a good breakfast. Only, when she peeped at him while he was greeting Margaret, she saw that there were tired lines around his eyes. He caught her staring at him when he turned to bid her good morning and she blushed a little. He watched the pretty colour pinken her cheeks and smiled. It was a kind and friendly smile and she was taken by surprise by it.

'Your patient? Was the operation successful?' She went even pinker; perhaps she shouldn't have asked—it wasn't any of her business.

'Entirely, thank you—a good start to my day.' Thank heaven he hadn't sounded annoyed, thought Mary Jane.

The nurse led Margaret away then, and Mary Jane sat and looked at the glossy magazines scattered around her. The models in them looked as though they should still be at school and were so thin that she longed to feed them up on good wholesome food. Some of the clothes were lovely but since she was never likely to wear any of them she took care not to want them too much.

I'm the wrong shape, she told herself, unaware that despite her thinness she had a pretty, curvy figure and nice legs, concealed by the tweed suit.

The door opened and Sir Thomas showed Margaret back into the waiting-room, and it was quite obvious that Margaret was in a dreadful temper whereas he presented an impeturbable manner. He didn't look at Mary Jane but shook Margaret's reluctant hand, wished her goodbye with cool courtesy and went back into his consulting-room.

Margaret took no notice of the nurse's polite good-byes but flounced down to the street. 'I told you he was no good,' she hissed. 'The man's a fool, he says there is nothing wrong with me.' She gave a nasty little laugh. 'I'm to take more exercise, if you please—walk for an hour, mind you—each day, make beds, work in the garden, be active. I have suffered for years with my back, I'm quite unable to do anything strenuous; if you knew the hours I spend lying on the *chaise longue*…'

'Perhaps that's why your back hurts,' suggested Mary Jane matter-of-factly.

'Don't be stupid. You can drive me home and I shall tell Dr Fellowes exactly what I think of him and his specialist.'

'He must know what he's talking about,' observed Mary Jane rashly, 'otherwise he wouldn't be a consultant, would he?'

'What do you know about it, anyway?' asked Margaret rudely. They had reached the hotel. 'Get your bag and get someone to bring the car round. We're leaving now.'

It was a pleasant autumn day; the drive would have been agreeable too if only Margaret would have stopped talking. Luckily she didn't need any answers, so Mary Jane was able to think her own thoughts.

She wasn't invited in when they arrived at the house. Mary Jane, to whom it had been home for happy years, hadn't expected that anyway. 'You can drive the car round to the garage before you go,' said Margaret without so much as a thank-you.

'Oliver can do that whenever he comes back; if you mind about it being parked outside you can drive it round yourself, Margaret; I'm going home.' She added rather naughtily, 'Don't forget that hour's walk each day.'

'Come back,' ordered Margaret. 'How can you be so cruel, leaving me like this?'

Mary Jane was already walking down the short drive. She called over her shoulder, 'But you're home, Margaret, and Sir Thomas said that there was nothing wrong with you...'

'I'll never speak to you again.'

'Oh, good.'

Mary Jane nipped smartly out of the open gate and down to the village. It was still mid-afternoon; she would open the tea-room in the hope that some passing motorist would fancy a pot of tea and scones. First she would have a meal; breakfast was hours ago and Margaret had refused to stop on the way. Beans on toast, she decided happily, opening her door.

Brimble was waiting for her. She picked him up and

tucked him under an arm while she opened windows, turned the sign round to 'Open' and put the kettle on.

Brimble, content after a meal, sat beside her while she ate her own meal and then went upstairs to take a nap, leaving her to see that everything was ready for any customers who might come.

They came presently, much to her pleased surprise; a hiking couple, a family party in a car which looked as though it might fall apart at any moment and a married couple who quarrelled quietly all the while they ate their tea. Mary Jane locked the door with a feeling of satisfaction, got her supper and started on preparations for the next day. While she made a batch of tea-cakes she thought about Sir Thomas.

IT WAS TOWARDS the end of October, on a chilly late afternoon, just as Mary Jane was thinking of closing since there was little likelihood of any customers, that Sir Thomas walked in. She had her back to the door, rearranging a shelf at the back of the tea-room and she had neither heard nor seen the Rolls come to a quiet halt outside.

'Too late for tea?' he asked and she spun round, clutching some plates.

'No—yes, I was just going to close.'

'Oh, good.' He turned the sign round. 'We can have a quiet talk without being disturbed.'

'Talk? Whatever about? Is something wrong with Miss Potter? I do hope not.'

'Miss Potter is making excellent progress...'

'Then it's Margaret—Mrs Seymour.'

'Ah, yes, the lady you escorted. As far as I know she is leading her normal life, and why not? There is nothing wrong with her. I came to talk about you.'

'Me. Why?'

'Put the kettle on and I'll tell you.'

Sir Thomas sat down at one of the little tables and ate one of the scones on a plate there, and, since it seemed that he intended to stay there until he had had his tea, Mary Jane put the plates down and went to put on the kettle.

By the time she came back with the teapot he had finished the scones and she fetched another plate, offering them wordlessly.

'You wanted to tell me something?' she prompted.

He sat back in the little cane chair so that it creaked alarmingly, his teacup in his hand. 'Yes...'

The thump on the door stopped him and when it was repeated he got up and unlocked it. The girl who came in flashed him a dazzling smile.

'Hello, Mary Jane. I'm on my way to Cheltenham and it seemed a good idea to look you up.' She pecked Mary Jane's cheek and looked across at Sir Thomas. 'Am I interrupting something?'

'No,' said Mary Jane rather more loudly than necessary. 'This is Sir Thomas Latimer, an orthopaedic surgeon, he—that is, Margaret went to see him about her back and he has a patient in the village.' She glanced at him, still standing by the door. 'This is my sister, Felicity.'

Felicity was looking quite beautiful, of course; she dressed in the height of fashion and somehow the clothes always looked right on her. She had tinted her hair, too, and her make-up was exquisite, making the most of her dark eyes and the perfect oval of her face. She smiled at Sir Thomas now as he came to shake her hand, smiling down at her, holding her hand just a little longer than he need, making some easy light-hearted remark which made Felicity laugh.

Of course, he's fallen for her, reflected Mary Jane; since Felicity had left home to join the glamorous world of fashion she had had a continuous flow of men at her beck and call and she couldn't blame Sir Thomas; her sister was quite lovely. She said, 'Felicity is a well-known model…'

'I can't imagine her being anything else,' observed Sir Thomas gravely. 'Are you staying here with Mary Jane?'

'Lord, no. There's only one bedroom and I'd be terribly in the way—she gets up at the crack of dawn to cook, don't you, darling?' She glanced around her. 'Still making a living? Good. No, I'm booked in at the Queens at Cheltenham, I'm doing a dress show there tomorrow.' She smiled at Sir Thomas. 'I suppose you wouldn't like to come? We could have dinner…?'

'How delightful that would have been, although the dress show hardly appeals, but dinner with you would be another matter.'

The fool, thought Mary Jane fiercely. She had seen Felicity capture a man's attention a dozen times and not really minded but now she did. Sir Thomas was like the rest of them but for some reason she had thought that he was different.

Felicity gave an exaggerated sigh. 'Surely you could manage dinner? I don't know anyone in Cheltenham.'

'I'm on my way back to London,' he told her. 'Then I'm off to a seminar in Holland.'

Felicity said with a hint of sharpness, 'A busy man— are you a very successful specialist or something, making your millions?'

'I am a busy man, yes.' He smiled charmingly and she turned away to say goodbye to Mary Jane.

'Perhaps I'll drop in as I go back,' she suggested.

He opened the door for her and then walked with her to her car. Mary Jane could hear her sister's laughter before she drove away. She began to clear away the tea tray, she still had to do some baking ready for the next day and Brimble was prowling round, grumbling for his supper.

'We didn't finish our tea,' observed Sir Thomas mildly. He looked at her with questioning eyebrows.

Well, he is not getting another pot, reflected Mary Jane, and told him so, only politely. 'I've a lot of baking to do and I expect you want to get back to London.'

Sir Thomas's eyes gleamed with amusement. 'Then I won't keep you.' He picked up the coat he had tossed over a chair. 'You have a very beautiful sister, Mary Jane.'

'Yes, we're not a bit alike, are we?'

'No, not in the least.' A remark which did nothing to improve her temper. 'And I haven't had the opportunity to talk to you...'

'I don't suppose it was of the least importance.' She spoke tartly. 'You can tell me if we meet again, which isn't very likely.'

He opened the door. 'You are mistaken about a great many things, Mary Jane,' he told her gravely. 'Goodnight.'

She closed the door and bolted it and went back to the kitchen, not wishing to see him go.

She washed the cups and saucers with a good deal of noise, fed Brimble and got out the pastry board, the rolling pin and the ingredients for the scones. Her mind not being wholly on her work, her dough suffered a good deal of rough treatment; notwithstanding, the scones came from the oven nicely risen and golden brown. She cleared away and went upstairs, having lost all appetite for her supper.

Felicity hadn't said when she would come again but she seldom did, dropping in from time to time when it suited her. When they had been younger she had always treated Mary Jane with a kind of tolerant affection, at the same time making no effort to take much interest in her. It had been inevitable that Mary Jane should stay at home with her aunt and uncle and, even when they had died and she had inherited the cottage, Felicity had made no effort to help in any way. She was earning big money by then but neither she nor, for that matter, Mary Jane had expected her to do anything to make life easier for her young sister. Mary Jane had accepted the fact that Felicity was a success in life, leading a glamorous existence, travelling, picking and choosing for whom she would work and, while she was glad that she had made such a success of her life, she had no wish to be a part of it and certainly she felt no envy. Common sense told her that a plain face and a tendency to stay in the background would never earn her a place in the world of fashion.

Not that she would have liked that, she was content with her tea-room and Brimble and her friends in the village, although it would have been nice to have had a little more money.

The Misses Potter came in for their usual tea on the following day.

Miss Mabel was walking with a stick now and was a changed woman. They had been to Cheltenham on the previous day, they told Mary Jane, and that nice Sir Thomas had said that she need not go to see him anymore, just go for a check-up to Dr Fellowes every few months.

'He's going away,' she explained to Mary Jane, 'to some conference or other, but we heard that he will be going to the Radcliffe Infirmary at Oxford when he gets back. Much sought-after,' said Miss Mabel with satisfaction.

Of course, the village knew all about him calling at the tea-room and, Mary Jane being Mary Jane, her explanation that he had merely called for a cup of tea on his way back to London was accepted without comment. Felicity's visit had also been noticed with rather more interest. Very few people took *Vogue* or *Harpers and Queen* but those who visited their dentist or doctor and read the magazines in the waiting-room were well aware of her fame.

She came a few days later during the morning, walking into the tea-room and giving the customers there a pleasant surprise. She was wearing a suede outfit in red with boots in black leather and a good deal of gold jewellery. Not at all the kind of clothes the village was used to; even the doctor's wife and Margaret, not to mention the lady of the manor, wouldn't have risked wearing such an outfit. She smiled around her, confident that she was creating an impression.

'Hello, Mary Jane,' she said smilingly, pleased with the mild sensation she had caused. 'Can you spare me a cup of coffee? I'm on my way back to town.'

She sat down at one of the tables and Mary Jane, busy with serving, said, 'Hello, Felicity. Yes, of course, but will you help yourself? I'm quite busy.'

The customers went presently, leaving the two sisters alone. Mary Jane collected up cups and saucers and tidied the tables and Felicity said rather impatiently,

'Oh, do sit down for a minute, you can wash up after I've gone.'

Mary Jane fetched a cup of coffee for herself, re-filled Felicity's cup and sat. 'Did you have a success-ful show?' she asked.

'Marvellous. I'm off to the Bahamas next week—*Vogue* and *Elle*. When I get back it will be time for the dress show in Paris. Life's all go...'

'Would you like to change it?'

Felicity gave her a surprised stare. 'Change it? My dear girl, have you any idea of the money I earn?'

'Well no, I don't think that I have...' Mary Jane spoke without rancour. 'But it must be a great deal.'

'It is. I like money and I spend it. In a year or two I intend to find a wealthy husband and settle down. Sooner, if I meet someone I fancy.' She smiled across the little table. 'Like that man I met when I was here last week. Driving a Rolls and doing very nicely and just my type. I can't think how you met him, Mary Jane.'

'He operated on a friend of mine here and I met him at the hospital. He stopped for a cup of tea on his way back to London. I don't know anything about him ex-cept that he's a specialist in bones.'

'How revolting.' Felicity wrinkled her beautiful nose. 'But of course, he must have a social life. Is he mar-ried?'

'I've no idea. I should think it must be very likely, wouldn't you?'

'London, you say? I must find out. What's his name?'

Mary Jane told him but with reluctance. There was no reason why she should mind Felicity's interest in him, indeed she would make a splendid foil for his magnifi-cent size and good looks and presumably he would be able to give Felicity all the luxury she demanded of life.

'He said he was going abroad—to Holland, I think,' she volunteered.

'Good. That gives me time to track him down. Once I know where he lives or works I can meet him again—accidentally of course.'

Well, thought Mary Jane in her sensible way, he's old enough and wise enough to look after himself and there's that other woman who came here with him...

She didn't mention her to her sister.

Felicity didn't stay long. 'Ticking over nicely?' she asked carelessly. 'You always liked a quiet life, didn't you?'

What would Felicity have said if she had declared that she would very much like to wear lovely clothes, go dancing and be surrounded by young men? Mary Jane, loading a tray carefully, agreed placidly.

Since it seemed likely that the quiet life was to be her lot, there wasn't much point in saying anything else.

CHAPTER THREE

OCTOBER, SLIDING TOWARDS November, had turned wet and chilly and customers were sparse. Mary Jane turned out cupboards, washed and polished and cut down on the baking. There were still customers glad of a cup of tea, home from shopping expeditions—or motorists on their way to Cheltenham or Oxford stopped for coffee. More prosperous tea-rooms closed down during the winter months and their owners went to Barbados or California to spend their summer's profits, but Mary Jane's profits weren't large enough for that. Besides, since she lived over the tea-room she might just as well keep it open and get what custom there was.

On this particular morning, since it was raining hard and moreover was a Monday, she was pleased to hear the doorbell tinkle as she set the percolator on the stove. It wasn't a customer, though. Oliver stood there, just inside the door.

She wasn't particularly pleased to see him but she wished him a cheerful good morning.

'I'm just back from the States,' declared Oliver pompously. 'Margaret tells me that you have behaved most unkindly towards her. I should have thought that you could at least have stayed with her and made sure that she was quite comfortable.'

'But she is not ill—Sir Thomas Latimer said so.

He said that she should take more exercise and not lie around.'

Oliver's eyes bulged with annoyance. 'I consider you to be a heartless girl, Mary Jane. I shall think twice before asking you to do any small favour...'

'You'd be wasting time,' said Mary Jane matter-of-factly, 'for you're quite able to find someone else if Margaret insists on feeling poorly all the time. I've my living to earn, you know.'

Oliver's eyes slid away from hers. 'As a matter of fact, I have to go away again very shortly...'

'Then you can arrange for someone to be with Margaret. Don't waste your time with me, Oliver.'

'You ungrateful...'

She came and stood before him. 'Tell me, what am I ungrateful for?' she invited.

Oliver still didn't meet her eyes. 'Well,' he began.

'Just so, go away, Oliver, before I bang you over the head with my rolling pin.'

'Don't be ridiculous,' he blustered. All the same he edged towards the door.

Which opened to admit the giant-like person of Sir Thomas, his elegant grey suit spattered with rain. He said nothing, only stood there, his eyebrows slightly raised, smiling a little.

Mary Jane had gone pink at the sight of him; blushing was a silly habit she had never quite conquered. She was pleased to see him. Oliver, after a first startled glance, had ignored him. 'You've not heard the last of this, Mary Jane—your own flesh and blood.'

'Ah,' said Sir Thomas, in the gentlest of voices. 'You are, I believe, Mrs Seymour's husband?'

Oliver goggled. 'Yes—yes, I am.' He puffed out his

chest in readiness for a few well-chosen words but he was forestalled.

'Delighted to meet you,' said Sir Thomas with suave untruthfulness. 'It gives me the opportunity to tell you that there is nothing wrong with your wife. A change of lifestyle is all that she needs—rather more activity.'

Oliver looked from him to Mary Jane, who in her turn was studying the row of glass jars on the shelf on the further wall. 'Really, surely this is hardly the place,' he began.

'Oh, Miss Seymour was with your wife and of course already knows what I have told Mrs Seymour. I thought it might reassure you to mention it. You will, of course, get a report from your own doctor in due course.'

He opened the door invitingly, letting in a good deal of wind and rain, and Oliver, muttering that he was a busy man, hurried out to his car without a word more than a cursory good morning.

Sir Thomas brushed a few drops of rain off his sleeve and Mary Jane said, 'You're wet.'

He glanced at her. 'I was passing in the car and saw you talking to your—cousin? You looked as though you were going to hit him and it seemed a good idea to—er—join you.'

'I threatened him with a rolling pin,' said Mary Jane in a satisfied voice.

'Admirable. A very handy weapon. Do you often use it?' He added gravely, 'As a weapon?'

'Well, of course not. He was annoying me. Do you want coffee?'

'I was hoping that you would ask me. And are there any scones?'

She set a plate on the table and a dish of butter and he spread a scone and bit into it.

'Are you hungry?' asked Mary Jane pointedly.

'Famished. I've been at the Radcliffe all night…'

She poured coffee for them both and sat down opposite him. 'But you're going the wrong way home.'

'Ah, yes. I thought I'd take a day off. I've a clinic at six o'clock this evening. It crossed my mind that it would be pleasant if we were to spend it together. Lunch perhaps? A drive through the countryside?'

'Oughtn't you to go to bed?'

'If you were to offer me a boiled egg or even a rasher or two of bacon I'll doze for ten minutes or so while you do whatever it is you do before you go out for the day.'

'The tea-room…'

'Just for once?' He contrived to look hungry and lonely, although she suspected that he was neither.

'Bacon and eggs,' she told him before she could change her mind. 'And I'll need half an hour.'

'Excellent. I'll come and watch you cook.'

He sat on the kitchen table, Brimble on his knee, while she got out the frying pan and, while the bacon sizzled, sliced bread and made more coffee.

'Two eggs?' She looked up and found him staring at her. It was a thoughtful look and she wondered about it until he spoke.

'Yes, please. Where is your beautiful sister, Mary Jane?'

She cracked the eggs neatly. For some reason his question had made her unhappy although she had no intention of letting it show. 'Well, she went to Barbados but she should be back by now—I think it's the Paris dress shows next week. She lives in London, though. Would you like to have her address?'

'Yes, please, I feel I owe her a dinner. If you remember?'

'Yes, of course.' She wrote on the back of the pad, tore off the page and gave it to him. 'That's her phone number, too.'

She didn't look at him but dished up his breakfast and fetched the coffee-pot.

'I'll go and change while you eat,' she told him. 'Brimble likes the bacon rinds.'

Upstairs she inspected her wardrobe. It would have to be the jersey dress, kept for unlikely occasions such as this one, and the Marks & Spencer mac. Somewhere or other there was a rainproof hat—if only she had the sort of curly hair which looked enchanting when it got wet...

She went downstairs presently and found Sir Thomas, his chair balanced precariously against the wall, his large feet on the table, asleep. He had tidied his breakfast plate away into the sink and Brimble, licking the last of the bacon rinds from his whiskers, was perched on his knees.

Mary Jane stood irresolute. It would be cruel to wake him up; on the other hand he looked very uncomfortable.

'A splendid breakfast,' said Sir Thomas, his eyes still closed. 'I feel like a new man.'

He opened his eyes then. No one would have known that he had been up all night.

'Have you really been up all night?' asked Mary Jane. She blinked at the sudden cold stare.

'I have many faults, but I don't lie.' His voice was as cold as his eyes and she made haste to make amends.

'I'm sorry, I wasn't doubting you, only you look so—so tidy!' she finished lamely.

'Tidy? I have showered and shaved and put on a clean shirt. Is that being tidy?' He lifted Brimble gently from his knee and stood up, towering over her. His gaze swept over her person. 'Most suitably dressed for the weather,' he observed, and she bore his scrutiny silently, aware that the hat, while practical, did nothing for her at all.

She turned the sign to 'Closed', coaxed Brimble into his basket, shut windows and locked doors and pronounced herself ready. The rain was still sheeting down. 'You'll get wet,' she told him. 'I've an umbrella…'

He smiled and took the key from her and locked the tea-room door and went to unlock the car door, bundled her in, gave himself a shake and got in beside her. 'Oxford?' he asked and, when she nodded happily, smiled.

Mary Jane, suddenly shy, was relieved when he started an undemanding conversation, and he, versed in the art of putting people at their ease, kept up a flow of small talk until they reached Oxford. The rain had eased a little, and, with the car safely parked, they set out on a walk around the colleges.

'Did you come here?' asked Mary Jane, craning her neck to see Tom Tower.

'I was at Trinity.'

'Before you trained as a doctor—no, surgeon.'

'I took my MD, and then went over to surgery—orthopaedics.'

She lowered her gaze from Tom Tower to her companion. 'I expect you're very clever.'

'Everyone is clever at something,' he told her, and took her arm and walked her to the Radcliffe Camera.

'May we go inside?'

'To the reading rooms if you like. It houses the Bodleian Library.'

He took her to the Eastgate Hotel and gave her coffee in the bar, a cheerful place, crowded with students, and then walked her briskly down to the river before popping her back into the car.

'There's a rather nice place for lunch,' he told her casually, 'a few miles away.'

An understatement, Mary Jane decided when they reached Le Manoir aux Quat' Saisons at Great Milton; it was definitely a grand place and the jersey dress was quite inadequate. However, she was given no time to worry about that. She was whisked inside, led away to tidy herself and then settled in the bar with a glass of sherry while Sir Thomas, very much at his ease, sat opposite her studying the menu. He glanced at her presently.

'Dublin Bay prawns?' he suggested. 'And what about *poulet Normand*?'

Mary Jane agreed, she had never tasted Dublin Bay prawns but she was hungry enough to try anything; as for the chicken, she had read the recipe for that in her cookery book—egg yolks and thick cream and brandy, butter and onions—it sounded delicious.

It was. She washed it down with spa water and, when invited, chose an orange cream soufflé—more cream, and Curaçao this time. Over coffee she said, in her sensible way, 'This is a delightful place and that was the most gorgeous meal I've had for a long time. You're very kind.'

She caught his eye and went a little pink. 'Oh, dear, I've made it sound like a half-term treat with an…' She stopped just in time and the pink deepened.

'Uncle? Godfather?' he suggested, and she let out a sigh of relief when he laughed. 'I've enjoyed my day too, Mary Jane, you are a very restful companion; you haven't rearranged your hair once or powdered your nose or put on more lipstick and you really enjoyed Oxford, didn't you?'

'Oh, very much. It's a long time since I was there.' She fell silent, remembering how her father used to take Felicity and her there, walking the streets, pointing out the lovely old buildings, and Sir Thomas watched her with faint amusement and vague pity. So independent, he reflected, making a life for herself, and so different from her rather beautiful sister. He must remember to mention her funny little tea-room to his family and friends; drum up some customers for her so that she would have some money to spend on herself. A new hat for a start. No rain hat was becoming but at least it need not be quite as awful as the one she had been wearing all day.

Her quiet voice interrupted his thoughts. 'If you are to be back in London this evening ought we not to be going? I don't want to go,' she added childishly and smiled at him, her violet eyes glowing because she was happy.

'I don't want to go either, but you are quite right.' He had uttered the words almost without thinking and realised to his surprise that he had meant them; he had really enjoyed her company, undemanding, ready to be pleased with everything they had seen and done.

He drove her back to the tea-room, talking about nothing much, at ease with each other, but when she offered him tea he refused. 'I've played truant for long enough. It has been a delightful day, Mary Jane—thank you for your company.'

She offered a small gloved hand. 'Thank you for asking me. It was a treat and so much nicer because I hadn't expected one. I hope you're not too busy this evening so that you can get a good night's sleep, Sir Thomas.'

He concealed a smile. The evening clinic was always busy and there was a pile of work awaiting him on his desk at home.

'I have no doubt of it,' he told her cheerfully, and got into his car and drove away.

She stood at the door until he was out of sight and then took off her outdoor things, fed a peevish Brimble and put the kettle on. It had been a lovely day; she thought about it, minute by minute, while she sipped her tea. She had too much common sense to suppose that Sir Thomas had actually wished for her company—he had needed a companion to share his day and she had been handy and it was obvious that he had called that morning so that he might get Felicity's address. His invitation had been on the spur of the moment and she was quite sure that she fell far short of his usual companions. And she had seen the look he had cast at the rain hat. She got up and went to examine her face in the small looking glass on the kitchen wall. It was rosy from her day out of doors but she didn't see how her skin glowed with health and how her eyes shone. All she saw was her hair, damp around the edges where it had escaped from the hat, and the lack of make-up.

'You're a plain girl,' she told her reflection, and Brimble looked up from his grooming to mutter an agreement.

Promptly at six o'clock, Sir Thomas sat himself down behind his desk in the clinic consultation-room and listened patiently as one patient after the other took the seat opposite to him, to be led away in turn to be carefully examined by him, and then told, in the kindest possible way, what was wrong and what would have to be done. It was almost nine o'clock by the time the last patient had been shown out and he and his regis-

trar and houseman prepared to leave too. Outpatients
Sister stifled a yawn as she collected notes—she hated
the evening clinic but she had worked with Sir Thomas
for several years now and if he had decided to have a
clinic at three o'clock in the morning, she would have
agreed cheerfully. He was her—and almost all of the
nursing staff's—ideal man, never hurried, always polite, unfailingly patient, apparently unaware of the devotion accorded him. For such a successful man he was
singularly unconceited.

He bade everyone goodnight and drove himself to
his home; a house in a row of similar elegant houses
in Little Venice, facing the Grand Union Canal. It had
stopped raining at last and the late evening was quiet.
He opened his front door and as he did so an elderly
man, rather stout and short, came into the hall.

'Evening, Tremble,' said Sir Thomas, and tossed his
coat on to an elbow chair beside a Georgian mahogany
side-table.

Tremble picked up the coat and folded it carefully
over one arm. 'Good evening, sir. Mrs Tremble has a
nice little dinner all ready for you.'

'Thank you.' Sir Thomas was looking through his
post. 'Give me ten minutes, will you?'

He took his post and his bag into the study at the
back of the hall and sat down to read the letters before
going up to his room, to return presently and sit by the
fire in the big drawing-room at the front of the house.
He was greeted here by a Labrador dog, who got to elderly feet and lumbered happily to meet him.

Sir Thomas sat down, a glass of whisky beside him,
the dog's head on his knee. 'A pity you weren't with
us, old fellow,' he said. 'I rather fancy you would have
liked her.'

Tremble's voice reminded him that dinner was served and he crossed the hall with the dog to the dining-room, a room beautifully furnished with a Regency mahogany twin pedestal table surrounded by Hepplewhite chairs; there was an inlaid mahogany sideboard of the same period against one wall and the lighting was pleasantly subdued from the brass sconces on the walls. There were paintings too—Dutch flower studies and a number of portraits.

Sir Thomas, being a very large man, ate his dinner with good appetite, exchanging a casual conversation with Tremble as he was served and offering his dog the last morsel of his cheese.

'Watson had his supper an hour ago, sir,' said Tremble severely.

'We are told that cheese is good for the digestion, Tremble; I suppose that applies to dogs as well as humans.'

'I really couldn't say, sir. Will you have your coffee in the drawing-room?'

'Please, and do tell Mrs Tremble that everything was delicious.'

He went to his study presently with Watson as company, and worked at his desk. He had quite forgotten Mary Jane.

EVEN IF MARY Jane had wanted to forget him she wasn't given that chance. Naturally, in a village that size, she had been seen getting into Sir Thomas's Rolls-Royce, a news item flashed round the village in no time at all, so that when she got out of it again that late afternoon, several ladies living in the cottages on either side of her saw that too.

Trade was brisk the following morning and it was

only after she had answered a few oblique questions that she realised why. Since some of the ladies in the tea-room were prone to embroider any titbit of news to make it more exciting, she told them about her day out in a sensible manner which revealed not a whiff of romance.

She was well-liked; disappointed as they were at her prosaic description of her day with Sir Thomas, they were pleased that she had enjoyed herself. She had little enough fun and no opportunity of getting away from the village and meeting young people of her own age. They lingered over their coffee and, when the Misses Potter joined them, the talk turned, naturally enough, to Sir Thomas.

'Such a nice man,' declared Miss Mabel. 'As mild as milk.'

'Even milk boils over from time to time,' muttered Mary Jane, offering a plate of digestive biscuits. The scones had all been eaten long-since.

Sir Thomas, arriving at his consulting-rooms in Wigmore Street the following morning, wished Miss Pink, his secretary and receptionist, a cheerful good morning and paused at her desk.

'What have I got this weekend?' he wanted to know.

'You're making a speech at that dinner on Saturday evening. Miss Thorley phoned and asked would you like to take her to dinner on Sunday evening; she suggested a day out somewhere first.' Miss Pink's voice was dry.

For a moment Mary Jane's happy face, crowned with the deplorable hat, floated before Sir Thomas's eyes. He said at once, 'I intend to go down to my mother's. Would you phone Miss Thorley and tell her I shall be away?'

Miss Pink gave him a thoughtful look and he returned it blandly. 'I'm far too busy to phone her myself.'

Miss Pink allowed herself a gentle smile as Sir Thomas went into his consulting-room; Miss Thorley, on the rare occasions when she had seen her, had looked at her as though she despised her and Miss Pink, of no discernible age, sharp-nosed and spectacled, objected strongly to that.

There was just time before the first patient was announced for Sir Thomas to phone his mother and invite himself for the weekend.

Her elderly, comfortable voice came clearly over the wires. 'How nice, dear. Are you bringing anyone with you?'

He said that no, he wasn't and the fleeting thought that it would be interesting to see his mother and Mary Jane together whisked through his head, to be instantly dismissed as so much nonsense.

MARY JANE'S DAY out, while not exactly a nine-day wonder, kept the village interested for a few days until the local postman's daughter's wedding. An event which caused the village to turn out *en masse* to crowd into the church and throw confetti afterwards. It brought some welcome custom to Mary Jane, too, for somewhere was needed afterwards where the details of the wedding, the bride's finery and speculation as to the happy couple's future happiness could be mulled over. She did a roaring trade in coffee and scones and, for latecomers, sausage rolls.

She went to bed that night confident that, with luck, she would be able to get a new winter coat.

IT WAS ALMOST midnight by the time Sir Thomas, resplendent in white tie and tails, returned from the banquet which he had been invited to attend. He had made

his speech, brief and to the point, and it had been well
received and now it was just a question of changing into
comfortable clothes, collecting a sleepy Watson and getting into his car once more. It would be late by the time
he reached his mother's house, but he had a key. At that
time of night, with the roads quiet and a good deal of
them motorway, he should be there in little over an hour.

Which he was; he slowed down as he entered the village, its inhabitants long since in bed, and took the car
slowly past the church and then, a few hundred yards
further, through the open gates of the house beyond.

The night was chilly with a hint of frost and there
was bright moonlight. The low, rambling house was in
darkness save for a dim light shining through the tran-
som over the door. Sir Thomas got out quietly, opened
the door for Watson and stood for a moment while his
companion trotted off into the shrubbery at the side of
the house, to reappear shortly and, as silent as his master, enter the house.

The hall was square, low-ceilinged and pleasantly
warm. There was a note by the lamp on the side-table.
Someone had printed 'Coffee on the Aga' on a card and
propped it against the elegant china base of the lamp.
Sir Thomas smiled a little and went soft-footed to the
baize door beside the staircase and so through to the
kitchen door, where he poured his coffee, gave Watson
a drink and presently took himself up to his bed, leaving Watson already asleep on the rug before the Aga.

Four hours later he was up and dressed, drinking
tea in the kitchen and talking to his mother's housekeeper, Mrs Beaver.

'And how's that nasty old London?' she wanted to
know.

'Well, I don't see a great deal of it, I spend most

of my days either at the hospital or my rooms. I often wonder why I don't resign and come and live in peace and quiet here.'

'Go on with you, Sir Thomas, leaving that clever brain of yours to moulder away doing nothing but walking the dog and shooting pigeons. That's not you. Now if you was to ask me, I'd say get yourself a wife and a clutch of children—no question of you giving up then with all them mouths to feed.'

He put down his mug and gave her a hug, 'You old matchmaker,' he told her, and whistled to Watson. It was a fine, chilly morning; there was time to go for a walk before breakfast.

His mother was at the table when he got back, sitting behind the coffee pot; a small, slim woman with pepper and salt hair done in an old-fashioned bun and wearing a beautifully tailored suit.

'There you are, Thomas. How nice to see you, dear, I suppose you can't stay for a few days?'

He bent to kiss her. 'Afraid not, Mama—I'm rather booked up for the next week or so, I'll have to go back very early on Monday morning.'

He helped himself to bacon and eggs, added mushrooms and a tomato or two and sat down beside her. 'The garden looks pretty good…'

'Old Dodds knows his job, though he's a bit pernickety when I want to cut some flowers.' She handed him his coffee. 'Well, what have you been doing, my dear—other than work?'

'Nothing much. A banquet I couldn't miss yesterday evening and one or two dinner parties…'

'What happened to that gorgeous young woman who had begged a lift from you—oh, some weeks ago now?'

He speared a morsel of bacon and topped it neatly with a mushroom.

'Ingrid Bennett. I have no idea.' He smiled suddenly, remembering. 'She insisted on stopping for tea and we did, at a funny little tea-room in a village near Stow-on-the-Wold, run by a small tartar with a sharp tongue.'

'Pretty?'

'No. A great deal of mousy hair and violet eyes.'

His mother buttered toast. 'How unusual—I mean the eyes. One never knows the hidden delights of remote villages until one has a reason to go to them.' She peeped at him and found him watching her, smiling.

'She interested you?'

'As a person? Perhaps; she was so unlike the elegant young women I usually meet socially. But more than that, I imagine she scratches a bare living from the place and yet she seemed quite content with her lot.'

'No family?'

'A sister. A beautiful creature—a top model, flitting about the world and making a great deal of money, I should imagine.'

'Then she might give something to the tea-shop owner.'

Sir Thomas reached for the marmalade. 'Somehow, I don't think that has occurred to her. Do we have to go to church?'

'Of course. We will have a lovely afternoon reading the Sunday papers and having tea round the fire.'

MARY JANE, ALWAYS hopeful of customers even on a Monday morning, was taking the first batch of teacakes from the oven when the doorbell rang. She glanced at the clock on the wall; half-past eight and she hadn't even turned the sign round to 'Open' yet. Perhaps it was the postman with a parcel…

Sir Thomas was standing with his back to the door, his hands in his pockets, but he turned round as she unlocked the door and opened it.

She would have turned the sign round too but he put a large hand over hers to prevent that. 'Good morning, Mary Jane. May I beg a cup of coffee from you? I know it's still early.' He sounded meek, not at all as he usually spoke and she jumped at once to the wrong conclusion as he had anticipated.

'You're on your way back to London? You've been up all night?'

Her lovely eyes were soft with sympathy. She didn't wait for an answer, which saved him from perjury, but went on briskly. 'Well, come on in. Coffee won't take more than a few minutes—I could make you some toast…'

'Something smells very appetising.' He followed her into the kitchen.

'Teacakes. I've just made some.' She looked at him over her shoulder. 'Do you want one?'

'Indeed I do.' He wandered back to the door. 'I have my dog with me. Might he come in? Would Brimble object?'

'A dog?' She looked surprised. 'Of course he can come in. Brimble isn't up yet, but I'll shut the stairs door anyway.'

Watson, his nose twitching at the prospect of something to eat, greeted her with gentle dignity. 'Whenever possible he goes everywhere with me,' said Sir Thomas.

Mary Jane fetched a bowl and filled it with water and offered a digestive biscuit. 'The poor lamb, he'll be glad to get home, I expect.' She added shyly, 'You too, Sir Thomas.'

'I'll drop him off before I go to my rooms.'

She poured his coffee, offered a plate of buttered teacakes and poured coffee for herself. 'But you'll have to have some rest—you can't possibly do a day's work if you've been up all night. You might make a wrong diagnosis.'

Sir Thomas swallowed a laugh. He should, he reflected, be feeling guilty at his deception, actually he was enjoying himself immensely.

Over his second cup of coffee he asked, 'How's business? And is that cousin of yours bothering you?'

'I make a living,' she told him seriously. 'Oliver hasn't been again—I think that was the second time I've seen him in years. He isn't likely to come again.'

'No other family?' he asked casually.

'No—there's just Felicity and me. He quite likes her though because she's quite famous.'

'And you, Mary Jane, have you no wish to be famous?'

'Me? Famous? What could I be famous for? And I wouldn't want to be, anyway.' She added with a touch of defiance, 'I am very happy here. I've got Brimble and I know almost everyone in the village.'

'You don't wish to marry?'

She got up to refill his cup. 'I've not met many men—not in a village as small as this one. It would be nice to marry but it would have to be someone I—I loved. Could you eat another teacake?'

'I could, but I won't. I must be on my way.'

She watched him drive away, Watson sitting beside him, and went back to make more teacakes and fresh coffee. She didn't expect to be busy on a Monday morning but it was nice to be prepared.

As it turned out, she had several customers; early though it was and after a brief lull the Misses Potter came—most unusually for them on a Monday, to tell her over coffee that their nephew from Canada would be coming to visit them. They in their turn were followed by Mrs Fellowes, to ask her over still more coffee if she would babysit for them on the following Saturday as Dr Fellowes had got tickets for the theatre in Cheltenham. Mary Jane agreed cheerfully; the doctor's children were small and cuddly and once they were asleep they needed very little attention. Mrs Fellowes had been gone only a few moments before two cars stopped, disgorging children and parents and what looked like Granny and Grandpa. They ate all the teacakes and most of the scones, drank a gratifying amount of coffee and lemonade and went away again with noisy cheerfulness, leaving her to clear away, close the tea-room for the lunch-hour and, after a quick sandwich, start on another batch of scones.

No one came during the early afternoon and in a way she was glad for it gave her time to return everything to its usual pristine order. It was almost four o'clock and she was wondering if she should close for the day when a car drew up and a lady got out, opened the door and asked if she might have tea.

'Have a table by the window,' invited Mary Jane. 'It's a nice afternoon and I like this time of day, don't you? Indian or China, and would you like scones or teacakes?'

'China and scones, please. What a charming village.' The lady smiled at her and Mary Jane smiled back; her customer wasn't young but she was dressed in the kind of tweeds Mary Jane would have liked to be able to afford and her pepper and salt hair was stylishly dressed. She had a very kind face, full of laughter lines.

Mary Jane brought the tea and a plate of scones, butter and a dish of strawberry jam, and Sir Thomas's mother engaged her in idle talk while she studied her. So this was the girl with the violet eyes; the tartar with a sharp tongue. She approved of what she saw and the eyes were certainly startlingly lovely.

'I don't suppose you get many customers at this time of year?' she asked casually.

'Well, no, although today I've been quite busy...'

'You don't open until mid-morning, I suppose,' asked Mrs Latimer, following a train of thought.

'About nine o'clock—I opened early today, though—someone who had been up all night and needed a hot drink.'

Mary Jane's cheeks went nicely pink at the thought of Sir Thomas. To cover her sudden confusion at the thought of him, she went on lightly, 'He had a dog with him—he was called Watson...'

'What an unusual name,' said Mrs Latimer, and silently congratulated herself on her maternal instincts. 'For a dog, I mean. What delicious scones.' She smiled at Mary Jane. 'I am so glad I came here.'

CHAPTER FOUR

THE EVENINGS WERE closing in and the mornings were crisp. Mary Jane, locking the door after another day almost devoid of customers, thought of Felicity in London, from whom she had had a card that morning. The Paris show had been a resounding success and she was having a few days off before another week or so of modelling, this time in the Seychelles. Mary Jane, reading it without envy, wondered why they had to go so far to take photos of clothes which only a tiny percentage of women wore. She wondered who paid for it all—perhaps that was why the clothes were so wildly expensive.

She fed Brimble, had her supper and spent the evening shortening the hem of the jersey dress. Short skirts were the fashion and she had nice legs even if there was no one to notice that.

THE MORNING BROUGHT several customers, the last of whom, an elderly man, looked so ill she gave him a second cup of coffee without charging for it. He had a dreadful cough, too, watering eyes and a face as white as paper.

As he got up to go she said diffidently, 'You have got a frightful cold; should you be out?'

'Got a job to do,' he said hoarsely. 'No good giving in, miss.'

Poor fellow, thought Mary Jane, and then forgot him. Closing up for the day later, she peered out into the cold, wet evening and thought with sympathy of Dr and Mrs Fellowes, who had gone to London for a few days. It was no weather for a holiday.

She woke up in the night with a sore throat and when she got up she had a headache. There were no customers all day and for once she was glad because she was beginning to feel peculiar. She closed early, locking the door thankfully against persistent rain and a rising wind and, since she wasn't hungry, she fed Brimble, made herself a hot drink and went to bed after a hot bath, but even its warmth and that of the hot water bottle she clasped to her made no difference to the icy shivers running down her spine. Brimble, that most understanding of cats, got on to the bed presently and stretched out against her and soon she slept, fitfully, relieved when it was morning. A cup of tea teamed with a couple of Panadol would make her feel better. She crept downstairs, gave Brimble his breakfast, drank her tea and went back to bed. The weather had worsened during the night and there was no one about; there would certainly be no customers. She went to sleep again, to wake every few hours with a blinding headache and a chest which hurt when she breathed. It was late afternoon when she crawled out of bed again to feed Brimble, wash her face and put on a clean nightie. A night's sleep would surely get her back on her feet, she thought. She ought to make herself a drink, but the very idea of going downstairs again made her feel ill. She got back into bed…

She woke several times aware that she was thirsty, that she should feed Brimble, put on some clothes and knock on Mrs Adams's door and get her to ask Dr Fel-

lowes's locum to come, but somehow she couldn't be
bothered to do anything about things. She was dimly
aware that Brimble was mewing but she was by now so
muddled that she quite thought she had been downstairs
to put out his food. She fell into an uneasy doze, not
heeding the rain and the wind rattling at the windows.

SIR THOMAS, DRIVING himself back from a consultation in
Bristol, turned off the motorway at Swindon. He would
have to stop for lunch somewhere and he might as well
go a little out of his way and have it at Mary Jane's. He
had no appointments for the rest of the day and driving
was tiring in the appalling weather. It was more than a
little out of his way; from the village he would have to
drive to Oxford but he had reasoned that he could pick
up the M40 there, a mere fifty miles or so from London.

It was just after one o'clock when he stopped at the
tea-room. There was no one around and no traffic, not
that there was ever very much of that and he wasn't
surprised to see the 'Closed' sign on the door. Mary
Jane would be having her lunch. He got out of the car
and went to the door and rang the bell and, since no
one came, peered into the little room. Brimble was sitting on the little counter at the back, looking anxious,
and when Sir Thomas tapped on the glass he jumped
down and came to the door, standing on his hind legs,
mewing urgently.

Sir Thomas rang again and knocked for good mea-
sure, standing patiently in his Burberry, the rain drench-
ing his head. He stood back from the door and looked up
to the windows above but there was no sign of anyone
and after a moment he walked to the end of the little
terrace and went down the narrow alley which led to the
back gardens. Mary Jane's cottage was halfway along,

he opened the flimsy gate, crossed the small garden and went to peer through the kitchen window. The kitchen was untidy, not at all in its usual state with a pan full of milk on the stove and the kettle and dishes and cutlery lying around. As he looked, Brimble jumped on to the draining board by the sink and scratched at the window, which, since he had his own cat-flap, seemed unnecessary. The cottages on either side were unlit and silent; Sir Thomas took out his Swiss Army penknife, selected one of its versatile components and eased it into the window frame.

The window opened easily for the hasp was loose, and he swung it wide so that Brimble might go out. He didn't want to. Instead he jumped down and went to the door leading to the stairs standing half-open.

Sir Thomas took off his Burberry, threw it into the kitchen and squeezed through the window, no easy task for a man of his splendid size. He gained the floor and stood for a moment, listening. When he called, 'Mary Jane,' in a quiet voice, there was silence and he started up the narrow little stairs.

As he reached the tiny landing Mary Jane came wobbling out of the bedroom. She was barefoot and in her nightie and her hair hung down her back and over her shoulders in an appalling tangle. Her pinched face was a nasty colour and her eyelids puffy. Not a pretty sight.

'Oh, it's you,' she said in a hoarse whisper.

Sir Thomas bit back strong language, scooped her up and laid her back in the tumbled bedclothes. She was in no state to answer questions; he went back downstairs, out of the door this time, fetched his bag from the car, paused long enough to fill Brimble's bowl with what he took to be cold milk-pudding in the top of the fridge and took the stairs two at a time.

Mary Jane hadn't moved but she opened her eyes as he sat down on the side of the bed. She was too weary to speak, which was just as well, for he popped a thermometer under her tongue and took her wrist in his large cool hand. It felt comforting and she curled her hot fingers round it and closed her eyes again.

Her temperature was high and her breaths rapid and so was her pulse. He said with reassuring calm, 'You have a nasty bout of flu, Mary Jane. Who's your doctor?'

She opened an eye. 'He's away.'

'Is there anyone to look after you?'

She frowned, not wanting to bother to answer him. 'No.'

He tucked her in firmly. 'I'll be back,' he told her and went out of the back door again and round to the front, to bang on the doors on either side of the tea-room. No one came to answer his thumps and he went to his car and picked up the phone.

Back in the cottage he set to work with quiet speed, clearing the kitchen, shutting and locking the kitchen door, fastening the window and then going upstairs again to fetch his bag. Mary Jane opened her eyes once more. 'Do go away,' she begged. 'I've such a headache.'

'You'll feel better presently,' he assured her, and then asked, 'Have you a box or basket for Brimble?'

'On top of the wardrobe.' She sat up suddenly. 'Why? He's all right, he's not ill?'

'No, but you are. I'm taking you to someone who will look after you both for a day or two. Now be a good girl and stay quiet until I get organised.'

Brimble wasn't pleased to be stuffed gently into his basket, but the hands which picked him up and stowed him away were gentle and he had been easily mellowed by the milk-pudding. He was borne into the tea-room and the basket put on top of one of the tables, next to the bag Sir Thomas had brought downstairs. He unlocked the shop door next and went back upstairs, rolled Mary Jane in the quilt and carried her downstairs. The stairs, being narrow, made things a bit difficult, but Mary Jane was small and slight even if the quilt was bulky. He opened the tea-room door and with some difficulty the car door and arranged his bundle beside his seat, strapped her in and went back for Brimble and his bag before locking the door of the tea-room. He was very wet by now since he hadn't bothered to put his Burberry on again but thrown it into the back of the car, but before he got into the car he stood a moment looking up and down the street. There was no sign of anyone; presumably everyone was indoors, sitting cosily by the fire, no doubt with the TV on very loud to drown the sound of the wind and the rain. He got in, gave a quick look at Mary Jane's sickly face and drove off.

After a minute or so Mary Jane opened her eyes. She felt very ill but she knew vaguely that there were some things she needed to know.

'Not hospital,' she muttered. 'Brimble...'

'Don't fuss,' advised Sir Thomas. 'You're going somewhere so that you can lie in bed for a day or two and get well, and Brimble will be right by you.'

'Oh, good,' said Mary Jane, and, remembering her manners, 'thank you, so sorry to be such a nuisance.'

She dozed off, lulled by his grunt, a reassuring commonplace sound which soothed her. She stirred only slightly when he stopped before his mother's front door and lifted her out as though she had been a bundle of feathers and carried her in. Mrs Latimer, waiting in the hall, took one look at Mary Jane. 'Oh, the poor child.

Upstairs, Thomas, the garden room—there's a balcony for the cat.'

He paused for a second by her. 'Bless you, you've thought of everything.'

He went on up the staircase and she received Brimble in his basket and went up after him at a more leisurely pace.

Sir Thomas laid Mary Jane on the bed and carefully unrolled her out of the quilt and Mrs Beaver tucked the bedclothes around her. 'There, there,' she said comfortably, 'the poor young thing. Just you go away, Sir Thomas, and I'll have her put to rights in no time at all. A nice wash and a clean nightie and some of my lemonade.'

Mrs Latimer, coming into the room, nodded her head, set Brimble's basket down on the covered balcony and put a hand on her son's sleeve. 'Shall I get Dr Finney?'

'I'll have a look at her when you've tidied her up. The sooner I get her on to antibiotics the better. You might get him up tomorrow if you would, Mother.'

'Yes, dear. Now go away and have a drink or something and we'll let you know when we are ready for you.'

When he went upstairs again Mary Jane was awake; save for her eyes there was no colour in her face but her hair had been brushed and hung, neatly plaited, over one shoulder and she was wearing one of Mrs Latimer's nighties.

'That's better.' He came and sat on the edge of the bed and felt her pulse. It was galloping along at a fine rate and he frowned a little. 'I'm going to start you off on an antibiotic,' he told her. He spoke with pleasant

remoteness, a doctor visiting his patient. 'An injection.
I'll get it ready while Mrs Beaver turns you over.'

She couldn't be bothered to answer him; now that
she was clean and in a warm bed all she wanted to do
was sleep. 'Where's Brimble?' she asked suddenly, and
rolled over obedient to Mrs Beaver's kind hands.

'Having a snack on the balcony,' said Sir Thomas,
sliding in the needle as Mrs Beaver drew back the bedclothes and ignoring Mary Jane's startled yelp.

'There, dearie, all over,' said Mrs Beaver. 'You just
turn over on to the other side and have a little nap.'

'It's sore.' Mary Jane's hoarse voice sounded ag-
grieved; tears weren't far off.

'Here's Brimble,' said Sir Thomas. She heard his
voice, remote and kind and felt Brimble's small furry
body beside her, closed her eyes on threatening tears
and went to sleep.

Sir Thomas stood for a moment looking down at her.
She looked not a day over fifteen…

Downstairs he found his mother sitting in the drawing-room. 'I think I will ring Finney,' he told her, 'explain the circumstances.'

She agreed, 'Yes, dear. I'll take good care of her—
it is flu?'

'Yes, but I suspect that there's a mild pneumonia as
well. I have no idea how long she was lying there ill.'

'You would have thought that the neighbours would
have noticed that the tea-room was closed.'

'Normally, yes, but with this bad weather it would
seem normal enough for her not to open, don't you
think?'

When he came back from phoning they went to a be-
lated lunch and as they drank their coffee Mrs Latimer

asked, 'Has she no family at all? Did you not mention a sister? She should be told.'

'Felicity—yes, of course, if she is in London. I gather that she seldom is, but I have her address and phone number.' He saw his mother's look of surprise and smiled a little. 'I'll look her up. I'm free for the rest of today.'

'If you do see her, Thomas, and she is anxious about Mary Jane, do tell her that she is very welcome to come here and make sure that she is all right.'

'Thank you, dear.' They were back in the drawing-room and Mrs Latimer began to talk about other things until presently Sir Thomas said, 'I think I'll just take a quick look at Mary Jane before I go. Is Mrs Beaver in the kitchen or in her own room?'

Mrs Latimer glanced at the clock. 'In the kitchen getting the tea-tray ready.'

He went first to look at Mary Jane, deeply asleep now, one arm flung around Brimble. Her washed out face had a little colour now and her breathing was easier; he took her pulse and put a hand on her forehead and then went downstairs to find Mrs Beaver. 'Wake her and wash her and give her plenty to drink and something to eat if she fancies it—yoghurt or something similar. Dr Finney will come in the morning and give you fresh instructions. Thank you, Mrs Beaver—it will only be for a couple of days; I believe she is through the worst of it.'

He drank his tea, promised his mother that he would phone her that evening and drove back to London, leaving his parent thoughtful.

Mary Jane, unaware of his departure and indeed rather hazy as to whether she had seen him at all, woke to find Mrs Latimer sitting by the bed. She still felt ill and weary but her headache was better and she was warm.

When she tried to sit up Mrs Latimer said, 'No, dear, just lie still. We are going to wash your face and hands and make you comfortable and then you are going to eat a little something. Thomas told me to be sure that you did and presently he will telephone to find out if I have done as he asked.'

She smiled so kindly that Mary Jane, to her shame, felt tears fill her eyes and spill down her cheeks. Mrs Latimer said nothing, merely wiped them away and told her that she was getting better and then Mrs Beaver came in with a basin and towels and Brimble was coaxed away to eat his supper on the balcony while she was washed and her hair combed. She lay passive while the two ladies tidied her, fighting a fresh desire to burst into tears; she had looked after herself for so long that she had forgotten how marvellous it was to be cosseted with such care and gentleness.

Mrs Latimer saw the tears. 'Cry if you want to, my dear. I'm sure you're not a watering pot normally, it's just the flu. You're going to feel so much better in the morning.'

She was quite right. Mary Jane woke feeling as though she had been put through a mangle, but her head was clear; she even wished to get up, to be sternly discouraged by Mrs Beaver, standing over her while she drank her tea and ate some scrambled egg.

'If you would tell me,' began Mary Jane.

'All in good time, miss, you just lie there and get well—bless you, a day or two in bed'll do you all the good in the world and you could do with a bit of flesh on those bones.'

Sir Thomas telephoned as his mother was sitting

down to breakfast; he had phoned on the previous evening to tell her that he had rung Felicity and was taking her out to dinner later; now he wanted to know how Mary Jane was and Mrs Latimer said carefully, 'Well, Thomas, I don't know much about it, but she seems better. Very limp and still rather hot but she's had several cups of tea and a few mouthfuls of scrambled egg. I gave her the pills you left for her to take. What did her sister say?'

He didn't answer at once. Felicity had been charming when he had phoned, expressed concern about Mary Jane and begged him to go and see her at her flat. He hadn't wanted to do that; instead he had arranged to take her out to dinner and over that meal he had told her about Mary Jane. She had listened for a few minutes and then smiled charmingly at him across the table. 'She'll be all right, she's awfully tough—it's very kind of you to bother.' She had put out a hand and touched his on the table. 'Could we go somewhere and dance?'

He had refused with beautiful manners, pleading patients to see and the hospital to visit and had driven her back to her flat, and when she had asked him where he lived he had evaded her question.

'She told me that Mary Jane would be all right, that she was tough—oh, and that it was kind of us to bother.'

'I see,' said Mrs Latimer, who didn't. 'Dr Finney will be here presently, will you be at your rooms? He could phone you there.'

'Yes, ask him to do that, will you? I'll phone you this evening— I don't think I'll have time before then.'

He rang off and Mrs Latimer finished her breakfast and went back to Mary Jane. 'My doctor is coming to see you presently; perhaps we can tidy you up first?'

'I could get up,' began Mary Jane. 'I feel much better. I'm giving you so much trouble and you are so kind…'

'It's delightful to have someone to fuss over, my dear. Thomas, as you can imagine, has long outgrown any attempts of mine to cosset him. How would you like a nice warm bath before Dr Finney comes and then pop back into bed?'

Mary Jane was sitting up very clean and fresh in another of her hostess's nighties, still pale and limp but doing her best to appear her normal self, when Dr Finney came. He was elderly and rather slow and very kind.

He examined Mary Jane very thoroughly, tapping her chest and thumping her gently and bidding her say 'nine nine nine' and put out her tongue. All these things done, he said thoughtfully, 'A narrow squeak, young lady; another day and you would have been in hospital with pneumonia. Most fortunate that Thomas found you and acted quickly. Another two days in bed and then you may return to your home. You don't have a job?'

'I run a tea-room.'

'Do you, indeed? How interesting. By all means return to it but don't attempt to exert yourself for a few more days. Take the pills which Thomas has left you and there's no reason why you shouldn't get out of bed from time to time and walk round.' His eye lighted on Brimble, who had just come in and had jumped on to the bed. 'A cat? Bless my soul!'

'He is mine, Sir Thomas brought him here with me.'

'Of course. I shall come and see you again in two days' time, young lady, and I expect to find you very much better.'

When Mrs Latimer came back presently Mary Jane said, 'I can't think why Sir Thomas brought me here.

That sounds awfully rude but you do understand what I mean, Mrs Latimer. I could have gone to…' She paused because she couldn't think of anywhere, only Margaret, who wouldn't have had her anyway, and Miss Kemble, who would have had her and nursed her, too, but only because of a strong sense of duty. All her other friends lived in small houses with children or elderly grannies or grandpas in the spare bedrooms.

'I think,' said Mrs Latimer carefully, 'that Thomas realised that by the time he had found someone in the village who could spare the time to look after you you would have been fit only for the hospital and that would have been such an upheaval, wouldn't it, dear?'

'If I had some clothes I could go home as soon as Dr Finney says I may. I don't want to put you to any more trouble, I can never thank you enough.'

'We can talk about that in two days' time; now you are going to have a nap and presently Mrs Beaver will bring you a little lunch. Remember, my dear, that we are really enjoying having you here even though you aren't well. Allow two elderly ladies to spoil you.'

Mrs Latimer smiled at her and went away and Mary Jane closed her eyes and slept, with the faithful Brimble curled up against her.

It was amazing what two days of good food and ample rest did for Mary Jane. Her hair, washed by Mrs Beaver, shone with soft brown lights, her face lost its pinched look and its colour returned and her eyes regained their sparkle. Not pretty, but nice to look at, reflected Mrs Latimer.

After Dr Finney had been to see her again Mary Jane asked diffidently if someone could possibly get her clothes so that she might return home, 'For I have trespassed on your kindness too long,' she pointed out.

'If only I had the key, Mrs Adams could go and get me the clothes and send them at once.'

Mrs Latimer looked vague. 'Well, I suppose that Thomas has the key, my dear, but since he will be coming tomorrow, I'm sure he will know what is best to be done.'

So Mary Jane, wrapped in one of her hostess's quilted dressing-gowns, spent a happy day being shown round the house and sitting in Mrs Latimer's pretty little sitting-room at the back of the hall, listening to that lady talking about Thomas. She longed to ask why, at the age of thirty-four, he wasn't married. Perhaps he was divorced or loved someone already married to another man, perhaps she had died young... Mary Jane, with a lively imagination, allowed it to run riot.

He arrived the next day after lunch and he wasn't alone. Felicity got out of the car and accompanied him into the house, was introduced to his mother and made a pretty little speech to her; she had found that she had a couple of days free and on the spur of the moment she had telephoned to Sir Thomas and asked if she might accompany him if and when he next went to his home. 'I have been anxious about Mary Jane,' she added with one of her charming smiles. Mrs Latimer hid her doubts about that, welcomed her warmly and suggested that she might like to go and see Mary Jane at once.

'Oh, yes, please. She isn't infectious, is she? I have several bookings next week; I have to be careful...'

Mrs Latimer led her upstairs, leaving Sir Thomas to go into the drawing-room with Watson, where presently she joined him.

'What a very pretty girl,' she observed, sitting down by the fire. Her voice was dry and he looked at her, smiling a little.

'Beautiful. I'm sorry not to have let you know, but I had no time, I was on the point of leaving when she phoned. I could do nothing else but suggest that she could come.'

'Of course, dear. She expects to stay the night, I dare say.'

'She has an overnight bag with her—said something about putting up at the local pub.'

'No, no, she must stay here. I dare say Mary Jane is delighted to see her.' She didn't look at her son. 'The dear child is so anxious to go back to her tea-room but of course she has no clothes. What do you suggest?'

'I'll drive over presently, take Mrs Beaver with me and fetch what she needs. The place was in a mess; perhaps we could tidy it up a little before I take her back.'

'Do you suppose her sister will go with her and stay a day or two?'

'Unlikely...' He broke off as Felicity came into the room.

'May I come in? Mary Jane is resting so I didn't stay long. What a lovely house you have, Mrs Latimer. I do love old houses; I'd love to see round it.'

She sat down near Sir Thomas and smiled enchantingly at him, and he wondered how two sisters could be so unlike each other. 'I'll go and take a look at her,' he said blandly, 'see if she's fit to go home.'

'I'll come with you,' said Felicity.

'No, no. If she is resting, the fewer visitors she has, the better.'

He took no notice of her pretty little *moue* of disappointment and went away. First to the kitchen to see Mrs Beaver and then upstairs, where he found Mary Jane not resting at all but sitting in a chair with Brimble on her knee, looking out of the window at the dull weather outside.

'Not resting?' he asked, and pulled up a chair to sit beside her. 'Felicity said that you were. How are you?'

'I'm quite well, thank you, Sir Thomas. It was very kind of you to invite Felicity.'

He didn't answer that but observed, 'I hear that you would like to get back to your cottage. I'm going to take Mrs Beaver over there now. Make a list of what you need and we'll bring your things back and I'll drive you over first thing tomorrow morning.'

'I could go as soon as you come back...'

'And so you could, but you're not going to. Another night here won't do you any harm and my mother is loath to let you go.' He got out his pocket-book and a pen and handed them to her. 'Make your list. Mrs Beaver is waiting.'

He was brisk and businesslike so she did her best to be the same, making a careful list with directions as to where everything was. Handing it to him, she tried once more. 'I could go back this afternoon if you wouldn't mind taking me, really I could.'

'Don't be obstinate,' said Sir Thomas, and went away to come back within a few minutes with Mrs Beaver, hatted and coated in case Mary Jane had forgotten something. 'There's no reason why you shouldn't come downstairs and have tea with my mother and Felicity,' he said kindly, and pulled her gently out of her chair. 'Bring Brimble; it's time he and Watson met.'

So she went downstairs and met Watson waiting patiently at the bottom of the stairs for his master. He sniffed delicately at Brimble and Brimble eyed him from the shelter of Mary Jane's arms and muttered before they went into the drawing-room.

'Mary Jane's coming down for tea—we'll be back in good time for dinner.'

'You're not taking Mary Jane back?' Felicity sounded flurried. 'She hasn't any clothes here?'

'We're going to fetch them now.'

'Oh, then I'll come with you…' Felicity had jumped up.

'Mrs Beaver is coming, she knows what to get, but it's good of you to offer.'

He whistled to Watson and went away, leaving the three of them to chat over their tea. At least Felicity did most of the talking, relating titbits of gossip about the people she had met, the glamorous clothes she modelled and the delightful life she led. 'Of course,' she told Mrs Latimer airily, 'I shall give it all up when I marry but it will be so useful—I mean, knowing about clothes and make-up and being social.'

'You are engaged?' asked Mrs Latimer.

'No, not yet. I've had ever so many chances but I know the kind of man I intend to marry—plenty of money, because I'm used to that, a good social background, good looks.' She gave a little tinkling laugh. 'I'll make a good wife to a man with a successful career.'

All the while she talked Mary Jane sat quietly. Sir Thomas, she reflected, was exactly the kind of husband her sister intended to marry, and she was pretty and amusing enough for him to fall in love with her—and he had invited her to come to his mother's home, hadn't he? He had not answered her but he hadn't denied it either. Mrs Latimer quietly took the conversation into her own hands presently and suggested taking Felicity to her room so that she might tidy herself. 'We dine at eight o'clock,' she told her. 'I do hope you will be comfortable; if there is anything you need, do please ask.'

Mary Jane, left alone with Brimble, began making resolute plans for her return. There would be the baking to see to and the place to clean up, for as far as she could remember it had been in something of a pickle when Sir Thomas had fetched her away. He had been so kind and she had put him to a great deal of trouble, she hoped that Mrs Beaver had been able to find everything easily so that he hadn't had to wait too long. The cottage would be cold; she should have asked him to light the gas fire in the sitting-room and sit there…

HE HADN'T EVEN been into the sitting-room. He and Mrs Beaver had gone into the cold tea-room and through to the kitchen which was indeed in a pickle.

'You go upstairs and get the clothes,' he told Mrs Beaver. 'I'll tidy up here.'

He had taken off his coat and his jacket and rolled up his shirt-sleeves and boiled several kettles of water, washed everything he could see that needed it, dried them and put them away, found a broom and swept the floor and looked in the cupboard. There was tea there, and sugar and a packet of biscuits, cat food and some porridge oats. The fridge held butter and lard, some rather hard cheese and a few rashers of bacon. He went to the foot of the stairs and called up to Mrs Beaver who was trotting to and fro and she peered down at him from the tiny landing. Before he could speak she observed, 'It's a shocking shame, Sir Thomas, that dear child— two of everything, beautifully washed and ironed and mended to death and a cupboard with almost nothing to wear in it. Good stuff, mind you, but dear knows when she went shopping last.' She drew a breath. 'And that sister of hers in them silks and satins—blood's thicker than water, I say and I don't care who hears me say it.'

'Perhaps something can be done about that. I'm going over to the village shop—it should be open still, there's almost no food in the house. Surely the milk-man calls…'

'Look outside the back door, sir…'

The milk was there; he fetched it in and put it in the fridge, got into his coat and walked to the shop where he bought what he hoped were the right groceries and bore them back to stack them in the cupboard.

Mrs Beaver was ready by then; they got back into the car and he half listened to Mrs Beaver's indignant but respectful remarks about young girls being left to fend for themselves. She paused for breath at last and added apologetically, 'I do hope I've not put you out, sir, letting me tongue run away with me like that and you likely as not sweet on the young lady. I must own she's pretty enough to catch any gentleman's eye.'

Sir Thomas agreed placidly.

HE FOUND HIS mother and Mary Jane in the drawing-room, bent over a complicated piece of tapestry. They looked up as he went in and Mary Jane got to her feet. 'I'll go and dress,' she said. 'And thank you very much indeed, Sir Thomas.'

He smiled. 'You look very nice as you are, but I dare say you will feel more yourself in a dress.' He held the door for her as she went into the hall. 'Mrs Beaver's taken your case upstairs. Would you like to leave Brim-ble here? Watson won't hurt him.'

He took the cat from her and watched her go up the staircase before going back into the room.

'Where is our guest?' he asked.

'She went upstairs to tidy herself. Is the cottage all right for Mary Jane to go back?'

'As clean and tidy as we could make it. I fetched some food from the shop—the lady who owns it said they were beginning to wonder where Mary Jane had gone—no one had been out much because of the bad weather and those that had had supposed that she had closed the tea-room since there was no chance of customers. Her neighbours had been away and the Misses Potter, who call regularly, had been indoors with bad colds. A series of unfortunate events.' He sat down opposite her. 'I'm sure that once she is back the village will rally round—she is very well-liked.'

'I'm not surprised...' Mrs Latimer broke off as the door opened and Felicity came into the room. She had changed into a silk sheath of vivid green, its brevity allowing an excellent view of her shapely legs, its neckline, from Mrs Latimer's point of view, immodest. She walked slowly to join them, giving Sir Thomas time to study her charming if unsuitable appearance. It was a pity that he got to his feet almost without a glance and went to get her a drink.

Ten minutes later Mary Jane joined them, wearing the skirt of her suit and a Marks and Spencer blouse, and this time Sir Thomas allowed his gaze to dwell upon her prosaic person. What he thought was nobody's business; all he said was, 'Ah, Mary Jane, come and sit down and have a glass of sherry.'

CHAPTER FIVE

MRS LATIMER SPOKE. 'Come and sit by me, Mary Jane. How nice to see you dressed and well again. You have recovered so quickly, too. I'm glad for your sake but we shall miss you. Once you are settled in I shall drive over and have tea with you again.'

Mary Jane's quiet answer was drowned by Felicity's voice. 'How I wish that I could live away from London—I do love the country and the quiet life. Sometimes I wish that I would never need to travel so much again. How I envy you, Mary Jane.'

Not easily aroused to bad temper, Mary Jane found these sentiments too hard to swallow. 'Well, I don't suppose it would matter much if you gave up your modelling—there must be dozens of girls… I could do with some help, especially in the summer.' She spoke in a matter-of-fact voice, smiling a little. No one would have known that she was seething; first her dull, sensible clothes, highlighted pitilessly by Felicity's *couture* and now this nonsense about wanting to live in the country. Why, she had run away from it just as soon as she could… Sir Thomas, watching her quiet face from under his eyelids, had a shrewd idea of her thoughts. The contrast between her and her sister was too striking to overlook, especially the clothes; on the other hand, he conceded, Felicity hadn't beautiful eyes the colour of violets.

He said smoothly, 'You would probably find living in the country very dull, Felicity. Are you working at present?'

'Next week—here in London—perhaps we could meet? And then I'm off to New York for the shows. I was there last year and I had a marvellous time. The parties—you have no idea…'

She embarked on a colourful account of her visit and the three of them listened, Mary Jane with understandable wistfulness, Mrs Latimer with an apparent interest because she had never been ill-mannered in her life, and Sir Thomas with an inscrutable face which gave away nothing of his true feelings.

During dinner, however, Felicity was forced to curb her chatter; Sir Thomas kept the conversation firmly upon mundane matters, and, after drinking coffee with the ladies, he pleaded telephone calls to make and went away to the library, presumably not noticing Felicity's sulky face.

He returned just as Felicity, bored with her companions, declared herself ready for bed.

'Is eight o'clock too early for you?' asked Sir Thomas of Mary Jane. 'I need to be back in town by lunchtime.'

'That's fine,' said Mary Jane. 'But surely I could catch a bus or something…' She frowned. 'All the trouble…'

Felicity had been listening. 'I'll come with you…'

'It would mean getting up at half-past six,' Sir Thomas pointed out suavely.

She hesitated. 'Oh, well, perhaps not. It isn't as if Mary Jane needs anyone any more. I'll be waiting here for you when you get back.'

She smiled her most bewitching smile, quite lost on Sir Thomas who had turned away to speak to his mother.

IT WAS ONE of those mornings in autumn when night was reluctant to give way to morning. It was raining, too. They left exactly at eight o'clock and Mrs Latimer had come down to see them off. She had embraced Mary Jane warmly and promised to see her again shortly, and now they were in the car driving back to the tea-room, she beside Sir Thomas, Brimble in his basket, indignantly silent on the back seat. There seemed no need for conversation; Mary Jane sensed that her companion had no wish to listen to chatter, not that she was much good at that and at that time of day small talk seemed out of place. However, although for the most part they were silent, it wasn't uneasy. She sat quietly, planning her week while Sir Thomas thought his own thoughts. Presumably they were amusing, for once or twice he smiled.

At the tea-room he took no notice of her protests that she was quite able to be left at its door. He got out, opened the door, reached into the car for Brimble's basket, took her key from her and ushered her into her home.

It was chilly and unwelcoming. 'Wait here,' he told her and went upstairs to light the gas fire, switch on the kitchen light and set Brimble's basket down on the table. He fetched her case then, took it upstairs and found her in the kitchen. 'How very clean and tidy it is,' she told him. 'I'm sure I left it in a frightful mess. Will you have a cup of coffee before you go?'

'I wish I could but I must get back.' He took her hand

in his, smiling down at her very kindly. 'Take care of yourself, Mary Jane.'

She stared at him. 'You've been very kind, I can never thank you or Mrs Latimer enough, and thank you for bringing me back.' She offered a hand and he took it, bending to kiss her cheek as he did so. She watched him drive away, wondering if she would ever see him again. Probably not. On the other hand, if he should fall in love with Felicity, she would.

She went into the kitchen and released Brimble, made herself a pot of tea, unpacked her few things and put on her pinny. Customers were unlikely. On the other hand, she had to be ready for them if they did come. She went to turn the sign to 'Open' and only then saw the box on the table by the door. There was a bunch of flowers on it, too—chrysanthemums, the small ones which lasted for weeks, just what was needed to cheer up the tea-room...

She took the lid off the box then, and discovered a cooked chicken, straw potatoes and salad in a covered container, egg custard in a pottery dish and a crock of Stilton cheese; there was even a small bottle of wine.

Much cheered, she arranged the flowers on the tables, got the coffee going and got out her pastry board. As soon as she had made some scones she would sit down and write to Mrs Latimer—Mrs Beaver too— and thank them for their kindness.

THERE WAS NO sign of Felicity by the time Sir Thomas reached his mother's house. He went to bid his mother goodbye and went in search of Mrs Beaver. He found her in the kitchen. 'Ask Rosie or Tracey—' the girls who came from the village each day to help in the house '—to go to Miss Seymour's room and tell her that I am leaving in five minutes. If she is unable to be ready by then, Mrs Latimer will get a taxi for her so that she can get to Banbury and get a train to town.'

Felicity was in the hall with a minute to spare and very put out. 'My make-up,' she moaned prettily, 'I haven't had time, and I've thrown my things into my case...' She pouted prettily at Sir Thomas who remained impervious. 'Perhaps we could stop on the way...'

He had beautiful manners. 'I'm so sorry, but there won't be time—I must be at the hospital. Shall we go?'

She bade Mrs Latimer goodbye with the hope that she would see her again. 'For I haven't had time to see your lovely home, have I?' But Mrs Beaver she ignored, sweeping past her to get into the car.

'You'd never know that they were sisters,' declared Mrs Beaver sourly. A thought echoed by Sir Thomas as he swept the Rolls out of the gate and through the village.

Felicity, accustomed to the admiration of the men she met, worked hard to attract Sir Thomas, but although he was a charming companion he remained aloof, and when he stopped the car outside her flat she had the feeling that she had made no impression on him whatsoever. It was a galling thought and a spur to her determination to get him interested in her. Obviously, he had no interest in her success as a model or the glamorous life she led. She would have to change her tactics. She bade him goodbye in a serious voice, with no suggestion that they might meet again and added a rider to the effect that she hoped Mary Jane would be all right. 'I shall take the first opportunity to go down and see her,' she assured him, and he murmured suitably, thinking that the likelihood of that seemed remote. One could never tell, however; beneath that frivolous manner there might be a heart of gold. He thought it unlikely, but he was a tolerant man, ready to think the best of everything and everyone. He dismissed her from his mind and drove to the hospital.

MARY JANE WAS taking the first batch of scones out of the oven when her first customers came in. A young couple barely on speaking terms, the girl having misread the map and directed her companion in entirely the wrong direction. They sat eyeing each other stormily over the little vase of flowers. Mary Jane brought the coffee and they wanted to know just where they were. She told them and the man muttered, 'We're miles out of our way thanks to my map-reader here.' He glared at the girl.

'No, you're not,' said Mary Jane. 'Just keep on this road and turn right at the first crossroads—you're only a few miles in the wrong direction.'

She left them to their coffee and presently the door opened and the Misses Potter came in.

'Not our usual time, my dear,' said Miss Emily, 'but we were on our way to the stores and saw that you were back. Have you had a nice little break?'

Mary Jane said that, yes, she had and fetched the coffee pot just as Miss Kemble came in. 'I see you're back,' she said briskly. 'You have enjoyed your holiday, Mary Jane?'

It didn't seem worthwhile explaining. Mary Jane said that yes, she had, and poured more coffee. The young couple went presently, on speaking terms once more, and a tall, thin man with a drooping moustache came in and asked for lunch.

She hadn't had time to make sausage rolls and the demand for lunch during the winter was so small that she could only offer soup and sandwiches. She went to the kitchen to open the soup and slice bread, reflecting as she did so that someone had stocked up the fridge while she had been away. She would have to ask Mrs Latimer...

By one o'clock everyone had gone; she made herself some coffee, ate biscuits and cheese, fed Brimble and went upstairs. Beyond a quick look round she had had no time to put anything away and the bed would have to be made up.

That had been done and very neatly too, and so, when she looked, had her nightie been washed and ironed and folded away tidily. The bathroom was spotless and there wasn't a speck of dust anywhere. It was like having a fairy godmother.

She got into her outdoor things and went to the stores, exchanged the time of day with its owner and asked to use the phone. Mrs Latimer sounded pleased to hear from her and Mary Jane thanked her again for her kindness and then asked, 'Someone cleaned the cottage for me and the fridge is full of food and everything is washed and ironed. Did Sir Thomas...no sorry, I'm being silly, I'm sure he's never ironed anything in his life or bought groceries.'

Mrs Latimer chuckled. 'He certainly brought the food and I'm sure if he had to iron he would, and very well too. No, my dear, he took Mrs Beaver with him, she sorted out your things and together they tidied your cottage. Thomas is a dab hand at washing up.'

'Is he really?' said Mary Jane, much astonished. 'If I write him a note could you please send it on to him? And will you thank Mrs Beaver? As soon as I have time I'll write to you and her as well.'

'We look forward to that, my dear. Have you opened your tea-room yet?'

'Yes, and had customers too. I'm going back now to open until five o'clock although I don't expect anyone will come.'

They wished each other goodbye and she rang off and hurried back to her cottage. No one came that afternoon; she locked the door and went to get her supper, carrying the delicacies upstairs to the sitting-room to eat by the gas fire, with Brimble, on the lookout for morsels of chicken, sitting as close as he could get.

Her supper finished, she sat down to write her letters. Those to Mrs Latimer and Mrs Beaver were quickly done, but the note to Sir Thomas needed both time and thought. He had been kind and very helpful but not exactly friendly; it was hard to strike the right note and it took several wasted sheets of paper before she was satisfied with the result. By then it was time to go to bed.

She saw few customers during the following days. Doing her careful sums each evening, she decided that she was barely paying her way; there was certainly nothing to spare once her modest bills were paid. The winter always was a thin time, of course; it was just a question of hanging on until the spring. Looking out of the window at the dull autumn day, the spring looked a long way off. Luckily, there was Christmas; it might not bring more customers but those who came were usually full of the Christmas spirit and inclined to spend more. She was a neat-fingered girl and not easily depressed; in the tiny loft there was an old-fashioned trunk stuffed with old-fashioned clothes which had belonged to her mother. She got on to a chair and poked her head through the narrow opening. The loft was very small and cold and she wriggled into it and heard the scrab-

ble of mouse feet, but mice or no mice she wasn't going
to be put off. She leaned in as far as she was able and
dragged the trunk over to the opening. She wouldn't be
able to get it down into the cottage but she could open
it and see if there was anything she could use.

There was. A gauzy scarf, yards of lace, bundles of
ribbons, a watered silk petticoat, balls of wool still us-
able. She dragged them out, closed the trapdoor and
examined her finds at her leisure. The wool was fine
and in pale colours, splendid for dolls' clothes, even
baby clothes, and the lace and ribbons and silk could be
turned into the kinds of things people bought at Christmas: pincushions, lavender bags, beribboned nightdress
cases—rather useless trifles but people bought them
none the less. She went to bed that night, her head full
of plans.

There was a card from Felicity in the morning: she
was off to New York in two days' time and she had had
a meal with Thomas—they would meet again when she
got back. She didn't ask how Mary Jane was but Mary
Jane hadn't expected that, anyway. She read the card
again; she wasn't really surprised that Sir Thomas had
been seeing Felicity, but it made her vaguely unhappy.
'And that's silly,' she told Brimble, his whiskered face
buried in his breakfast saucer. 'For she's such a very
pretty girl and her clothes are lovely. Perhaps she'll
come and see us before Christmas,' and then, because
that was what she had really been thinking about, she
added, 'I wonder what meal it was and where they
went?'

SIR THOMAS COULD have told her if he had been there; he
had been waylaid—there was no other word for it—by
Felicity, who had taken pains to find out where he lived

and had just happened to be walking past his house as he returned from the hospital. That she had done this three evenings running without success was something she didn't disclose but she evinced delighted surprise at seeing him again. 'Perhaps we could have dinner together?' she had suggested. 'You must need cheering up after a hard day's work.'

Sir Thomas had been tired, he had wanted his dinner and a peaceful evening with no one but Watson for company while he caught up with the medical journals, but his manners were too nice to have said so; instead he had suggested that they had a drink in a pleasant little bar not too far away, 'For I have to go back to the hospital shortly and I have any amount of work to do this evening.'

She had pouted prettily and agreed and jumped into the car; she had great faith in her charm and good looks, and had no doubt that once they sat down she could persuade him to take her on to dinner—let the hospital wait, he was an important man and must surely do what he wanted to do; he wasn't some junior doctor at everyone's beck and call.

She was, of course, mistaken, and half an hour later she had found herself being put into a taxi with no more than a brisk handshake and regrets that he must cut short an enjoyable meeting. 'I had hoped you could drive me to my flat,' she had complained prettily, and turned her lovely face up to his. 'I do hate going home alone.'

Sir Thomas had handed the cabby some money. 'You must have many friends, Felicity; I'm sure you won't be alone for long.' He had lifted a hand in casual salute as the taxi drove off.

Tremble had come fussing into the hall as he opened
the door of his house and Watson had come to meet him.

'You're late, Sir Thomas—a bad day, perhaps?'

'No, no, Tremble, only the last hour or so. Give me
ten minutes, will you, while I go through the post?'

He had gone into his study with the faithful Watson
and leafed through his letters without paying much attention to them. He had had to waste part of an evening
listening to Felicity's airy chatter, and he had found her
tedious. 'A beautiful girl,' he told Watson. 'There's no
denying that, and charming too. Perhaps I am getting
middle-aged...'

It was much later that evening, standing by the
French windows leading to the small garden behind
the house, waiting for Watson to come in, that he had
decided that he would drive down to see how Mary
Jane was getting on. Her stiff little note of thanks had
amused him, it had so obviously taken time and thought
to compose, but she had given no hint as to how she
was. It would, he told himself, be only civil to go and
see her and make sure that she was quite well again.
He was free on Sunday...

CUSTOMERS HAD BEEN thin on the ground that week; the
Misses Potter came, as usual, of course, and one or
two women from the village on their way home from
shopping and the very occasional car. Mary Jane told
herself that things would improve and started on her
needlework. She had neat, clever fingers and a splendid
imagination; in no time at all she had a row of mice,
fashioned from the petticoat and wearing lace caps on
their tiny heads and frilly beribboned skirts. Quite useless but pretty trifles that she hoped someone would
buy. She was rather uncertain what she should ask for

them and settled on fifty pence, which Miss Emily Potter told her was far too low a price. All the same she bought one and told Miss Kemble about them. That lady bought one too, declaring it was just the thing for a birthday present for her niece. Mary Jane thought it rather a poor sort of present but perhaps she didn't like the niece very much. Selling two of the mice so quickly gave her the heart to continue with her sewing. She sat them on the counter so that anyone paying for their coffee would see them and, very much encouraged by a passing motorist buying three of them, began on a series of frivolous heart-shaped pincushions.

When Sir Thomas drew up outside the tea-room she was standing on the counter stowing away the potted fern which was usually on it so that there was more room for the mice. She had left the 'Open' sign on the door in the hope that a customer or two might come and she turned round as the door was opened and the bell rang.

Sir Thomas's bulk, elegantly clothed in cashmere, filled the doorway. His, 'Good morning, Mary Jane,' was pleasantly casual, which gave her time to change the expression of delight on her face to one of nothing more than polite surprise. But not before Sir Thomas had seen it.

He wasn't a man to mince his words. 'I thought we might have lunch together; may I bring Watson in?'

'Of course bring him in. It's warm in the kitchen. Brimble's there.'

Sir Thomas fetched the dog, shut the door behind him and took off his coat. 'Where would you like to go?' he asked.

'Well, thank you all the same, but I've made a chicken casserole—Mrs Fellowes keeps poultry and she gave me one—already killed, of course. It's in the oven now and I wouldn't like to waste it. It's a French recipe, thyme and parsley and a bay leaf and a small onion. There should be brandy too, but I haven't any so I used the cooking sherry left over from last Christmas.'

Sir Thomas, who had never before had an invitation refused, listened, fascinated. His magnificent nose quivered at the faint aroma coming from the kitchen. With commendable promptness he said, 'Delicious. May I stay to lunch?'

Mary Jane was still standing on the counter. She looked down at him a little uncertainly. 'Well, if you would like to…'

'Indeed I would.' He crossed the room and stretched up and lifted her down, reflecting that she was a little too thin. He saw the mice then and picked one up. 'And what exactly are these bits of nonsense?'

'Well, I'm not very busy at this time of year, so I thought I'd make something to sell—for Christmas you know.'

He studied it and held it in the palm of his hand. 'My mother would love one, and Mrs Beaver. May I have two—how much are they?'

Mary Jane went very pink. 'I would prefer to give them to you, if you don't mind. If you will choose two I will wrap them up.'

He would have to be more careful, Sir Thomas told himself, watching her wrap the mice in tissue paper. Mary Jane was proud-hearted; she might have few possessions but she had the right kind of pride. He asked casually after the Misses Potter, wanted to know if her cousin had been annoying her lately and had her laughing presently over some of Watson's antics.

'Do you mind sitting in the kitchen?' She led the way

to where the two animals were sitting amicably enough side by side before the cooking stove. 'I'll make some coffee and put the fire on upstairs.'

'I'll do that,' he said, and when he was downstairs again, he asked, 'Are there any odd jobs to be done while I'm here?'

'Would you reach up and get two plates from that top shelf? I don't often use them but they belonged to my mother.'

He reached up and put them on the table. 'Coalport—the Japan pattern—eighteenth-century? No, early nineteenth, isn't it? Delightful and very valuable, even just two plates.'

'Yes, we always used them when I was a little girl. I never discovered what happened to them all when we came to live with Uncle Matthew. When I came here Cousin Oliver told me that I could take a few plates and cups and saucers with me so I took these. I found them at the back of the china pantry.'

'The casserole will taste twice as good on them. Do you want me to peel potatoes or clean these sprouts?'

She gave him an astonished look. 'But you can't do that. At least, what I mean is you mustn't, you might cut your hands and then you couldn't operate.'

'Then I'll make the coffee...'

The little kitchen was very crowded, what with Sir Thomas and his massive frame taking up most of it and Watson and Brimble getting under their feet. He made the coffee and carried it up to the sitting-room, closely followed by Watson, Mary Jane and Brimble. He had switched on the little reading lamp and the room looked cosy. Sir Thomas stretched out his long legs and drank his coffee. He thought that Mary Jane was very restful; there was no need to talk just for the sake of talking and she was quite unselfconscious. Presently he suggested, 'Would you like to drive around for a while this afternoon? Even in the winter the Cotswolds are always delightful.'

'That would be nice, but isn't there something else you'd rather do?'

He hid a smile, 'No, Mary Jane, there isn't.'

'Well, then, I'd like that very much.' She put down her mug. 'There's the bell.'

Three elderly ladies nipped with the cold, wanting coffee and biscuits and, when the aroma from the casserole reached them, wanting lunch as well. Sir Thomas could hear Mary Jane apologising in her pretty voice and reflected that if he hadn't been there she would have probably offered to share her dinner with them. As it was, she gave them very careful instructions as to how to get to Stow-on-the-Wold where, she assured them they could get an excellent lunch at the Union Crest.

When they had gone Sir Thomas went downstairs and locked the door and turned the notice to 'Closed'. 'For nothing,' he explained, 'must hinder my enjoyment of the casserole.'

It was certainly delicious; Mary Jane had creamed the potatoes and cooked the sprouts to exactly the right moment, grated nutmeg over them and added a dollop of butter, thus adding to the perfection of the chicken.

Mary Jane had laid the kitchen table with care and, although they drank water from the tap and everything was dished up from the stove, the meal was as elegant as any in a West End restaurant. Mary Jane didn't quite believe him when he said that, but it was nice of him to say so.

They washed up together while Watson and Brimble ate their own hearty meal and, since the days were getting short now and the evenings came all too quickly, Sir Thomas took Watson for a brisk walk while Mary Jane got into her elderly winter coat, made sure that Brimble was cosy in his basket and, being a good housewife, went round turning off everything that needed to be turned off, shut windows and locked the back door securely.

Sir Thomas ushered her into the car, settled Watson on the back seat and went to lock the tea-room door.

'Have you any preference as to where we should go?' he asked her.

Mary Jane, very comfortable in the leather seat and quietly happy at the prospect of his company for an hour or so, had no preference at all.

He turned the car and went out of the village on the Gloucester road to turn off after a mile or so into the country. The road was narrow and there were few villages and almost no traffic. The big car went smoothly between the hedges, allowing them views on either side.

'You know this part of the country?' asked Sir Thomas.

'No, not well; I've never been on this road before. It's delightful.'

'It will take us to Broadway. There's another very quiet road from there to Pershore…'

At Pershore he turned south to Tewkesbury, where he stopped at the Bell and gave her a splendid tea with Watson under the table, gobbling up the morsels of crumpets and cake which came his way. 'Your scones are much better,' declared Sir Thomas.

She thanked him shyly and took another crumpet.

It was already dusk and, in the car once more, he turned for home, still keeping to the side-roads so that it was almost dark by the time they got back to the tea-room.

When she would have thanked him and got out of the car he put a hand over hers on the door-handle. 'No, wait.' And he took the key and went in to switch on the lights and go upstairs to turn on the fire. Only then did he come back to the car.

They went in together and Mary Jane said, 'I don't suppose you would like a cup of coffee?' And when he shook his head, 'I expect you've got something to do this evening.' She spoke cheerfully, thinking that he must have found her dull company. Perhaps he would have a delightful evening with some beautiful witty girl who would have him laugh. He hadn't laughed much all day, only smiled from time to time...

He stood watching her. Her unexpected outing had given her a pretty colour and her eyes shone. She offered her hand now. 'It was a lovely day—thank you very much. Please remember me to your mother and Mrs Beaver when you see them.' She smiled up at him. 'Did you have a pleasant evening with Felicity? She sent me a card. She's great fun.'

Sir Thomas, versed in the art of concealing his true feelings under a bland face, agreed pleasantly while reflecting that no two sisters could be more unlike each other and why had Felicity made a point of telling Mary Jane that she had spent the evening with him? A gross exaggeration to begin with, and what was the point? To make Mary Jane jealous? That seemed to him to be most unlikely; his friendship with her was of the most prosaic kind, brought about by circumstances.

He got into his car and drove back to London to his quiet house and a long evening in his study, making notes for a lecture he was to give during the coming week. But presently he put his pen down and sat back in his chair. 'You enjoyed your day?' he enquired of Watson, lying half-asleep before the fire. 'Delightful, wasn't it? I think that we must do it again.' He opened his diary. 'Let me see, when do I next go to Cheltenham?'

Watson opened an eye and thumped his tail. 'You agree? Good. Now let me see, whom do we know living not too far from the village?'

MARY JANE WATCHED the tail-lights of the Rolls disappear down the village street and then locked the door and went to feed Brimble. She wasn't very hungry but supper would be something to do. She poached an egg and made some toast and a pot of tea and took the tray upstairs and sat by the gas fire while she ate her small meal. It had been a lovely day but she mustn't allow herself to get too interested in Sir Thomas. The thought occurred to her that perhaps since Felicity wasn't there to be taken out, he had taken the opportunity to see more of her. If he was falling in love with her sister then he would want to be on good terms with herself, wouldn't he? She should have talked more about Felicity so that if he had wanted to, he could have talked about her too. For some reason she began to feel unhappy, which was silly since Sir Thomas and Felicity would make a splendid couple. Perhaps she was being a bit premature in supposing that he had fallen in love, but he was bound to if he saw more of her sister; all the men she met fell in love with her sooner or later. Mary Jane was sure of that, for Felicity had told her so.

AUTUMN HAD GIVEN way to winter without putting up much of a fight and everyone was thinking about Christmas. The village stores stocked up on paper chains for the children to make and a shelf full of sweet biscuits and boxes of sweets. Mary Jane made a cake and iced it and stuck Father Christmas at its centre and put it in her window with two red candles and a 'Merry Christmas' stuck on to the window. Christmas was still a few weeks off, but with the red lampshades she had made the tea-room look welcoming. Surprisingly, for the next day or two she had more customers than she had had for weeks. She sold the mice too, stitching away each evening, replenishing her stock.

She had another card from Felicity. She was back in London to do some modelling for a glossy magazine but she intended to spend Christmas at her flat. There was no point in asking Mary Jane to join her there, she had written, for she knew how much she hated leaving the cottage. She wouldn't have gone, she told herself, even if she had been invited, for she knew none of Felicity's friends and hadn't the right clothes. All the same, it would have been nice to have been asked.

The next day Mrs Latimer came, bringing with her a little dumpling of a woman with a happy face. The Misses Potter were sitting at their usual place but there was no one else there. Mrs Latimer went over to the counter to where Mary Jane was getting out cups and saucers. 'How nice to see you again, my dear, and looking a lot better, too. I've come for tea—some of your nice scones? And come and meet someone who knows about you and your family...

'Mrs Bennett, this is Mary Jane Seymour—Mary Jane, Mrs Bennett was a friend of your mother's.'

The little lady beamed. 'You were a very little girl—you won't remember me, your mother and I lost touch. I heard that you and your sister had gone to live with your uncle and of course Felicity is quite famous, isn't she? However, I had no idea that you were here. I wrote once or twice to your uncle but he never answered. It's lovely to see you again, and with a career too!'

'Well, it's only a tea-room,' said Mary Jane, liking her new customer. 'Do sit down and I'll bring you your tea.'

The Misses Potter, too ladylike to stare, had been listening avidly. Now they had no excuse to stay any longer for the scones were eaten and the teapot drained. They paid their bill, bowed to the two ladies and went home; news of any sort was welcome, and they looked forward to spreading it as soon as possible.

It was long after closing-time when Mrs Latimer and her friend left and the latter by then had wheedled Mary Jane into accepting her invitation to the buffet supper she was giving in ten days' time. It would mean a new dress, but Mary Jane, feeling reckless, had accepted.

That evening Mrs Latimer phoned her son. 'We had tea with Mary Jane—she's coming to Mrs Bennett's party. Tell me, Thomas, how did you discover that she had known Mary Jane's parents?' She paused. 'Or, for that matter, how did you discover Mrs Bennett? A most amiable woman, apparently not in the least surprised to have a visit from a friend of a friend...'

'Easily enough. Felicity mentioned her and I remembered the name—and phoned a few friends around that part of the country. Thank you for your help, my dear.'

Mrs Latimer was frowning as she put down the phone. Thomas was going to a good deal of trouble to liven up Mary Jane's sober life, she hoped it wasn't because he had fallen in love with Felicity. A man in love would go to great lengths to please a girl, and yet, somehow, he wasn't behaving as though he were. He could of course be sorry for Mary Jane. Mrs Latimer smiled suddenly. That young lady wouldn't thank him for that.

CHAPTER SIX

THE PROBLEMS OF a dress kept Mary Jane wakeful for a few nights. She would have to close the tea-room and go to Cheltenham. She couldn't afford to buy a dress; she would have to find the material and make it herself. There wasn't much time for that, especially as she hadn't a sewing-machine. Mrs Stokes had one and so did Mrs Fellowes and now was no time to be shy about asking to borrow from one of them.

Mrs Fellowes agreed to lend hers at once; moreover, when she heard why Mary Jane wanted it, she offered to give her a lift on the following day to Cheltenham.

She found what she wanted: ribbed silk in a soft dove-grey, just right for the pattern she had chosen, a simple dress with a full skirt, a modest neckline and elbow-length sleeves. She bought matching stockings and, in a fit of recklessness, some matching slippers in grey leather. They could be dyed black, she told herself, so they weren't an extravagance.

Customers were few and far between, which was a good thing, for she was able to cut out the dress and sew it. She had a talent for sewing and the dress, when it was finished, would pass muster just as long as it didn't come under the close scrutiny of someone in the world of fashion. She hung it in her bedroom and spent an evening doing her nails and washing her hair, half wishing that she weren't going to the party. Mrs Bennett seemed friendly and sweet but they didn't really know each other; she had said that there would be a lot of people there and Mary Jane wondered if there would be dancing. She loved to dance, but supposing no one wanted to dance with her?

She would be fetched, Mrs Bennett had told her in a letter; friends who lived in Shipton-under-Wychwood would collect her on their way to Bourton-on-the-Hill, where Mrs Bennett lived.

She was ready long before they arrived, wrapped in her elderly winter coat, cold with sudden panic at the idea of meeting a great many strange people. She need not have worried; the estate car which pulled up at her door was crammed with a cheerful family party, quite ready to absorb her into their number, and if they found the winter coat not quite in keeping with the occasion, no one said so. She was made to feel at home and by the time they arrived she had forgotten her sudden fright and went along to the bedroom set aside for their coats, to be further braced by the two girls and their mother admiring her dress. She needed their reassurance, for she could see that, compared with the dresses the other girls were wearing, hers, while quite suitable, was far too modest. Bare shoulders, tiny shoulder straps and bodices which stayed up by some magic of their own seemed to be the norm. She went down the staircase with the others and into the vast drawing-room in Mrs Bennett's house where her hostess was greeting her guests.

Sir Thomas, talking to his host, watched Mary Jane, a sober moth among the butterflies, pause by Mrs Bennett and exchange brief greetings. Her dress, he considered, suited her very well, although he surprised himself by wondering what she would look like in something pink and cut to show rather more of her person. No jewellery either. A pearl choker, he reflected, would look exactly right around her little neck. He listened attentively to his companion's opinion of modern politics, made suitable replies and presently made his way to where Mary Jane, swept along by her new acquaintances, stood with a group of other young people.

She saw him coming towards her and quite forgot to look cool and casual. Her gentle mouth curved into a wide smile and she flushed a little. He took her hand. 'Hello, Mary Jane, I didn't know that you knew the Bennetts.'

She didn't take her hand away. 'I didn't either. Your mother came the other day and brought Mrs Bennett with her. I think she's a friend of a friend and she remembered me when I was a little girl—she knew my mother.'

'What a delightful surprise for you,' said Sir Thomas gravely, not in the least surprised himself. 'Who brought you?'

'Mr and Mrs Elliott—they live at Shipton-under-Wychwood and called for me. They've been very kind...'

'Ah, yes— I've met them. My mother's here—have you seen her yet?'

'No.' She added rather shyly, 'I don't know anyone here.'

'Soon remedied.' He took her arm and made his way round the room, greeting those he knew and introducing her and finally finding his mother.

'There you are, Thomas—and Mary Jane. How pretty you look, my dear, and what a charming dress—I have never seen so many exposed bosoms in all my life and many of them need covering.' She eyed Mary Jane and added, 'Although I don't think your bosom needs to be concealed; you have a pretty figure, my dear.'

Mary Jane, very pink in the cheeks, thanked her faintly and Sir Thomas, standing between them, stifled a laugh. His mother, a gentle soul by nature, could at times be quite outrageous.

'You agree, Thomas?' She smiled up at her son. 'No, probably you don't. Go away and talk to someone; I want a chat with Mary Jane.'

When they were alone she said, 'My dear, I wanted to ask you—where will you be at Christmas? Not alone, I hope?'

'Me? No, Mrs Latimer, Felicity is in London, you know, and I'm going there. I'm looking forward to it.' She told the lie, valiantly glad that Sir Thomas wasn't there to hear her. She was normally a truthful girl but this, she considered, was an occasion when she must bend the truth a little. After all, there was still time for Felicity to invite her...

'I'm glad to hear that. What do you do with your cat?'

Mary Jane was saved from replying by a dashing young man in a coloured waistcoat. 'I say, if I'm not interrupting, shall we dance? They're just starting up. Sir Thomas introduced us just now—Nick Soames? Remember?'

'Run along, dear,' said Mrs Latimer. 'But don't leave without coming to say goodbye, will you?'

So Mary Jane danced. Nick was a good partner and she had always loved dancing and when the dance finished he handed her over to someone called Bill, who didn't dance very well but made her laugh a lot. Now and then she saw Sir Thomas, head and shoulders above everyone else, circling the room with a succession of beautifully dressed girls. From the look of them he certainly hadn't agreed with his mother about the over-exposure of bosoms. They're not decent, decided Mary Jane, swanning round the room in the arms of someone called Matt, who talked of nothing but horses.

Mrs Bennett had drawn the line at a disco. It was her party, she had pointed out; the young ones could go somewhere and dance their kind of dancing whenever they liked; in her house they would foxtrot and waltz or not dance at all. The band was just striking up a nice old-fashioned waltz when Sir Thomas whisked Mary Jane away from an elderly gentleman who was on the point of asking her to dance with him.

'I was going to dance with that gentleman,' she pointed out tartly.

'Yes, I know, but he's a shocking dancer; your feet would have been black and blue.' He was going round the edge of the big room. 'Are you enjoying yourself?'

'Yes, very much, thank you. I—I was a bit doubtful at first, I mean, I don't know anyone, but Mrs Bennett has been so kind. She's coming to see me one day after Christmas so that we can talk about my mother and father. Uncle Matthew didn't talk to us much, you know; I dare say he didn't like children, although he was a very kind man.'

The music stopped but he didn't let her go and when it started again he went on dancing with her. She was a little flushed now, but her pale brown hair, pinned in its heavy coil, was as neat as when she had arrived and her small person, so demurely clad, was light in his arms.

He waltzed her expertly through an open door and into a small room, where a fire was burning and chairs grouped invitingly.

He sat her down by a small table with an inviting display of tasty bits and pieces in little dishes and a bottle of white wine in a cooler. 'Spare me five minutes of your time and tell me how you are.'

'I'm very well thank you, Sir Thomas.' She popped an olive into her mouth—she had had a sketchy lunch and almost no tea and the buffet supper was still an hour or so away.

'Busy?' He poured wine into two glasses. 'I suppose you will be going to Felicity's for Christmas?' His tone was casual though he watched her carefully from under his lids.

'Christmas.' Mary Jane stalled for a time while she thought up a good fib. 'Oh, yes, of course; I always go each year. It's great fun.'

He didn't believe her but nothing in his calm face showed that.

'How do you go?' he wanted to know, still casual.

'Oh, Felicity fetches me,' said Mary Jane, piling fib upon fib. She hadn't looked at him but had busied herself sampling the potato straws. She flashed him a brief smile. 'I expect you go to Mrs Latimer's?'

'Or she comes to stay with me with various other members of the family.'

He handed her a dish of little biscuits and she selected one carefully.

'I'm glad to see you looking so well.' Sir Thomas handed her her glass. 'Let us drink to your continued good health.'

The wine was delicious and very cold. 'And you,' said Mary Jane. 'I hope you have a very happy Christmas and don't have to work. I don't suppose you do, anyhow.'

'You suppose wrongly. People break arms and legs

and fracture their skulls every day of the year, you know.'

'Well, yes, of course they do but surely you're too important…' She stopped because he was smiling.

'Not a bit of it; if I'm needed to operate or be consulted then I'm available.'

'Do you ever go to other countries?'

'Frequently.'

She had polished off the potato straws and most of the olives.

'May I have the supper dance?' asked Sir Thomas.

'Will that be soon? I'm awfully hungry…'

He glanced at his watch. 'Half an hour; that will soon pass if you are dancing.'

They went back to the drawing-room and he handed her over quite cheerfully to the horsey Matt, who danced her briskly round the room and gave her a detailed account of his last point-to-point. It was a relief when the music stopped and she was claimed by a tall young man with a melancholy face who had no idea how to dance but shambled round while he told her, in gruesome detail, about his anatomy classes. He was a medical student in his third year and anxious to impress her. 'I saw you dancing with Sir Thomas—do you know him?'

'We're acquainted.'

'He's great—you've no idea—to see him fit a prosthesis…'

'Yes, he seems well-known,' said Mary Jane quickly, anxious to avoid the details.

'Well-known? He's famous!' He trod on her foot and she hoped that he hadn't laddered her stockings or ruined her shoe. 'There's no one who can hold a candle to him. I watched him do a spinal graft last week…' He embarked on the details—every single drop of blood and splinter of bone. Sir Thomas, guiding his hostess round the floor, saw Mary Jane's face and grinned to himself.

The supper dance came next and he went to find her, still listening politely to her companion's description of the instruments needed for the grisly business. Sir Thomas put a large hand on her arm and nodded affably at the young man. 'Our dance, Mary Jane?' he said and led her away.

'It seems you're quite famous,' she observed, her small nose buried in his white shirt-front. 'You never talk about it.'

He said, seriously, 'I don't think I've ever met any-one who would want to hear.'

'How dreadful for you, having to keep it all to your-self.'

'Indeed it is at times but most of my companions wouldn't wish to hear about anything to do with hos-pitals or patients.'

'No? Well, I wouldn't mind. I'm sure it couldn't be worse than that boy's description of a meni—mensis...'

'Meniscectomy—the removal of the cartilage of the knee. An operation performed with considerable suc-cess and not in the least dramatic.'

He smiled down at her. 'Next time I feel the urge to unburden myself I shall come and see you, Mary Jane.'

She didn't think that he was serious but she said cheerfully, 'You do—I'm not in the least squeamish.'

They went in to supper then, sharing a table with at least half a dozen other guests, eating lobster pat-ties, tiny sausages, cheesey morsels and little squares of toast spread with pâtés and dainty trifles which left Mary Jane feeling hungry still. She drank two glasses of wine, though, and her eyes became an even deeper violet. She would have accepted a third glass of wine if Sir Thomas hadn't pulled her gently to her feet.

'A little exercise?' he suggested suavely, and danced her round the room in a leisurely manner, and when the music stopped took her to where his mother was sitting talking to Mrs Bennett.

'There you are, my dears.' Mrs Latimer beamed at them both. 'Thomas, go away and dance with some of the lovely girls here, I want to talk to Mary Jane.' She realised what she had said, and added, 'I put that very badly, didn't I? Mary Jane is lovely, too.'

Mary Jane smiled a little and sat down and didn't watch Sir Thomas as he went away. It was kind of Mrs Latimer to call her lovely, although it was quite untrue. It would have been nice if Sir Thomas had told her that but of course he never would; she had no illusions as to her mediocre face.

Presently, she was whisked away to dance once more—never mind her lack of looks, she danced well and the men had been quick to see that. She didn't lack partners and she was still full of energy when someone announced the last waltz and she found Sir Thomas beside her.

'I'll take you back,' he told her. 'Will you explain to the people who brought you?'

'Won't they mind?'

'I don't suppose so.' He was holding her very correctly, looking over her head with the air of a man who wasn't very interested in what he was doing. Most of the other couples were dancing very close together in a very romantic fashion but of course, she told herself, there was nothing about her to inspire romance. Perhaps he was wishing it was Felicity in his arms. He'd be holding her a lot tighter...!

She thanked him as the dance ended and after a few minutes of goodbyes went off to fetch her coat. It stood out like a sore thumb among the elegant shawls and cloaks in the hall and she wondered if he was ashamed of her and dismissed the thought as unworthy of him. His place was so sure in society that he had no need to worry about such things.

Mrs Latimer kissed her goodbye. 'We must see you again soon, Mary Jane,' a wish echoed by Mrs Bennett. 'We shall all be busy with Christmas,' she added, 'but in the New Year you must come and spend the day.'

Mary Jane thanked them both and got into the car and sat quietly as Sir Thomas drove away.

Clear of the village, he slowed the car. 'A pleasant evening,' he observed. 'Do you go to many parties at this time of year?'

She couldn't remember when she had last attended a party—the church social evening, of course, and the Misses Potters' evening—parsnip wine and ginger nuts—but they were hardly parties.

'No.' She sought for some light-hearted remark to make and couldn't think of any.

He didn't seem to notice her reticence but began to talk about their evening, a casual rambling talk which needed very little reply.

It was profoundly dark when he drew up before her cottage. He said, 'Stay where you are, and give me the key,' and went and opened the door before coming back for her. At the door he said, 'Hot buttered toast and tea would be nice...'

She turned a startled face to his. 'It's half-past two in the morning.' She smiled suddenly. 'Come in, you can make the toast while I put the kettle on.'

They had it in the kitchen, with Brimble, refreshed by a sleep, sitting between them.

'You don't have to go back to London, do you?' asked Mary Jane.

'No, I'm spending the rest of the night at my mother's. I must be back in town by Monday morning, though. And you?'

'Me? Oh, I'm not doing anything. The tea-room will be open, of course, but there won't be many customers.'

'That will give you time to get ready for your trip to London,' he observed smoothly.

She agreed rather too quickly.

He bade her goodnight presently, bending to kiss her cheek with a casual friendliness. 'I dare say we shall see each other again,' and when she looked puzzled, 'At Felicity's.'

She wished then that she could tell him that she would not be there, that she had allowed him to suppose that she would be with her sister, but somehow she couldn't think of the right words. He had gone before she had conjured up another fib.

She had rather more customers than she had hoped for in the last weeks before Christmas and the mice sold well; she began to cherish the hope that she might go to the January sales and look for a coat. The Misses Potter had invited her for Christmas dinner as they had done for several years now and the church bazaar gave her the opportunity to bake some little cakes for Miss Kemble's stall. And on Christmas Eve the postman handed in a big cardboard box from Harrods. It contained caviar, a variety of pâtés, a tin of ham, a small Christmas pudding and a box of crackers, chocolates and a half-bottle of claret. The slip of paper with it contained a message from Felicity; she knew that Mary Jane would have a lovely Christmas, she herself was up to her ears in parties and there was a wonderful modelling job waiting for her in Switzerland in the New Year. There was a PS 'Saw Thomas yesterday'.

Which was to be expected, reflected Mary Jane, shaking off a sudden sadness.

She went to church at midnight on Christmas Eve and lingered afterwards exchanging greetings with everyone there and then went back to the cottage to drink hot cocoa and go to bed with Brimble heavy on her feet. She wasn't sorry for herself, she told herself stoutly; several people had given her small gifts and she was going to spend the day with the Misses Potters'. She wondered what Sir Thomas was doing, probably with Felicity... She fell into a troubled sleep which would have been less troubled had she known that he was bent over the operating table, carefully pinning and plating the legs of a young man who had, under the influence of the Christmas spirit, jumped out of a window on to a concrete pavement.

She took the wine, the crackers and the chocolates with her when she went to the Misses Potter. Brimble she had left snug in his basket, a saucer of his favourite food beside him. Her elderly friends liked her to stay for tea and by the time she had washed the delicate china they used on special occasions, it would be evening. She had put a little Christmas tree in the cottage window and switched on the lights before she left; it would be welcoming when she went home.

Miss Emily had roasted a capon and Miss Mabel had set the table in the small dining-room with a lace-edged cloth, the remnants of the family silver and china and wine glasses and had lighted a branched candlestick.

Mary Jane wished them a happy Christmas, kissed their elderly cheeks and handed over the wine.

'Crackers,' declared Miss Emily. 'How delightful, my dear, and chocolates—Bendick's—the very best, too. Let us have a small glass of sherry before lunch.'

It had been a very pleasant day, thought Mary Jane, letting herself into the cottage. Tomorrow she would go for a good walk in the morning and then have a lazy afternoon reading by the fire.

IT WAS RAINING in the morning and not a soul stirred in the village street. 'It'll be better out than in,' she told Brimble and got into her wellies, her elderly raincoat and tied a scarf over her hair, crammed her hands into woolly gloves and then set out. She took the country road to Icomb, past the old fort, on to Wick Rissington and then she turned for home, very wet and, despite her brisk walking, rather cold.

It was a relief to reach the path at the side of the church, a short cut which would bring her into the main street, opposite the tea-room. She nipped down it smartly and came to a sudden halt. The Rolls was standing before her door and Sir Thomas, apparently impervious to the wind and rain, was leaning against its bonnet, the faithful Watson beside him.

His, 'Good afternoon, Mary Jane,' was austere and she had the suspicion that he was concealing ill-humour behind his bland face. It was just bad luck that he should turn up; she was, after all, supposed to be in London, enjoying the high life with Felicity.

She stood in front of him, feeling at a disadvantage; she was wet and bedraggled and the sodden scarf did nothing for her looks.

'Hello, Sir Thomas—how unexpected...'

He took the key from her and opened the door and stood aside to let her enter before following her in. Watson shook himself thankfully and went straight through to the kitchen and Sir Thomas, without asking, took off his coat.

'I expect you'd like a cup of tea,' said Mary Jane, wringing out her headscarf over the sink and kicking off her wellies.

'I expect I would.' He took her raincoat from her and hung it on the hook behind the back door and she went to put on the kettle. It was a little unnerving, she reflected, being confronted like this; she would have to think something up.

She wasn't given the time. 'Well,' said Sir Thomas, 'perhaps you will explain.'

'Explain what?' She busied herself with cups and saucers, wondering if a few more fibs would help the situation. Apparently not.

'Why you are here alone when you should be with Felicity in London.'

'Well…' She spooned tea into the pot and couldn't think of anything to say.

'You told me that you were staying with your sister, and yet I find you here.'

'Yes, well,' began Mary Jane and was halted by his impatient response.

'For heaven's sake stop saying "Yes, well"—forget the nonsense and tell me the truth for once.'

She banged the teapot on to the table. 'I always tell you the truth…' She caught his cold stare. 'Well, almost always…'

She sat down opposite him and poured out their tea, handed him a plate of scones and offered Watson a biscuit as Brimble jumped on to her lap.

She decided to take the war into the enemies' camp. 'Why aren't you in London?'

His stern mouth twitched. 'I spent most of Christmas Day with my mother and I'm on my way back to town.'

'You're going the wrong way.'

'Don't be pert. I am well aware which way I am travelling. And now, Mary Jane, since you are unable to string two sentences together, perhaps you will answer my questions.'

'I don't see why I should…'

He ignored this. 'Did Felicity invite you to go to London for Christmas?'

'It's none of your business.' She gave him a defiant look and saw that he had become Sir Thomas Latimer, calm and impersonal and quite sure that he would be answered when he asked a question. She said in a small voice, 'Well, no.' She added idiotically, 'I expect she forgot—you know, she has so many friends and she leads a busy life.'

'Did you not hear from her at all?'

'Oh, yes. She sent me a hamper from Harrods. I don't expect that I would like to go to London anyway, I haven't the right clothes and her friends are awfully clever and witty and I'm not.'

'So why did you lie to me?'

'Well…'

'If you say well just once more, I shall shake you,' he observed pleasantly. 'Tell me, have you ever been to stay with Felicity?'

'W… Actually, no.'

'So why did you lie to me?'

'They were fibs,' she told him sharply. 'Lies hurt people but fibs are useful when you don't want—to interfere or make people feel that they have to help you if you're getting in the way.' She added anxiously, 'Have I made that clear?'

'Oh, yes, in a muddled way. Tell me, Mary Jane, why should you not wish me to know that you would be staying here on your own for Christmas?'

'I have just told you.'

'You think that I have fallen in love with Felicity?'

She looked at him then. 'Everyone falls in love with her, she's so beautiful and she is fun to be with and so successful. Whenever she sends me a card she mentions you so you must know her quite well by now. So you must...yes, I think you must love her.'

She wasn't sure if she liked his smile. 'Would you like me for a brother-in-law, Mary Jane?'

She wondered about the smile; she wouldn't like him for a brother-in-law; she would like him for a husband, and why should she suddenly discover that now of all times, sitting opposite him, being cross-examined as though she were in a witness-box and fighting a great wish to nip round the table and fling her arms round his neck and tell him that she loved him? She would have to say something, for he was watching her.

'Yes, oh, yes, that would be delightful.' She bent to pat Watson so that he shouldn't see her face and was surprised and relieved when Sir Thomas got up.

'Well, I must be off.' He added smoothly, 'Shall I give your love to Felicity when I see her?'

'Yes, please.' She went to the door with him and she held out her hand. 'Drive carefully,' she told him. 'Goodbye, Sir Thomas.'

His hand on the door, he paused. 'There is something you should know. Falling in love and loving are two quite different things. Goodbye.'

He drove away, Watson sitting beside him, and she

went back to the kitchen and began to tidy up. She told herself that it was extremely silly to cry for no reason at all, but she went on weeping and Brimble, wanting his supper and jumping on to her lap to remind her of that, got a shockingly damp coat.

Presently she dried her eyes. 'Well—no, I mustn't say well; what I mean to say is I shall forget this afternoon and take care not to see Sir Thomas again unless I simply must.'

Brimble, drying his fur, agreed.

IT WAS DIFFICULT, though, the tea-shop was open, but for several days no one came to drink the coffee or eat the scones she had ready, she filled her days with odd jobs around the cottage, turning out cupboards and drawers with tremendous zeal, making plans for the year ahead; perhaps she should branch out a bit— do hot lunches? But supposing no one ate them? She couldn't afford to waste uneaten meals and her freezer was too small to house more than bare necessities. Felicity, on one of her flying visits, had suggested, half laughingly, that she should sell the cottage and train for something. Mary Jane had asked what and she had said, carelessly, 'Oh, I don't know—something domestic—children's nurse or something worthy— a dietician at a hospital or a social worker, at least you would meet some people. This village is dead or hadn't you noticed?'

Mary Jane recalled the conversation clearly enough now and gave it her serious consideration, deciding that she didn't want to be any of the people Felicity had suggested and, moreover, that the village wasn't dead. Quiet, yes, but at least everyone knew everyone else...

IT WAS THE last day of December when Mrs Bennett came. She trotted in, her good natured face wreathed in smiles. 'I'm so glad I found you at home,' she declared, 'and I do so hope you are not doing anything exciting this evening, for I've come to take you back with me—to see the New Year in, my dear.'

She sat herself down and Mary Jane sat down on the other side of the table. 'How very kind of you, Mrs Bennett, but you see it's a bit difficult—there's Brimble and I'd have to come home again...'

Mrs Bennett brushed this aside. 'Put on the coffee-pot, my dear, and we'll put our heads together.' She unbuttoned her coat and settled back in her chair. 'Someone will come over for you at about half-past seven and we'll dine at half-past eight, and I promise you that directly after midnight someone shall bring you back here. There won't be many people, just a few close friends and the family.' She added firmly, 'You can't possibly stay here by yourself, Mary Jane.' She glanced around. 'Your sister isn't here?'

Mary Jane brought the coffee and passed the sugar and milk. 'No, I'm not sure if she is in England—she travels all over the place, you know.'

'So, that settles it,' said Mrs Bennett comfortably. 'Wear that pretty dress you had on at the party, I dare say we shall all be feeling festive, and please don't disappoint me, my dear.'

'I'd love to come, Mrs Bennett, if it's not being too much of a bother collecting me and bringing me back. You're sure the grey dress will do?'

'Quite positive. Now I must be off home and make sure that everything is ready for this evening.'

Mary Jane wasted no time; the contents of a cupboard she had intended to turn out were ruthlessly returned higgledy-piggledy before she set about making her person fit for the evening's entertainment. Her hair washed and hanging still damp down her back, she studied her face, looking for spots. There were none, she had a lovely skin which needed little make-up which was a good thing for she couldn't have afforded it anyway. Her hands needed attention, too…

She was ready long before she needed to be, her hair shining, her small nose powdered, sitting by the little fire with her skirts carefully spread out and Brimble perched carefully on her silken knee. A cheerful tattoo on the door sent her downstairs to open the door to discover that the same family who had taken her to the dance were calling for her. They greeted her with a good deal of friendly noise, waited while she fetched her coat and bade Brimble goodbye and wedged her on to the back seat between the two girls and drove off all talking at once. Such fun, she was told, just a few of us, nothing like the Christmas party but Mrs Bennett always has a splendid meal and lashings of drinks.

They sat down sixteen to dinner and Mary Jane found herself between two faces she recognised, the horsey Matt, who it seemed was a nephew of Mrs Bennett's and the medical student, both of whom were in a festive mood and didn't lack for conversation. Dinner lasted a very long time and by the time they had had coffee it was getting on for eleven o'clock and more people were arriving. Mary Jane, listening to an elderly man with a very red face explaining the benefits of exactly the right mulch for roses, allowed her eyes to rove discreetly. It was silly, but she had hoped that perhaps Sir Thomas would be there…but he wasn't.

She was wrong. Calm and immaculate in his dinner-jacket, he arrived with five minutes to spare, just in nice time to take the glass of champagne he was offered and thread his way through the other guests to stand beside her.

CHAPTER SEVEN

MARY JANE SAW him coming, and delight at seeing him
again swamped every other feeling. She could feel
herself going pale, as indeed she was, and her heart
thumped so strongly that she trembled so that the glass
she was holding wobbled alarmingly. He reached her
side, took the glass from her and wished her good evening, adding, 'Did you think that I would not be here?'

He was smiling down at her and she only stopped
herself just in time from telling him how wonderful it
was to see him. She said instead, 'Well, it's a long way
from London and I dare say you've been busy with your
patients and—and had lots of invitations to spend the
evening there.'

'Oh, yes, indeed, but I wished to spend the evening
with my mother—she came over with me.'

She followed her train of thought. 'Isn't Felicity in
London?'

He was still smiling but his eyes were cold. 'Yes,
she sent you her love.' He might have added that she
had wanted him to take her to a party at one of the big
hotels and he had made the excuse that he was going
to his mother's home. She had said sharply, 'How dull
for you, Thomas. I don't suppose you'll see Mary Jane,
but if you do or if you meet anyone who knows her send
my love, will you?'

Mary Jane said in a wooden voice, 'It's a pity she isn't here…' She was unable to finish for there was a sudden hush as Big Ben began to strike the hour. At its last stroke there were cries of 'Happy New Year!' as the champagne corks were popped and everyone started kissing everyone else. Mary Jane looked at the bland face beside her and said, meaning every word, 'I hope you have a very happy New Year, Sir Thomas.'

He smiled suddenly. 'I hope that we both shall, Mary Jane.' He bent and kissed her, a swift, hard kiss as unlike a conventional social peck as chalk from cheese. It took her breath but before she could get it back Matt had caught her by the hand and whirled her away to be kissed breathless by all the men there. She disentangled herself, laughing, and found Mrs Latimer standing close by.

'My dear, a happy New Year,' said Sir Thomas's mother, 'and how nice to see you enjoying yourself. You lead far too quiet a life.'

Mary Jane wished her a happy New Year in her turn. 'I've just been talking to Sir Thomas.' She blushed brightly, remembering his kiss, and Mrs Latimer just hid a smile.

'He drove down earlier this evening, and he will go back early tomorrow morning—he had made up his mind to be here.'

'He shouldn't work so hard,' said Mary Jane, and blushed again, much to her annoyance. 'What I mean is, he must get so tired.' She added, 'It's none of my business, please forgive me.'

'You're quite right,' observed Mrs Latimer. 'His work is his whole life although I think, when he marries, his wife and children will always come first.'

The very thought hurt; Mary Jane murmured suitably and said that she would have to find her hostess. 'Mrs Bennett kindly said that someone would drive me back as soon after midnight as possible.' She wished her companion goodbye and found Mrs Bennett at the far end of the room talking to Sir Thomas. As Mary Jane got within hearing, she said, 'There you are, my dear. What a pity that you must go but I quite understand…was it fun?'

'I've had a marvellous evening, Mrs Bennett, and thank you very much. I'll get my coat. Shall I wait in the hall and would it be all right if you said goodbye to everyone for me?'

'Of course, child. Sir Thomas is taking you home.'

'Oh, but Mrs Latimer is here, he'll—that is, you will have to come back for her.' She looked at him and found him smiling.

'The Elliots are driving her back presently.' He spoke placidly but she couldn't very well argue with him. She fetched her coat and got into the Rolls without speaking, only when they were away from the house and out of the village she said, 'I'm sorry to break up your evening.'

He said coolly, 'Not at all, Mary Jane, I had no intention of staying and it is only a slight detour to drop you off before I go back.'

A damping remark which she found difficult to answer but when the silence got too long she tried again. 'Did you bring Watson with you?'

'No—I'm only away for the night and I'll be back to take him for his run tomorrow before I go to my rooms. Tremble will look after him.'

'Won't you be tired?' She added hastily, 'I don't mean to be nosy.'

'I appreciate your concern. I'm not operating tomorrow and I have only a handful of private patients to see later in the day.'

The conversation, she felt, was hardly scintillating. The silence lasted rather longer this time. Presently she ventured, 'It was a very nice party, wasn't it?'

He said mildly, 'Do stop making light conversation, Mary Jane...'

'With pleasure,' she snapped. 'There is nothing more—more boring than trying to be polite to someone who has no idea of the social niceties.' She paused to draw an indignant breath, rather pleased with the remark, and then doubtful as to whether she had been rather too outspoken. His low laugh gave her no clue. She turned her head away to look out at the dark nothingness outside. Where was her good sense, she thought wildly; how could she have fallen in love with this taciturn man who had no more interest in her than he might have in a row of pins? She would forget him the moment she could get into her cottage and shut the door on him.

He drew up gently before her small front door, took the key from her hand and got out and opened it before coming back to open the door of the car for her.

Switching on the tea-room lights, he remarked, 'A cup of tea would be nice.'

'No, it wouldn't,' said Mary Jane flatly. 'Thank you for bringing me home, although I wish you hadn't.' She put a hand on the door, encouraging him to leave, a useless gesture since the door wasn't over-sturdy and his vast person was as unyielding as a tree trunk.

He laughed suddenly. 'Why do you laugh?' she asked sharply.

'If I told you you wouldn't believe me. Tell me, Mary Jane, why did you wish that I hadn't brought you home?'

She said soberly, 'I can't tell you that.' She held out a hand. 'I'm sorry if I've been rude.'

He took her hand between his. 'Goodnight, Mary Jane.' His smile was so kind that she could have wept.

He went out to his car and got in and drove away and she locked up and turned off the lights, gave Brimble an extra supper and took herself off to bed. It was another year, she thought, lying in bed, warmed by the hot water bottle and Brimble's small body. She wondered what it might bring.

IT BROUGHT, SURPRISINGLY, Felicity, sitting beside a rather plump young man with bags under his eyes in a Mercedes. Felicity flung open the tea-shop door with a flourish. 'I just had to wish you a happy New Year,' she cried, and then paused to look around her. The little place was empty except for Mary Jane, who was on her knees hammering down a strip of torn lino by the counter. She got to her feet and turned round and the young man, who had followed Felicity said, 'Good lord, is this your sister, darling?'

Mary Jane eyed him; this was not the beginning of a beautiful friendship, she reflected, but all the same she wished him good morning politely and kissed her sister's cheek. 'I'm spring cleaning,' she explained.

Felicity tossed off the cashmere wrap she had flung over her *haute couture* suit. 'Darling, how awful for you, isn't there a char or someone in this dump to do it for you?'

There didn't seem much point in answering that. 'Would you like a cup of coffee?' She waved at two chairs upended on to one of the tables. 'If you'd like to sit down it won't take long.'

Felicity said carelessly, 'This is Monty.' She went

over to the table. 'Well, darling, give me a chair to sit on...'

Mary Jane thought that he didn't look capable of lifting a cup of tea let alone a chair and certainly he did it unwillingly. She went into the kitchen and collected cups and saucers while the coffee brewed and presently she went back to ask. 'Are you going somewhere or just driving round?'

'Riding round. It's very flat in town after New Year and I've no bookings until next week. Then it will be Spain, thank heaven. I need the sun and the warmth.'

Mary Jane let that pass, poured the coffee and took the tray across to the table and poured it for the three of them, rather puzzled as to why Felicity had come. She didn't have to wonder for long. 'Have you seen anything of Thomas?' asked Felicity. 'Well, I don't suppose you have but you may have heard something of him—after all, his mother doesn't live so far away, does she? She made a great fuss of you when you had the flu.'

She didn't wait for an answer, which was a good thing. 'I see quite a lot of him in town; I must say he's marvellous to go around with...'

'I say, steady on,' said Monty. 'I'm here, you know.'

Felicity gurgled with laughter. 'Of course you are, darling, and you're such fun.' She leaned across the table and patted his arm. 'But I do have my future to think of—a nice steady husband who adores me and can keep me in the style I've set my heart on...'

'You said you loved me,' complained Monty, and Mary Jane wondered if they had forgotten that she was there, sitting between them.

'Of course I do, Monty—marrying some well-heeled eminent surgeon won't make any difference to that.'

Mary Jane went into the kitchen. Felicity must be

talking about Sir Thomas. If Felicity had been alone she might have talked to her about him and discovered if she were joking; her sister was selfish and uncaring of anyone but herself but there was affection between them; she could at least have discovered if she loved Sir Thomas. But the presence of Monty precluded that. She went back into the tea-room and found Felicity arranging the cashmere stole. 'Well, we're off, darling—lunch at that nice restaurant in Oxford, and then home to the bright lights.' She kissed Mary Jane. 'I'll send you a card from sunny Spain. I must try to see Thomas, I'm sure he could do with a day or two in the sun.'

Monty shook Mary Jane's hand. 'I would never have guessed that you two were sisters.' He shook his head. 'I mean to say...' He had a limp handshake.

Mary Jane put the 'Closed' sign on the door and went back to knocking in nails. Thoughts, most of them unhappy as well as angry, raced round her head. Surely, she told herself, Sir Thomas wasn't foolish enough to fall in love with Felicity, but of course if he really loved her—hadn't he said that loving and being in love were two different things? She forced herself to stop thinking about him.

After a few days customers began to trickle in; the Misses Potter came as usual for their tea and several ladies from the village popped in on their way to or from the January sales; life returned to its normal routine. Mary Jane sternly suppressed the thought of Sir Thomas, not altogether successfully, when a card from Felicity came. She had written on the back, 'Gorgeous weather, here for another week. Pity he has to return on Saturday. Be good. Felicity'.

Mary Jane ignored the last few words, she had no other choice but to be good, but, reading the rest of the scrawled words, she frowned. Felicity had hinted that she would see Sir Thomas and persuade him to go to Spain with her. It looked as though she had succeeded.

'I suppose the cleverer you are the sillier you get,' said Mary Jane in such a venomous tone that Brimble laid back his ears.

She was setting out the coffee-cups on Saturday morning when the first of the motorcyclists stopped before her door. He was joined by two others and the three of them came into the tea-room. Young men, encased in black leather and talking noisily. They took off their helmets and flung them down on one of the tables, pulled out chairs and sat down. They weren't local men and they stared at her until she felt uneasy.

'Coffee?' she asked. 'And anything to eat?'

'Coffee'll do, darlin', and a plate of whatever there is.' He laughed. 'And not much of that in this hole.' The other two laughed with him and she went into the kitchen to pour the coffee. Before doing so she picked up Brimble and popped him on the stairs and shut the door on him. She wasn't sure why she had done it; she wasn't a timid girl and the men would drink the coffee and go. She put the coffee on the table, then fetched a plate of scones and went back to the kitchen where she had been making pastry for the sausage rolls. She could see them from where she stood at the kitchen table and they seemed quiet enough, their heads close together, talking softly and sniggering. Presently they called for more coffee and ten minutes later they scraped back their chairs and put on their helmets. She took the bill over with an inward sigh of relief, but instead of taking it, the man she offered it to caught her hand and held it fast. 'Expect us to pay for that slop?' he wanted to know.

'Yes,' said Mary Jane calmly. 'I do, and please leave go of my hand.'

'Got a tongue in 'er 'ead, too. An' what'll you do if we don't pay up, Miss High and Mighty?'

'You will pay up. You asked for coffee and scones and I gave you them, so now you'll pay for what you've had.'

'Cor—got a sharp tongue, too, 'asn't she?' He tightened his grip. ''Ave ter teach 'er a lesson, won't we, boys?'

They swept the cups and saucers, the coffee-pot and the empty plates on to the floor and one of them went around treading on the bits of china, crushing them to fragments. The chairs went next, hurled across the room and then the tables. The little vases of dried flowers they threw at walls and all this was done without a word.

She was frightened but she was furiously angry too, she lifted a foot, laced into a sensible shoe, and kicked the man holding her hand. It couldn't have hurt much through all that leather, but it took him by surprise. He wrenched her round with a bellow of rage.

'Why, you little...'

SIR THOMAS, ON his way to spend a weekend with his mother and at the same time call upon Mary Jane, slowed the car as the tea-room came into view and then stopped at the sight of the motorbikes. He got out, saw the anxious elderly faces peering from the cottages on either side of Mary Jane's home, crossed the narrow pavement in one stride and threw open her door. A man who kept his feelings well under control, he allowed them free rein at the sight of her white face...

Mary Jane wished very much to faint on to a comfortable sofa, but she sidled to the remains of the counter and hung on to it. This was no time to faint; Sir Thomas had his hands full and apparently he was enjoying it, too. The little room seemed full of waving arms and legs. The man who had been holding her was tripped up neatly by one of Sir Thomas's elegantly shod feet and landed with a crash into the debris of tables and chairs which left Sir Thomas free to deal with the two other men. Subdued and scared by this large, silent man who knocked them around like ninepins, they huddled in a corner by their fallen comrade, only anxious to be left alone.

'Any one of you move and I'll break every bone in his body,' observed Sir Thomas in the mildest of voices, and turned his attention to Mary Jane.

His arm was large and comforting and as steady as a rock. 'Don't, whatever you do, faint,' he begged her, 'for there's nowhere for you to lie down.' Nothing in his kind, impersonal voice and his equally impersonal arm hinted at his great wish to pick her up and drive off with her and never let her go again. 'The police will be along presently; someone must have seen that something was wrong and warned them.' He looked down at the top of her head. 'I'll get a chair from the kitchen…'

She was dimly aware of someone coming to the door then, old Rob from his cottage by the church, where he lived with his two sons. 'The Coats lad came running to tell something was amiss. The police is coming and my two boys'll be along in a couple of shakes.' He cast an eye over the three men huddled together. 'Varmints!' He turned a shrewd eye upon Sir Thomas. 'Knock 'em out, did yer? Nice bit of work, I'd say.'

The police, Rob's two sons and the rector arrived together. Not that Mary Jane cared. Let them all come, she reflected; a cup of tea and her bed was all she wanted.

The bed was out of the question, but the rector, a meek and kindly man, made tea which she drank with chattering teeth, spilling a good deal of it, thankful that Sir Thomas was dealing with the police so that she needed to answer only essential questions before they marched the three men away to the waiting van. 'You'll need to come to the station on Tuesday morning, miss,' the senior office said. 'Nine o'clock suit you? Have you got a car?'

'I'll bring Miss Seymour, Officer,' said Sir Thomas and he nodded an affable goodbye and turned to old Rob. 'Will you wait while I see Mary Jane up to her bed?'

'I do not want…' began Mary Jane pettishly, not knowing what she was wanting.

'No, of course you don't.' Sir Thomas's voice was soothing. 'But in half an hour or so when you have got over the nasty shock you had, you will think clearly again. Besides, I want to have a look at that wrist.'

She went upstairs, urged on by a firm hand on her back, and found Brimble waiting anxiously on the tiny landing. The sight of his small furry face was too much; she burst into tears, sobbing and sniffing and grizzling into Sir Thomas's shoulder. He waited patiently until the sobs petered out, offered a handkerchief, observing that there was nothing like a good cry and at the same time tossing back the quilt on her bed.

'Half an hour,' he told her, tucking it around her and lifting Brimble on to the bed. 'I'll be back.'

Downstairs, he found old Rob and his sons waiting. 'Ah, yes, I wonder if I might have your help…?' He talked for a few minutes and when old Rob nodded, money changed hands and they bade him goodbye and went off down the village street. Sir Thomas watched them go and then went to let the patient Watson out of the car and get his bag, let himself into the tea-room again and go soft-footed upstairs with Watson hard on his heels.

Mary Jane had fallen asleep, her hair all over the place, her mouth slightly open. She had a little colour now and her nose was pink from crying. Sir Thomas studied her lovingly and then turned his attention to her hand lying outside the quilt. The wrist was discoloured and a little swollen. The man's grasp must have been brutal. He suppressed the wave of rage which shook him and sat down to wait for her to wake up.

Which she did presently, the long lashes sweeping up to reveal the glorious eyes. Sir Thomas spent a few seconds admiring them. 'Better now? I'd like to take a look at that wrist. Does it hurt?'

'Yes.' She sat up in bed and dragged the quilt away. 'But I'm perfectly all right now. Thank you very much for helping me. I mustn't keep you...'

He was holding her hand, examining her wrist. 'This is quite nasty. I'll put a crêpe bandage on for the time being and we'll see about it later. Can you manage to pack a bag with a few things? I'm taking you to stay with my mother for a few days.'

She sat up very straight. 'I can't possibly, there's such a lot to do here, I must get someone to help me clear up and I must see about tables and chairs and cups and saucers and...' She paused, struck by the thought that she had no money to buy these essentials and yet she would have to have them, they were her very livelihood. She would have to borrow, but from whom? Oliver? Certainly not Oliver. Felicity? She might offer to help if she knew about it.

Sir Thomas, watching her, guessed her thoughts and

said bracingly, 'There is really nothing you can do for a day or two.' He added vaguely, 'The police, you know. Far better to spend a little time making up your mind what is to be done first.'

'But your mother...'

'She will be delighted to see you again.' He got up and reached down the case on the top of the wardrobe. 'Is Brimble's basket downstairs? I'll get it while you pack—just enough for a week will do. Do you want to leave any messages with anyone? What about the milk and so on?'

'Mrs Adams next door will tell him not to call, and there's food in the fridge...'

'Leave it to me.'

She changed into her suit, packed the jersey dress, undies and a dressing-gown, her few cosmetics, then she did her hair in a perfunctory fashion and found scarf and gloves, out-of-date black court shoes, well-polished, and she burrowed in the back of a drawer and got the few pounds she kept for an emergency. By then, Sir Thomas was calling up the stairs to see if she was ready. He came to fetch her case while she picked up Brimble, carried him down to his basket and fastened him in. She was swept through the ruins of the tea-room before she had time to look round her, popped into the car with the animals on the back seat while he went back to lock the door. He came over to the car then. 'I think it might be a good idea to leave the key with Mrs Adams,' he suggested and she agreed readily, her thoughts busy with ways and means.

A tap on the window made her turn her head. The rector was there, so was his sister, Miss Kemble and Mrs Stokes and hurrying up the street was the shopkeeper. Mary Jane opened the window and a stream of

sympathy poured in. 'If only we had known,' declared
Miss Kemble, 'we could have come to your assistance.'

'But you did, at least the rector did. A cup of tea was
exactly what I needed most! It was all a bit of a shock.'

The shopkeeper poked her head round Mrs Stokes's
shoulder. 'A proper shame it is,' she declared. 'No one is
safe these days. A good thing you've got the doctor here
to take you to his mum. You 'ave a good rest, love—
the place'll be as good as new again, don't you worry.'

They clustered round Sir Thomas as he came back
to the car and after a few minutes' talk he got into his
seat, lifted a hand in farewell and drove away. 'I like
your rector,' he observed, 'but his sister terrifies me.'

Which struck her as so absurd that she laughed,
which was what he had meant her to do.

He didn't allow her to talk about the disastrous morning either but carried on a steady flow of remarks to
which, out of politeness, she was obliged to reply. When
they arrived at his mother's house, she was met by that
lady with sincere pleasure and no mention as to why she
had come. 'We've put you in the room you had when
you were here,' she was told. 'And have you brought
your nice cat with you?'

Mrs Latimer broke off to offer a cheek to her son
and receive Watson's pleased greeting. 'Would you like
to go up to your room straight away? Lunch will be in
ten minutes or so. Come down and have a drink first.'

The house was warm and welcoming and Mrs Beaver, coming into the hall, beamed at her with heartwarming pleasure. It was like coming home, thought
Mary Jane, skipping upstairs behind that lady, only of
course it wasn't, but it was nice to pretend…

No one mentioned the morning's events at lunch.
The talk was of the village, a forthcoming trip Sir

Thomas was to make to the Middle East and whether
Mrs Latimer should go to London to do some shopping.
Somehow they contrived to include Mary Jane in their
conversation so that presently she was emboldened to
ask, 'Are you going away for a long time?'

'If all goes well, I should be away for a week, perhaps less. I've several good reasons for wanting to get
back as soon as possible.'

Was one of them Felicity? wondered Mary Jane,
and Mrs Latimer put the thought into words by asking, 'Have you seen anything of that glamorous sister
of yours lately, Mary Jane?'

'No. I'm not sure where she is—she was in Spain but
I don't know how long she will be there.'

Sir Thomas leaned back in his chair, his eyes on
her face. 'Felicity is in London,' he observed casually.

It was quite true, thought Mary Jane, love did hurt, a
physical pain which cut her like a knife. Somehow she
was going to have to live with it. 'Perhaps you would
like to go and see her?' Sir Thomas went on.

She spoke too quickly. 'No, no, there's no need, I
mean, she's always so—that is, she works so hard she
wouldn't be able to spare the time.'

She had gone rather red in the face and he said
blandly, 'I don't suppose she could do much to help
you,' and when his mother suggested that they have
their coffee in the drawing-room she got up thankfully.

They had had their coffee and were sitting comfortably before the fire when Sir Thomas asked abruptly,
'Have you any money, Mary Jane?'

She was taken by surprise; there was no time to think
up a fib and anyway, what would be the point of that?
'Well, no, I mean I have a few pounds—I keep them
hidden at the cottage but I've brought them with me

and there's about forty pounds in the post office.' She achieved a smile. 'I shall be able to borrow for the tea-room.' She added hastily, 'I'm not sure who yet, but I've friends in the village.'

'Good. As I said, there's nothing to be done for a day or two; besides, I think that wrist should be X-rayed. I'll take you up to town when I go on Monday morning—I'm operating all day but I'll bring you back in the evening. Someone can take you to my house and Mrs Tremble will look after you until I'm ready.'

He smiled at her. 'You are about to argue but I beg you not to; I'm not putting myself out in the least.'

'It only aches a little.'

'You may have got a cracked bone.' He glanced at her bandaged wrist. He asked mildly, 'What had you done to annoy the man?'

'I kicked him.'

'Quite right too,' said Mrs Latimer. 'What a sensible girl you are. I would have done the same. Do you suppose it hurt?'

He went away presently to make some phone calls and Mrs Latimer said cosily, 'Now, my dear, do tell me exactly what happened if you can bear to talk about it. What a brave girl you are. I should never have dared to ask for my money.'

So Mary Jane told her and discovered that talking about it made it seem less awful than she supposed. True, the problem of borrowing money and starting up again was at the moment impossible to solve but as her companion so bracingly remarked, things had a way of turning out better than one might expect. On this optimistic note she bore Mary Jane away to the conservatory at the back of the house to admire two camellias in full bloom.

The three of them had tea round the fire presently and sat talking until Sir Thomas was called to the phone and Mrs Latimer suggested that Mary Jane might like to unpack and then make sure that Mrs Beaver had prepared the right supper for Brimble, who had spent a day after his heart, curled up before the fire. Mary Jane went to her room, bearing him with her; there was some time before dinner and perhaps mother and son would like to be alone. So she stayed there, spending a lot of time before the looking-glass, trying out various hair-styles and then, disheartened by the fact that they didn't improve her looks in the slightest, pinning it in her usual fashion, applied lipstick and powder and, when the gong sounded, went downstairs, leaving Brimble asleep on the bed.

Sir Thomas and his mother were in the drawing-room and he got up at once and invited her to sit down and offered her a drink.

'But the gong's gone…'

He smiled. 'I don't suppose anything will spoil if we dine five minutes later. Did you fall asleep?'

He was making it easy for her and Mrs Latimer said comfortably, 'All that excitement—you must have an early night, my dear.'

They dined presently and Mary Jane discovered that she was hungry. The mushrooms in garlic sauce, beef Wellington and *crème brulée* were delicious and just right—as was the conversation; about nothing much, touching lightly upon any number of subjects and never once on her trying morning. As they got up from the table, Sir Thomas said casually, 'Shall we go for a walk tomorrow, Mary Jane? I enjoy walking at this time of year but perhaps you don't care for it?'

'Oh, but I do.' The prospect of being with him had sent the colour into her cheeks. 'I'd like that very much.'

'Good—after lunch, then. We go to church in the morning—come with us if you would like to.'

'I'd like that, too.'

'Splendid, I've fixed up an appointment for you on Monday morning—half-past nine—we'll have to leave around seven o'clock. I'm operating at ten o'clock.'

'I get up early. Would someone mind feeding Brimble? He'll be quite good on the balcony.'

'Don't worry about him, my dear.' Mrs Latimer was bending her head over an embroidery frame. 'Mrs Beaver and I will keep an eye on him. Thomas, did you bring any work with you?'

'I'm afraid so—there's a paper I have to read at the next seminar.'

'Then go away and read it or write it, or whatever you need to do. Mary Jane and I are going to have a nice gossip—I want to tell her all about Mrs Bennett's daughter—she's just got engaged...'

The rest of the evening passed pleasantly. Sir Thomas reappeared after an hour or so and shortly afterwards, in the kindest possible manner, suggested that she might like to go to bed. 'Rather a dull evening for you,' he apologised.

'Dull? It was heavenly.' Had he any idea what it was like to spend almost every evening on one's own even if one were making pastry or polishing tables and chairs? Well, of course he hadn't, he would spend his evenings with friends, going to the theatre, dining out and probably seeing as much of Felicity as possible. The sadness of her face at the thought caused him to stare at her thoughtfully. He wanted to ask her why she was sad, but, not liking him enough to answer, she would give him a chilly look from those lovely eyes and murmur something. He still wasn't sure if she liked him, and even if she did, she had erected an invisible barrier between them. He was going to need a great deal of patience.

She hadn't been expected to sleep but she did, to be wakened in the morning by Mrs Beaver with a tray of tea and the news that it was a fine day but very cold. 'Breakfast in half an hour, miss, and take my advice and wear something warm; the church is like an ice-box.'

She had brought her winter coat with her but it wouldn't go over her suit. It would have to be the jersey dress. She dressed under Brimble's watchful eye and went down to breakfast.

THAT NIGHT, CURLED up in her comfortable bed, she reviewed her day. It had been even better that she had hoped for. The three of them had gone to church and, despite the chill from the ancient building, she had loved every minute of the service, standing between Sir Thomas and his mother, and after lunch she had put on her sensible shoes, tied a scarf over her head and gone with him on the promised walk. It was a pity, she reflected, that they had talked about rather dull matters: politics, the state of the turnip crop on a neighbouring farm, the weather, Watson. She had wanted to talk about Felicity but she hadn't dared and since he hadn't mentioned the tea-room she hadn't liked to say anything about it. After all, he had done a great deal to help her; she was a grown woman, used to being on her own, capable of dealing with things like loans and painting and papering. Women were supposed to be equal to men now, weren't they? She didn't feel equal to Sir Thomas, but she supposed that she would have

to do her best. He had been kind and friendly in a detached way but she suspected that she wasn't the kind
of girl he would choose for a companion. She would
have to go to London with him in the morning to have
her wrist X-rayed, although it didn't seem necessary to
her, but once she was back here she would go back to
her cottage and then she need never see him again. She
went to sleep then, feeling sad, and woke in the small
hours, suddenly afraid of the future. It would be hard
to begin again and it would be even harder never to
see Sir Thomas, or worse—if he married Felicity, she
would have to see him from time to time. She wouldn't
be able to bear that, but of course she would have to.
She didn't go to sleep again but lay making plans as to
how to open the tea-room as quickly as possible with
the least possible expense. She would need a miracle.

CHAPTER EIGHT

IT WAS STILL dark when they left the next morning. They had breakfast together, wasting no time and, with Watson drowsing on the back seat, had driven away, with no one but Mrs Beaver to see them off. Until they reached the outskirts of the city there was little traffic and they sat in a companionable silence, making desultory conversation from time to time. Crawling through the London streets, Mary Jane thanked heaven that she lived in the country. How could Felicity bear to live in the midst of all the noise and bustle? She asked abruptly, 'Do you like living in London?'

'My work is here, at least for a good part of the time. I escape whenever I can.'

They were in the heart of the city now and the hospital loomed ahead of them. At its entrance he got out, led her across the entrance hall and down a long tiled passage to the X-ray department, where he handed her over to a nurse.

'I'll see you later at my house,' he told her as he prepared to leave.

'Oh, won't you be here?' She was suddenly uncertain.

'I am going home now, but I shall be back presently. By then you will be taken care of by someone. Then Mrs Tremble is expecting you.'

She wanted to ask more questions, but the nurse was watching them with interest and besides, she could see that he was concealing impatience. She said goodbye and went with the nurse to take off her coat and have the bandage taken off her wrist.

The radiographer was young and friendly and she was surprised to find that he knew how her wrist had been injured. 'Sir Thomas phoned,' he told her airily, 'and of course he had to give me a history of the injury. Said you were a brave young lady. Does it bother you at all?'

'It aches but it doesn't feel broken.'

'There may be a bone cracked, though. Let's get it X-rayed—I'll get the radiologist to take a look at it and let Sir Thomas know as soon as possible.'

That done, he bade her goodbye, handed her over to the nurse to have the bandage put on again and then be taken back to the entrance hall.

There was a short, stout man talking to the porter but as she hesitated he came towards her. 'Miss Seymour, Sir Thomas asked me to drive you to his house. I'm Tremble, his butler.'

She offered a hand. 'Thank you, I'm afraid I'm being a nuisance…'

'Not at all, miss. You just come with me. Mrs Tremble has coffee waiting for you. Sir Thomas asked me to tell you that he may be delayed this evening and he hopes that you will dine with him before he drives you back to Mrs Latimer.'

He had ushered her out to the forecourt and into a Jaguar motor car, and as they drove away she asked, 'Where are we going?'

'To Sir Thomas's home, miss.' He had a nice, fatherly manner. 'Me and my wife look after him, as you might

say. Little Venice, that's where he lives, nice and quiet
and not too far from the hospital.'

It wasn't the country, she reflected, but it was certainly quiet and even on a winter's day it was pleasant,
with the water close by and the well-cared-for houses.
Tremble ushered her in, took her coat and opened a
door. Watson came to greet her as she went into the
room.

She had found Mrs Latimer's house charming but
this drawing-room was even more so. There were easy-
chairs drawn up to a blazing fire, a vast sofa between
them, covered as they were in a tawny red velvet. A
Pembroke table stood behind it and on either wall were
mahogany bow-fronted cabinets, filled with porcelain
and silverware. At the window facing the street there
was a Georgian library table, flanked by two side-chairs
of the same period, and here and there, just where they
would be needed, were tripod tables, bearing low ta-
ble-lamps.

'Just you sit down,' said Tremble, 'and I'll bring you
your coffee, miss.'

He went away, leaving her to inspect the room at her
leisure with Watson pressed close to her, until she sat
down in one of the chairs as Tremble came back. 'Sir
Thomas said for you to make yourself at home, miss.
There's the library across the hall if you should like
to go there presently. Mrs Tremble will be along in a
few minutes to make sure that what she's cooking for
lunch suits you.'

'Please don't let her bother—I'm sure whatever it
is will be delicious. I'm putting you to a great deal of
trouble.'

'Not at all, miss. It's a pleasure to have you here. If

Watson gets tiresome just open the French window and let him into the garden.'

Left alone, she drank her coffee, shared the biscuits with Watson and presently went to the French window at the back of the room to look out into the garden beyond. It was quite a good-sized garden with a high brick wall and, even on a grey winter day, was a pleasant oasis in the centre of the city. She went and sat down again and presently Mrs Tremble came into the room.

She was a tall, very thin woman with a sharp nose and a severe hairstyle, but she had a friendly smile and shrewd brown eyes. 'You'll be wanting to know where the cloakroom is, miss; I'm sure Tremble forgot to tell you. Forget his own head one day, he will! Now, as to your lunch; I've a nice little Dover sole and one of my castle puddings if that'll suit? Tremble will bring you a sherry and suggest a wine.'

So, later, Mary Jane sat down to her lunch and afterwards went to the library to choose something to read. The shelves were well-filled, mostly by ponderous volumes pertaining to Sir Thomas's work but she found a local history of that part of London and took it back to read by the fire. Her knowledge of London was scanty and it would be nice to know more about Sir Thomas's private life, even if it was only through reading about his house in a book.

Tremble brought her tea as dusk fell, and drew the red velvet curtains across the windows. 'I'll give Watson his tea now, miss, and take him for a quick run. When Sir Thomas is late home I do that, then the pair of them go for a walk later in the evening.'

Mary Jane ate her tea and, lulled by the warmth of the fire and the gentle lamp-light, she closed her eyes and went to sleep. Voices and Watson's bark woke her and she sat up as the door opened and Sir Thomas came in.

The thought of him had been at the back of her mind all day, mixed in with worried plans for the future of the tea-room. Now the sight of him, calm and self-assured, sent a wave of happiness through her insides.

She remembered just in time about Felicity and greeted him in a sober manner quite at variance with her sparkling eyes.

He wished her good evening in a friendly voice, enquired after her day and voiced the hope that she hadn't found it too tiresome that he had been delayed in driving her back to his mother's house.

'Tiresome? Heavens, no. I've had a lovely day. You can have no idea how delightful it is to eat a meal you haven't cooked for yourself. Such delicious food too! How lucky you are to have Mrs Tremble to cook for you, Sir Thomas—and I've done nothing all day, just lounged around with Watson.' She beamed at him. 'I expect you've been busy?'

He agreed that he had, in a bland voice which didn't betray a long session in Theatre, a ward round, outpatients clinic and two private patients he had seen when he should have been having lunch.

He had sat down opposite her. He had poured her a drink and was sitting with a glass of whisky on the table beside him. She looked exactly right sitting there in her unfashionable clothes; she would be nice to come home to. He dismissed the thought with a sigh; he wanted her for his wife, but only if she loved him, and he wasn't even sure if she liked him! She was grateful for his help, but gratitude was something he chose to ignore.

It was a pity that Mary Jane couldn't read his thoughts. She sat there, making polite conversation until Tremble came to tell them that dinner was served and at the table, sitting opposite him, she continued to make small talk while she ate her salmon mousse, beef *en croûte* and Mrs Tremble's lavish version of Queen of Puddings.

The excellent claret had loosened her tongue so that by the end of their meal she felt emboldened to ask, 'Will you be seeing Felicity? I expect—'

He said silkily, 'I do not know what you expect, Mary Jane, but rid yourself of the idea that I have any interest in your sister. Any meetings we have had have not been of my seeking.'

'Oh, I thought—that is, Felicity said…that you—that you got on well together.'

'In plain terms, that I had fallen in love with her, is that what you are trying to say?' He was suddenly coldly angry. 'You may believe me, Mary Jane, when I tell you that I have no wish to dangle after your sister. I am no longer a callow youth to be taken in by a pretty face.'

She had gone rather red. 'I'm sorry if I've annoyed you. It's none of my business,' and, at his questioning raised eyebrows, she added, 'your private life.'

He debated whether to tell her how mistaken she was and decided not to, and the conversation lapsed while Tremble brought in the coffee tray. When he had gone again, Mary Jane, for some reason, probably the claret, allowed her tongue to run ahead of her good sense. 'Haven't you ever been in love?' she wanted to know.

'On innumerable occasions from the age of sixteen or so. It is a normal habit, you know.'

'Yes, I know. I fell in love with the gym instructor when I was at school and then with the man who came to tune the piano at home. I actually meant enough to want to marry someone…?'

He said gently, 'Yes, Mary Jane. And you?'

'Well, yes.'

'Still the piano-tuner?' He was laughing at her.

She said quickly, 'No,' and managed to laugh too; of course he had found her silly and rather rude, 'I dare say you're wedded to your work.' She spoke lightly.

'Certainly it keeps me fully occupied.' He glanced at his watch. 'Perhaps we had better go…'

She got up at once. 'Of course, I'm sorry, keeping you talking and you've had a long day already.'

She made short work of bidding the Trembles good-bye, saying just the right things in her quiet voice, shaking their hands and smiling a little when Tremble voiced the hope that he would see her again. 'Most unlikely.'

With Watson, drowsy after a good supper and a quick run, on the back seat, Sir Thomas drove away.

Mary Jane, still chatty from the claret, asked, 'Do you like driving?'

'Yes. It is an opportunity to think, especially at this time of night when the roads are fairly clear.'

She kept quiet after that. If he wanted to think then she wouldn't disturb him and if it came to that she had plenty to think about herself. She tore her eyes away from his hands on the wheel and stared ahead of her into the road, lit by the car's headlights. That way she could pretend that he wasn't there sitting beside her and concentrate on her own problems. When eventually he broke the silence it was to remind her that she had an interview with the police in the morning, something she had quite forgotten. 'I've arranged for an officer to come to Mother's house and interview you there,' he added.

'Thank you—I'd forgotten about it. Perhaps he could

drive me back to the cottage? I really must start clearing up and getting it ready to open again.' A fanciful remark if ever there was one; she hadn't any idea at the moment how to find the money to start up once more, but he wasn't to know that.

Sir Thomas, who did know, gave a comforting rumble which might have meant anything and said briskly, 'Mother will be disappointed if you don't stay for a few days, and besides, although your wrist has no broken bones, it would be foolish of you to use it for anything more strenuous than lifting a tea-cup. Please do as I ask, Mary Jane, and wait another few days. If it won't bore you too much, I'll take you back home on Saturday morning.'

'Bored?' She was horrified at the thought. 'How could I possibly be bored in that lovely house, and your mother is so kind—I'd almost forgotten how nice mothers are.' There was a wistful note in her voice, and Sir Thomas sternly suppressed his wish to stop the car and comfort her in a manner calculated to make her forget her lack of a parent. Instead, he said in his quiet way, 'Good, that's settled, then.'

It was after ten o'clock when they reached Mrs Latimer's house and found the welcoming lights streaming from the windows and her waiting for them. So was the faithful Mrs Beaver, bustling in with a tray of coffee and sandwiches. 'And there's your bed waiting for you, Mary Jane, and you'd best be into it seeing that Constable Welch'll be here at nine o'clock sharp.'

Mary Jane drank her coffee obediently, ate a sandwich and, although she very much wanted to stay with Sir Thomas, bade them both goodnight.

'I dare say you'll be gone in the morning,' she observed as they walked together to the door.

'I'll be gone in ten minutes or so,' he told her.

She stopped short. 'You're never going back now? You can't—you mustn't, you've been at the hospital all day and driven here and now you want to drive straight back?'

He said placidly, 'I like driving at night and I promise you I'll go straight to bed when I get home.'

She put a hand on his coat sleeve. 'You'll take care, Thomas, do be careful.'

His eyes glinted under their lids. 'I'll be very careful, Mary Jane.' He bent and kissed her then. It was a quick, hard kiss, not at all like the very occasional peck she received from friends. She didn't know much about kisses, but this was definitely no peck. The look she gave him was amethyst fire.

'Oh, Thomas,' she muttered, and flew across the hall and upstairs, happily unaware that she had called him Thomas twice. She woke in the night, however, and she remembered. 'I am a fool,' she told Brimble, curled up on her feet. 'What a good thing he's not here and I must, simply must go away from here before he comes again.'

She had no chance against Mrs Latimer's gentle insistence that she should stay, or Mrs Beaver's more emphatic opinion that she needed more flesh on her bones and, over and above that, Constable Welch, when he came, assured her that there was no need for her return. 'Those men are to stay in custody for a few more days until we get things sorted out,' he told her. 'And there's nothing you can do for a bit.'

So she stayed in the nice old house, keeping Mrs Latimer company, eating the nourishing food Mrs Beaver insisted upon and discovering something of Sir Thomas. For his mother was quick to show her the family photo albums: Thomas as a baby, Thomas as a boy, Thomas as a student, Thomas receiving a knighthood…

'Why?' asked Mary Jane.

'Well, dear, he has done a great deal of work—around the world, I suppose I could say—teaching and getting clinics opened and lecturing, and, of course, operating. His father was a surgeon, too, you know.'

During the next few days she learnt a good deal about Sir Thomas, information freely given by his mother. By the time Saturday came around, Mary Jane felt that she knew quite a lot about him. At least, she told herself, she would have a lot to think about…

Watson's cheerful bark woke her the next morning and a few minutes later Mrs Beaver came in with her morning tea. 'He doesn't get enough rest,' she said, as she pulled back the curtains, revealing a grey February morning. 'Got here in the early hours, and he's up and outside before I could put the kettle on.' She shook her head. 'There's no holding him.'

When she had gone, Mary Jane got out of bed and went to look out of the window. Sir Thomas was at the end of the garden, throwing a ball for Watson. Whatever Mrs Beaver thought, he appeared to be well-rested and full of energy.

He wished her good morning with detached friendliness when she went down to breakfast, and asked if she would be ready to leave after breakfast and applied himself to his bacon and eggs. They had reached the toast and marmalade when he asked, casually, 'Have you any plans, Mary Jane?'

'I'll get cleared up,' she told him, summoning a cheerful voice. 'I can distemper the walls if they're marked, then I'll go to Cheltenham and borrow some money.' She didn't enlarge upon this and he didn't ask

her to, which was just as well, because she had no idea
how to set about it. She had spent several anxious hours
during the nights going over her problems without much
success and had come to the conclusion that if the solicitor who had attended to her uncle's affairs was unable to advise her there was nothing for it but to ask
Felicity for some money.

They had almost finished when Mrs Latimer joined
them. 'I shall miss you, dear,' she told Mary Jane. 'You
must come and stay again soon— with Brimble, of
course. Do take care of yourself. I shall come and see
you and I'll bring Mrs Bennett with me.'

They left shortly after with Watson and Brimble
sharing the back seat and Mary Jane very quiet beside
Sir Thomas. There seemed nothing to say and since it
was still only half light there was no point in admiring the scenery. It wasn't an awkward silence, though,
she had the feeling that speech wasn't necessary, that
he was content to drive silently, that to make conversation for its own sake was unnecessary. They were almost there when he observed casually, 'I shall be away
all next week—Austria. I'll see you when I get back.'

He looked at her and smiled. It was a tender smile
and a little amused and she looked away quickly. Then,
for something to say, she asked, 'Have you been to Austria before?'

'Several times. Vienna this time—a seminar there.'

He had slowed the car down the village street and
he stopped before her cottage, got out and opened the
door and let Watson out as he reached in for Brimble's
basket. Mary Jane stared.

'Someone's painted the outside—look…'

'So they have,' observed Sir Thomas, showing only

a faint interest as he took the key from a pocket and opened the door.

She went in quickly and then stood quite still. 'Inside too,' she said. 'Look at the walls, and there's a new counter and tables and chairs.' She turned to look at him. 'Did you know? But how could…there's no money to pay for it.' She stared into his quiet face. 'It's you, isn't it? You arranged it all.'

'Mr Rob and his sons have done all the work, your friends in the village collected tables and chairs and I imagine that every house in the village contributed the china.'

'You arranged it, though, and you paid for it, too, didn't you?' She smiled widely at him. 'Oh, Sir Thomas, how can I ever thank you? And everyone else of course, and as soon as I've got started again I'll pay you back, every penny.'

'You called me Thomas.' He had come to stand very close to her.

'I expect I forgot,' she told him seriously. 'I hope you didn't mind.'

'On the contrary, I took it as a sign that we were becoming friends.'

She put a hand on his arm. 'How can I ever be anything else after all you've done for me?' She reached up and kissed his cheek. 'I'll never forget you.'

'I rather hope you won't!'

He stared down at her with such intensity that she said hurriedly, 'Will you have a cup of coffee? It won't take a minute.'

He went to fetch her case from the car and she let an impatient Brimble out of his basket and put on the kettle and saw that there were cups and saucers arranged on the kitchen table and an unopened tin of biscuits, sugar in a bowl and milk in the fridge. She knew the reason a moment later for when Sir Thomas came in he was followed by the rector, his sister, old Rob and his sons, the shopkeeper and the Misses Potter.

There was a chorus of, 'Welcome back, Mary Jane,' and a good deal of talk and laughter as she made the coffee and handed round the cups. No one intended to hurry away; they all sat around, admiring their efforts, telling Mary Jane that she had never looked so plump and well. 'And we would never have done any of this if it hadn't been for Sir Thomas,' declared Miss Emily in her penetrating voice. 'He had us all organised in no time.'

It was a pity that presently he declared that he had to go and in the general bustle of handshaking and good-byes Mary Jane had no chance to speak to him. She did go out to the car with him and stood there on the pavement, impervious to the cold, her hands held in his.

'We can't talk now, Mary Jane, and perhaps it is just as well, but I'm coming to see you. You want to see me, too, don't you?'

'Yes, oh, yes, please, Thomas!'

His kiss was even better than the last one. She stood there watching the Rolls disappear out of sight and would have probably gone on standing, freezing slowly, if Miss Kemble hadn't opened the door and told her to come inside at once. Mary Jane, who never took any notice of Miss Kemble's bossy ways, meekly did as she was told.

She was borne away presently to eat her lunch at the rectory and to be given a great deal of unheeded advice by Miss Kemble. That lady said to her brother later in the day, 'I have never known Mary Jane to be so atten-tive and willing to take my advice.'

Mary Jane had heard perhaps one word in ten of Miss

Kemble's lectures; her head was full of Sir Thomas, going over every word he had said, the way he had looked, his kiss.

Back in her cottage once more, she assured Brimble that she would be sensible, at least until she saw him again. He had said that he wanted to see her again... she forgot about being sensible and fell to daydreaming again.

She was up early the next morning, polishing and dusting, setting out cups and saucers and making a batch of scones. Sunday was a bad day usually, and she seldom opened, only in the height of the tourist season, but she had a feverish wish to get back to her old life as quickly as possible. Her efforts were rewarded, for several cars stopped and when she opened again after lunch there were more customers. It augured well for the future, she told herself, counting the takings at the end of the afternoon.

Her luck held for the first few days, and a steady trickle of customers came; if it continued so, she could make a start on paying back Sir Thomas. She had no idea how much it would be and probably she would be in his debt for years.

Thursday brought Oliver. He marched into the tea-room and stood looking around him. 'Who paid for all this?' he wanted to know.

Mary Jane, her hands floury from her pastry making, stood in the kitchen doorway, looking at him. 'So you did hear about the—incident? The rector told me that he had let you know...'

Oliver blew out his cheeks. 'Naturally, it was his duty to inform me.'

Mary Jane put her neat head on one side. 'And what did you do about it?'

'There was no necessity for me to do anything. The place was being put to rights.' He looked around him. 'It must have cost you a pretty penny. You borrowed, of course?'

'That's my business. Have you just come to see if I'm still here or do you want something?'

'Since your regrettable treatment of Margaret I would hesitate to ask any favours of you.'

'Quite right too, Oliver. So it's just curiosity.'

He said pompously, 'I felt it my duty to come and see how things were.'

'Oh, stuff,' said Mary Jane rudely. 'Do go away, Oliver, you're wasting my time.'

'You've wasted enough time with that surgeon,' he sneered. 'We hear the village gossip as well as everyone else. Hoping to catch him, are you? Well, I'll tell you something—even if you were pretty, and knew how to dress you wouldn't stand a chance. That sister of yours has him hooked. We've been to town and met her—just back from Vienna. She means to marry him, and I must say this for the girl, she always gets what she wants.'

She put her hands behind her back because they were shaking and, although she had gone pale, she said steadily enough, 'Felicity is beautiful and famous and she works hard at her job. She deserves to have whatever she wants.'

'Well, from all accounts he's a great catch—loaded, well-known and handsome. What more could a girl want?' He laughed nastily. 'So you can stop your silly dreaming and look around for someone who's not too fussy about looks.'

'Oh, do go. I'm busy.' She added, 'You're getting fat, Oliver—you ought to go on a diet.'

If he didn't go quickly, she reflected, she would

scream the place down. He was sly and mean and she had no doubt at all that he had come intending to tell her about Felicity and Sir Thomas; he had obviously known all about the tea-room being vandalised and what Sir Thomas had done to help her. Thankfully, he went with a last, sniggering, 'I don't expect Felicity will ask you to be a bridesmaid, but you wouldn't like that, would you? Seeing the man of your dreams marrying your sister.'

It was too much; she had been cutting up lard to make the puff pastry for the sausage rolls, and she scooped up a handful and threw it at him as he opened the door. It caught him on the side of his head and slid down his cheek, oozed over his collar and down on to his overcoat.

Rage and surprise rendered him speechless. 'Bye bye, Oliver,' said Mary Jane cheerfully.

She locked the door when he had gone, turned the sign to 'Closed' and went upstairs, where she sat down and had a good cry. It had been foolish of her, she told Brimble, to imagine, even for a moment, that Sir Thomas had any deeper feelings for her than those of friendliness and—regrettably—pity, but he could have told her...and he was coming to see her; he wanted to talk. Well, of course he did, he wanted to tell her about Felicity and himself, didn't he? But why couldn't he have told her sooner and only kissed her in a casual manner, so that she couldn't get silly ideas into her head? She blew her red nose, bathed her eyes and went back to her pastry making. Perhaps Oliver had been lying; he was quite capable of that. The thought cheered her so that by the time she had taken the sausage rolls from the oven she felt quite cheerful again.

She had some more customers calling in for coffee and sausage rolls. Several of them remarked upon her heavy cold and she agreed quickly, conscious that her eyes were still puffy and her nose still pink.

Sir Thomas had thoughtfully caused a telephone to be installed when the tea-room had been done up, arguing that as she lived alone it was a sensible thing to have. She had thanked him nicely, wondering how she was going to pay for its rental, let alone any calls she might make.

When it rang just before closing time she lifted the receiver—only he and possibly Mrs Latimer would know the number and, even if her friends in the village knew it, too, they would hardly waste money ringing her up when they only needed to nip down the road. 'Thomas,' she said happily to Brimble, disturbed from a refreshing nap.

It was Felicity.

'Felicity,' said Mary Jane. 'How did you know I had a phone?'

'Thomas told me. Back with your nose to the pastry-board again? What a thrill for you, darling. I'm just back from Vienna and in an absolute daze of happiness, darling. I told you I'd marry when I found the right man—good looks, darling, lots of lovely money and dotes on me.'

Mary Jane found her voice. 'What wonderful news and how exciting. When will you get married?'

'I've one or two modelling dates I can't break but very soon—a few weeks. I wanted to move in with him, but he wouldn't hear of it.' She giggled. 'He's very old-fashioned.'

Mary Jane wasn't sure about Sir Thomas being old-fashioned but she was quite sure that allowing Felicity to move in with him would be something he would never agree to.

'Will you have a big wedding?'

'As big as I am able to arrange in a few weeks. There's a nice little church close by—we've dozens of friends between us and I shall wear white, of course. Bridesmaids, too. A pity you're so far away, darling.'

Which remark Mary Jane took, quite rightly, to be a kinder way of saying that she wasn't expected to be a bridesmaid or even a guest.

'What would you like for a wedding present?'

Felicity laughed. 'Oh, darling, don't bother, I'm sending a list to Harrods. Besides, you haven't any money.'

Mary Jane was pleased to hear how bright and cheerful her voice sounded. 'Let me know the date of the wedding, anyway,' she begged. 'And I'm so glad you're happy, dear.' She was going to burst into tears any minute now. 'I must go, I've scones in the oven.'

'You and your scones,' laughed Felicity, and rang off. Just in time. She locked the door and turned the notice round and switched off the lights, not forgetting to put the milk bottles outside the back door and checking the fridge before polishing the tables ready for the morning. All the while she was weeping quietly. Oliver, with his nasty, snide remarks, had been bad enough and she had almost persuaded herself that he had just been malicious, but now Felicity had told her the same story.

Moping would do no good, she told herself presently, and started to clean the stove—a job she hated, but anything was better than having time to think.

She pushed her supper round and round her plate and went to bed. It was a well-known adage that things were always better in the morning.

They were exactly the same, except that now she never wanted to see Thomas again. He had been amusing himself while Felicity was away, playing at being the Good Samaritan. She ground her little white teeth at the thought. If it took her the rest of her life she would pay him back every penny. How dared he kiss her like that, as though he actually wanted to…?

He had said that he would be away for the whole of the week and it was still only Friday; she would have the weekend to decide how she would behave and even if he had to go to the hospital or see his patients he might not come for some days. He might not come at all.

'Which, of course, would be far the best thing,' she told Brimble.

He came the next day just as she was handing a bill to the last of the few people who had been in for tea. She stared at him across the room, her heart somersaulting against her ribs. He looked as he always did, calm and detached, but he was smiling a little. Well he might, reflected Mary Jane, ushering her customers out of the door which Sir Thomas promptly closed, turning the sign round.

'It is not yet five o'clock,' said Mary Jane frostily. Talking to him wasn't going to be difficult at all because she was so angry.

'I got back a day early,' said Sir Thomas, still standing by the door. 'It has been a long week simply because I want to talk to you.'

'Well, you need not have hurried. Felicity phoned me. She's—she's very happy, I hope you will be too.' Despite her efforts her voice began to spiral. 'You could have told me… You've been very kind, more than kind, but I can understand that you wanted to please her.'

'What exactly are you talking about?' he wanted to know, his voice very quiet.

'Oh, do stop pretending you don't know,' she snapped. 'I knew that you would fall in love with her but you didn't tell me, you let me think…did you have a nice time together in Vienna?'

His voice was still quiet but now it was cold as well. 'You believe that I went straight from you to be with Felicity? That I am going to marry her? That I was amusing myself with you?'

'Of course I do. Oliver told me and I didn't quite believe him and then she phoned.'

'Is that what you think of me, Mary Jane?' And when she nodded dumbly he gave her a look of such icy rage that she stepped back. If only he would go, she thought miserably, and had her wish.

CHAPTER NINE

MARY JANE STOOD in the middle of the sitting-room, listening to the faint whisper of the Rolls-Royce's departure, regretting every word she had uttered. She hadn't given Sir Thomas a chance to speak, and her ingratitude must have shocked him. She should have behaved like a future sister-in-law, congratulated him and expressed her delight. All she had done was to let him see that she had taken him seriously when all the time he was merely being kind. Well, it was too late now. She had cooked her goose, burnt her boats, made her bed and must lie on it. She uttered these wise sayings out loud, but they brought her no comfort.

She felt an icy despair too deep for tears. The thought of a lifetime of serving tea and coffee and baking cakes almost choked her. She could, of course, sell the cottage and go right away, but that would be running away, wouldn't it? Besides, she must owe him a great deal of money...

Leaving church the next morning, Miss Kemble took her aside. 'You must have your lunch with us,' she insisted, overriding Mary Jane's reasons for not doing so. 'Of course you must come, you are still too pale. Do you not sleep? Perhaps you are nervous of being alone?'

Mary Jane said very quickly that she wasn't in the least nervous—only at the thought of Miss Kemble moving in to keep her company. 'Besides,' she pointed out, 'I have a telephone now.'

'Ah, yes, that charming Sir Thomas Latimer, what a good friend he has been to you. I hear from all sides how thoughtful he is of others—always helping lame dogs over stiles.' An unfortunate remark unintentionally made.

They were kind at the rectory. She was given a glass of Miss Kemble's beetroot wine and the rector piled her plate with underdone roast beef which she swallowed down, wishing that Brimble were there to finish it for her. I don't mean to be ungrateful, she reflected, but why does Miss Kemble always make me feel as if I were an object for charity?

She left shortly after their meal with the excuse that she intended to go for a brisk walk. 'For I don't get out a great deal,' she explained, and then wished that she hadn't said that, for Miss Kemble might decide to go with her.

However, there was a visiting parson coming to tea and staying the night, so Miss Kemble was fully occupied. Mary Jane thanked the pair of them sincerely; they had been kind and going to the rectory had filled in some of the long day. Sunday was always a bad day with time lying heavy on her hands, and today was worse than usual. She tired herself out with a long walk; as the days went by it would get easier to forget Sir Thomas and the chances of seeing much of him were slight; Felicity didn't like a country life. She let herself into her cottage, shed her coat and scarf, fed Brimble and spent a long time cooking a supper she hardly touched.

There was a spate of customers on Monday morning to keep her busy and she had promised to make a cake for the Women's Institute meeting during the week, so the baking of it took most of the afternoon.

'Another day gone,' said Mary Jane to Brimble.

Mrs Latimer and Mrs Bennett came the next day. 'We thought we would have a little drive round, dear,' explained Mrs Latimer, 'and we'd love a cup of coffee.'

They sat down, her only customers—and begged her to join them.

'I must say I'm disappointed,' observed Mrs Latimer. 'You don't look at all well, dear. You were quite bonny when I last saw you. Are you working too hard? A few days' rest perhaps? Thomas is back from wherever it was he went to…'

'Vienna.'

'That's right. Has he been to see you?'

Mrs Latimer's blue eyes were guileless.

'Yes.'

For the life of her, Mary Jane couldn't think of anything to add to that. And if Mrs Latimer expected it she gave no sign but made some observation about the life her son led. 'It is really time he settled down,' she declared, which gave Mrs Bennett the chance to talk about her recently engaged daughter, so that any chance Mary Jane had of finding out more about Thomas and Felicity was squashed.

'You must come and see us,' said Mrs Bennett. 'On a Sunday, when you're free. How nice that you're on the telephone—very thoughtful of Thomas to have it put in. I must say it has all been beautifully redecorated.'

'He's been very kind,' said Mary Jane woodenly. 'And the village gave me the china and the tables and chairs. I don't think I could have managed to start again without help. I'm very grateful.'

'My dear child,' said Mrs Latimer, 'I don't know of

many girls who would have carved themselves a living out of an old cottage and the pittance your uncle left you, and as for that wretched cousin of yours...'

'I don't see Oliver very often,' said Mary Jane, adding silently, Only when he wants something or has news which he knows might upset me.

The two ladies left presently and, save for a man on a scooter who had taken a wrong turning, she had no more customers that day.

Sir Thomas immersed himself in his work, as calm and courteous and unflappable as he always was, only Tremble was disturbed. 'There's something up,' he confided to Mrs Tremble. 'Don't ask me what, for I don't know, but there's something wrong somewhere.'

'That nice young lady...' began his wife.

'Now don't go getting sentimental ideas in your head,' begged Tremble.

'Mark my words,' said Mrs Tremble, who always managed to have the last word.

That same evening Felicity arrived on Thomas's doorstep. Tremble, opening the door to her, tried not to look disapproving; he didn't like flighty young ladies with forward manners but he begged her to go into the small sitting-room behind the little dining-room while he enquired if Sir Thomas was free.

Thomas was at his desk writing, with Watson at his feet. He looked up with a frown as Tremble went in. 'Something important, Tremble?'

'A young lady to see you, sir, a Miss Seymour.'

The look on his master's face forced him to remember his wife's words. If this was the young lady who was giving all the trouble then he for one was disappointed.

There was no accounting for taste, of course, but somehow she didn't seem right for Sir Thomas.

He followed his master into the hall and opened the sitting-room door and let out a sigh of relief when Sir Thomas exclaimed, 'Felicity—I thought it was Mary Jane.'

'Mary Jane? Whatever would she be doing in London? You might at least look pleased to see me, Thomas. I've news for you—it will be in the papers tomorrow but I thought you might like to know before then. I'm engaged, isn't it fun? A marvellous man—a film director, no less. I've had him dangling for weeks—a girl has to think very carefully about her future, after all. He went to Vienna with me and I decided he'd do. He is in the States now, coming back tomorrow. You'll come to the wedding, of course. I phoned Mary Jane—she won't be coming, she'd be like a fish out of water and she hasn't the right clothes.'

Sir Thomas was still standing, looking down at her, sitting gracefully in a high-backed chair. He said evenly, 'I think it is unlikely that I shall be free to come to your wedding, Felicity. I hope that you will both be very happy. I expect Mary Jane was surprised.'

Felicity shrugged. 'Probably. You were in Vienna, too, were you not? We might have met but I suppose you were lecturing or something dull.'

'Yes. May I offer you a drink?'

'No, thanks, I'm on my way to dine with friends.' She smiled charmingly. 'Do you know, Thomas, I considered you for a husband for a while but it would never have done; all you ever think of is your work.'

He smiled. He didn't choose to tell her how mistaken she was.

ON THURSDAY AFTERNOON the Misses Potter came for tea, as usual. There had been a handful of customers but now the tea-room was empty and Miss Emily said in a satisfied voice, 'I am glad to find that you have no one else here, Mary Jane, for we have brought the newspaper for you to read. There is something of great interest in it. Of course, the *Telegraph* only mentions it, but I persuaded Mrs Stokes to let me have her *Daily Mirror* which has more details.'

The ladies sat themselves down at their usual table and Mary Jane fetched tea and scones and waited patiently while the ladies poured their tea and buttered their scones. This done, Miss Emily took the newspapers from her shopping basket and handed them to her. The *Telegraph* first, the page folded back on 'Forthcoming Marriages'.

Mary Jane's eyes lighted on the announcement at once. 'Mr Theobald Coryman, of New York, to Miss Felicity Seymour of London.' She read it twice just to make sure, and then said, 'I don't understand—is it a mistake?'

'In the *Telegraph*?' Miss Emily was shocked. 'A most reputable newspaper.' She handed over the *Daily Mirror*, which confirmed the *Telegraph*'s genteel announcement in a more flamboyant manner. 'Famous Model to Wed Film Director' said the front-page and under that a large photo of Felicity and a man in horn-rimmed glasses and a wide-brimmed hat. They were arm in arm and Felicity was displaying the ring on her finger.

'It must be a mistake,' said Mary Jane. 'Felicity said…!'

She remembered with clarity what her sister had said—word for word, and Thomas's name had not been mentioned. It was she herself who had made the mis-

take, jumped to the wrong conclusion and accused Sir
Thomas of behaviour in a manner which had been nothing short of that of a virago. She had indeed cooked
her goose; worse, she had wronged him in a manner
he wasn't likely to forgive or forget. She hadn't given
him a chance to say anything, either.

The Misses Potter were looking at her in some astonishment. 'You are pleased? Felicity seems to have
done very well for herself.'

'Yes, I'm delighted,' said Mary Jane wildly. 'It's
marvellous news. I'm sure she'll—they—will be very
happy. He looks…!' She paused, at a loss to describe
her sister's future husband; there wasn't much of him
to see other than the hat and the glasses. 'Very nice,'
she finished lamely.

'They seem very suitable,' remarked Miss Emily
drily. 'He is, so they say, extremely rich.'

'Yes, well, Felicity likes nice things.'

The elderly sisters gave her a thoughtful glance. 'I
think we all do, dear,' said Miss Mabel. 'You look a bit
peaked—have a cup of tea with us.'

Which Mary Jane did; a cup of tea was the panacea
for all ills, at least in the United Kingdom, and it gave
her time to pull herself together.

The Misses Potter went presently, and she was left
with her unhappy thoughts. Would it be a good idea,
she wondered, to write to Sir Thomas and apologise; on
the other hand, would it be better to do nothing about
it? Had she the courage, she wondered, to write and tell
him that she loved him and would he forgive her? She
went upstairs and found paper and pen and sat down
to compose a letter. An hour later, with the wastepaper
basket overflowing, she gave up the attempt. Somehow
her feelings couldn't be expressed with pen and ink.

'In any case,' she told Brimble, 'I don't suppose he has given me a thought.'

In this she was mistaken; Sir Thomas had thought about her a great deal. Although he shut her away to the back of his mind while he went about his work, sitting in Sister's office after a ward round, apparently giving all his attention to her tart remarks about lack of staff, the modern nurse, the difficulties she experienced in getting enough linen from the laundry—all of which he had heard a hundred times before, he was thinking that he would like to wring Mary Jane's small neck and then, illogically, toss her into his car and drive away to some quiet spot and marry her out of hand. How dared she imagine for one moment that he was amusing himself with her when he loved her to distraction? That he had never allowed his feelings to show was something he hadn't considered.

He promised Sister that he would speak to the hospital committee next time it met, and wandered off to be joined presently by his registrar wanting his opinion about a patient. Stanley Wetherspoon was a good surgeon and his right hand, but a bit prosy. Halfway through his carefully expressed opinion, Sir Thomas said suddenly, 'Why didn't I think of it before? Of course, we were in Vienna at the same time. Naturally...'

Stanley paused in mid-flow and Sir Thomas said hastily, 'So sorry, I've lost the thread—this prosthesis—what do you suggest that we do?'

Presently, Stanley went on his way, reassured, wondering all the same if his boss was overworking and needed a holiday.

Sir Thomas, outwardly his normal pleasantly assured

self, went to his rooms, saw several patients and then requested Miss Pink to come into his consulting-room.

'How soon can I get away for a day?'

'Well, it's your weekend on call, Sir Thomas—I could ask your patients booked for Monday to come on Saturday morning—since you'll be here anyway—if you saw them then you could have Monday off.'

'And Tuesday? I know I've got a couple of cases in the afternoon, but is the morning free?'

'It will be if I get Mrs Collyer and Colonel Gregg to come in the afternoon—after three o'clock? That'll give you time to get back to your rooms from hospital and have a meal.'

'Miss Pink, you are a gem of real value to me. Do all that, will you? Then let me know when you've fixed things.'

At the door she asked, 'You'll leave an address, Sir Thomas?'

'Yes. I'll go very early in the morning; if you need anything, get hold of Tremble.'

'Well, well,' said Miss Pink, peering out of the window to watch him getting into his car, and she went in search of his nurse, tidying up in the examination-room. A lady of uncertain age, just as she was, and devoted, just as she was, to Sir Thomas's welfare.

'He looked so happy,' said Miss Pink, and, after a cosy chat of a romantic nature, she went away to reorganise his days for him. A task which necessitated a good deal of wheedling and coaxing, both of which she did most willingly; Sir Thomas had the gift of inspiring loyalty and, in Miss Pink's case, an abiding devotion.

Mary Jane spent the next three days composing letters in her head to Sir Thomas, but somehow when she wrote them down they didn't seem the same. By Sunday evening she had a headache, made worse by a visit from Oliver.

'Well, what do you think of Felicity?' he wanted to know when she opened the door to him.

'I'm very pleased for her, Oliver. You had it all wrong, didn't you?'

He gave her a nasty look. 'I may have been mistaken with the name of her future husband, but there's no denying that she has done very well for herself.'

'Why have you come?' asked Mary Jane, not beating about the bush and anxious for him to go again.

'Margaret and I have had a chat—now that this place is tarted up and equipped again, we think that it might be a good idea if we were to buy you out. You can stay here, of course—the cottage is yours anyway, more's the pity—you can run the place and we will pay you a salary. A little judicial advertising and it should make it worth our while.' He added smugly, 'We can use the connection with Felicity—marvellous publicity.'

'Over my dead body,' said Mary Jane fiercely. 'Whatever will you dream up next? And, if that is why you came, I'll not keep you.'

She opened the door and ushered him out while he was still arguing.

When he had gone, however, she wondered if that wouldn't have solved her problem. Not that she would have stayed in the cottage. There was no doubt that he would buy the place from her even if it meant getting someone in to run it. She would have money and be free to go where she wanted. She couldn't think of anywhere at the moment, but no doubt she would if she gave her mind to it. The trouble was, she thought only of Sir Thomas.

The sun was shining when she got up on Monday

morning; February had allowed a spring day with its blue sky and feathery clouds to sneak in. Mary Jane turned the door sign to 'Open', arranged cups and saucers on the four tables and made a batch of scones. The fine weather might tempt some out-of-season tourist to explore and come her way. Her optimism was rewarded: first one table, then a second and finally a third were occupied. Eight persons drinking coffee at fifty-five pence a cup and eating their way through the scones. She did some mental arithmetic, not quite accurate, but heartening none the less, and made plans to bake another batch of scones during the lunch hour. It was still only mid-morning and there might be other customers.

The family of four at one of the tables called for more coffee and she was pouring it when the door opened and Sir Thomas came in, Watson at his heels. It was difficult not to spill the coffee, but she managed it somehow, put the percolator down on the table and, heedless of the customers' stares, stood gaping at him. He sat down at the remaining empty table, looking quite at his ease, and requested coffee. Watson, eager to greet Mary Jane, had, at a quiet word from his master, subsided under the table. Sir Thomas nodded vaguely at the other customers and looked at Mary Jane as though he had never seen her before, lifting his eyebrows a little because of her tardy response to his request.

The wave of delight and happiness at the sight of him which had engulfed her was swamped by sudden rage. How could he walk in as though he were a complete stranger and look through her in that casual manner? Coffee, indeed. She would like to throw the coffee-pot at him…

She poured his coffee with a shaky hand, not looking at him but stooping to pat the expectant Watson's head, and then, just to show him that he was only a customer like anyone else, she made out the bill, laid it on the table and held out her hand for the money.

He picked the hand up gently. It was a little red and rough from her chores, but it was a pretty shape and small. He kissed it on its palm and folded her fingers over it and gave the hand back to her.

What would have happened next was anybody's guess, but the two women who had arrived in a small car, having taken a wrong turning, asked loudly for their bill. When they had gone, Mary Jane made herself as small as possible behind the counter, taking care not to look at Sir Thomas, very aware that he was looking at her. The young couple on a walking holiday went next, looking at her curiously as they went out, frankly staring at Sir Thomas, and that left the family of four, a hearty, youngish man, his cheerful loud-voiced wife and two small children. They had watched Sir Thomas with avid interest, in no hurry to be gone, hoping perhaps for further developments. Sir Thomas sat, quite at his ease, silent, his face a blank mask, his eyes on Mary Jane. Unable to spin out their meal any longer, they paid their bill and prepared to go. His wife, looking up from fastening the children's coats, beamed at Mary Jane. 'You'll be glad to see the back of us, love—I dare say he's dying to pop the question—can't take his eyes off you, can he?'

They all went to the door and she turned round as they went out. 'Good luck to you both, bye bye.'

They got into their car and Sir Thomas got up, turned the sign to 'Closed', locked the door and stood leaning against it, his hands in his pockets.

Mary Jane, standing in the middle of the room, waited for him to speak; after a while, when the si-

lence became unbearable, she said the first thing to
come into her head.

'Shouldn't you be at the hospital?'

'Indeed I should, but, owing to Miss Pink's zealous
juggling of my appointments book, I have given myself
the day off.' He smiled suddenly and her heart turned
over. 'To see you, my dearest Mary Jane.'

'Me?'

'You believed that I had gone to Vienna to be with
Felicity?' He asked the question gravely.

'Well, you see, Oliver told me and then Felicity
phoned and she didn't say who it was and I thought
it would be you—she said you were famous and rich
and good-looking and you are, aren't you? It sounded
like you.'

'And then?' he prompted gently.

'Miss Emily showed me two newspapers and one
of them had a photo of Felicity and—I've forgotten his
name, but he wears a funny hat, and I tried to write you
a letter but it was too difficult...'

'You supposed that I had helped you to set this place
to rights because you are Felicity's sister?'

She nodded. 'I was a bit upset.'

'And why were you upset, Mary Jane?'

She met his eyes with an effort. 'I'd much rather not
say, if you don't mind.'

'I mind very much. I mind about everything you
say and do and think. I am deeply in love with you, my
dearest girl, you have become part—no, my whole life. I
want you with me, to come home to, to talk to, to love.'

Mary Jane was filled with a delicious excitement,
and a thankful surprise that sometimes dreams really
did come true. She said in a small voice, 'Are you quite
sure, Thomas? I love you very much, but Oliver...'

Sir Thomas left the door and caught her close. 'Oliver can go to the devil. Say that again, my darling.'

She began obediently, 'Are you quite sure…?' She peeped at him and saw the look on his face. 'I love you very much.'

'That's what I thought you said, but I had to make sure.'

'But I must tell you…'

'Not another word,' said Sir Thomas, and kissed her. Presently, Mary Jane, a little out of breath, lifted her face to his. 'That was awfully nice,' she told him.

'In which case…'

'Thomas, there's a batch of scones in the oven.' She added hastily, 'It isn't that I don't want you to kiss me, I do, very much, but they'll burn.'

Sir Thomas, quite rightly, took no notice of this remark but presently he said, 'Pack a bag, my love, and urge Brimble into his basket. You may have ten minutes. I will see to things here. No, don't argue, there isn't time—you may argue as much as you wish once we're married.'

She reached up and kissed his chin. 'I'll remember that,' she said and slipped away up the stairs to do as she was told.

He watched her go before going into the kitchen and rescuing the scones, the faithful Watson beside him. Brimble was on the kitchen table, waiting.

'What must I take with me, Thomas?' Mary Jane's voice floated down the little stairs. 'You didn't say where we are going?'

He stood looking up at her anxious face. 'Why, home, of course, my love.' And saw her lovely smile.

* * * * *

The Daughter of the Manor

CHAPTER ONE

THE VILLAGE OF Pont Magna, tucked into a fold of the Mendip Hills, was having its share of February weather. Sleet, icy rain, a biting wind and a sharp frost had culminated in lanes and roads like skating rinks, so that the girl making her way to the village trod with care.

She was a tall girl with a pretty face, quantities of dark hair bundled into a woolly cap, her splendid proportions hidden under an elderly tweed coat, and she was wearing stout wellies—suitable wear for the weather but hardly glamorous.

The lane curved ahead of her and she looked up sharply as a car rounded it, so that she didn't see the ridge of frozen earth underfoot, stumbled, lost her footing and sat down with undignified suddenness.

The car slowed, came to a halt and the driver got out, heaved her onto her feet without effort and remarked mildly, 'You should look where you're going.'

'Of course I was looking where I was going.' The girl pulled her cap straight. 'You had no business coming round that corner so quietly...'

She tugged at her coat, frowning as various painful areas about her person made themselves felt.

'Can I give you a lift?'

She sensed his amusement and pointed out coldly,

'You're going the opposite way.' She added, 'You're a stranger here?'

'Er-yes.'

Although she waited he had no more to say; he only stood there looking down at her, so she said matter-of-factly, 'Well, thank you for stopping. Goodbye.'

When he didn't answer she looked at him and found him smiling. He was good-looking—more than that, handsome—with a splendid nose, a firm mouth and very blue eyes. She found their gaze disconcerting.

'I'm sorry if I was rude. I was taken by surprise.'

'Just as I have been,' he replied.

An apt remark, she reflected as she walked away from him, but somehow it sounded as though he had meant something quite different. When she reached the bend in the lane she looked back. He was still standing there, watching her.

Pont Magna wasn't a large village; it had a green, a church much too big for it, a main street wherein was the Village Stores and post office, pleasant cottages facing each other, a by-lane or two leading to other cottages and half a dozen larger houses—the vicarage, old Captain Morris's house at the far end of the street, and several comfortable dwellings belonging to retired couples. A quiet place in quiet countryside, with Wells to the south and Frome to the east and Bath to the north.

Its rural surroundings were dotted by farms and wide fields. Since the village was off a main road tourists seldom found their way there, and at this time of the year the village might just as well have been a hundred miles from anywhere. It had a cheerful life of its own; people were sociable, titbits of gossip were shared, and, since it was the only place to meet, they were shared in Mrs Pike's shop.

There were several ladies there now, standing with their baskets over their arms, listening to that lady—a stout, cheerful body with a great deal of frizzy grey hair and small, shrewd eyes.

'Took bad, sudden, like!' she exclaimed. 'Well, we all knew he was going to retire, didn't we, and there'd be a new doctor? All arranged, wasn't it? I seen 'im when 'e came to look the place over. 'Andsome too.' She gave a chuckle. 'There'll be a lot of lady patients for 'im, wanting to take a look. Lovely motor car too.'

She beamed round her audience. 'Would never 'ave seen 'im myself if I 'adn't been coming back from Wells and stopped off to get me pills at Dr Fleming's. There 'e was, a great chap. I reckon 'e'll be taking over smartish, like, now Dr Fleming's took bad and gone to 'ospital.'

This interesting bit of news was mulled over while various purchases were made, but finally the last customer went, leaving Mrs Pike to stack tins of baked beans and rearrange packets of biscuits. She turned from this boring job as the door opened.

'Miss Leonora—walked, 'ave you? And it's real nasty underfoot. You could 'ave phoned and Jim could 'ave fetched whatever you wanted up to the house later.'

The girl pulled off her cap and allowed a tangle of curly hair to escape. 'Morning, Mrs Pike. I felt like a walk even though it's beastly weather. Mother wants one or two things—an excuse to get out…'

I'm not surprised, thought Mrs Pike; poor young lady stuck up there in that great gloomy house with her mum and dad, and that young man of hers hardly ever there. She ought to be out dancing.

She said out loud, 'Let me have your list, miss, and I'll put it together. Try one of them apples while you're waiting. Let's hope this weather gives over so's we can get out and about. That Mr Beamish of yours coming for the weekend, is 'e?'

'Well, I shouldn't think so unless the roads get better.' The girl twiddled the solitaire diamond on her finger and just for a moment looked unhappy. But only for a moment. 'I dare say we shall have a glorious spring...'

Mrs Pike, weighing cheese, glanced up. 'Getting wed then?' she wanted to know.

Leonora smiled. Mrs Pike was the village gossip but she wasn't malicious, and although she passed on any titbits she might have gleaned she never embellished them. She was a nice old thing and Leonora had known her for almost all of her life.

'We haven't decided, Mrs Pike.'

'I like a nice Easter wedding meself,' said Mrs Pike. 'Married on Easter Monday, we were—lovely day it was too.' She gave a chuckle. 'Poor as church mice we were too. Not that that matters.'

It would matter to Tony, reflected Leonora; he was something in the City, making money and intent on making still more. To Leonora, who had been brought up surrounded by valuable but shabby things in an old house rapidly falling into disrepair, and who was in the habit of counting every penny twice, this seemed both clever and rather daunting, for it seemed to take up so much of Tony's life. Even on his rare visits to her home he brought a briefcase with him and was constantly interrupted by his phone.

She had protested mildly from time to time and he had told her not to fuss, that he needed to keep in touch with the markets. 'I'll be a millionaire—a multimillionaire,' he told her. 'You should be grateful, darling—think of all the lovely clothes you'll be able to buy.'

Looking down at her tweed skirt and wellies, she supposed that her lack of pretty clothes sometimes irked him and she wondered what he saw in her to love enough to want to marry her. The family name, perhaps—they had no hereditary title but the name was old and respected—and there was still the house and the land around it. Her father would never part with either.

It was a thought which scared her but which she quickly dismissed as nonsense. Tony loved her, she wore his ring, they would marry and set up house together. It was a bit vague at present but she hoped they wouldn't have to live in London; he had a flat there which she had never seen but which he assured her he would give up when they married. And he had told her that when they were married he would put her home back on its original footing.

When she had protested that her father might not allow that, he had explained patiently that he would be one of the family and surely her father would permit him to see to it that the house and land were kept as their home should be. 'After all,' he had pointed out to her, 'it will eventually be the home of our son—your parents' grandson…'

She had never mentioned that to either her mother or her father. How like Tony, she thought lovingly—so generous and caring, ready to spend his money on restoring her home…

Mrs Pike's voice interrupted her thoughts. 'Pink salmon or the red, Miss Leonora?'

'Oh, the pink, Mrs Pike—fishcakes, you know.'

Mrs Pike nodded. 'Very tasty they are too.' Like the rest of the village she knew how hard up the Crosby family were. There never had been much money and Sir William had lost almost all of what had been left in some City financial disaster. A crying shame, but what a good thing that Miss Leonora's young man had plenty of money.

She put the groceries into a carrier bag and watched Leonora make her way down the icy street. She had pushed her hair back under her cap and really, from the back, she looked like a tramp. Only when you could see her face, thought Mrs Pike, did you know she wasn't anything of the sort.

Leonora went into the house through one of the side doors. There were several of these; the house, its oldest part very old indeed, had been added to in more prosperous times and, although from the front it presented a solid Georgian façade with imposing doors and large windows, round the back, where succeeding generations had added a room here, a passage there, a flight of unnecessary stairs, windows of all shapes and sizes, there were additional doors through which these various places could be reached.

The door Leonora entered led through to a gloomy, rather damp passage to the kitchen—a vast room housing a dresser of gigantic proportions, a scrubbed table capable of seating a dozen persons, an assortment of cupboards, and rows of shelves carrying pots and pans. There was a dog snoozing before the Aga stove but he got up, shook himself and came to meet her as she put her bag on the table.

She bent to fondle him, assuring him that no doubt the butcher's van would be round and there would be

a bone for him. 'And as soon as it's a bit warmer we'll
go for a real walk,' she promised him. He was an old
dog, a Labrador, and a quick walk in the small park at
the back of the house was all that he could manage in
bad weather.

The door on the other side of the kitchen opened and
a short, stout woman came in, followed by a tabby cat,
and Leonora turned to smile at her.

'It's beastly out, Nanny. I'll take Wilkins into the
garden for a quick run.' She glanced at the clock. 'I'll
see to lunch when I get back.'

Nanny nodded. She had a nice cosy face, pink-
cheeked and wrinkled, and grey hair in a tidy bun. 'I'll
finish upstairs. I've taken in the coffee—it's hot on the
Aga when you get in.'

Wilkins didn't much care for the weather but he trotted obediently down one of the paths to where a door
in the brick wall opened onto the park—quite a modest park with a small stream running along its boundary and clumps of trees here and there. They went as
far as the stream and then turned thankfully for home.

The house was a hotchpotch of uneven roofs and
unmatched windows at the back but it had a certain
charm, even in winter months. Of course many of its
rooms were shut up now, but Leonora conceded that if
you didn't look too closely at peeled paint and cracks
it was quite imposing. She loved it, every crack and
broken tile, every damp wall and creaking floorboard.

Back in the kitchen once more, Wilkins, paws wiped
and his elderly person towelled warm, subsided before
the Aga again, and Leonora hung her coat on a hook
near the door, exchanged her wellies for a pair of scuffed
slippers and set about getting lunch—soup, already sim-

mering on the stove, a cheese soufflé and cheese and biscuits.

Carrying a tray of china and silver to the dining room, she shivered as she went along the passage from the kitchen. It would be sensible to have their meals in the kitchen, but her mother and father wouldn't hear of it even though the dining room was as cold as the passage, if not colder.

'Mustn't lower our standards,' her father had said when she had suggested it. So presently they sat down to lunch at an elegantly laid table, supping soup which had already been cooling by the time it got to the dining room. As for the soufflé, Leonora ran from the oven to the table, remembering to slow down at the dining-room door, and set it gently on the table for her mother to serve, thankful that it hadn't sunk in its dish.

'Delicious,' pronounced Lady Crosby. 'You are such a good cook, darling.' She sighed faintly, remembering the days when there had been a cook in the kitchen and a manservant to wait at table. What a blessing it was that Leonora was so splendid at organising the household and keeping things running smoothly.

Lady Crosby, a charming and sweet-tempered woman who managed to avoid doing anything as long as there was someone else to do it, reflected comfortably that her daughter would make a good wife for Tony—such a good man, who had already hinted that once they were married he would see to it that there would be someone to take Leonora's place in the house. She was a lucky girl.

She glanced at her daughter and frowned; it was unfortunate, but Leonora was looking shabby.

'Haven't you got anything else to wear other than that skirt and sweater, dear?' she asked.

'Well, Mother, it's awful outside—no weather to dress up. Besides, I promised Nanny I'd help her with the kitchen cupboards this afternoon.'

Her father looked up. 'Why can't that woman who comes up from the village see to them?'

Leonora forbore from telling him that Mrs Pinch hadn't been coming for a month or more. Her wages had been a constant if small drain on the household purse, and when her husband had broken an arm at work she had decided to give up her charring and Leonora had seen the chance to save a pound or two by working a bit harder herself.

She said now, 'Well, Father, I like to go through the stores myself once in a while.' A remark which dispelled any faint doubts her parents might have had.

'Do wear gloves, dear,' observed her mother. 'Remember it's the Willoughbys' dinner party this evening—your hands, you know!'

The Willoughbys lived just outside the village in a small Georgian house in beautiful grounds, and since they had plenty of money it was beautifully maintained. They were elderly, good-natured and hospitable and Leonora enjoyed going there.

The cupboards dealt with, she got tea with Nanny and carried the tray through to the drawing room. Even on a cold winter's day it looked beautiful, with its tall windows, plaster ceiling and vast fireplace in which burned a log fire that was quite inadequate to warm the room. The furniture was beautiful too, polished lovingly, the shabby upholstery brushed and repaired.

Her mother was playing patience and her father was

sitting at a table by the window, writing. She set the tray down on a small table near her mother's chair and went to put more logs on the fire.

'I thought we might give a small dinner party quite soon,' observed Lady Crosby. 'We owe several, don't we? You might start planning a menu, darling.'

'How many?' asked Leonora, humouring her parent, wondering where the money was to come from. Dinner parties cost money. They could pawn the silver, she supposed with an inward chuckle; on the other hand she could make an enormous cottage pie and offer it to their guests...

'Oh, eight, I think, don't you? No, it would have to be seven or nine, wouldn't it? We can't have odd numbers.'

Lady Crosby sipped her tea. 'What shall you wear this evening?'

'Oh, the blue...'

'Very nice, dear, such a pretty colour; I have always liked that dress.'

So did I, reflected Leonora, when I first had it several years ago.

Getting into it later that evening, she decided that she hated it. Indeed, it was no longer the height of fashion, but it was well cut and fitted her splendid shape exactly where it should. She added the gold chain she had had for her twenty-first birthday, slipped Tony's ring on her finger and took a last dissatisfied look at her person, wrapped herself in a velvet coat she had worn to her twenty-first-birthday dance, and went downstairs to join her parents.

Sir William was impatiently stomping up and down the hall. 'Your mother has no idea of time,' he complained. 'Go and hurry her up, will you, Leonora? I'll get the car round.'

Lady Crosby was fluttering around her bedroom looking for things—her evening bag, the special hanky which went with it, her earrings...

Leonora found the bag and the hanky, assured her mother that she was wearing the earrings and urged her down to the hall and out into the cold dark evening, while Nanny went to open the car door.

The car, an elderly Daimler which Sir William had sworn that he would never part with despite the drain on his income, was at the entrance; Leonora bundled her mother into the front seat and got into the back, where she whiled away the brief journey thinking up suitable topics of conversation to get her through dinner. She would know everyone there, of course, but it was as well to be prepared....

The Willoughbys welcomed them warmly, for they had known each other for a long time. Leonora glanced round her as they went into the drawing room, seeing familiar faces, smiling and exchanging greetings; there was the vicar and his wife, old Colonel Howes and his daughter, the Merediths from the next village whose land adjoined her father's, Dr Fleming, looking ill, and his wife and, standing with them, the man in the car who had witnessed her undignified tumble.

'You haven't met our new doctor, have you, dear?' asked Mrs Willoughby, and saved Leonora the necessity of answering by adding, 'James Galbraith.' Mrs Willoughby smiled at him. 'This is Leonora Crosby— she lives at the Big House—you must come and meet her parents.'

Leonora offered a hand. Her 'How do you do?' was

uttered with just the right amount of pleasant interest, but it had chilly undertones.

His hand was large and cool and firm and she felt compelled to look at him. Very handsome, she conceded—rather sleepy blue eyes and very fair hair, a splendid nose and a rather thin mouth. He was tall too, which was nice, she reflected; so often she found herself looking down on people from her five feet ten inches. Now she had to look up, quite a long way too!

'Six foot four?' she wondered out loud.

The Flemings had turned away to speak to someone else. Dr Galbraith's mouth quivered faintly. 'Five, actually. Are you feeling sore?'

She said austerely, 'I hardly think that is a question I need to answer, Dr Galbraith.'

She had gone rather pink and glanced around her, on the point of making an excuse to go and talk to the vicar. She was stopped by his saying, 'I speak in my professional capacity, Miss Crosby; presumably you will be one of my patients.'

'I am never ill,' said Leonora, unknowingly tempting fate.

Mrs Willoughby had joined them again. 'Getting to know each other?' she wanted to know. 'That's nice—take Leonora in to dinner, will you, James?' She tapped his sleeve. 'You don't mind if I call you James? Though if ever I need your skill I'll be sure to call you Doctor.'

Leonora had been sipping her sherry; now she put the glass down. 'I really must circulate, and Nora Howes is dying to come and talk to you.'

He looked amused. 'Oh? How do you know that?'

'Woman's intuition.' She gave him a brief smile and

crossed the room and he watched her go, thinking that a splendid creature such as she deserved a better dress.

She had been right about Nora Howes, who laid a hand on his sleeve, threw her head back and gave him an arch look. Older than Leonora, he supposed, as thin as a washboard and wearing a rather too elaborate dress for a dinner party in the country. But he could be charming when he liked and Nora relinquished him reluctantly as they went in to dinner, and he turned with relief to Leonora as the soup was served. Not a girl he could get interested in, he reflected—far too matter-of-fact and outspoken—but at least she didn't simper.

It was a round table so conversation, after a time, became more or less general. He had Mrs Fleming on his other side, a quiet, middle-aged woman, a good deal younger than her husband and anxious about him.

'I didn't want him to come,' she confided quietly, 'but he insisted. 'He's not well; he's going into hospital tomorrow.'

He said gently, 'You mustn't worry too much, Mrs Fleming. If he leads a quiet life for the next few months and keeps to his treatment he'll get a great deal better.'

She smiled at him. 'If anyone else had said that I should have supposed them to be pulling the wool over my eyes, but because it's you I believe what you've told me.'

'Thank you. I wish all patients were as trusting. Don't hesitate to call me if you're worried.'

'I won't. It's so nice that you're going to live at Buntings—such a lovely old house and it's been empty far too long.'

She turned to speak to her neighbour and presently everyone went back to the drawing room to drink coffee and gossip. It might be a small village but there was always something happening.

The party broke up shortly before eleven o'clock and since it was cold outside no one lingered to talk once they'd left the house. Sir William unlocked his car door and glanced at the Rolls-Royce parked beside him.

Who's the lucky owner? he wondered, and saw Dr Fleming getting in.

'Good Lord, Bill, have you come into a fortune?' he called.

'No, no, James owns it. Rather nice, isn't it?' He disappeared inside and Sir William got behind his wheel and backed the car. 'Lucky young devil,' he said to no one in particular. 'Come up on the pools, has he?'

Leonora made some vague reply. She was thinking about Tony. She hadn't seen him for a week or so; perhaps he would come at the weekend. She hoped so; she felt strangely unsettled and just seeing him would reassure her—she wasn't sure why she wanted to be reassured, but that didn't matter; Tony would set her world to rights again.

He did come, driving up on Saturday afternoon in his Porsche, and if his kiss and hug were lacking the fervour of a man in love she didn't notice because she was glad to see him.

He went indoors with her to meet her parents and make himself agreeable and then they went for a walk. He took her arm and talked and she listened happily to his plans. They would marry—he was a bit vague as to exactly when—and he would set about restoring her father's house. 'There's a chap I know who knows exactly what needs to be done. It'll be a showplace by the time it's finished. We can have friends down for the weekend…'

Leonora raised a puzzled face. 'But Tony, we shan't be living here; Mother and Father wouldn't much like a great many people coming to stay—even for a weekend.'

He said rather too quickly, 'Oh, I'm thinking of special occasions—Christmas and birthdays and so on; it's usual for families to get together at such times.' He smiled at her. 'Tell me, what's been happening since I was last here?'

'Nothing much. The Willoughbys' dinner party, and—I almost forgot—the new doctor to take over from Dr Fleming—he had a heart attack—not a severe one but he's got to retire.'

'Someone decent, I hope. Local chap?'

'Well, no, I don't think so. I don't know where he comes from. He's bought Buntings—that nice old house at the other end of the village.'

'Has he, indeed? Must have cost him a pretty penny. Married?'

'I've no idea. Very likely, I should think. Most GPs are, aren't they?'

Tony began to talk about himself then—the wheeling and dealing he had done, the money he had made, the important men of the business world he had met. Leonora listened and thought how lucky she was to be going to marry such a clever man.

They went to church the following morning and she stood beside Tony in the family pew, guiltily aware that she was glad the new doctor was there too and could see her handsome fiancé.

Dr Galbraith was handsome too, and his height and

size added to that, but he was… She pondered for a moment. Perhaps it was the way he dressed, in elegant, beautifully tailored clothes, sober ties and, she had no doubt, handmade shoes—whereas Tony was very much the young man about town with his waistcoats and brightly coloured ties and striped shirts. She took a peep across the aisle and encountered the doctor's eyes, and blushed as though she had spoken her thoughts out loud and he had heard her.

She looked away hastily and listened to the Colonel reading the lesson, with a look of rapt attention, not hearing a word, and she took care not to look at the doctor again.

It was impossible to avoid him at the end of the service; he was standing in the church porch with the Flemings, talking to the vicar, and there was no help for it but to introduce Tony to him.

'The new GP,' observed Tony. 'I don't suppose there's much work for you around here. Wouldn't mind your job—peace and quiet in the country and all that. You fellows don't know when you're lucky. I'm in the City myself…'

The doctor said drily, 'Indeed? One of the unlucky ones? You must be glad to spend the weekend in this peaceful spot.'

Tony laughed. 'Not even a weekend—I must go back after lunch, try and catch up with the work, you know.'

'Ah, well, it's a pleasant run up to town. I dare say we shall meet again when next you're here.' The doctor smiled pleasantly and turned away to talk to the vicar's wife, who had joined them, and presently when he and the Flemings left the little group he did no more than nod affably at Leonora, who gave him a decidedly chilly smile.

'A bit of a stiff neck, isn't he?' asked Tony as they walked back to the house. He gave his rather loud laugh. 'I don't need to have qualms about the two of you!'

'If that's a joke,' said Leonora, 'I don't think it's funny. And why do you have to go back after lunch?'

'Darling—' he was at his most cajoling '—I simply must. There's no let-up, you know, not in my world— the business world. Keeping one step ahead is vital…'

'Vital for what?'

'Making money, of course. Don't bother your pretty head; just leave it to me.'

'Will it always be like this? I mean, after we're married? Will you be dashing off at all hours of the day, and do we need a lot of money? Don't you earn enough for us to get married soon?'

He gave her a quick kiss. 'What a little worrier you are. I am that old-fashioned thing—comfortably off. We could marry tomorrow and live pleasantly, but I don't want to be just comfortably off; I want to be rich, darling—a flat in town, decently furnished, money to go abroad when we want to, all the clothes you want to buy, dinner parties, the theatre. I want you to have the best of everything.'

'Tony, I don't mind about any of that. I'm not a town girl; at least, I don't think I am. I like living in the country and I don't care if we haven't much money. After all, I'm used to that.' She added thoughtfully, 'Perhaps you've fallen in love with the wrong girl…'

He flung an arm around her. 'Darling, what nonsense. The moment I set eyes on you when we met at the Willoughbys I knew you were what I was looking for.'

Which was quite true—she was a very pretty girl, had been ready to fall in love, and was an only child, with no large family to complicate matters. She lived in a lovely old house with plenty of land, which would be worth a fortune once he could get his hands on it.

He would have to go slowly, of course, and naturally he couldn't do anything to make Leonora unhappy. Her parents would be just as happy in a smaller house, somewhere close by, and he and Leonora could live in the big house. It would be a splendid focal point for meeting influential men and their wives—men who would give him a helping hand up the financial ladder.

Decently dressed, Leonora would prove an asset; she had lovely manners and a delightful voice. A bit outspoken at times and a good deal more intelligent than he had expected, but he was sure that he could persuade her to his way of thinking.

It was a couple of days later when Leonora met the doctor again. The icy weather had become quite mild and it rained from a dull sky. Sir William had caught cold and sat morosely by the fire, while his wife fussed around him and Nanny offered hot drinks and aspirin, which left Leonora looking after the household and doing the shopping, for, much as she loved her father, she could see that two females hovering over him was just about as much as he could stand. So she made the beds and hoovered and did most of the cooking and now they were running out of groceries.

In a mackintosh even older than the tweed coat, a hat, shapeless with age, rammed down onto her head, she picked up her basket, announced that she was going to the village and, accompanied by Wilkins, set out.

'At least we won't skid on ice,' she observed to

Wilkins, who was plodding along beside her. 'Though we are going to get very wet.'

Mrs Pike's shop was empty, which was a good thing for she allowed Wilkins to come in out of the rain, offering a sheet of newspaper which he was to sit on while Leonora took out her list.

A visit to Mrs Pike's was a leisurely affair unless she had a great many customers; she chatted while she collected bacon, cheese, the loaf the baker left each day, the marmalade Sir William preferred, tea and coffee, sugar and flour. Not that there was much to gossip about: Mrs Hick's new baby, the Kemp's youngest boy with a broken arm—'What do you expect from boys, anyway?' asked Mrs Pike—and Farmer Jenkins making a bit of trouble about his milk quota. 'Whatever that is, Miss Leonora; I'm sure I don't know what the world's coming to!'

This was one of Mrs Pike's frequent observations and the preliminary to a lengthy monologue of a gloomy nature, so it was a relief when two more customers came in together and Leonora was able to gather up her shopping and start for home.

It was still raining. Dr Galbraith, driving out of the village, saw Leonora's bedraggled figure ahead of him, marching along briskly, Wilkins beside her. He passed them and then pulled in to the side of the road, opened the door and said, 'Get in—I'm going past your place. Your dog can sit at the back.'

'Good morning, Doctor,' said Leonora pointedly. 'Please don't bother. We are both very wet; we shall spoil your car.'

He didn't answer but got out of the car and walked round to where she stood. 'Get in,' he said pleasantly, and opened the door for Wilkins, who was only too glad to get out of the rain.

'Oh, well, all right,' said Leonora ungraciously, and slid into the front of the car. 'I have warned you that we are both very wet.'

'Indeed you have, and now I'm wet as well.' He glanced at her. 'A waste of time, Leonora...'

'What's a waste of time?'

'Trying to get the better of me.' He was driving now and turned to smile at her. 'How are your mother and father?'

'They're very well—no, that's not quite true. Father's got a very bad cold; he's a shocking patient when he's not well and Mother gets worried.'

'In that case, perhaps it might be as well if I took a look at him. An antibiotic might get him back on his feet—colds can drag on at this time of year.'

'Yes, but aren't you on your rounds or something?'

'No.' He swept the car through the gates and up the neglected drive to the front door and got out to go round the bonnet and open her door and then free Wilkins.

'Do come in,' said Leonora, all at once minding her manners, 'and take off your coat. I'll fetch Mother.' She turned round as Nanny came down the staircase.

'Oh, good, here's Nanny. This is Dr Galbraith, our new doctor; he's kindly come to see Father.'

Nanny eyed the doctor. 'And that's a mercy. How do you do, Doctor? And a fine, well-set-up young man you are, to be sure. Give me the coat; I'll dry it out while Miss Leonora takes you to see the master.'

She turned her attention to Leonora then. 'And you too, Miss Leonora—off with that coat and that old hat and I'll give Wilkins a good rub down. There'll be coffee when you come down.'

Dismissed, the pair of them went upstairs to find her father sitting in a chair by a brisk fire with his wife bending over him. She looked up as they went in and gave a relieved sigh. 'Dr Galbraith, I was wondering if I should ask you to call. You met Leonora…'

'Yes, Lady Crosby, and it seemed sensible to take a look at Sir William, since I was passing.' He went to look at his patient and Leonora discovered that he was no longer a man who persisted in annoying her but an impersonal doctor with his head stuffed full of knowledge, and to be trusted. His quiet voice and his, 'Well, sir, may I take a look at you?' was reassuring.

CHAPTER TWO

Sir William coughed, blew his nose, coughed again and spoke.

'Nothing much wrong—just this infernal cold—cough keeps me awake, makes me tired.'

Leonora helped him off with his dressing gown and followed her mother to the door. She paused to ask, 'Do you need me to stay?'

She was surprised when the doctor said, 'Please,' in an absent-minded voice as he bent over his patient.

She stood by the window and glanced out at the rain-sodden landscape, listening to the doctor's quiet voice and her father's querulous answers. He wasn't well; perhaps they should have called the doctor sooner, she thought worriedly.

She loved her parents and got on well with them; indeed, she had been perfectly happy to stay home with them. Before her father had lost his money, there had been plans afoot to send her to friends in Italy, suggestions that she might train for a career, have a flat in town—the world had been her oyster.

She hadn't regretted the loss of any of these, although she sometimes longed for new clothes, a visit to the theatre, evenings out at some famous restaurant. The longings weren't deep enough to make her unhappy, and now that she and Tony were to marry it seemed to her that she would have the best of both worlds—living with Tony, sharing his social life, and coming home whenever she wanted to.

Dr Galbraith's voice disturbed her thoughts. 'If you would help your father with his dressing gown?'

He didn't look up as he wrote out a prescription. 'If you could get this made up? It's an antibiotic. And a couple of days in bed. Flu can hang around for a long time if it isn't treated promptly.'

He handed her the prescription and closed his bag. 'I'll call again in a day or so, but if you're bothered about anything don't hesitate to call me.'

'Hope I haven't given it to my wife,' observed Sir William.

'As I said, let me know if you are worried about anything.' He glanced at Leonora. 'Forewarned is forearmed.'

'Obliged to you for coming,' said Sir William. 'I'm sure there'll be coffee downstairs for you. Busy, are you?'

The doctor, who had been up all night with a premature baby, replied that no, he wasn't unduly so.

'Probably a good deal easier than a city practice,' said Sir William, blithely unaware that the doctor's practice extended for miles in every direction. Some of the outlying farms were well off the main roads, and the lanes leading to them were, as often as not, churned into muddy ruts.

Downstairs Lady Crosby was waiting for them in the drawing room, looking anxious.

'Fetch the coffee, Leonora; Nanny has it ready. Come and sit down, Doctor, and tell me if Sir William is ill or if it's just a bad cold.'

'Flu, Lady Crosby. He will need to keep to his bed for a few days and take the antibiotic I have prescribed. He should be perfectly all right within a week, provided he keeps warm and quiet; he isn't as young as he was.'

He smiled at her and she smiled back. 'Sixty-one— I'm a good deal younger.' Lady Crosby, who had been a very pretty girl, wasn't averse to a little admiration and her smile invited it.

She was disappointed and a little put out; she had been spoilt and pampered for most of her life, only during the last difficult years she had had to forgo the comforts and luxuries she had taken for granted. She loved her husband and daughter, but took their care and attention as her right. The expected compliment from the doctor wasn't forthcoming. All he said was, 'I'm going to Bath; perhaps your daughter might come with me and get the prescription I have written up for Sir William. I shall be returning within the hour and will give her a lift back.'

Leonora, coming in with the coffee, heard the last part of this and said, in her matter-of-fact way, 'Oh, there is no need for that. I can take the car—I might hold you up.'

'Nonsense, dear,' said her mother. 'Why take the car when you can get a lift? Dr Galbraith is coming back to the village. You'll probably have time to pop into that wool shop and see if you can match my embroidery silks...'

She poured the coffee. 'Have you taken a tray up to your father, dear? I dare say he would like a hot drink.' She smiled charmingly at the doctor. 'We shall take the greatest care of him, Doctor.'

He glanced from mother to daughter; Leonora had

inherited her mother's good looks on a more generous scale; he fancied she had inherited her father's forthright and strong-willed nature. It was no life for a girl such as she—living with elderly parents and, he suspected, bearing the burden of the household management in the down-at-heel, still beautiful house. Still, he remembered, she was engaged; presumably she would marry shortly. Not that he had liked the man.

Leonora, wrapped up against the weather, got into the car presently. He was glad to see that she had found a decent hat and her gloves and handbag were beyond reproach. Not that he cared in the least about her appearance, but with her striking looks she deserved the right clothes.

Glancing at her profile, he set himself out to be pleasant and had the satisfaction of seeing her relax. Gradually he led the conversation round to more personal matters, putting a quiet question here and there so casually that she answered freely, unaware that she was talking about things that she had kept tucked away at the back of her head because neither her mother nor her father would want to hear about them, and nor would Tony: small niggling doubts, little worries, plans she had little hope of putting into effect.

They were on the outskirts of Bath when she said abruptly, 'I'm sorry, I must be boring you. I expect you get enough moaning from your patients.'

'No, no, talking never bores me, unless it is the kind of chat you encounter at parties. I'm going to park at the Royal National Hospital. There are several chemists in Milsom Street; fetch the prescription and come back to the car. There's a quiet restaurant by the abbey—I hope you'll take pity on me and have lunch.' When she opened her mouth to refuse he said, 'No, don't say that you have to go home at once; you would be too late for lunch anyway, and I promise you I'll get you home within the next hour or so.' He smiled suddenly. 'I have an afternoon surgery…'

'Well, that would be nice; thank you. I don't like to be away from home for very long because of Father…'

He had stopped the car by the hospital and got out to open her door. 'I'll be fifteen minutes. If I'm longer than that, go and wait in the entrance hall…'

He watched her walk away. She was just as nice to look at from the back as from the front. He smiled a little as he went into the hospital.

When she got back he was there, waiting for her. 'We'll leave the car here; it's only a few minutes' walk. You know Bath well?'

The restaurant was small, quiet, and the food was excellent. Leonora, savouring a perfectly grilled sole, thought she must remember to tell Tony about it; it was a long time since they had been out together for a meal— he was happy to stay at home with her, he always told her, and she spent hours in the kitchen conjuring up a meal he would like from as little of the housekeeping money as possible.

She wished that he were sitting opposite her now instead of Dr Galbraith and despised herself for the mean thought. After all, he had no reason to give her lunch and she had to admit he was a pleasant companion. All the same, she had the sneaking feeling that behind that bland face there was a man she wouldn't care to cross swords with.

They talked as they ate, exchanging views on Bath,

Pont Magna and its inhabitants, and the various houses in it.

'I used to go to Buntings when I was a little girl,' Leonora told him. 'It's a lovely old house. Are you happy there?'

'Yes. It is the kind of place where you feel instantly at home. I expect you feel that about your own home?'

'Oh, yes. It's badly in need of repairs, though. Some rich American wanted to buy it last year, but Father wouldn't hear of it. His family have lived in it for a very long time. It would break his heart to leave.'

'I can understand that. It is a delightful house. Rather large to look after, though.'

'Yes, but quite a few rooms are shut and Nanny and I can manage the rest.'

She frowned and he said smoothly, 'Nannies are marvellous, aren't they? Shall we go? I must get you back before someone wonders where you are.'

Less than an hour later he stopped the car at her home, got out to open her door and waited until she had gone inside. He had beautiful manners, she thought, and hoped that she had thanked him with sufficient warmth.

Her mother was in the drawing room. 'There you are, dear. Have you got those pills for your father? He's rather peevish so I came down here to have a little rest—I find looking after someone ill so very tiring. We'll have tea soon, shall we? Perhaps Nanny could make a few scones.'

Leonora said, 'Yes, Mother,' and went to look for Nanny.

In the kitchen Nanny asked, 'Have you had some lunch, Miss Leonora? There's plenty of that corned beef—'

'Dr Galbraith gave me lunch, Nanny—a rather splendid one too. Mother wants tea a bit earlier—and scones? I'll come and make them, but first I must go and see about Father.'

Sir William, back in his bed, was glad to see her.

'I've got your pills and you can start them straight away,' she told him cheerfully. 'And how about a cup of tea and some of that thin bread and butter Nanny cuts so beautifully?'

She sat down on the side of the bed. 'I don't suppose you feel like sausages for supper. How about scrambled eggs and creamed potato and jelly for pudding?'

'That sounds good.' Her father smiled at her. 'We shall be lost without you when you marry, my dear.' He paused to cough. 'You are quite sure, aren't you? Tony is a successful young man—he'll want to live in London.'

She shook her head. 'Not all the time—he was talking about coming down here whenever we could. He loves this house, you know.'

Her father said drily, 'It is a gold-mine for anyone with enough money to put it in order. As it is, it's mouldering away. At least it will be yours one day, Leonora.'

'Not for years, Father.' She got up and fetched a glass of water and watched him while he swallowed his pill. 'Every four hours,' she warned him. 'Now I'm going to get your tea.'

She dropped a kiss on his head and went down to the kitchen, where, since Nanny was making the scones, she got her father's tea-tray ready and presently bore it upstairs.

Back in the drawing room with her mother, she drew a chair closer to the fire. 'I must say that Dr Galbraith seems to be a very pleasant man. Charming manners, too. We must invite him to dinner one evening, Leonora—remind me to make a list of guests. We must think of something delicious to give them.'

Leonora said, 'Yes, Mother,' and bit into a scone. 'I dare say Father will enjoy that once he's feeling better.'

Her mother said vaguely, 'Oh, yes, of course, dear. What did you have for lunch? So kind of the doctor to give you a meal.'

When Leonora had told her she added, 'Ah, yes, I know the restaurant you mention. The food there is good but expensive. I dare say that, being a single man, he can afford such places. I'm surprised that he isn't married, but I expect he is merely waiting until he is settled in at Buntings. A doctor, especially one with a country practice, needs a wife.'

Leonora murmured an agreement, and wondered why he should need one more than a GP with a town practice.

'He would have done very well for you,' went on Lady Crosby, 'but of course you've already got a fiancé in Tony. Most suitable and such a charming man.'

Leonora thought about Tony. He was charming and fun to be with. He teased her a good deal, told her that she was old-fashioned and strait-laced. 'I'll forgive you that,' he had told her, laughing. 'You'll change once I get you up to town.'

She had pointed out that she didn't want to change. 'I wouldn't be me,' she'd told him, aware that she had irritated him. The next moment, however, he had been laughing again; perhaps she had mistaken the look on his face. They would be happy together, she felt sure; she looked at the diamond on her finger and told herself how happy she was at that very moment just thinking about him.

That night she dreamt of Dr Galbraith, and the dream persisted in staying in her head all next day. She did her best to dispel it by writing a long letter to Tony.

Her father was feeling a little better, although he was still coughing a good deal and looked tired. She wondered uneasily what would be done if the antibiotic didn't do its good work; Dr Galbraith hadn't said that he would call again...

He came the next morning and, since she was upstairs with the Hoover, it was her mother who opened the door to him.

'Dr Galbraith—how kind of you to call again. Just in time for coffee. I'll get Leonora or Nanny to bring it to the drawing room.' She smiled her charming smile. 'I do hate having it by myself...'

Any opinion the doctor might have had about this remark he kept to himself.

'I called to see Sir William and, much though I would enjoy a cup of coffee, I can't spare the time—I have quite a few visits to make this morning.' He smiled in his turn. 'If I might go up?'

'Oh, dear, we could have had a nice little chat. Do you want me to come up with you? Leonora is hoovering the bedrooms; I'm sure she'll see to anything you may want.'

The Hoover was making a good deal of noise; he had time to study Leonora's back view before she turned round. She was wearing a sensible pinny and had tied her hair in a bright scarf; the Hoover, being past its prime, tended to raise almost as much dust as it sucked up.

She switched it off when she saw him, wished him a good morning and said, 'You want to see Father? He had quite a good night but he's chesty…'

She whipped off the pinny and also the scarf and led him into her father's room.

The doctor pronounced himself satisfied with his patient but added that he would need to remain in bed for several days yet. 'Get up for an hour or so, if you wish,' he said, 'but stay in this room. I'll come and see you again in a couple of days or so.'

Going downstairs with Leonora, he observed, 'Your father is by no means out of the woods. He has escaped pneumonia by a whisker and anything other than rest and a warm room, plenty to drink and plenty of sleep is liable to trigger off a more serious condition. He'll do well if he stays where he is—don't let him get out of bed for much more than an hour or so.'

He sounded just like the family doctor, thought Leonora waspishly, but then that was exactly what he was. Did he need to be quite so impersonal, though? After all, they had had lunch together…

Her mother came into the hall as they reached it and he bade her a pleasant goodbye, added a few reassuring words about Sir William's condition, smiled briefly at Leonora and drove away, leaving her feeling vaguely unsettled.

Tony came at the weekend, breezing into the house, explaining that he had torn himself away from his work to take them by surprise.

'You look as though you need a bit of cheering up,' he told Leonora, who certainly didn't look her best after four days of coping with her irascible parent. 'How is Sir William? Not too bad, I hope?'

'He is better, but he has a bad chest; he's getting up today for a few hours but he mustn't go outside until his cough has cleared up.'

'Where is that delightful mother of yours?'

'She went to Colonel Howes's for coffee.' Leonora hesitated. 'Tony, would you mind awfully if I left you for a bit? I'll get some coffee for you and there are the morning papers in the drawing room. I haven't quite finished the bedrooms and I must make a bed for you. You are staying?'

'Well, of course, if it's too much bother...' He contrived to look hurt and she said quickly, 'No, no, of course it's not, and I shan't be long.'

'I'll go and have a chat with your father,' suggested Tony, getting out of the chair into which he had flung himself.

'No— Oh, dear, I keep saying no, don't I? He is shaving and getting dressed. We'll both be down presently. I'll just fetch the coffee. Did you have a good trip here?'

He said sulkily, 'Not bad. It's the deuce of a long way from town, though.'

I ought to be so pleased to see him, reflected Leonora, putting china on a tray and listening to Nanny's opinion of those who came for the weekend uninvited, but he might have phoned first. 'I'll have to go to the butcher's and get some chops.' She interrupted Nanny's indignant flow. 'Have we plenty of eggs?' she asked.

'No. We have not. Mr Beamish will have bacon for his breakfast and one or two of those mushrooms Mrs Fleming sent over. The cake's almost finished too.'

'Oh, I'll make another one, Nanny—there'll be time before lunch...'

'There's the doorbell,' said Nanny in a voice which

suggested that she was much too busy to answer it. So
Leonora opened the door, to find Dr Galbraith towering over her. She stared up into his calm face and felt a
ridiculous urge to burst into tears. She didn't say anything and presently he said placidly, 'I've come to see
your father.'

'Yes, but—yes, of course. Do come in…'

'You were doing something urgent. If I'm interrupting do go and finish.' He looked her over slowly. 'You
look put upon. What's the matter?'

As Tony came into the hall, the doctor said, 'Ah,
yes, of course,' in a very quiet voice, and added a much
louder, 'Good morning.'

'Ah, the local GP. Good morning to you. Come to
check on the invalid, have you?'

'Yes.' Dr Galbraith turned towards Leonora. 'Shall
we go up?'

'I'll come along too—the old chap's always glad to
see me.'

The doctor was saved the necessity of answering as
Nanny came into the hall with the coffee-tray.

'I'm putting your coffee in the drawing room, Mr
Beamish; you'll need to drink it while it's hot.'

Tony, although he didn't like her, did as he was told,
mentally promising himself that once he was married
to Leonora one of the first of his acts would be to get
rid of Nanny.

Going up the staircase, the doctor noted that Leonora looked less than her best; her hair was tied back
and hung in something of a tangle down her back, and
she was without make-up, not that that mattered for
she had clear skin and a mouth which didn't need lipstick; moreover, she was wearing an elderly skirt and a

sweater with the sleeves rolled up. But none of this really detracted from her undoubted good looks.

'Is Lady Crosby at home?' he asked casually.

'No, I'm sorry, but she's having coffee with the Howeses—you've met the Colonel and his daughter...'

He had dined with them on the previous evening but he didn't say so.

'Don't you care for visiting?' he wanted to know.

'Me? Oh, yes, it's nice meeting people. But today—well, the weekend, you know, and then I didn't know Tony was coming so there's a bit more to do.'

They had reached her father's door and the doctor didn't answer.

Her father was sitting in his dressing gown, looking out of the window. He turned as they went in, saying, 'Leonora? Is that my coffee? It's past ten o'clock.'

He saw the doctor then. 'Good morning. You see how much better I am. I shall get dressed presently and go downstairs for lunch.'

'Why not?' The doctor sat down beside him. 'Such a delightful view from this window even at this time of the year. How is the cough?'

'Better—much better—and I've taken those pills you left for me. Leonora sees to that, don't you, my dear?'

Leonora said, 'Yes, Father,' and admired the back of the doctor's head.

'A splendid nurse,' her father went on. 'We are indeed lucky to have a daughter who takes such good care of us both.'

'You will miss her when she marries,' observed the doctor, taking his patient's pulse.

'Yes, yes, of course, although Tony has a great liking for this house; I'm sure they will visit us as often as possible.'

The doctor didn't hurry but tapped Sir William's chest, listened to his heart, asked a number of leisurely questions and finally pronounced himself satisfied. 'Stay indoors for another day or so,' he advised, 'and when you do go out wrap up warm.'

Tony came out of the drawing room as they reached the hall.

'Well, what's the verdict? I'm not surprised that Sir William has been ill—this house may look a thing of beauty but it's riddled with damp. Needs money spent on it. More sense if he found something smaller and modern.'

Leonora gave him a surprised look. 'Tony, you know as well as I do that Father and Mother will never move. Why should we? We're happy here—it's our home.'

He took her arm. 'Darling, of course it is. Come and have some coffee.' He nodded at Dr Galbraith. 'Nice to meet you,' he observed.

Leonora frowned. Tony was being rude. 'Thank you for coming, Doctor. I'll keep an eye on Father. You won't need to come again?'

'I think not, but do give me a ring if that cough doesn't clear up within the next week or ten days.' He shook hands, ignored Tony and went out to his car, got in and drove away.

'You were rude,' said Leonora, leading the way to the drawing room.

'Sorry, darling. I can't stand the fellow, looking down that long nose of his. Thinks he knows everything— I've met his sort before.'

'He's a good doctor,' said Leonora, 'and everyone likes him—except you.'

'Let's not argue about him. I've come to spend the weekend with you, so let's enjoy ourselves. Heaven knows, it's hard enough to get away.'

Tony had sat down again. 'How about getting into something pretty and we'll go out to lunch?'

'Tony, I'd love to, but I can't. When you got here I was making beds—and when I've done that I must get lunch and see about making a cake and getting something made for this evening. Father has to have his coffee and his lunch, and Mother will be back presently. They like their tea at half past four and dinner has to be cooked…'

'For heaven's sake, Leonora…can't Nanny deal with all that?'

'No, she can't. The kitchen has to be cleaned, food has to be prepared, she has to answer the door and Father's bell if I'm busy and one of us will have to go to the village and do some extra shopping.'

'Well, I thought I would be welcome,' said Tony sulkily, 'but it seems I'd better leave as quickly as possible!'

'Don't be silly,' said Leonora briskly. 'You know how glad I am to see you, but what's the use of pretending that I can sit here, nicely dressed and made up, when it's simply not possible? We could go for a walk in the afternoon.'

She saw his irritable frown. 'I'm sorry, Tony…'

'Let's hope that next time I manage to get here you'll be looking more like my fiancée and not the home help.' He laughed as he spoke and she laughed with him, hiding her hurt. He was delightful and charming, she told herself, and she loved him, and she reminded herself that he worked very hard and had little time to enjoy his leisure.

All the same the beds had still to be made. It was fortunate that her mother returned, delighted at the sight of Tony, grumbling prettily at the awful coffee she had had to drink at Colonel Howes's. 'Darling,' she begged Leonora, 'do make me a cup—you make such good coffee.'

She settled down in her chair and turned to Tony. 'Now, tell me all the latest gossip…'

Her father wasn't best pleased to learn that Tony had come for the weekend. He loved his daughter dearly, was aware that she was missing the kind of life a girl of her age should be enjoying but was not sure what to do about it. When Tony had swept her off her feet and he had seen the happiness in her face, he had been glad for her sake, although he had had to bury the vague dislike he had for him. If Leonora loved him and he would make her happy, then that was more important than his own feelings. Tony, after all, was a successful young man, able to give Leonora the comforts and small luxuries which he, her father, had been unable to afford.

He expressed a pleasure he didn't feel and told her he would be down to lunch and she whisked herself away to finish the beds and tidy first the rooms and then herself. There wasn't time to change into something more eye-catching than the sweater and skirt but at least she could do something to her face and hair.

Going downstairs a little later, she could hear her mother and Tony laughing and talking in the drawing room, which gave her the chance to go to the kitchen and see what Nanny had found for lunch.

Cheese omelettes, they decided, and there was a tin

of mushroom and garlic soup which they could eke out with some chicken stock. Melba toast and a salad.

'We'll worry about dinner presently,' promised Leonora. 'I'll do the table in a minute and after lunch I'll go down to the village. It had better be a joint, I suppose—five of us—roast this evening, cold tomorrow.'

That would make a hole in the housekeeping, she reflected, going to sit in the drawing room and listen to Tony being amusing about his life in London.

A good-looking man, she reflected lovingly, and such fun to be with. She hoped that once they were married she would make him happy—live his kind of life, like his friends, enjoy the dinner parties and theatres and social occasions which he had assured her were so very important to his work.

Presently she slipped away to see to lunch and give Nanny a hand, half hoping that he would go with her. But he merely smiled and waved a hand.

'Don't be too long, darling; I miss you.'

Perhaps it was as well that he had stayed talking to her mother and father, she decided, beating eggs, making a salad, laying the table...

After lunch she told him that she was going to the village. He frowned for a moment then smiled. 'A chance for us to talk,' he told her. 'Not paying visits, I hope.'

'No, no, just some shopping. It'll give you an appetite for tea.'

They met the vicar in the village street and she left them talking while she bought the meat. They were still talking when she joined them again.

Tony put an arm around her shoulders. 'Do we know when we want to get married, darling?' he asked. 'It all depends, actually, but it won't be long now. A June wedding, perhaps. That is, if the bride agrees to that.'

The vicar looked pleased. 'We haven't had a wedding for some time,' he observed, 'and June is a delightful month in which to be married.'

'A nice old man,' said Tony as they started back home. 'Very keen to see us married, isn't he?'

'Did you mean that—June—you said…?'

He took her free hand in his. 'Why not, darling? It will be a bit of a rush—but I suppose we could get the place tidied up by then.'

'What place?'

He stopped and turned to look at her. 'Leonora, surely you can see for yourself that that great house is too much for your father and mother? Suppose we move them out to something smaller? There's a nice little property a couple of miles away on the road to Bath. I'll have the house completely refurbished and it'll be a marvellous headquarters for me—us. Weekends for clients and friends. We'll have a flat in town, of course, but it's an easy run. I might even give you a car of your own so that you can go to and fro whenever you want.'

Leonora stared at him. 'You don't mean any of that, do you? I mean, turning Mother and Father out of their home? It's been in the family for almost two hundred years; Father would die; it's—it's his blood. Mother has all her friends here and she loves the house too—she came here when she married Father. It's a joke, isn't it?'

He put his arm round her shoulders. 'Darling, it's not a joke, it's common sense—can't you see that? Your father isn't exactly in the best of health, is he? Supposing he were to die—what would your mother do? Try and run this place on her own? She hasn't the faintest idea how to do it...'

'You forget me.' Leonora had twisted away from him. 'It's my home too and I won't leave it. And Father's almost well again—you heard what Dr Galbraith said—'

'A country GP?' Tony sounded derisive. 'He'll say whatever he thinks his patients want to hear.'

'That isn't true. What an abominable thing to say.' She began to walk on and he caught up with her and took her arm.

'Darling, I'm sorry if I've made you cross. All right, I won't say another word about your parents leaving home, but you must know that your father is in financial difficulties, and what will happen if they foreclose the mortgage?'

That brought her up short. 'Mortgage? I didn't know...'

'How do you suppose he's been able to stay here for so long?'

'How did you know?'

'I make it my business to know these things. Besides, I am concerned for you, Leonora.'

'Oh.' She felt guilty then for suspecting him. Suspecting him of what? she wondered. 'I'm sorry, Tony. Don't let's talk about it any more. Father will get things sorted out once he is feeling quite well. Do please believe me when I say that nothing on earth will make Father or Mother move from the house, and that goes for me too!'

He caught her arm again. 'Darling, you're going to marry me, remember?' He laughed a gentle laugh which made her smile and then laugh with him.

They went on their way and just as they reached the

open gates to the house Dr Galbraith drove past. He raised a hand in salute, wondering why the sight of Leonora apparently so happy in Tony's company should disturb him.

Probably because I don't like the fellow, he decided, and forgot about them.

The weekend went too quickly for Leonora. Of course, having Tony there made a lot of extra work; he had admitted soon after they'd met that he was quite useless around the house and since there was no need for him to do anything for himself at his flat—a service flat where he could get his meals and a cleaner came each day—he made no effort to help. Not that Leonora expected him to make his bed or wash up, but it would have been nice if he hadn't given Nanny his shoes to clean and expected his trousers pressed—or even if he'd carried a tray out to the kitchen...

It would be better when they were married, reflected Leonora; she was sure that he would be only too willing to help out when necessary once he realised that help was needed.

He went back very early on Monday morning, which meant that Leonora got up and cooked his breakfast first. It also meant that he used up almost all the hot water from the boiler and woke everyone up.

'I'll be down again just as soon as I can spare the time,' he told Leonora. 'And when I come do be ready for me, darling, and we'll have an evening out. Bath, perhaps? A decent meal and we could dance after.'

She agreed happily, ignoring the bit about the decent meal. Sunday lunch had been excellent, she had thought—roast beef, Yorkshire pudding, baked potatoes, vegetables from the garden and an apple tart for pudding. That was surely a decent meal? She kissed him goodbye and begged him to phone when he had time. 'Or write.'

'Write? My dear girl, when do I ever have time to write letters?' He squeezed her arm and gave her a charming smile. 'Be good.'

She gravely said, 'Yes, Tony,' and he laughed as he got into the car.

'Not much chance of being anything else, is there?' he shouted at her as he started the engine.

He would have to go carefully, he decided as he drove; no more mention of moving her mother and father out of the house. Perhaps it might be a good idea to wait until they were married. He had no doubt at all that he could persuade her to do anything he asked of her once she was his wife.

A few weeks of comfortable living, new clothes, new faces, meals out—once she had a taste of all the things a girl wanted in the way of a carefree life she would come round to his way of thinking. The more he saw of the house, the more he intended to have it…

Leonora, happily unaware of his schemes, went indoors, placated her parents with very early morning tea, soothed a grumpy Nanny and went up to the attics to see if the rain had come in during the night. It had.

CHAPTER THREE

At about the same time as Tony was getting into his car to drive back to London, Dr Galbraith was letting himself into his house. He had been called out in the very early hours to a farm some miles away from the village, where the farmer's elderly father had suffered a stroke and he'd waited with him until the ambulance had come to take him to Bath. He had followed it to the hospital, made sure that his patient was in good hands and then driven himself back home.

There was no question of going back to bed; he had morning surgery and a scattered round before mothers and babies' clinic in the early afternoon. He went quietly across the square hall and up the uncarpeted oak staircase to his room at the front of the old house. He had his hand on the door when another door at the far end of the passage opened and a tall, bony man emerged.

He was middle-aged, with a long, narrow face, dark hair streaked with grey, combed carefully over a bald patch, and an expression of gloom.

'Good morning, sir. You'll need a cup of coffee. I'll bring it up at once. Breakfast in an hour suit you?'

'Admirably, Cricket. I'm famished.'

Cricket went back to his room, shaking his head in a disapproving manner. He never failed to disapprove when the doctor was called out at night, but that didn't prevent him from making sure that there was a hot drink and a meal waiting for him. He had been with the doctor for a number of years now, running his house to perfection, cooking delicious meals, making sure that the cleaning lady did her work properly. In fact, he was a treasure.

The doctor drank his coffee, showered, dressed and went downstairs to his breakfast. It was light now, a chilly, breezy March morning, and he opened the door to the garden before going into the small sitting room at the back of the house, where Cricket had laid his breakfast.

It was a charming room, facing the rising sun, furnished comfortably with some nice old pieces and decidedly cosy, unlike the drawing room which was rather grand with its magnificent carpet, vast bow-fronted cabinets and the pair of sofas, one at each side of the marble fireplace. The drawing room also had comfortable chairs arranged here and there and a beautiful drum table in the bay window overlooking the front garden. It was a room the doctor used seldom, for dinner parties and on the occasions when his friends came to stay.

There was a dining room too, on the opposite side of the hall, with its Regency mahogany table and chairs and the splendid sideboard, and at the back of the hall his study, the room he used most of all.

It was a large house for an unmarried man but he was a big man and needed space around him. Besides, he loved the old place, having first seen it some years earlier when he had come to visit Dr Fleming, whom he had known for some time. It had seemed an act of

Providence when he had agreed to take over Dr Fleming's practice and Buntings had been on the market.

He had his surgery in the village—a cottage which had been converted into a consulting room and a waiting room—although he saw patients at his home if necessary.

This morning there were more patients than usual: neglected colds which had settled on chests, elderly people with arthritis and rheumatism, a broken arm, a sprained ankle, septic fingers. Nothing dramatic, but they kept him busy for most of the morning; he was late starting his round.

He was barely a mile out of the village when his car phone rang. Mrs Crisp, his part-time receptionist and secretary, sounded urgent.

'There's a call from Willer's Farm. Mrs Willer—she's on her own except for a farm lad. The tractor driver has had an accident—a bad one, she says. Mr Willer's away—gone to a cattle market. She phoned Beckett's Farm but couldn't get an answer. There's no one else nearby.'

'Tell her I'm on my way. I should be there in twenty minutes.'

He put his large foot down and sent the car speeding along the road and then braked hard to avoid Leonora with Wilkins, coming round the curve in the middle of the road.

She nipped to one side, dragging Wilkins with her, and shouted sorry and would have gone on. He had come to a halt, though, and had the car door open, so that she felt compelled to repeat her apologies.

'Never mind that,' said the doctor impatiently. 'You're just what I need. You know Willer's Farm.

There's been an accident there. I'm on my way and it seems there's no one there except Mrs Willer and a lad. I shall need help. Jump in, will you? I could use another pair of hands.'

'Wilkins?'

'In the car.' He leaned over and opened the door and Wilkins got in without being asked; a lazy dog by nature, he thought the chance of a ride wasn't to be missed.

Leonora got in beside the doctor, remarking calmly, 'I don't know anything about first aid, or at least not much, but I'm strong. I was going to the shop for Nanny; would you mind if I phoned her? She's waiting for some braising steak.'

The doctor handed her the phone without speaking and listened to her quiet voice telling Nanny that she might be home rather later than expected and perhaps someone else could go to the village. 'I've got Wilkins with me and we'll be back when you see us.'

She replaced the phone and sat quietly as he drove through the narrow, high-hedged lanes, wondering what they would find when they got to the farm.

Mrs Willer came running out to meet them as the doctor slowed the car across the farmyard, which was rutted and muddy and redolent of farmyard smells.

'He's on Lower Pike. The boy's with him; I came down to show you the way. He's real bad. It's 'is foot— got it caught in the tractor as 'e fell out.'

The doctor was bending over the car's boot, handing things to Leonora. He said merely, 'We'll take a look. How long has he been lying there? Is he conscious?'

'Now 'e is, Doctor... Not at first, 'e wasn't. Banged 'is 'ead.'

They were crossing the yard now, making for the

open fields beyond, which sloped gently uphill to Higher Pike, and going at a good pace. Leonora, a splendid walker, found herself making an effort to keep up with the doctor's strides.

The next twenty minutes were like a very unpleasant dream. The tractor had reared up and toppled backwards and although Ben, the driver, had been flung free his foot had been trapped by the superstructure.

The doctor got down beside him and opened his bag. 'Pain bad?' he asked, and when Ben nodded he filled a syringe and plunged its contents into the arm he had bared. Presently, as the dope took effect, he examined his patient and then bent over his foot, trapped by a heavy iron crossbar.

'Open that bag,' He nodded towards the zippered bag he had been carrying. 'Hand me the things from it as I ask for them.' He looked over his shoulder. 'And you, boy, fetch me a spade, two spades, anything to dig with.'

He busied himself cleaning and covering the crushed foot, and Leonora, very much on her mettle, handed things from the bag when he asked for them. Most of them she had never seen before—forceps and probes and some nasty-looking scissors. Most of the time she managed not to look too closely…

All the while he worked, the doctor talked to Ben—a soothing flow of words uttered in a quiet, reassuring voice. 'We're going to dig the earth from under your foot to relieve the pressure on it,' he explained. 'I'm going to phone for an ambulance and help now; you'll soon be comfortable.'

Leonora listened to him talking into his phone; it seemed hours since they had arrived but when she glanced at her watch she saw that it was barely fifteen minutes.

The boy came back then with the spades. Dr Galbraith took one, handed him the other and told him what they were going to do, then he said to Leonora, 'Come here and kneel by Ben's foot. Don't touch it yet, but be ready to steady it.'

She knelt gingerly. The tractor loomed huge above her and she tried not to think what would happen should it shift. The foot was swathed in a protective covering, bloodstained but not frighteningly so. She crept nearer and held her hands ready.

They dug cautiously, inch by inch, so that presently there was a bit of space between Ben's foot and the crossbar. It would need far more room than that to free the foot, she thought; the tractor would have to be righted.

The digging stopped then and the doctor took her place, his arm sheltering the foot as far as possible. If the tractor moves…thought Leonora, and didn't dare think further.

'Take Mrs Willer to the house and help her pack a bag for Ben,' said the doctor. 'Everything he'll need at the hospital. And then come back here.'

She led a shocked Mrs Willer back to the house, found a bag and together they packed it. They had done that when they heard the high-pitched wail of the ambulance and the louder, deeper note of the fire engine, and by the time they had got back to the tractor there were men everywhere.

It took time to right the tractor and more time to inspect Ben's foot thoroughly. Finally he was on a stretcher, being carried to the ambulance.

In answer to his, 'Come along, Leonora,' she followed the doctor to the car and got in. Wilkins, snoozing on the back seat, opened an eye in greeting and went back to sleep and she sat watching the doctor as he spoke to Mrs Willer.

Getting in beside her, he said, 'You have been a great help; thank you, Leonora. Ben is going to the Royal National at Bath; I must go there and speak to the casualty officer.' He picked up the phone. 'I'll explain to Nanny...' Which he did before handing the phone to her.

Nanny sounded anxious. 'Miss Leonora, are you all right? Am I to tell your ma and pa?'

'I'm fine, Nanny, really I am. I shan't be home for a little while. If you tell them that without any details...'

'Anyway, you're safe enough with Dr Galbraith and you've got the phone.'

At the hospital she got out with Wilkins and walked round with him while the doctor went inside. She was hungry and untidy and her skirt was covered with dried earth from the ploughed field but she felt happy; she had made herself useful even in a humble capacity and Dr Galbraith's brisk thanks had warmed her. Presently she saw him leave the hospital and went back to the car, into which Wilkins scrambled with evident relief. He had walked enough.

'Ben—that foot?' said Leonora, getting into the car. 'Will he be all right?'

'He's in Theatre now. If anyone can save it, it's the man who's operating.'

'Oh, good.' She added fiercely, 'He needs his feet—it's his livelihood...'

When he didn't answer, she said, 'What about your

other patients? You had just started your round, hadn't you?'

'Mrs Crisp has sorted them out for me; there's nothing really urgent. I've a surgery this evening and I can do a round this afternoon. We'll go back now and clean up and have a meal.'

He picked up the phone again. 'Cricket? I'm bringing Miss Crosby back with me for lunch. We'll need to clean up first—say half an hour? Something quick.'

'Who's Cricket?' asked Leonora. 'And you don't have to ask me to lunch. Drop me off at the gate as you go past.'

'Cricket is my manservant; he runs my home. I should be totally lost without him. And will you lunch with me, Leonora? It is the least I can do to make amends for spoiling your quiet day.' He glanced at her. 'Besides, you're badly in need of a wash and brush-up.'

It was hardly a flattering reason for being asked to lunch. She had half a mind to refuse but curiosity to see his house and find out something about him got the better of her resentment, and then common sense came to the rescue and she laughed. He was offering practical help and she was hungry and, as he had pointed out, badly in need of a good wash.

'Thank you; that would be nice,' she told him sedately.

It was as he drew up before his door that Leonora spoke again.

'What about Wilkins? Do you have a dog?'

He came round the car to open her door. 'He's welcome to come in. I have a dog. My sister has borrowed him for a week or two while her husband is away. He'll be back next week. Cricket has two cats. I hardly think they will be in any danger from Wilkins; a remarkably mild animal, isn't he?'

'He's a darling,' said Leonora warmly, 'and he's partial to cats.'

Cricket opened the door, shook the hand she offered and instantly approved of her. Even with a smudge on her cheek and dirty hands she was a very pretty girl. Plenty of her, too; he liked a woman to look like a woman and here was one who, he decided, lived up to his strict ideals of what a young lady should be.

He ushered her indoors, tut-tutted gently at the state of her skirt and led her to the downstairs cloakroom. Halfway across the hall the doctor called after them.

'Get Miss Crosby a dressing gown, Cricket, and see if you can get some of that mud off her skirt, will you?'

'Certainly, sir. Is ten minutes too soon for lunch?'

'Just right. If I'm not down show Miss Crosby into the sitting room, will you? Thanks!'

Then he went up upstairs two at a time and Cricket ushered Leonora into the cloakroom, begged a moment's grace and came back within a minute with a bathrobe. 'If you would let me have your skirt, Miss Crosby, I'll have it as good as new before you leave.' He smiled at her. 'I will keep an eye on your dog, miss.'

She thanked him and, left alone, began on the task of getting clean again. Her skirt was horribly stained and it smelled, naturally enough, of the farm.

Presently, with a nicely washed face and her hair neatly pinned up, she got into the robe, opened the door cautiously and peered round it. Cricket had said that he would show her where to go...

Dr Galbraith was in the hall, lounging against the wall, Wilkins panting happily beside him.

'Come on out,' he invited. 'Cricket has lunch ready and I have to be at the surgery in less than an hour.'

He sounded, reflected Leonora, like someone's brother, and she did as she was told, following him, a little hampered by the robe, across the hall and into the sitting room overlooking the garden. Their lunch had been laid on a round table near the open fire and something smelled delicious. She pushed the over-long sleeves up her arms and sat down without further ado to sample Cricket's artichoke soup.

The doctor had made no comment about her appearance but he smiled a little at the sensible way she had tucked up the sleeves and wrapped the yards of extra material around her person, and he liked her lack of self-consciousness.

The soup was followed by a cheese pudding and a salad and they drank tonic water before Cricket brought in the coffee-tray. Since there wasn't much time and it was obvious to her that this wasn't a social occasion, Leonora made no attempt to make conversation.

The moment they had drunk their coffee she said, 'I'll go and put my own clothes on again. You'll want to be going.' She smiled at him. 'Thank you for lunch; it was delicious.'

He got up with her. 'I'll be in the garden with Wilkins,' he told her, and watched her gather up the trailing robe as she crossed the hall. A sensible girl, he thought; no nonsense about her. Beamish was a lucky man. He frowned. She was too good for the fellow.

Cricket had worked wonders with the stains on her skirt. Really, they had almost gone; he had pressed it too. How wonderful to have someone like that to look after you, Leonora mused. No wonder the doctor wasn't married; he must be very comfortable as he was. She hurried into her clothes, thanked Cricket for his help and got into the car once more.

'Drop us off in the village,' she told the doctor. 'Anywhere along the main street will do.'

'I shall drive you home.' His voice dared her to argue about it and she sat silent for a moment, trying to think of something to say. At length she said, 'You told me you had a dog; what do you call him?'

'Tod.'

'Unusual—is it a foreign name?'

She saw his slow smile. 'No, no. It isn't a name of my choosing but a young lady for whom I have an affection named him and Tod it is.'

Ha, thought Leonora, the girlfriend—there was bound to be someone. Her fertile imagination was already at work. Small and fragile and blue-eyed. Fair hair beautifully dressed, and wearing the very latest in fashion. She would have one of those sickening voices that made one squirm. Leonora, disliking this figment of her imagination, reflected that she would be the kind of girl to call a dog by such a silly name.

She said inadequately, 'How nice,' and waved to Mrs Pike standing outside her shop.

When he stopped before her home she said frostily, still influenced by her fancies, 'Thank you so much, Doctor. I do hope you won't be too busy for the rest of the day. And I hope that poor man will get better.'

He got out to open her door and stood beside her, looking at her thoughtfully. 'I'll let you know, and it is I who thank you for your help.'

He waited while she opened the door, and Wilkins rushed past her, intent on getting to the warmth of the kitchen. 'Well, goodbye,' said Leonora awkwardly, and went indoors.

Her mother and father were in the drawing room.

'Darling, where have you been? So awkward—I mean, Nanny had to leave everything and go down to the village. Why ever should Dr Galbraith want you? An accident at Willer's Farm, Nanny says. Surely they could have managed without you?'

Leonora opened her mouth to explain but her mother went on, 'Your Tony phoned. He was quite annoyed because you weren't here. Perhaps you had better give him a ring presently and explain.'

'Did he say why he had phoned?'

'No, dear. We were chatting for a while and I quite forgot to ask.'

Leonora went to the kitchen and found Nanny preparing oxtail for supper.

'I'm sorry, Nanny, but Dr Galbraith didn't give me a chance to refuse...'

'Quite right too. Bad accident, was it? He wouldn't have asked for your help if he hadn't needed it. Tell me about it. It's too early for tea but you could get the tray ready while I finish this and get it into the oven.'

So Leonora recited her morning's activities, not leaving anything out, detailing her lunch and the perfections of the doctor's house.

'Sounds nice,' said Nanny. 'And that man of his—was he nice?'

'Yes, very. He took my skirt and cleaned it. You've no idea how filthy it was—he pressed it too.'

'I'm sorry about Ben, but the doctor will see him right and the Willers will keep an eye on him—give him light work if he can't manage his usual jobs.'

Leonora ate a scone from the plate Nanny had just put on the table.

'You'll get fat,' said Nanny. 'Your young man rang up. Put out, he was.' She shot a quick glance at Leonora. 'Won't do no harm just for once…'

'What do you mean, Nanny?'

'Well, love, the men like to do a bit of chasing. It's not a bad idea to be difficult to get at times.'

'Nanny, you naughty old thing, where did you learn to play fast and loose with the gentlemen?' Leonora was laughing.

'Never you mind! It's sound common sense. No need to say you're sorry you weren't waiting here by the phone in the hopes he'd ring up.'

She picked up the plate of scones. 'They're for tea, Miss Leonora, and I'm not making another batch. You'd best go and tidy yourself. What the doctor thought of you I'll never know.'

The doctor was a man to keep his thoughts to himself so Nanny was never likely to find out. All the same she would have been pleased if she had found out; she had never taken a fancy to Tony Beamish—not good enough for her Miss Leonora, but clever enough to make her think she was in love with him.

'No good'll come of it!' said Nanny, buttering scones.

Leonora, feeling guilty but bearing Nanny's advice in mind, made no attempt to phone Tony, although once or twice during the rest of the afternoon and evening she very nearly did. She was on the point of going to bed when he rang up.

He was still annoyed. 'Where were you?' he wanted to know. 'What's all this about going to an accident and why didn't you phone me as soon as you got home?'

'Well, I am never quite sure where you are. It was a bad accident—one of the men on Willer's Farm—the tractor overturned—'

'Spare me the details,' begged Tony impatiently. 'And why you had to have anything to do with it I can't imagine.'

She told him, leaving out quite a bit because he was getting impatient again.

'Utterly ridiculous,' said Tony. 'That doctor must be thoroughly incompetent.'

'Don't be silly!' Leonora heard his indrawn breath. She had never called him silly before.

'I'm busy,' snapped Tony, 'and obviously you're overwrought. I hope you will have the good sense to keep out of the man's way in future.' He rang off without saying goodbye, confident that he would get a letter from her in the morning begging forgiveness for being such a bad-tempered girl.

Leonora, however, had no intention of putting pen to paper. Love was blind but not as blind as all that; Tony hadn't sounded like Tony at all. Was there a side to him which she hadn't yet discovered? It wasn't as though she particularly liked Dr Galbraith. For that matter, he didn't particularly like her, ordering her around and telling her what to do and that she needed a wash.

Despite the horror of the accident, she had enjoyed herself. Being useful—really useful—had made her feel quite different. She would drive to Bath and visit Ben. Perhaps there was something that her father could do for him—not financial help, of course, that wasn't possible, but influence with authority, perhaps.

She drove over to Bath two days later with a box of

fruit and some flowers and found her way to the ward where Ben was lying.

He was in bed, propped up by pillows, his leg under a cradle, his weather-beaten face pale and lined, although he greeted her cheerfully.

She sat down beside his bed, offered the fruit and flowers and asked how he was getting on.

"Ad me foot put together again,' he told her. 'Take a bit of time, it will, but I'll be able to walk, so they tell me. Mustn't grumble.'

'How long will you be here?'

'A while yet. Got to learn to walk again, 'a'n't I?'

'Yes, of course. You'll go back to Willer's?'

'Mr Willer, 'e'll see me right...'

'I think you can claim compensation, Ben.'

'So 'tis said. Mr Willer, 'e'll attend to that.' He said awkwardly, 'I'm downright thankful for your help, Miss Crosby. Dr Galbraith told me as 'ow you gave a hand. 'E's been a trump too. Comes to see me regular; knows the surgeon who done me foot.'

'That's nice. Ben, is there anything that you want? Money? Books? Clothes?'

'I'm fine, thank you, miss. Proper good treatment I'm getting too. Pretty nurses and all.'

She stayed for an hour, dredging up bits of local gossip to interest him, but when the tea-trolley arrived she bade him goodbye. 'I'll be back,' she told him. 'The Willers are coming to see you in a day or two—I'll come again next week.'

She left the ward and was walking along the long corridor which led to the main staircase when she saw Dr Galbraith coming towards her. He wasn't alone; there were a couple of younger men in white jackets and a white-coated man with him, and although he wasn't wearing a white coat Leonora had the feeling that he was as remote as his companion, the possessor of knowledge she knew nothing of and therefore someone difficult to get to know, to be friends with.

Face to face, she wished him a good afternoon and made to walk on, but he put out an arm and caught her gently by the wrist.

'Leonora? You have been to see Ben? This is Mr Kirby who operated on his foot.'

He looked at his companion. 'This is Miss Crosby, who very kindly came to my aid at the farm.'

She shook hands and murmured that she mustn't keep them.

'How did you come? I'll give you a lift back...'

'I drove over, but thank you all the same.' She included everyone in her goodbye, aware that she wasn't behaving in her usual calm and collected manner. The look of amusement on Dr Galbraith's face sent the colour into her cheeks, which made things even worse.

It was two days later when her mother looked up from her letters over breakfast.

'Our little dinner party, Leonora. I thought twelve of us—just a nice number, don't you agree? We'll ask Colonel Howes and Nora, the Willoughbys, of course, the Merediths, the vicar—Dulcie Hunt is visiting her mother so he'll be glad of a little social life—and Dr Galbraith, and Tony simply must manage to come. We'll have it on a Saturday; that should make it easy for him.'

She counted on her fingers. 'With us that's twelve—'

'Mother,' said Leonora, 'I don't think it's a good idea to ask Dr Galbraith if Tony comes. They don't like each other...'

'Nonsense, darling, of course they do.' She made a great business of buttering her toast. 'Anyway, I've already invited them.' She gave Leonora a quick glance. 'Well, I hadn't much to do yesterday so I wrote the invitations and your father gave them to the postman in the afternoon.'

'When for?' asked Leonora. 'And have you any ideas about feeding them?'

'Darling, what a funny way of putting it... Saturday week. That gives Tony lots of time to arrange his work. I thought we might have artichoke soup. You did say there were a lot still in the garden. Willer sent over two brace of pheasants—a kind of thank-you for your help, he said; wasn't that nice? There must be some kind of vegetables still in the kitchen garden to go with them, and I'm sure Nanny will think of some delicious sweet. Thank heaven there are at least a couple of bottles of claret in the cellar.'

She smiled, well pleased with herself. 'So you see, darling, there's almost nothing to do and it'll cost hardly anything, and if we use the best silver and those lace table mats and you concoct one of your centrepieces it will all look much more than it is, if you see what I mean.'

'Yes, Mother,' said Leonora. Of course it would cost something—the best coffee beans, cream, cranberries for the sauce, more cream for the soup, after-dinner mints, sherry—two bottles at least—and a bottle of whisky for any of the men who wanted it. Her father wouldn't take kindly to her using his...

Then there would be bacon and baby sausages to go with the pheasant, and the 'delicious sweet' still to be decided upon. They couldn't afford it but it was too late

to tell her mother that. Leonora cleared up the breakfast things and went to the kitchen to give a hand with
the washing-up and confer with Nanny about a suitable pudding.

Tony phoned during the week. He had managed to
squeeze out a weekend, he told her, and would be down
at teatime on the Saturday, adding the rider that he
hoped her father would be up to a dinner party. 'He's
not as young as he was!' he cautioned. 'We must keep
an eye on him.'

He was in such good humour that she thought it prudent not to mention that Dr Galbraith was to be one of
the guests. After all, there would be twelve of them
there and they didn't need to do more than bid each
other a civil good evening. She must remember to make
sure that they were as far apart at the table as possible.

She went once more to see Ben, anxious not to meet
the doctor in the hospital but disappointed nonethe-
less when she didn't. Ben was doing well. He had been
out of bed on crutches and was having physiotherapy.
It would take a bit of time, he assured her, but he'd be
as good as new by the time they'd finished with him.

She left him a bag of fruit and some magazines and
drove home. When she saw Dr Galbraith again she must
ask him just how fit Ben would be. The thought struck
her that she might not have the chance to speak to him
at the dinner party, not if Tony was there...

Saturday week came and with it a dozen or more
things to see to. The floral arrangement she had already
contrived from various bits of greenery, some daffodils
and primroses and aconites from the neglected border
at the front of the house. She polished the table, helped
Nanny put in the extra leaf and arranged the lace mats.

The silver was old, kept in a baize bag in what had once been the butler's pantry, and she had polished it to a dazzling gleam; she had done the same with the crystal glasses and had washed the Coalport dinner service. They combined to make an elegant dinner table, and her mother, coming to see that things were just as she liked them, gave a satisfied sigh.

'We may be poor,' she observed, 'but we can still show the world a brave face. It looks very nice, dear.'

Leonora filled the Georgian salt cellars and went to the kitchen to start the syllabub. A dozen eggs was an extravagance; on the other hand the yolks could be made into *créme brûlée*, which if it wasn't all eaten at dinner could be used up on the following day...

She went upstairs after tea and looked through her wardrobe. Her clothes were good, for they had been bought when there had been enough money to have the best. They still looked good, too, but were sadly out of date. There was a silver-grey velvet somewhere at the back of the cupboard...

She hauled it out and tried it on and it didn't look too bad—very plain, with its modest, unfashionable neckline and long sleeves, but it fitted her nicely. She had a quick shower and got dressed; Tony had said that he would arrive in plenty of time for drinks and there were still one or two jobs to do in the kitchen, where Nanny was working miracles with the pheasants.

Downstairs she put on a pinny, tucked up her sleeves and began to whip the cream. The evening should be a success, she thought; her mother was pleased, her father was better, though somewhat irascible, Tony was coming...

He had come; he stood in the doorway looking at

her. Frowning. She looked up, smiling as he came in and then puzzled.

'My dear girl, do you have to spend your time in the kitchen? The guests will be here in ten minutes or so and I expected to be met by an elegant fiancée sitting in the drawing room doing nothing.'

She made the mistake of thinking that he was joking. 'Tony, don't be so absurd. Of course I have to be here. Nanny can't possibly manage on her own; she's doing two people's work as it is. I'm almost ready. Go and pour yourself a drink; Father and Mother should be down at any minute.'

He turned away without another word, and since the cream had reached the peak of perfection she hardly noticed his going. The fleeting thought that he hadn't kissed her or even said how glad he was to see her passed through her head, but just at that moment she had a lot to think about if the dinner party was to be a success.

Ten minutes later she slipped into the drawing room to find that everyone had arrived, and she went from one to the other, exchanging greetings. They were all old friends—excepting Dr Galbraith, elegant in black tie, talking to Nora. He smiled down at her and she offered a hand, and since Tony had made no effort to speak to her, had barely glanced in her direction she let it lie in his firm grasp for longer than necessary and gave him a bewitching smile in return.

'I'm glad you could come. Have you got your dog—Tod—home yet?'

'Yesterday. He brought my sister with him. She had to return home at once, though—her youngest has the measles.'

'Oh, what bad luck, but nice to get it over with when you're young. We had it at about the same time, didn't we, Nora? We must have been seven or eight…'

The doctor stared down at her; she must have been an engaging small girl with those enormous eyes, he thought.

'Yes, well,' said Leonora, aware of the stare. 'I must just nip along to the kitchen—the soup, you know…'

They watched her go. 'She's such a dear,' said Nora. 'She practically runs this great place on her own. If it wasn't for Nanny she could never cope.'

Mrs Sims from the village, who occasionally obliged with the heavy cleaning, was waiting in the kitchen ready to carry in the soup tureen; the pheasants were done to a turn, everything was fine, declared Nanny.

Leonora went back to the drawing room, bent to whisper to her mother and everyone crossed the hall to the dining room. Leonora had had a fire burning in its elegant grate all day, sighing over every shovelful of coal and every log, but appearances had to be kept up and the room was nicely warm now. She took her seat beside Tony and watched Mrs Sims place the tureen in front of her mother. So far, so good…

CHAPTER FOUR

THERE WAS A good deal of lively conversation over the soup. Leonora, listening to Colonel Howes describing the delights of a genuine Indian curry, hardly noticed Tony's silence on her other side. When she was free to turn to him, he was talking to Nora beside him.

She glanced down the table; Dr Galbraith was sitting beside her mother, who was talking animatedly, and the vicar and her father were discussing the local fishing.

The soup plates were removed and her father began to carve the pheasants—quite a lengthy business, but the claret had loosened tongues and everyone was chatting, relaxed among friends...

'Will you stay until Monday?' she asked Tony. She smiled at him, no longer vexed; he was probably tired after a busy week and he hated to see her working around the house.

'There doesn't seem to be much point if you're going to be in the kitchen all day.'

She refused to get needled. 'Well, I shan't be. We might go for a good walk—blow the London cobwebs away.'

'London at this time of year is rather delightful. How is your father? I thought he looked very tired.'

'Did you?' She frowned. 'He's so much better—'

'I shall have a word with that doctor of his before I go—make sure he's getting proper treatment.'

Leonora helped herself to sprouts. 'Quite unnecessary, Tony; Father is in good hands.'

'It seems to me that that fellow has cast a spell over you all—he's probably quite incompetent!'

Leonora's eyes glittered with temper. 'That's an abominable thing to say. Would you have known how to get a man with a crushed foot free from a farm tractor?'

She turned back to Colonel Howes and began an animated conversation about the extension to be built to the village hall, and the doctor, watching her from under lowered lids and replying suitably to Lady Crosby's chatter, wondered what she and Tony were quarrelling about. They were being very discreet about it, but they were quarrelling.

In due course the pheasant was replaced by syllabub and the *crème brûlée,* and since Lady Crosby refused to accede to modern ideas the ladies were led away to the drawing room while the men remained to drink the port Sir William had brought up from the cellar.

Leonora slid away as the ladies went into the drawing room, to reappear presently with the tray of coffeepot, cream and sugar. The small table had already been placed by her mother's chair, bearing the Worcester coffee-cups and the silver dishes of after-dinner mints. By the time the men joined them, they were deep in comfortable talk—clothes, the price of food, their grandchildren, and the difficulty of getting a gardener.

When the men came in there was a good deal of rearranging of seats and Leonora was kept busy offering more coffee and refilling cups, and by the time she had seen to everyone Tony was sitting between Nora and

Mrs Willoughby on one of the old-fashioned sofas. So she went and sat by the vicar and listened to him talking about his wife, to discover after a few minutes that Dr Galbraith had joined them. A moment later her father walked over.

'Come along to my study,' he invited the vicar. 'I'll show you that new trout fly I've just tied.' Which left Leonora and the doctor together.

'A pleasant evening, Leonora.'

'Thank you.'

'Why were you and young Beamish quarrelling?' He smiled. 'Still are?'

She was getting used to the way he eschewed the soft approach. 'Well, you see, I was in the kitchen when he got here—and he was disappointed because I wasn't in the drawing room.'

'Quite.'

'I should have thought of that but I had the cream to whip. I didn't think it mattered much. I mean, would you have minded?'

'In the circumstances, and seeing that the success of the dinner party largely rested on the cream being properly whipped, no!' He put down his coffee-cup. 'But there was something else, wasn't there?'

'Well, yes. He thinks Father doesn't look well.' She went pink. 'He—he wondered if…'

'Ah—he doubts my expertise.'

'I'm so sorry. I mean, no one else does; we all trust you and think you're a very good doctor.'

He hid a smile. 'Thank you. I won't let it worry me.'

'He said that he would talk to you.'

'Splendid. And since he is coming to join us now, what could be a better opportunity?' He glanced at her troubled face. 'Go and talk to someone else,' he suggested quietly, and turned a bland face to Tony.

He stood up as Leonora moved away and Tony frowned, put at a disadvantage by the doctor's height and size.

'You wanted to talk to me?' the doctor enquired pleasantly.

'Look here,' began Tony, 'I'm not at all happy about Sir William…'

Dr Galbraith said nothing.

'He isn't a young man.'

The doctor inclined his head; he looked so exactly like an eminent doctor listening with courteous patience to one of his patients that Tony's face darkened with annoyance.

'Isn't it ridiculous that Sir William should go on living in this great house? He needs to be in something smaller and modern where he would be properly looked after.' He caught the doctor's eye. 'Oh, Leonora looks after him very well, I know, but she's limited— no money. Now, if he were to sell the place or hand it over to her, I could restore it.'

'Yes?' queried the doctor gently. 'Would you live in it—with Leonora, of course?'

Tony said rudely, 'Oh, of course. We'd have a flat in town but we could come for weekends, bring guests.' He stopped, aware that he was talking too much. He essayed a smile. 'My dear chap, I'm sure you could persuade Sir William to settle in something more suitable to his age and lifestyle.'

The doctor said evenly, 'No, I couldn't do that. It isn't my business. Sir William lives here, it is his home, his ancestor's home, he loves it. Surely if you intend to restore the place there is no reason why he and Lady Crosby shouldn't live here? Why move? There is ample room for them, is there not?'

'I can't see that it is any concern of yours,' said Tony sulkily.

The vicar had joined them again and presently Tony went away. The talk hadn't been very successful, he reflected, and went in search of Leonora. He found her talking to Nora, who finally drifted away, so that he was able to give her his version of his talk with Dr Galbraith.

'Well,' said Leonora in a matter-of-fact way, 'he's quite right; there's no reason why Father should move from here. It's a silly idea. It would break his heart, besides being an enormous undertaking. You have no idea of the stuff that's stored in the attics.'

She saw his annoyance and said quickly, 'It's very good of you to bother, Tony—I'm sure Father appreciates your concern; we all do.' She added soberly, 'I suppose in due time I shall inherit the place, but not for a long while yet. If you want to restore it then, I won't mind...'

Tony said soberly, 'My dear girl, we shall probably be in our dotage. The place needs a complete overhaul now but it can't be done while your mother and father are still here.'

Leonora gave him a puzzled look and he saw that he had said too much. He took her arm and smiled at her. 'Darling, don't let's worry about it. As you say, your parents are very happy here. It is a lovely old place, just the right background for a dinner party. I must say it's a splendid evening and dinner was delicious. I can see that I am going to be very proud of my wife.'

They were words which dulled the faint feeling of

unease Leonora had been trying to ignore. She told him about the pheasants and the artichoke soup. 'So, you see, it cost hardly anything...'

He squeezed her arm and laughed with her and Dr Galbraith, watching them from the other side of the room, thought it was a great pity that a sensible girl like Leonora should be taken in by young Beamish. She was too good for him and too honest, and once she had married him and found out about him, as she was bound to do eventually, she would keep her marriage vows and be a loyal wife and quietly break her heart. A pity that some decent man couldn't come along and marry her before Beamish had a chance to complete his plans.

It seemed strange to the doctor that Sir William hadn't seen what was happening, with all this talk about his health and the need to move away from his home. Could he not see that Beamish wanted to get his hands on the lovely old place and use it for his own ends? The doctor frowned; it seemed likely that the man was going to marry Leonora for that very reason.

He shrugged his enormous shoulders; it was none of his business.

Cricket, advancing to meet him as he let himself into his house later that evening, enquired as to whether he had had an enjoyable time. 'A very pleasant young lady, Miss Crosby,' said Cricket. 'I have had occasion to have a few words with Miss South—her old nanny, sir—and she told me that she is a most capable person and shortly to be married.'

'You old gossip,' said the doctor cheerfully. 'I had a very pleasant evening and now I am going to take Tod for a quick walk. I'll lock up when I get back.'

Presently he did just that, saw Tod into his basket in

the kitchen and took himself off to bed. He had had a long and busy day and he slept the sleep of a tired man, never once thinking of Leonora.

However, Leonora, tired though she was, didn't sleep well. Tony had sewn the seeds of doubt in her mind; perhaps her father would be better off living in a smaller house where there was no need of buckets to catch the drips when it rained and the plumbing was up to date. What did Tony intend to do with her house after they were married? He had been enthusiastic about restoring it but for what reason? He had made it plain on several occasions that they would live in London because of his work.

She shook up her pillows and tried to settle down. They would have to have a talk about it, fix the date of the wedding and discuss their future. She closed her eyes and presently slept uneasily.

There was no chance to talk to Tony in the morning; when they got back from church he went with her father to the library and over lunch the talk was of nothing much. She suggested over their coffee that they might go for a walk but he told her that he would have to go back to London within the hour. 'You should see the pile of work on my desk,' he told her. 'But I was determined to come to your dinner party, darling. It was a great success. I'll be down again just as soon as I can manage it.'

She said soberly, 'Tony, I think we must have a talk—about the wedding and where we're to live and—oh, a whole lot of things I'm not sure about.'

'Of course, darling. We will the very next time I come.' He bent to kiss her. 'You're my darling girl and we are going to be very happy.' He spoilt it for her by adding, 'And very rich...'

'I don't care about being rich, Tony.'

'You will. Lovely clothes, and theatres, and meeting all the right people.'

She said coolly, 'The right people live here too, Tony!'

He kissed her again. 'Yes, of course they do. I'll phone you this evening.'

It was later in the week, when she had walked down to the village to Mrs Pike's shop, that that lady leaned over the counter to say confidentially, 'Those gentlemen staying over at the Blue Man—they've not been bothering you, Miss Leonora?'

'Bothering me? I didn't know there was anyone staying in the village, Mrs Pike, and why should they bother me?'

'Well, they been asking questions about the house, wanting to know how many rooms there was and how much land there was with it. When Mr Bowles over at the Blue Man spoke up and asked them why they didn't go to the house and ask Sir William since they were so anxious to know, they shut up like clams, said as how they were just curious. All the same, they've been sitting in the bar of a night, dropping questions here and there. Your pa's not thinking of selling, like?'

'Absolutely not, Mrs Pike. What sort of men are they?'

'Oh, gents, miss, quite the city men, if you get my meaning; they wears ties and carries umbrellas. Nicely spoken too.'

'You don't know where they're from? I mean, has some house agent got it into his head that my father is going to sell the house? I can't understand it. Perhaps I'd better go across and tell them that they are mistaken.'

'Oh, I wouldn't do that, miss,' said Mrs Pike, 'seeing as how they'd know at once who you was. You leave it to me; I'll get my George to go over for a pint this evening. He's a sharp one; perhaps he can ferret something out.'

'Would he? That would be very kind. Mrs Pike, you won't talk about this to anyone, will you? I can assure you that my father has absolutely no intention of leaving the house.' She picked up her shopping. 'I'll come down in the morning...'

She went back home wishing there were someone she could talk to about it, but that wasn't possible; her parents would be upset and worried and Nanny would probably go down to the Blue Man and demand to see these men and give them a piece of her mind. A pity that she wasn't on better terms with Dr Galbraith, she reflected; he was someone one could confide in and get sensible advice from in return.

She worried about it all day and half the night and, making some excuse about fetching a particular brand of biscuits Mrs Pike was getting for her, went to the village directly after breakfast.

There were several people in the shop, and when it was empty at last Mrs Pike seemed very reluctant to talk.

'Mr Pike heard something?' she asked Mrs Pike. 'Something you don't like to tell me?'

'Well, yes, miss. Mind you, it's only gossip; you can't believe half you hear these days. I dare say there's a good reason...'

Leonora smiled and looked so calm that Mrs Pike decided to talk after all.

'Well, it's like this, miss—these gentlemen has come here to look over the house and see if it's worth doing up and if the land is good for selling to build on…'

At Leonora's quick breath she paused. 'The house is to be a kind of headquarters for visiting business-men—them big nobs with millions.' She eyed Leonora carefully. 'I hates to say this, Miss Crosby, but the man who sent them is your Mr Beamish.'

Leonora had gone very pale but she said composedly, 'Mrs Pike, I can't thank you enough—or Mr Pike—for your help. I'm sure there's some misunderstanding but at least I know whom to see about it. I'm quite sure that my father knows nothing about this but I'll talk to Mr Beamish about it. There must be an explanation.'

'Yes, miss, that's what we thought. Mr Beamish seems such a nice gentleman…'

'Yes,' said Leonora, and added, 'I'll be off. I want to do some gardening.'

She made herself walk normally out of the shop, even turning to smile at Mrs Pike from the doorway, and somehow she had to go through the village look-ing the same as usual. If she could manage not to think about it until she got home… She gulped; when she got home she wouldn't be able to think about it either, let alone say anything.

She marched down the street, saying good morning and smiling as she went, with Wilkins close at her heels. She was going past the surgery when Dr Galbraith came out, shutting the door behind him. She would have gone past him with a brief greeting but he fell into step be-side her.

'What is the matter?' he asked, and added, 'No, don't

tell me for the moment. The car's across the street; we'll go back to Buntings.'

Because she would have burst into tears if she had attempted to speak just then, she went with him and got into the car and sat silently with Wilkins's elderly whiskers pressed into the back of her neck.

At the house the doctor got out, opened her door, let Wilkins out, and as Cricket came to the door said briskly, 'Could we have coffee, Cricket? In the sitting room, I think; Wilkins can go into the garden with Tod.'

Cricket cast a look at Leonora's face, murmured soothingly and went to the kitchen while the doctor led her across the hall and into the pleasant little room bright with sunshine.

The door to the garden was open and racing across the grass lawn came a dog, barking his pleasure at the sight of them. It was impossible to tell what kind of a dog he was, but there was a strong bias towards an Alsatian and more than a hint of retriever; he had a noble head and a curly coat and a feathery tail and liquid brown eyes.

'Tod,' said the doctor briefly. 'Sit down here; Wilkins can go into the garden too and make friends.' He said over one shoulder, 'Cry if you want to.'

'I have no intention of crying,' said Leonora stiffly, and burst into tears.

She hadn't wept like that for a long time, not since Bouncer, the family cat, had died of old age, lying in the sun at the back of the house. She sobbed and sniffed, hardly aware that she was making a fine mess of the doctor's jacket, her head buried against his shoulder while she muttered and mumbled and wept.

Presently she lifted a sodden face. 'I'm so sorry; I really am. I never cry—well, almost never.'

'A mistake; there's nothing like it for relieving the feelings.'

His voice was kind and his arms comforting. 'Now mop up and sit down and tell me all about it.'

He offered a large white handkerchief and nodded to Cricket to put the coffee-tray down on a side table, then he went to the door and stood watching the two dogs, who were still cautiously getting to know each other, not looking at her, giving her time to wipe away her tears and tuck back her hair. She gave a final sniff. 'I'll let you have your hanky back,' she told him. 'I'm quite all right now.'

He poured their coffee and gave her a cup and offered biscuits to the dogs.

'They seem to like each other,' said Leonora, anxious to get the conversation onto an impersonal footing again.

'Naturally. They are intelligent animals.' He sat down opposite her but not facing her directly. 'Begin at the beginning, Leonora.'

'It's all so silly; I mean, I don't believe a word of it. There must be some mistake.'

'If there is, we can, perhaps, discover it.' He was sitting back in his chair, quite at ease—a man, she reflected, who could solve the knottiest problem without fuss.

'Well,' she began, and poured it all out in rather a muddle, for, just for once, her common sense had forsaken her. 'I simply can't understand why Tony has sent these men. I'm quite sure he has said nothing to Father. Besides, Father wouldn't even listen to a plan like that—' she gulped '—to build houses on our land—and where are we supposed to live? It doesn't make sense.'

It made sense to the doctor although he didn't say so.

'Would you like to go to London and talk to Tony? Ask for an explanation? There may be a reason of which you know nothing. Perhaps he intends to surprise you in some way, but if you tell him that you are worried about the rumours he will tell you what he has in mind. Since he is to marry you, I imagine it is some scheme beneficial to you and your parents.'

He didn't imagine anything of the kind—Tony Beamish was capable of manipulating affairs to suit himself—but perhaps it wasn't as bad as Leonora thought it was. After all, the man loved her, presumably; he wouldn't want to hurt her in any way, even if it meant forgoing whatever ambitious plans he had.

Leonora said suddenly, 'I think you're right. I'll go up to town and see him. I'll not tell him I'm going. I've an aunt living in Chelsea—I can say I'm going to see her and go and see him after he gets back from work.'

'That sounds like a good idea. I have to go up to town myself tomorrow afternoon. I'll be there for a day or two. If you're ready to come back with me, well and good; otherwise you can get a train.'

'Thank you; I'd like that. I'll stay the night, perhaps two nights. I'm very grateful for your help.' She put down her coffee-cup. 'I'll go home…'

'I dare say you would like to wash your face first,' he observed in a matter-of-fact voice. 'Cricket will show you where to go.'

She was still pale when she rejoined him but quite composed. He doubted if her parents would notice anything amiss although Nanny probably would. She thanked Cricket for the coffee and waited while the doctor saw the dogs onto the back seat of the car.

As he drove the short distance to her home he told her, 'I'll be leaving around two o'clock—I'll call for you.'

At the house he got out to open her door and then allow a reluctant Wilkins to join her. 'You're quite sure that you want to go and see Beamish?'

She nodded. 'Oh, yes. Otherwise I'm going to fuss and fret, aren't I?'

He smiled down at her. 'You're a sensible woman, Leonora.'

After he had driven away she went slowly indoors, not sure that she liked being called 'a sensible woman' in that casual manner.

Her mother and father saw nothing unusual in her wish to visit Aunt Marion. 'A good idea, darling,' said her mother. 'It will make a nice change for you, and Aunt Marion loves company. Perhaps you'll see Tony. Don't stay too long, though; remember there's the village bazaar coming up and I've promised that we'll help—take a stall or something. Mrs Willoughby will tell you, I've no doubt. Lydia Dowling will be organising it so I expect you'll have to go to see her to talk about it.'

Nanny looked at Leonora sharply when she told her that she was going to visit her aunt for a day or two.

'A bit sudden, isn't it? Going to see that Mr Beamish, are you?'

'Well, yes, I expect so. Nanny, why don't you like him?'

Nanny bent over a saucepan, inspecting its contents. 'We all have our likes and dislikes,' she said reluctantly.

'I dare say I'll get around to liking him in a while.' She sniffed. 'Perhaps he'll improve with marriage.'

Leonora, packing an overnight bag later, hesitated as to what to take with her. She intended to see Tony on the following evening. There wouldn't be time to change when she reached her aunt's house but if she stayed for a second day she would need a dress, since Aunt Marion had old-fashioned notions about changing for dinner.

She crammed a stone-coloured jersey dress in with her night things and added a pair of high-heeled shoes. She would go in the tweed suit and easy shoes; both had seen better days but they had been good when new. Her handbag and gloves were beyond reproach. She had a very small income from a godmother's bequest—money she seldom touched, saving it for a rainy day. Well, that day had come; she would nip down to the village in the morning and get Mrs Pike to cash a cheque...

THE DOCTOR WAS punctual. He came into the house and spent five minutes talking to her mother and father before settling her in the car and getting in beside her. Beyond asking her if she was comfortable he had little to say as he drove along minor roads to reach the M4, and once on the motorway he shot smoothly ahead.

'Your aunt knows you are coming?'

'Yes, I phoned her last night. She's a very hospitable person and very sociable. She may not be there when I arrive but she has a marvellous housekeeper who's been with her for ages. I'm to stay for as long as I like.'

'Will you give me her phone number before I drop you off? I'll phone you when I'm ready to leave in case you would like a lift back.'

'That's very kind of you. I don't expect to be in London for more than a day or two. If Tony's free he might drive me home.' Before she could stop herself, she added, 'I'm sure it's a mistake—a misunderstanding. He'll explain…'

'There is always an explanation, Leonora, although sometimes we have to look for one. Will you see him this evening?'

'Yes, I'll go to his flat. I've never been there; it's in a street just off Curzon Street.'

The doctor raised his eyebrows. 'A very good address. He is a successful businessman, I should suppose.'

Somehow, talking about Tony made the whole puzzling business seem far-fetched. She said slowly, 'I wonder if I'm just being very silly…?'

'No. If the whole thing is, as you say, a misunderstanding, then the quicker it is put to rights the better. Five minutes' talk together and probably you will both be laughing over the matter.'

'Yes, I'm sure you're right. Are you going to be busy while you're in London?'

'A seminar and a couple of lectures I want to attend, friends to look up. A theatre, perhaps.'

He would have friends, she reflected, and since he was single, handsome and an asset to any dinner table he would be much in demand. Besides, perhaps he would see this girl who had called his dog by such a silly name. She switched her thoughts away from that; it was none of her business what he did in his private life.

Her aunt lived in a narrow street of small but elegant houses; the doctor, following Leonora's directions calmly, drew up before its pristine door, flanked by two bay trees in tubs, and got out to open Leonora's door.

She got out, waited while he fetched her overnight bag from the boot and then held out a hand. 'Thank you very much,' she told him. 'I hope I haven't brought you too much out of your way.'

'No, no. I'll wait until you are indoors…'

Her aunt's housekeeper answered her knock and she turned to smile at him as she went inside.

Mrs Fletcher, the housekeeper, greeted her placidly. 'The mistress is out, miss; I'm to show you to your room and give you tea. Mrs Thurston will be back around six o'clock.'

So Leonora tidied herself in the charming room overlooking the tiny back garden and had her tea in the elegant sitting room.

Aunt Marion, a childless widow, had been left comfortably off by a doting husband, so that she lived pleasantly in her little gem of a house, surrounded by charming furniture and leading the kind of life she enjoyed—shopping, bridge parties, theatres—at the same time retaining a warm heart and generous nature. Sir William was a good deal older than she and she saw very little of him, but years ago, when they were children, she had been his favourite sister, and still was.

She came home soon after Leonora had finished her tea, embraced her niece warmly and demanded to know why she had come on this unexpected visit.

'Not that I'm not delighted to have you, my dear— you know that—but it's not like you… Is there anything wrong at home?'

Leonora gave her reasons, carefully couched in neutral terms.

'Ah, yes, of course you must have a talk. The whole thing sounds preposterous to me, but I know what villages are—someone has got the wrong end of the stick.'

Leonora nodded, not at all certain about that; all the same, her aunt's bracing opinion put heart into her and when they had dined she declared her intention of going to Tony's flat.

'Now? Wouldn't you like to phone him first?'

'No, I don't think so. I mean, if I just walk in and ask him he'll tell me at once, if you see what I mean.'

Her aunt understood very well. She was another one who wasn't quite happy about Tony Beamish. Let the girl catch him on the hop, as it were!

'Take a taxi, dear,' she advised. 'Have you sufficient money?'

When the taxi stopped outside the block of flats where Tony lived, Leonora got out, paid the driver and stood a minute looking around her.

It was a dignified street, lined with large houses and sedate blocks of flats—the kind that had enormous porticos with a lot of glass and wrought iron and a uniformed man just inside the door. Tony had told her that he was on the first floor and she looked up as she reached the entrance, half expecting to see him at one of the windows.

The porter enquired whom she wished to visit and offered to phone Mr Beamish's flat and announce her.

She smiled at him. 'I'd rather you didn't; it's a surprise.' She declined the lift, walked up the wide stairs and knocked on the door bearing his name.

A sour-faced man opened it. She disliked him at once for no reason that she could think of and asked politely if she might see Mr Beamish.

'Tell him it is Miss Crosby,' she said, and went past him into a small hall, thickly carpeted, its walls hung with paintings and vases of flowers on the wall tables. A bit overdone, she thought, but probably Tony had a housekeeper as well as the sour-faced man. She sat down composedly on a small walnut hall chair and watched the door through which the man had gone.

Nothing happened for a few minutes, then the door was flung open and Tony came into the hall.

'What in heaven's name brings you here?' he demanded, and the happy excitement of seeing him again slowly shrivelled at the cold anger in his voice. He must have seen her face because he added quickly, 'Darling, what has happened? Is it your father—something dire?'

Leonora stayed on the chair. 'Hello, Tony. No, Father is very well. I want to talk to you.'

'My dear girl, why couldn't you have phoned?' He had controlled his annoyance now and bent to kiss her. 'I have guests—a dinner party. I simply can't leave them.' He glanced at the tweed suit and the sensible shoes. 'You aren't dressed…' he began.

Leonora got up. 'I'll come back tomorrow. Will you be here in the evening? About six o'clock? I won't keep you long and I shall be dining with Aunt Marion.'

'You do understand, Leonora? They're important people—colleagues in the business world.'

He kissed her again and she turned her cheek away and walked to the door. 'I'll see you tomorrow,' she told him in a rather small, polite voice, and went past the sour-faced man, who had appeared to open the door, and down the stairs.

At the entrance she asked the porter to get her a taxi, stood quietly until it arrived, then tipped the man and got in, outwardly serene while her thoughts were in chaos. Tony hadn't been pleased to see her; surely if he loved her he would have been only too glad to see her? She thought he had looked furiously angry; he had been, for a moment, a man she didn't know.

Her aunt was out when she got back, which meant that she could go to bed early, pleading tiredness after her journey—something which the housekeeper found understandable. Not that Leonora slept, not until the small hours. She pondered her few minutes with Tony, and because she loved him—well, she was going to marry him, wasn't she? So she must love him—she suppressed the doubt at once and convinced herself that he had been tired after his day's work. It had been her fault; she should have warned him of her coming. She must learn to accommodate her actions to suit his... She slept at last on this high-minded resolve.

In the morning, yesterday evening's meeting faded into something which had been regrettable and entirely her fault, and hard on this thought there followed the one that Tony would certainly have an explanation for the goings-on in the village.

She spent the morning at Harrods with her aunt, pretending that she had all the clothes she wanted while her aunt tried on hats, and in the afternoon she made a fourth at bridge, a game at which she was only tolerably good. However, since her aunt had been so kind as to have her for a guest, she could do no other than express pleasure at the prospect of several hours of anxious concentration.

They played for money too but, as Aunt Marion explained laughingly, the stakes would be very low, otherwise it wouldn't be fair to rob her niece.

Kindly fate allowed Leonora and her partner, a for-midable dowager in a towering hat, to win as often as they lost, so that she was a little better off by the time they stopped for tea.

Then it was time for her to go and see Tony once more.

CHAPTER FIVE

THE SOUR-FACED MAN admitted Leonora when she reached Tony's flat. This time he led her through the hall and into a large room overlooking the street. It was splendidly furnished and its tall windows were elaborately curtained but she hardly noticed this. Tony was coming towards her, his arms outstretched.

'Darling, how lovely to see you. I am so sorry about yesterday evening. Sometimes the only chance I have to discuss things with colleagues is over a meal. Come and sit down and tell me why you wanted to see me so urgently!'

He went to a small table against one wall. 'What would you like to drink?' He glanced over his shoulder. 'I have to go out shortly—you said you were dining with your aunt so I saw no reason to cancel it.'

'No, of course not.' All the same she felt chilled by his remark. It was as if he was fitting her in between more important engagements. She refused a drink and told herself not to be petty.

He came and sat down opposite her. 'This is delightful,' he told her, smiling. 'I have so often sat here and wished that you were here with me.' He sat back, at his ease. 'Now, what's all this about?'

She went straight to the point, already feeling confident that the whole business was a storm in a teacup.

'There are two men staying at the Blue Man; they have been asking questions—searching questions—about the house and our park. Two days ago I was told that they were there on behalf of someone who intends to buy the house and the land and build houses on it, as well as restoring the house. I was told that the someone was you, Tony.'

He was no longer smiling. His face was coldly angry and he didn't look at her.

'It's true,' said Leonora in a quiet voice. 'Why, Tony? Tell me why and perhaps I'll understand.'

He was smiling again, even laughing a little. 'Listen, darling. Your father's house needs to be restored; it's already half a ruin—no paintwork, faulty plumbing, doors broken, windows warped, floors uneven, brickwork crumbling. I intend to restore it and modernise it at the same time—new bathrooms, carpets, curtains, wallpapers, the lot.

'We will live on the top floor—a flat with its own entrance, of course—the rest will be used as a business centre. You have no idea of the number of clients I have who come here from Japan, the Middle East, the Continent. It's an ideal spot for them to come for conferences, make decisions, arrange mergers. It'll be run at a profit—I'll see to that.

'And yes, the park is useless as it is; the land will bring in a splendid amount of money and the village will benefit from an influx of new inhabitants. They will be decent-sized places and the people who buy them will bring money with them—the village will love that. Of course I'll see that your father and mother have a suitable house—something that gorgon of a nanny can run single-handed—and of course I'll see that your father is financially comfortable.'

Leonora, listening to this rigmarole, couldn't believe her ears. Rage had kept her silent—a rage strong enough to make her forget that her world was tumbling round her. Now she asked quietly, 'Is this why you wanted to marry me? So that you could do all this?'

She showed no sign of her strong feelings. so Tony said lightly, 'Well, I must admit that that was one of the reasons...'

'There must be any number of girls like me,' said Leonora, 'with elderly parents living in dilapidated old houses; you shouldn't have much difficulty in finding one.'

She stood up, took the ring off her finger and laid it gently on the table by her chair. 'I'm not going to marry you, Tony. I never want to see you again, and if you don't recall those men and drop the whole idea I shall get our solicitor to take the matter up.' She walked to the door. 'You're ruthless and wicked and greedy; I'm surprised that I didn't see that. Luckily I do now.'

He crossed the room and caught her arm. 'Leonora, darling, you can't go like this; I've taken you by surprise. Go away and think about it. It's a splendid scheme and you'll benefit from it—everything you could ever want.'

She turned to look at him. 'All I ever want is to live at Pont Magna amongst friends and people I've known all my life.'

'But you love me—'

'I thought I did, but there's a difference.'

She gave him a little nod and went into the hall and through the door, which the sour-faced man had opened.

She walked down the stairs, bade the porter a polite goodnight, asked him to get her a taxi and when it came got in.

When she got out at her aunt's house she was so white that the driver asked her if she felt ill and only drove away when she assured him that there was nothing wrong. She said the same to Mrs Fletcher and followed her obediently into the drawing room, feeling peculiar. I mustn't faint or cry, she thought.

Her aunt was there, sitting by the small, bright fire, and standing at the window was Dr Galbraith. They turned to look at her as she went in and she stood just inside the door, knowing that if she said anything she would burst into tears. But they had seen her face and understood.

'Come and sit down, Leonora,' said her aunt. 'Mrs Fletcher's bringing coffee. I'm sure you can do with a cup.'

So she sat down, still without speaking, until she asked in a tight voice, 'Why are you here, Doctor?'

He came and sat down, half turned away from her. 'I phoned to see if you wanted a lift home and Mrs Thurston suggested that I might come and wait for you here.'

'Oh—oh, I see. That's very kind of you…'

'Would you like to go home?' The casual friendliness of his voice was comforting.

She looked at her aunt.

'You would like it, wouldn't you, Leonora? Why not? You may be sure that I understand, my dear; you don't have to tell me anything.'

'Thank you, Aunt Marion. I'd like to go home very much if you don't mind. I—that is, Tony and I aren't getting married so I don't need to stay. It was very kind of you to have me… You don't think I'm rude? I don't mean to be!'

'Bless you, girl, of course I don't. I'd do the same in your shoes. Here's the coffee; drink it while it's hot, while Mrs Fletcher packs your bag for you. You'll be home by bedtime. So convenient that Dr Galbraith should be going back this evening.'

'Two days here is enough for me,' observed the doctor, which led to an exchange of views about London versus the country while Leonora drank her coffee, swallowing with it the tears she longed to shed.

Ten minutes later she wished her aunt goodbye and got into the car, her pretty face set in a rigid smile while she uttered her thanks once more.

'In a day or so, when you've had a good cry and found that life's worth living after all, you shall tell me all about it,' said Aunt Marion.

As he drove away the doctor observed casually, 'What a very sensible and delightful woman your aunt is. Do you want to phone your mother?'

'No, I don't think so; she might worry and wonder why I'm coming back…'

'We should be home well before bedtime. We'll stop on the way and have a meal.'

'I'm not hungry.'

He ignored that. 'There's rather a nice pub in a village just off the motorway once we've passed Reading. That should suit us nicely. There's plenty of time for you to have a good cry before we get there, and if I remember rightly the lighting is very dim there.'

She didn't know whether to laugh or cry. 'You think of everything,' she told him. 'I'd much rather go straight home.'

'Of course you would, but consider, Leonora. The moment you entered the door you would burst into tears, upset the household and make a complete muddle of explaining.'

She took an indignant breath. 'What a horrid thing to say. You seem to forget that I'm a grown woman and perfectly able to control myself.'

He said placidly, 'Well, it will take a little while to get to this pub; you can think about it and tell me what you want to do when we reach the turn-off.'

He had no more to say then, which meant that she had no way of ignoring her thoughts, so that presently her much vaunted self-control collapsed and she sat rigid while the tears rolled down her cheeks. It seemed that nothing would stop them; she looked sideways out of the window although it was already getting dark and there was nothing to see, swallowing the sobs.

They were bypassing Reading when the doctor handed her his handkerchief.

'Shall we go to the pub?' he asked with brisk friendliness.

She mopped her face, blew her pretty nose and said, 'Yes, please, only I must look a fright...'

'Does that matter? No one will know you there and they will be locals chatting over their pints—and I don't mind what you look like.'

Despite her misery, Leonora took exception to that remark.

The village was four or five miles off the motorway, a handful of cottages, one or two handsome houses and the church, and opposite it the pub—a quite small place with a solid door and small windows.

The doctor had been quite right—it was indeed

dimly lit and, although the bar was almost full, beyond a quick glance no one bothered to really look at them. Moreover, at one end of the bar there were tables, none of them occupied. He led her to a small table under the window.

'I'll fetch our drinks and see what we can have to eat. If you want the Ladies' it is in that far corner.'

He sounded exactly as she imagined a brother would sound—unfussed and casual. She nodded and took herself off and found the light in the cloakroom, unlike the one in the bar, was so powerful that it could show every wrinkle. No wrinkles in her case but certainly a rather tear-stained face, fortunately not beyond repair. She emerged presently, feeling a good deal better, and found the doctor sitting at the table reading the menu.

He got up as she reached him. 'I'd like you to drink what's in that glass,' he told her, 'and no arguing.'

'What is it?'

She took a sip since he didn't answer and said, 'Oh. Brandy, isn't it?'

He nodded. 'I am sure you would have liked a pot of tea—we'll have that later.'

She eyed his own glass. 'That looks like water...'

'Bottled water. I'm driving. Now, we have quite a choice.' He handed her the menu. 'Last time I was here I had a jacket potato piled high with baked beans—it was delicious. Soup first? No? Then I'll order.'

He wandered over to the bar, gave his order, stopped to exchange a few cheerful comments with the men there and then wandered back again.

'Drink your brandy and then start at the beginning. Never mind if it's all a bit muddled; the thing is to get it off your chest so that you can think clearly about what you want to do next.'

She said tartly, 'You sound like an agony aunt in a women's magazine...'

'God forbid, but I do have five sisters. I grew up steeped, as it were, in the female sex. In a position to offer humble advice if asked for it.'

She said quickly, 'That was a horrid thing I said about being an agony aunt. I'm sorry. I'm sure you must be a very nice brother.'

'Thank you. And now, having established my suitability as confidant, tell me what has happened to bring about this unfortunate situation.'

The brandy had been a great help. She related the whole sorry business in a voice which only wobbled occasionally and while she talked she ate the potato and beans with an appetite she hadn't realised she had.

The doctor said nothing at all, not even when she stopped to subdue a particularly persistent wobble. It wasn't until they had finished and a pot of tea and cups and saucers had been set before them that he observed, 'There is a possibility that Beamish will come hotfoot after you, beg your forgiveness and scrap his plans. Have you considered that he might have had the best intentions?'

Leonora gave him a cold look. 'He said one of the reasons for marrying me was so that he could get his hands on the house and land.' She drew a furious breath, looking quite beautiful despite the slightly reddened nose.

'I'm not sure any more if he ever loved me. How can I be?'

The doctor sighed gently. It would be tragic if young

Beamish could persuade her into thinking that the whole thing had been nothing but a misunderstanding—something he would be quite capable of doing—and it would be easy if he himself dropped sufficient hints as to the man's character to put her on her guard, but he had no right to interfere. In any case, he reminded himself, Leonora was no shy young girl; she must decide for herself what she wanted from life.

'I think that perhaps you will know that when you see him again.' At her look of doubt he added, 'Oh, you will, you know. You must follow your heart, Leonora.'

Back in the car, speeding along the motorway once more, sitting in a friendly silence, Leonora thought about the doctor's advice. It had been sound, unbiased and quite impersonal. She would take it, only she wished that he had been a little more sympathetic. There was no reason why he should be, she reminded herself; he had given her advice just as, doubtless, he gave advice to such of his patients who asked for it.

The lights were still on at the house when he drew up before it. He got out to open her door and said, 'I'll come in with you,' and she gave him a grateful look.

'I've my key,' she told him, and they went in together just as Nanny came into the hall from the kitchen end.

'Well, I must say that seeing you so sudden is a bit of a shock. You didn't phone.' She looked at the doctor as she spoke.

'Hello, Nanny,' said Leonora. 'I'm sorry if we made you jump. Dr Galbraith gave me a lift home. Are Mother and Father in the drawing room?'

Nanny nodded. 'You could do with a cup of coffee, the pair of you. I'll bring it presently.'

Lady Crosby was doing a jigsaw puzzle and Sir William was reading. It was Wilkins who came to meet them as they went in, delighted to see them.

'Leonora—we didn't expect you—you haven't phoned.' Her mother looked surprised. 'And Dr Galbraith.' She frowned. 'Tony isn't with you?' She glanced at her husband. 'Your father and I thought he might come back with you—you must have seen him.'

Her father had put down his book. 'Something's wrong?' he asked.

'I went to London to see Tony about something— something I had been told about him. We—that is, I decided that I don't want to marry him so we're not engaged any more.'

'There's more to it than that,' Sir William said sharply.

'Yes, but it can wait until tomorrow morning, Father. I had the chance to come back with Dr Galbraith. He most kindly gave me a lift.'

'Much obliged to you,' said her father. 'Come and sit down; I'm sure Nanny will have made us coffee.' He turned his head. 'Leonora, run and tell Nanny to bring it as soon as it's ready.'

When she had gone, relieved to be away from her mother's faint air of disapproval, he asked, 'All right, is she? More to it than she has said—'

'Yes, a good deal more, Sir William, but I am sure that Leonora will explain everything later. She has had a very trying time and she is tired.'

Sir William nodded. 'Then we won't pester her this evening. Good of you to bring her back. You know what happened, of course?'

The doctor looked grim. 'Yes, indeed I do.'

Leonora came in with the coffee-tray then, and

after ten minutes or so of desultory talk the doctor got up to go.

Leonora went with him to the door. 'Thank you again,' she said, and offered a hand. 'And thank you for listening. You were quite right—it's much easier to think sensibly now I've talked about it. You didn't mind?'

He was still holding her hand. 'No, Leonora, I didn't mind. I hope that if you should need a shoulder to cry on at any time you'll use mine.'

He gave her a brotherly thump on the shoulder and went out to his car and drove away.

Once she was back in the drawing room her mother said with a little *moue* of discontent, 'Your father says we are to wait until tomorrow before you tell us exactly what has happened to bring you rushing back like this. You say you are no longer engaged to Tony… You must have a very good reason—'

Sir William said sharply, 'That is enough, my dear; Leonora is tired; no doubt she has had a long day with things to worry her. She should go to bed and in the morning, if she wishes, she will tell us what happened.'

So Leonora went thankfully to bed and rather to her surprise went to sleep at once, to wake the next morning feeling that she was able to cope with the situation and determined that if Tony should want to see her she would refuse.

That would be the only way, she reflected as she dressed and went downstairs to the kitchen, for if they were to meet again she wasn't sure if she could withstand his charm, despite knowing now that he had never really loved her-not with the kind of love she wanted. He had thought of her as someone who went with the house and the land, someone he would possibly treat with casual affection, load with jewellery and dress in lovely clothes and who would be expected to agree to all his plans.

'Well, I won't,' said Leonora, putting on the kettle, and she wished Nanny a good morning. She opened the door for Wilkins and stood taking great breaths of the early-morning air.

'And what's all this I hear from your ma?' asked Nanny.

Leonora fetched a teapot and spooned in the tea. 'I haven't explained yet,' she said, 'and I'll tell you all about it, Nanny, but first I have to tell Father and Mother.'

Which, over the breakfast table, proved a difficult task. Her father stared with disbelief.

'This house? My land? The park? I cannot believe it, Leonora…'

'No, I know it's difficult, Father, but it's true. Tony had it all planned—you and Mother were to be moved to a smaller house—'

'I could not possibly live in a small house,' observed her mother, 'and what about the Sheraton chairs and the William and Mary display cabinet? And the other furniture—it would never fit into a small house. I think it was most inconsiderate of him to even suggest such a thing. Why were we not told?'

Sir William asked, 'These men staying in the village—you say that Tony sent them? Leonora, I find this very difficult to believe.'

'So did I, Father, but it's true. I told Tony that he was to recall the men and that there was no question of you selling the house and the land.'

'Quite right too, my dear.' Sir William, not the most sensitive of men, all the same added, 'I hope this hasn't upset you too much, Leonora.'

'I expect I'm as upset as any woman who expects to get married and then finds that she won't after all,' said Leonora.

Lady Crosby wiped away a tear. 'And I was planning the wedding. What will everyone think…?'

'I don't care what they think,' said Leonora with a snap, and took herself off to the kitchen before she lost her cool and burst into tears.

It was all right to cry against Nanny's elderly shoulder, pouring out her rage and disappointment and unhappiness in a jumble of words. She felt better then and sat down at the table with Wilkins pressed against her and drank the tea Nanny had made.

'He'll come after you,' said Nanny. 'If he wants the house and the land he'll not give them up without another try. And if you truly love him, dearie, it won't matter what he's done; you'll forgive him and he'll get his way. Even Sir William would give in eventually once you were wed and Tony could show him a good reason for parting with the house and giving it to you—and to him, of course.'

'I won't listen to him; I never want to see him again…'

'I dare say you'll have to, Miss Leonora; you can't run away if he comes here. Besides, you may have got over your rage by then and discovered that you love him enough to want to have him back.'

Leonora drank her tea. 'Nanny, have you ever been in love?'

'Bless the girl, of course I have. He was a deep-sea

fisherman—drowned, he was, years ago now. But we were in love and we loved each other. Being in love is one thing—it doesn't always last, but loving does.'

'Nanny, I didn't know. I'm so sorry. You never wanted to marry after that?'

'What for? I never met a man to touch my Ned.'

Nanny got to her feet. 'I'm going up to make the beds, if you'll tidy the drawing room. You'll be going to the village presently?'

'Yes, we want one or two things, don't we? I'm not sure what happens next.'

'Sir William will know what to do.'

Leonora hoovered and dusted and listened to her mother's gentle complaining. 'Of course,' she said, 'Tony is sure to come here and want to see you and no doubt explain everything.' Lady Crosby blew her nose daintily and glanced at Leonora. 'After all, he does love you.' She frowned at Leonora's wooden expression. 'Well, he does, doesn't he?'

'I think,' said Leonora carefully, 'that he loves this house and the land, and because he can only get them if I make up the package, as it were, he may be a little in love with me.'

'But you love him, darling?'

Leonora dusted a fragile porcelain figurine with great care. 'I'm not sure, Mother.'

Mrs Pike's shop was empty when Leonora went in, the faithful Wilkins at her heels. She gave her order and nibbled at the biscuit she was offered—a new line in slimming rusks—while Mrs Pike collected tea, sugar, rice and corned beef.

'They've gone,' she said, leaning over the counter and speaking in a loud whisper just as though they were surrounded by eavesdroppers. 'Them men at the Blue Man. Went first thing this morning. Had a phone call from London last night. Pike happened to be in the bar and couldn't help but hear. Very surprised they were too.'

Leonora finished the rusk. 'I'm not surprised; I saw Mr Beamish yesterday and—the matter has been settled.'

She took off a glove to tuck her hair back and Mrs Pike said sharply, 'Your ring, Miss Crosby—lost it, have you?'

Leonora went pink. 'No—no, Mr Beamish and I are not to be married after all.'

Mrs Pike wordlessly handed her another biscuit. 'Well, I never…and it were a whopping great diamond.'

'Yes, it was, wasn't it?' Leonora found to her surprise that she didn't mind not having it. On second thoughts she wasn't even sure that she liked diamonds.

She went back home presently and found her father in his study.

'They've gone, the two men.' She told him what Mrs Pike had said and then said, 'Father, do you suppose that Tony will want to see me or you and explain?'

'Yes, I do, my dear. You do not need to see him on your own unless you want to. I shall certainly want an explanation and an apology.'

There was no sign of Tony, however. No letter, no telephone call. After several days, Leonora stopped listening for the phone and looking through the post each morning, nor did she catch her breath each time a car went past the gates. She had phoned Aunt Marion to thank her for her visit and that lady had informed her that Tony had made no attempt to get in touch with her. 'Although why he should wish to do so I'm sure I don't know.'

The doctor, kept up to date with village gossip by Cricket, whose benevolent and discreet manner had quite won over the hearts and the confidences of the village ladies, knew better. Tony Beamish was no fool; he would bide his time, wait until Leonora had had the time to realise that her future was no longer the one she had been looking forward to. He was a conceited man and very sure of himself; he would bank on Leonora missing him and everything he stood for and at the right moment he would turn up to beg forgiveness and convince her that everything would be changed. If she loved him he would eventually get what he wanted.

He could do nothing about it, of course. Leonora wasn't some young, empty-headed girl; she could think for herself. All he could do was listen if she needed to talk.

It was a pity that he saw no sign of her for several days. He had a number of patients living on outlying farms and the surgery at that time of year was full with nasty chests, flu and a mild outbreak of chickenpox amongst the small fry. He drove to Bath to see Ben but, passing the gates to her home, he could see no sign of anyone.

Which was a shame, for Leonora needed to talk to someone. Her parents, outraged at Tony's behaviour, didn't wish to discuss the matter, and Nanny, friend and confidante though she was, had declared that she was in no position to give advice.

Tony arrived on Monday, ten days after Leonora had seen him in London. He drove up to the house, got out and looked it over before ringing the bell. Despite its shabby appearance, it was a lovely old place and he had no intention of giving it up lightly.

When Leonora opened the door he said eagerly, 'Hello, darling. Have you calmed down enough for us to have a talk? You didn't mean it, you know.' He smiled with charm. 'I've brought the ring with me...'

Leonora stood in the doorway, blocking his path.

'I've calmed down and I meant it,' she said, 'so you can go away again.'

He put a hand on her arm. 'You don't mean that, Leonora. Think of all the marvellous things you will miss—I'll be good to you—'

'No, you won't,' said Leonora. 'I don't want anything more to do with you, and if Father hears any more about your plans he intends to get our solicitor to deal with it.'

Tony laughed. 'I say—look here, old girl, you don't mean that. You can't have thought about it—the advantages...'

'To you, yes. Have you come to see Father?'

'No, no. At least, I thought if I saw you first then we might see him together and explain.'

'Explain what? That you deceived him as well as me? Go away, Tony.'

'I'm not going until we've had a talk, until I've been given the chance to explain.'

Leonora, not the nervous type, nevertheless didn't like the look on his face, and he had put his foot in the door so that shutting it in his face was no longer possible. I need help, she thought.

She got it. Dr Galbraith, on his way back from Bath, glanced as he always did at the house as he passed. He slowed, reversed and slid silently up the drive to the door. His good morning was uttered in a genial voice.

'As I was passing I thought I might just take a look at your father.'

He had, without apparent effort, got between Leonora and Tony and turned to smile at him now. 'Rather unexpected, isn't it?' he wanted to know cheerfully. 'You're not very popular around here, you know.' He shook his head in a disapproving fashion. 'You have got yourself a very bad name in the village.' He looked at Leonora. 'Is he bothering you, Leonora?'

At her eloquent look he added, 'If you've come to make your peace with Sir William I strongly advise against it. The best thing you can do, my dear chap, is to go back to wherever you came from and stay there!'

Tony found his voice. 'What business is it of yours? This is a private matter between Leonora and myself.'

The doctor shook his head. 'You're mistaken, Beamish; there's nothing private about it. The Crosbys have been here for a couple of hundred years, they're part of the village life, and, believe me, you haven't a single friend in Pont Magna.'

He smiled pleasantly but his eyes were blue ice and Tony was the first to look away. 'Don't think I am going to be intimidated by threats—' he began.

'Threats? No one is threatening you, Beamish—a friendly warning, perhaps.'

'There is no point in staying here,' said Tony. 'I shall come back when there is a chance to talk to you privately, darling.'

'Don't you "darling" me,' said Leonora frostily. 'I don't want to see you again and that is the last time I'll say it.'

'But you love me...' Tony infused a cajoling note into his voice.

'No, I don't. I thought I did, but I don't.'

A remark which the doctor found most satisfactory. Leonora was too good for that fellow, he reflected; some decent chap would come along and marry her sooner or later.

He watched Beamish go to his car and get in and drive away and then said briskly, 'Well, now that that's sorted out, shall I see your father?'

She had expected him to say something soothing, express satisfaction at the way she had dealt with Tony. She turned on her heel and led the way indoors, feeling hurt.

'I'm sure he'll be pleased to see you, Doctor,' she observed in a cool voice. 'I'll bring coffee; Father usually has a cup about now.'

She put her head round the study door. 'Father, here's Dr Galbraith to see you.'

Her father lowered *The Times*. 'Ask him to come in. I heard someone—I was wondering who it was.'

She stood aside to let the doctor pass then went into the kitchen and thumped cups and saucers down on a tray, knocked over the sugar bowl and used what Nanny called 'unsuitable language'.

'What's upset you, Miss Leonora?' asked her old friend. 'Who was that at the door? Leaving someone at the door is bad manners.'

'It was Tony Beamish and he did upset me and I had no intention of letting him come into the house,' said Leonora pettishly. 'Dr Galbraith's here; I'm taking coffee to the study. Where's Mother?'

'Up in her room, going through her wardrobe. A good thing too.'

Leonora found biscuits and put them on a plate and Nanny asked, 'That Tony of yours…?'

'He's not mine.'

'Good thing too. Making trouble, is he?'

'No—well, he wanted me to be engaged again.' She poured the coffee. 'Actually, he got a bit—well, awkward, but Dr Galbraith was passing and stopped.'

Nanny nodded in a satisfied way. 'And sent him right about.'

'Well, yes, but quite nicely, if you see what I mean.'

'Yes, I see,' said Nanny. 'Will you take a cup of coffee up to your mother when you come back?'

The two men were sitting chatting comfortably. The doctor got up and took the tray from Leonora as she went in but she didn't look at him as she went away again.

Her mother, occupied with her clothes, greeted her absent-mindedly.

'I do need new clothes,' she said plaintively. 'Did I hear someone talking in the hall?'

'Dr Galbraith is with Father. He called in as he was passing.'

'I'll come down and see him—perhaps he can give me something; I feel I need a change—a little holiday, perhaps, a few days in town with your aunt Marion. Breaking off your engagement to Tony has been a great disappointment to me, Leonora.'

'It was rather a disappointment to me, Mother.'

'Yes, dear, of course, and I suppose he has behaved very badly. Never mind, there are plenty more fish in the sea.'

'Perhaps I'm not a very good angler,' said Leonora, and went back to the kitchen.

She was still there, peeling potatoes with unnecessary ferocity, when the doctor came in.

'There you are. I've been talking to your mother; she
feels rather under the weather, she tells me. I've written a prescription for her; may I leave it with you, Leonora?' He watched her face. 'Your father is very well.
How about you?'

'I never need the doctor,' said Leonora, and began
on another potato.

He smiled. 'Don't tempt fate,' he said, and went away
as quietly as he had come.

CHAPTER SIX

AT LUNCH LADY Crosby said happily, 'Dr Galbraith has invited us to dine—rather short notice but he has friends coming down from London and he thought we might like to meet them. Next Saturday.'

Leonora remembered how she had sniffed and sobbed and made a fool of herself with the doctor. She said now, 'I'll have to refuse, Mother. I promised weeks ago that I'd babysit for Maggie—she and Gordon are going up to town to celebrate their anniversary. I said I'd spend the night.'

'For heaven's sake!' Her mother sounded impatient. 'They have a nursemaid, haven't they?'

'Yes, but she is very young and quite untrained. Did you accept for me as well as you and Father?'

'Yes, of course I did. Such a nice man, well connected too, and wealthy, I hear.'

'I'll write him a note,' said Leonora.

Which she did—a formal message of regret, couched in polite terms, which he read with some amusement and interest over his breakfast.

'Now why has she done that?' he enquired of the faithful Tod. 'Even if she had to refuse she could have phoned me or even called in at the surgery. We are, I suspect, to be Dr Galbraith and Miss Leonora Crosby again. A strange girl!'

He forgot about her then.

However, Leonora, who should by rights have been eating her heart out for the treacherous Tony, found herself thinking about the doctor. She liked him; he would be a splendid friend and she enjoyed his company and his matter-of-fact way of accepting events without fuss. But there was this vexed question of this young lady for whom he had a strong affection and, worse than that, her mother was making no secret of the fact that she would like it if Leonora and Dr Galbraith were to see more of each other. She would have to avoid him.

Luckily there would be a lot to do organising the fête, traditionally held in the park every year. Everyone had a hand in it, the practical making marmalade, cakes and sweets, embroidering small useless cushions and nightdress cases, knitting baby jackets, and the artistic painting local scenes.

Leonora, who drew and painted rather nicely, decided to shut herself in one of the attics and set to work. When she wasn't doing that she could go along to the Dowlings' and help with the writing of price tickets.

She took herself off to Maggie and Gordon's little house at the end of the village on Saturday afternoon and presently waved them goodbye as they drove off.

The house was charming, comfortably furnished and untidy. Leonora took her overnight bag up to the little guest room, had a chat with Sadie, the little nursery maid, and went about the business of making up feeds for three-month-old Tom. He was a placid baby, sleeping and feeding in a manner which would have delighted any writer of a childcare textbook.

The afternoon went by quickly, with a brisk walk in his pram, and feeding and bathing while Sadie got their tea and supper. And since Tom took his feed like a lamb at ten o'clock Leonora and Sadie went to bed and slept peacefully until the early morning.

It was a bright, chilly morning, and Leonora, sitting by the window in the little nursery, giving Tom his bottle, was content. It would be delightful to have a baby of her own, she reflected, small and cuddly like Tom—several babies in fact. If she had married Tony… She wondered then if he would have liked children. Certainly he wouldn't have had much time for them.

'I should like a husband,' she told Tom, 'who would get up in the night if the baby cried and who'd bring me a cup of tea without being asked and wouldn't mind babies dribbling onto his shoulder. He'd play cricket with the little boys and comfort the little girls when they cried…'

She tickled Tom under his chin to encourage him to finish his bottle. 'You don't have to listen to my nonsense,' she assured him. 'We'll go for a walk and blow away the cobwebs.'

She had enjoyed her day, she reflected as she walked home after Maggie and Gordon had returned. Sadie had had tea ready for them and she had sat listening to their account of their day, before bidding Tom a reluctant goodbye.

'He was so good,' she assured her friend. 'I'll babysit any time that you want me to.'

Her mother and father were in the drawing room, he behind the Sunday papers and her mother sitting at a small table with a half-finished jigsaw puzzle.

'Enjoyed yourself?' asked her father, glancing up.

She bent to kiss his cheek. 'Yes, thank you, Father. Little Tom is a darling baby and so good.'

Her mother turned away impatiently from the puzzle. 'Darling, such a pity you couldn't come with us yesterday. I must say Dr Galbraith has a lovely house; I quite envy him some of his furniture—handed down in the family, I should think. There is a bow-fronted cabinet in the drawing room... And that man of his—Cricket—the kind of servant one dreams of and never finds! Dinner was excellent and these friends of his very pleasant. Ackroyd is the name—and funnily enough Mr Ackroyd knew your father's brother-in-law, Aunt Marion's husband, you know—when he was alive. She was quite nice too—rather quiet, but friendly enough. A good deal older than Dr Galbraith but I believe their daughter and he are on good terms. He should marry, of course.'

'I dare say he will, when he wants to,' said Leonora. 'I'm glad you enjoyed the evening.'

She wandered off to the kitchen and found Nanny cutting up vegetables for soup. Into her willing ears Leonora poured every small detail of little Tom's day. 'He's such a darling baby, Nanny, and so good.'

She ate a carrot and went out into the garden, having called Wilkins, and then beyond into the park, feeling restless. She had, she supposed, got used to the idea of marrying Tony in the not too distant future—a future she had taken for granted. Now the future stretched ahead of her empty, and just for the moment there seemed little purpose in it. She had been happily filling in time, helping to organise various village functions, accompanying her parents to friends' houses for dinner, summer picnics and winter bridge afternoons, but now these seemed a waste of time.

What else could she do? For a few years after she had left school she had travelled a little, visited friends, spent a week or two with Aunt Marion going to theatres, dancing, shopping. Since her father had lost his money, though, none of these things had been possible and she'd found herself more and more involved in coping with the running of the house since Nanny was the only other person to do that.

She couldn't blame her mother, who had never done the household chores and had very little idea of what they involved anyway. It looked as though she was destined to stay at home, getting longer and longer in the tooth, making do with too little money, doing the odd repairs, and painting in an amateurish way.

She jumped across the little stream which ran along the boundary of the park and wandered into the woods beyond while Wilkins padded to and fro. When he stood still and began to bark she paused too.

'What's up, Wilkins? Rabbits?'

It was very quiet under the trees but presently she heard footsteps—unhurried and deliberate—and Wilkins raced back the way they had come to meet them. Leonora stayed where she was; it was someone the dog knew and liked and for a moment she wondered if it was Tony but then dismissed the thought; Wilkins and Tony had never been more than guarded in their approach to each other.

Perhaps it was Dr Galbraith...

It was. He came towards her, still unhurried, Wilkins jumping up on his elderly legs and running in circles around him. His, 'Hello, Leonora,' was casual and friendly. 'I should have brought Tod with me...

'Nanny told me that you might be here.' He had reached her by now and strolled along beside her. 'There is something about which I wish to talk.'

'What?' asked Leonora baldly.

'Mrs Crisp has broken her arm. Would you consider taking over from her from the time being, a few weeks? Morning surgery is half past eight until eleven o'clock or thereabouts. Evening surgery five o'clock until seven—sometimes later. No surgery on Saturday evenings or Sunday.'

Leonora had listened with her mouth open. 'I can't type,' she managed. 'I don't know anything...'

'You know everyone in the village and for miles around. You know where people live, the jobs they have. You can answer the phone intelligently and not fly into hysterics if something crops up. It's an easy job for you. If I have to get someone from an agency they won't know their way around or where the patients live.'

Leonora closed her mouth at last. 'But I can't. I mean, I do most of the housekeeping at home and the shopping—and odd jobs around the place.'

'You would be paid like anyone else who works for a living. Surely there is someone in the village who could go to the house each day and give Nanny a hand?'

When she hesitated he added, 'You would be working—let me see—between twenty and thirty hours a week. There's a standard rate of pay.' He mentioned a sum which caused her mouth to drop open again.

'All that?' asked Leonora. She paused just long enough to do some most satisfying mental arithmetic. 'If you think I'll do I'll come and work for you.'

'Good. Now that's settled, how about coming back with me and I'll explain just what you have to do?'

'Well, yes, all right. I'd better take Wilkins back home first and tell Mother.'

He walked back with her, saying little, not mentioning the job again until they were in the house once more. As they went in through the garden door he asked, 'Do you want me to come with you?'

She considered this. 'Well, it might be a good idea.' She glanced at him. 'If you see what I mean?'

He nodded gravely. That the daughter of the house should have a job was something Lady Crosby wouldn't allow, but as a favour to the local doctor, an emergency, as it were—that would be a different matter.

So it proved to be. Leonora could not help but admire the way in which the doctor convinced her mother that working for him at the surgery wasn't so much a job as a vital service to the community and that Leonora, being known in the village, was exactly the right person to undertake it.

'Well, I do see that as a member of the family Leonora has a certain duty. I mean, we have lived here for very many years, as you must know. I am sure it is a worthwhile undertaking since Mrs Crisp is unable to work for you.'

Lady Crosby frowned suddenly. 'There is one drawback—Leonora has undertaken the running of this house. I am rather delicate myself, Dr Galbraith; my poor health does not allow me to exert myself.'

She sighed. 'Such a pity, but I do not see how we are to manage if Leonora is away for most of the day.'

'Perhaps that is a problem which can be solved. Leonora will, of course, receive a salary. There must be someone in the village who would come here and work with Nanny while Leonora is away.'

Lady Crosby brightened. 'Well, yes. You say she will receive a salary?' She turned to look at the silent Leonora. 'That will be nice, my dear. I'm sure if you can find someone suitable to replace you for the time being neither your father nor I will have any objection to you helping the doctor.'

She smiled at him. 'You will stay to dinner? We dine late on Sundays.'

He refused with easy good manners and added, 'Perhaps I might take Leonora with me for an hour or so? I can give her some idea of her duties and we might share supper at the same time. The sooner she is able to start work, the better for me and my patients.'

'Yes, yes, of course. I can quite see that the matter is an urgent one. Leonora, will you go to your father—he is in his study—and tell him what we have arranged?' She turned back to the doctor. 'Perhaps while she is doing that you will advise me about this nasty little pain I get in my chest... My heart, you know...'

'I can hardly advise without a full examination; I suggest that you come down to the surgery one afternoon. I'm usually free then and you can tell me what is troubling you.' He added with brisk reassurance, 'You look extremely well.'

'Ah, but my looks have never pitied me,' said Lady Crosby in a resigned voice, 'and I don't complain.'

Leonora came back then, promised to be back in an hour or two and went out to the car with the doctor.

The drive to the surgery was so short that there was no need to talk and once they were there he set about explaining her work to her in a businesslike way which precluded any light-hearted chit-chat. She listened cheerfully, poked her nose into cupboards and drawers and asked intelligent questions.

'Like to start in the morning?' he wanted to know.

'Tomorrow? Well, why not? But you won't get too annoyed if I do everything wrong?'

'No, no.' He was laughing at her. 'I'm quite sure you will be able to cope well enough, and Mrs Crisp has promised that she will pop in just in case you need to know more about things. Half past eight, then?'

'All right. I'll ask Nanny if she knows of anyone who will come up to the house and help her. I could ask Mrs Pike too...'

'Good, that's settled. Now let us go and have our supper.'

Leonora said thoughtfully, 'There's no need, you know. I mean, you've explained everything to me here...'

He swept her out to the car. 'There's bound to be something I've forgotten,' he told her. 'I'll probably think of it during supper. There will be no time in the morning.'

A sensible observation to which she agreed. With pleasure and relief. She was hungry.

Cricket, accompanied by a boisterous Tod, admitted them, allowing his usual gloomy expression to be lightened with a smile at the sight of Leonora.

'Miss Crosby is having supper with me, Cricket,' said Dr Galbraith, and he took Leonora's jacket and ushered her across the hall and into the drawing room.

'Fifteen minutes, sir,' said Cricket, and melted away to the kitchen, where he set about adding one or two extra items to the supper menu. He approved of Miss Crosby; it was a pity he hadn't been given more notice, for she was worthy of his culinary skill. He had already made baked pears, standing ready in their dish with the flavoured syrup poured over them, but he decided now to save them for tomorrow and prepare something else... There was also time to prepare a dish of anchoïades. With commendable speed he assembled anchovies, garlic, olive oil and lemon juice, sliced bread and black pepper. Cricket fetched his pestle and mortar and set to work.

In the drawing room the doctor invited Leonora to sit down, opened the door to allow Tod to join them from the garden and offered her a drink. Then he began a rambling conversation about nothing much. Apparently her job wasn't to be discussed for the moment. Leonora sipped dry sherry and allowed herself to enjoy the moment. Since she was hungry, she allowed her thoughts to dwell on supper.

She was not to be disappointed. Presently, sated at the elegantly laid table, she enjoyed the anchovies followed by quiche Lorraine, embellished by a potato salad, green peas and mushrooms tossed in garlic and cream. She ate everything, rather surprised by the lavishness of what she had supposed would be a simple meal.

Dr Galbraith was surprised too, amused that Cricket had found the time to add to what would have been a well-cooked meal but without fancy trimmings. He wondered what they would be invited to eat for pudding and hid a smile when Cricket served them with ice cream, tastefully decorated with burnt almonds, glacé cherries and chocolate shavings, the whole topped with whipped cream—a dessert Cricket was well aware that the doctor would have spurned. As it was, he ate his portion with evident enjoyment, offered Leonora a second glass of wine and suggested that they should return to the drawing room.

302 THE DAUGHTER OF THE MANOR

'I should really go home,' said Leonora, not wishing to go.

'I'll drive you back presently, but you must have some coffee first. Cricket makes very good coffee.'

'There must be something else I should know,' suggested Leonora. Supper had been delicious and so had the wine. The lovely room was restful and Dr Galbraith was a soothing companion.

The doctor, sitting in his chair on the other side of the fireplace, with Tod pressed against his knee, replied easily, 'Oh, I'm sure you have got a good grasp of what has to be done. You know most of the patients, I would suppose, which should make things easy for you.'

He drove her home soon after and bade her a cheerful goodnight, refusing her offer to come in to see her parents, getting back into his car with a friendly wave and driving away.

Her mother and father were in the drawing room and Leonora couldn't help but contrast its shabbiness with the well cared for comfort of Buntings. Perhaps, she reflected, she could find another job when she was no longer needed at the surgery and save enough money to have something done to the house. That it needed thousands of pounds spent on it she chose to ignore; just to do the urgent repairs and paint over the worst bits would at least stave off the ravages of time.

As she went in her mother said, 'Ah, there you are, dear. Everything is settled, I hope? Your father agrees with me that you did quite rightly to offer to help Dr Galbraith; it behoves us all to give help when it is asked for.'

'Yes, Mother,' said Leonora, and caught her father's eye. Lady Crosby was quite sincere but they both knew that she was the last person anyone would ask for help. Indeed, she was more than likely the one who needed it.

She arrived in good time at the surgery in the morning after a quick breakfast in the kitchen with Nanny, to find the doctor's car outside and, when she went in, the waiting room almost full.

There was no sign of the doctor, though. She wished everyone a good morning, took off her jacket and set to work getting out patients' notes. She hadn't quite finished when the surgery bell pinged and she put her head round the door to answer it.

'I'm nearly ready,' she assured him. 'Shall I give you those I have?'

He said placidly, 'Good morning, Leonora. Yes, please do. Let me have the others later. There is no hurry. I spend about seven minutes with each patient, sometimes more.'

He held out his hand for the notes. 'Who is first? Mrs Dodge? Send her in, will you?'

Leonora withdrew her head and then poked it back again. 'I forgot to say good morning,' she said, and closed the door.

Once she got over her initial uncertainty, she began to enjoy herself. She knew everyone there, which made things easy, for they were eager to point out everything she didn't do correctly.

Mrs Crisp always put the patients' notes on the little shelf by the desk when they had been seen by the doctor, old Mr Trubshaw told her, and when a small girl became restless several voices advised her that the WC was down the passage, and as the last patient went in she paused to tell her to put the kettle on. 'For the doctor's coffee,' she pointed out kindly.

With the waiting room empty, Leonora found mugs and coffee and while the kettle boiled began to tidy the place.

She felt pleased with herself; she hadn't done so badly. True, there had been one or two hitches but she hoped that the doctor hadn't noticed them. As the surgery door opened she turned off the gas and looked round at him, hopefully expecting a few words of praise.

She was to be disappointed. He walked to the door with barely a glance in her direction. 'I may be delayed. Could you ring Mrs Crisp and ask her if she'll come here and take any calls? I'll do my best to get back by evening surgery.'

He gave her a brisk nod and closed the door behind him, so that she had no chance to say a word.

'Oh, well,' said Leonora, feeling deflated. 'Perhaps he's late on his rounds.' She made herself a cup of coffee and then phoned Mrs Crisp.

Mrs Crisp wasn't home. She had gone to Bath, her husband said, and probably wouldn't be back until the end of the week. Was there anything he could do?

Leonora said no, thank you and not to bother Mrs Crisp when she got back, and sat down to think what she should do. Obviously Dr Galbraith expected someone to be handy to take any calls or messages and he wasn't to know that Mrs Crisp, who had volunteered to come in in the afternoons, wasn't available.

'I can't leave here,' said Leonora, addressing the doctor's empty chair, and she picked up the phone again. Nanny answered it, which was a good thing for she only needed the barest explanation. 'I'll tell your ma. You've nothing to eat there?'

'No, but there's plenty of tea and coffee and a little milk.'

'Phone over to Mrs Pike and get her to make you a sandwich; the boy will bring it over for you.'

When Leonora said there was no need, Nanny replied, 'You do as I say, Miss Leonora. Otherwise you'll be flat on your back with hunger with the waiting room full of patients this evening.'

As usual, Nanny was right; as lunchtime approached Leonora's insides rumbled a reminder. She phoned Mrs Pike and ten minutes later sank her splendid teeth into the sandwiches that young Pike had brought over for her. She devoured the lot, made a pot of tea and planned her afternoon. If she had to sit there for several hours yet she might as well improve her mind and she had seen the books on the shelf in the surgery.

There had been several phone calls, none of them urgent, from patients wanting to make appointments, and it struck her suddenly that if the doctor was wanted urgently she had no idea where to find him.

'He should have told me,' said Leonora, talking to herself since there was no one else to talk to, and she went to see if there was a phone number she could ring. There was, tucked into the blotter on his desk, where, she supposed, if she had been trained for the job, she would have looked the moment he went out of the door. She was studying it when the phone rang.

Shirley Bates—Leonora recognised the voice at once. A cheerfully sluttish young woman living in one of the houses behind the main street. She had a brood of small children, a careless, easygoing husband and was known for her laziness.

'It's Miss Leonora, isn't it? My Cecil's that poorly.

Nasty cough and 'e's covered in pimples. Measles or the like. The others 'ave 'ad it, but 'e didn't. 'E's very 'ot, won't eat or drink.'

'The doctor's out,' said Leonora, 'but I'll ask him to call and see Cecil as soon as he can. Could you put him to bed and give him plenty to drink and keep him warm?'

''E's in the kitchen watching telly, but I'll get 'im up to bed as soon as I've seen to the baby.' She sounded quite cheerful. 'Bye.'

Leonora wrote it all down and wondered if Cecil was someone the doctor would think urgent enough to be told about. Mrs Bates's children were a remarkably healthy brood despite their diet of potato crisps and fish and chips; on the other hand, Cecil, if she remembered rightly, was only five years old and measles could turn nasty if neglected.

She was weighing the pros and cons when the door opened and an old lady came in. Leonora knew her too. Old Mrs Squires, seventy-odd, widowed, and what her neighbours charitably called 'difficult'. She was comfortably off and lived alone in a small house in the main street and, having nothing better to do with her days, imagined herself to be suffering from various illnesses. She was also the local purveyor of gossip and Leonora greeted her warily.

'Mrs Squires—I'm afraid the doctor isn't here. Surgery is at five o'clock.'

'Well, of course I know that.' Mrs Squires seated herself in the waiting room. 'But I am feeling ill; he must be fetched here to see me. It's his duty.'

'He is out on a case,' said Leonora. 'I should go home and rest and come back at five o'clock.'

Mrs Squires shot her a cross look. 'I shall complain about your treatment, Miss Crosby—the Patient's Charter, you know.'

'But I haven't treated you, Mrs Squires. I really should go home if I were you. I'll see that you are first in at five o'clock.'

'Very well.' But the old lady didn't budge. 'You're not wearing your ring. I did hear…well, never mind that. Broken it off, have you? Such a charming man too. Let's hope you get another chance.'

'Oh, I expect I shall,' said Leonora cheerfully, hiding her doubts and unhappiness. 'Now if you don't mind I must ask you to go. I have to turn out this room before the evening surgery.'

Mrs Squires tittered. 'Fancy you dusting and sweeping. The young lady from the house. I wonder what that Mr Beamish of yours would say to that?'

Leonora held her tongue and ignored a desire to shake Mrs Squires until her false teeth rattled in her head. Instead, she held the door open and smiled.

Mrs Squires, despite her rudeness a little in awe of the Crosby family, left, tottering dramatically on the step and hoping *sotto voce* that Leonora wouldn't regret her unkindness when she, a poor widow, was found dead in her bed.

Leonora shut the door and locked it and the phone rang.

It was Mrs Bates again. 'My Cecil, 'e's been sick all over the carpet; 'e's real poorly and 'e don't talk much. Gone all pale and limp.'

'I'll try and get the doctor at once, Shirley. Is Cecil in his bed?'

''E didn't want ter go. 'E's still in the kitchen.'

'Keep him warm and get him to drink a little. I'm sure the doctor won't be long. I'll phone him now.'

Leonora dialled the number on the desk and when someone answered she said with relief, 'Oh, it's you, Mr Willis. Is Dr Galbraith there? May I speak to him? It's urgent.'

'I'll fetch him, Miss Leonora. He's on the point of leaving.'

'Well?' said the doctor in her ear.

'I'm glad I caught you,' said Leonora, relief making her voice sharp. 'Mrs Bates—the council houses—you know? Her Cecil's ill.'

She recited his symptoms in a voice which she strove to keep level. 'Will you go there? Thank heavens you aren't miles away...'

'Phone Mrs Bates and tell her I'm on my way. Why are you still at the surgery?'

'Because Mrs Crisp is in Bath, isn't she? Gone to see her mother.'

All she had in reply was a grunt before he hung up.

'Miserable man,' said Leonora, and put the kettle on and rang Mrs Bates once more. She would have a cup of tea; heaven knew, she deserved it after such a trying day. In an hour it would be surgery again and by the time she had tidied the place she would be just in time for dinner at home.

All the same, she reflected, putting a teabag in the pot, the day had gone quickly and she had had no time to think. A week or two like this, she thought ruefully, and Tony would seem like a dream—rather a bad one. But, good or bad, she had to get over it, hadn't she? And make a future for herself. While she'd been engaged to Tony, her head had been largely filled with plans for the future, the wedding, new clothes—she had expected to be happy ever after!

It was almost five o'clock and the waiting room was half-full when the doctor came in. Leonora had laid the case notes on his desk and, the moment he rang, ushered in Mrs Squires.

She was ushered out again within five minutes and Leonora wondered what he had told her to make her look so pleased with herself. Leonora sent in the next patient and wondered what the doctor had been doing all day. He hadn't said a word to her, had barely glanced at her as he'd gone to his surgery. He had told her that it was an easy job. Well, she thought rebelliously, let him find another slave to do his work. She had agreed to help out purely from kindness of heart; she didn't need the money…

A small voice reminded her that the money was going to be very useful. Provided she could persuade her father to accept it, it would allow the more urgent roof repairs to be made.

The last patient went away and she began tidying up magazines and setting chairs back in their places. She was on her knees collecting up the toys kept in one corner of the room for the benefit of the smaller patients when Dr Galbraith opened his door.

'Tell me what happened today…'

She recited the day's events in a rather cross voice. 'If you had taken the time to tell me what I was supposed to do,' she observed, 'or where you were going, or how long you would be away…'

She got up from the floor. 'Cecil? Is he very ill? Shirley Bates was so worried but I wasn't sure if you would consider him urgent.'

'I've sent him to Bristol. He has meningitis.'

She gulped in horror. 'Oh, heavens, should I have phoned you earlier? Or got an ambulance or something?'

'You acted exactly as you should have done.' His calm voice reassured her, 'I think that he has a very good chance of recovery. I am sorry that you have had such a hard time of it. You must be famished...'

'Well, yes, I am, but Mrs Pike sent over some sandwiches for me at lunchtime. Did you get something to eat?'

He looked faintly surprised. 'Er—Cricket will have something for me when I get home.'

'Is Mrs Willis ill? She's not been well since her daughter left home.'

The doctor sat astride a chair and leaned on its back. 'Her daughter is home. She had twins this morning.' He smiled. 'That is why I was in a hurry. I got there just in time.'

Leonora said slowly, 'Her parents love her very much... Is she all right? And the babies?'

'All very fit. Tell me, was Mrs Squires very trying?'

'Yes. She came in and sat down and said she was ill. I do hope she's not...' She gave him an anxious look. 'You see, I've known her for years and years and she has been ill with almost everything under the sun and no one believes her any more.' She frowned. 'I expect she's lonely but she's a gossip.'

'There is nothing wrong with Mrs Squires. And she is a gossip—a malicious one, I rather think. She told me that your callous treatment of her was on account of you being broken-hearted at the ending of your engagement.'

'She said that? The whole village will have heard it in twenty-four hours.'

'I think not. I appealed to her good nature.'

She said coldly, 'There was no need for you to do that.'

'To interfere? Have you heard from Beamish, Leonora?'

'No, of course not. And I don't want to talk about it.'

'Naturally not,' he agreed blandly. 'I hope that when you do you will address him in the icy tones you are using on me.'

He got up, ignoring her indignant breath. 'I'll take you home. Do you think you can face another day after this one?'

'Of course I can. I've enjoyed myself,' said Leonora, still frosty. 'Mrs Crisp will be away for a few days; I'll bring sandwiches with me tomorrow.'

'No need. I'll come for you when I've done the morning round and we can have lunch at Buntings. I'll have the phone with me and take any calls.'

'There is no need,' began Leonora. 'I don't mind in the least.' She added ingenuously, 'The day has gone so quickly there was no time to think.'

'Good. You are beginning to recover your pride and courage. Only I do beg of you that when you see Beamish you remember to hang onto both at all costs.'

'I have no intention of seeing Tony again.'

'One never knows what is around the corner,' said the doctor placidly. 'Now let me drive you home before they send a search party for you.'

He got out of the car to open her door when they reached the house.

'Thank you for holding the fort so sensibly, Leonora.

Don't let your soft heart overrule your good sense when you see Beamish.'

'I'm not going to see him.'

He didn't answer her. Of course she would see him; he would even now be planning his visit, sure of its success. The doctor was very certain of that.

He was quite right.

CHAPTER SEVEN

LEONORA'S SECOND DAY at the surgery went smoothly. True, she wasn't very quick at finding the patients' notes in the filing cabinets but she was unfussed by the telephone and the appointments book.

The morning flashed by; she was surprised when the last patient went away and Dr Galbraith put his head round the door. 'How about coffee while I give you a list of where I'll be? If you need me and can't reach me from that, use the number on the desk—my own phone. When is Mrs Crisp coming home?'

'Mr Crisp thought at the end of the week.'

'Good. She'll take over here for the afternoons.'

He drank his coffee and drove away and she set about getting the notes out ready for the evening surgery. 'A man of few words,' she said, as usual talking to herself, and then wondered what he was really like when he wasn't being a doctor. She had had glimpses of that, but very briefly, and, for all she knew, his kindness and sympathy were all part of his being a doctor. Was he always calm and rather reserved? she wondered. Did he have a temper, get angry?

She washed the coffee-mugs and watered the potted plants on the waiting-room window-sill and after that there was a succession of phone calls—people wanting appointments, repeat prescriptions, a visit from the doctor—but there was nothing urgent and just before one o'clock he returned, popped her into the car and drove to Buntings.

Cricket was waiting for them, so was Tod, and they went briefly into the garden, going down to the end of it, throwing sticks for the dog and discussing bedding plants. It was a pretty garden, carefully tended but contriving to look as though everything growing in it had been there for ever and ever. Leonora stifled her envy. The garden at her house was twice as large and, despite her efforts, neglected.

Indoors again, they sat down to a cheese soufflé, salad, and a custard tart. They had their coffee at the table and Leonora, mindful of her duties, didn't linger over the meal.

'I must be getting back,' she said. 'Shall I ring you from the surgery so that you'll know I've taken the phone over again?'

'No—I'll drive you down. I want to see how Mrs Bates is coping. Cecil is going to be all right; she might like to visit him...'

'There isn't a bus until tomorrow.'

'I'm driving up to Bristol to see him. I'll take her with me.'

He's a kind man, reflected Leonora presently, watching him drive away from the surgery.

Another two days slipped by and Leonora now felt quite at home with the job. Indeed, she was vaguely regretful that Mrs Crisp would be home again tomorrow and would relieve her each afternoon, but despite the help Nanny had from Mrs Phelps from the village there was plenty to do when she was home, and her mother complained gently that while she was working the surgery took up so much time that it was impossible to have people to dinner; even an afternoon's bridge was difficult without Leonora being there to help with tea and make a fourth if needed.

'The bazaar, darling,' Lady Crosby had said with gentle reproach. 'Poor Lydia Dowling hasn't nearly enough helpers and you know what a great deal there is to do.'

Leonora had murmured a reply. Somehow, making pincushions and tray-cloths and sorting cast-off clothes for the jumble stall didn't seem important.

It was as the doctor was driving himself back from his morning rounds on Friday that he was passed on the road by a Porsche going too fast. Tony Beamish.

He glanced at his watch. Leonora would be back home by now; Mrs Crisp was always punctual and she had agreed to half past twelve as the time to take over for the afternoon. Any moment now Leonora would probably have to listen to Beamish's carefully planned explanations. Well, it was none of his business; she wasn't a child.

Later, as Cricket set his lunch before him, he gave a small, dry cough.

'Yes, Cricket?' Dr Galbraith was helping himself to ham but paused to look up.

'A message from Mrs Crisp, sir. She is unable to take over from Miss Crosby today. A migraine has laid her low.'

The doctor frowned. 'Miss Crosby is still at the surgery?'

'I presume so, sir. And Mrs Pike had occasion to telephone me a short time ago concerning your Bath Oliver biscuits which have arrived. Mr Pike was having a drink when Mr Beamish went to the pub. Very chirpy, she tells me, offered drinks all round and said he was on his way to see Miss Crosby. Unfortunately he was told that she was at the surgery.' Cricket paused to observe severely, 'It is regrettable how everyone knows everyone else's business in this village.' Then he resumed. 'Mr Beamish drank his whisky, asked if he could leave his car at the pub and was seen walking to the surgery.'

The doctor was about to sample the ham, but he put down his knife and fork, got to his feet and whistled to Tod.

'I'll be back presently, Cricket. You had better set another place.' He smiled at Cricket. 'I'll just take a look.'

Mrs Crisp's phone call, just as Leonora was getting ready to hand over to her, was tiresome but since there was nothing to be done about it she would have to stay at the surgery. Dr Galbraith should be home about one o'clock; she would ring him and ask what she was to do.

She made a pot of tea, sat down at her table in the waiting room and began to sort out the patients' notes for the evening surgery, and at the same time allowed her thoughts to dwell on the pay packet she expected the next day. She was to be paid by the hour and she had worked quite a few hours extra during the week. Even after paying for Mrs Phelps there would be a useful sum. Perhaps she could get her father to have Mr Sims, the local builder, round to take a look at the roof.

She looked up as the door opened and Tony walked in.

At the sight of him she gave a little gasp, put down her mug of tea and put her suddenly shaking hands in her lap out of sight.

'Darling, you didn't think I'd let you go, did you?

You see, here I am ready to go on my knees. I've no excuses, only that I was overwhelmingly busy when you came to see me and hardly knew what I was saying. Forgive me?' His smile was charming. 'Shall we start again? Just give me the chance to explain and you'll see how right I am. A marvellous future for us both—your parents will see what a splendid plan it is; it just needs a little persuasion from you—they listen to you, don't they?'

He came a little nearer, still smiling.

'Go away,' said Leonora. 'I'm working. Besides, I have no wish to speak to you ever again and I'll never forgive you—'

'Oh, come now, darling, you know you still love me.' His voice was beguiling.

'No, I don't. I can't bear the sight of you.'

He laughed then. 'Oh, you know you don't mean that.'

'Oh, but I do, and if you come a step nearer I'll throw this mug of tea at you.'

Tony laughed again, lunged forward and took the mug from her—just as the doctor came quietly through the door, tapped his elbow and sent hot tea pouring down his shirt and fashionable city suit. A few drops splashed his face too and he wiped them away furiously.

'You clumsy…'

He saw who it was then; he saw Tod too, standing by his master, all gleaming teeth and rumbling growls.

'Am I interrupting something?' asked the doctor genially. 'Is Mr Beamish annoying you, Leonora?'

She said, 'Yes. Please make him go away. I don't seem able to make him understand that I don't want to see or hear from him again.'

'Quite right,' agreed the doctor. 'Perhaps I should warn him that it might be as well if he did just that, for I don't like to see my friends harassed.'

He smiled at Tony, his eyes cold. 'I am a mild man, but if I get annoyed I can lose my temper. So be off with you, Beamish, and don't show your face here again or there might be trouble. You had better take that suit to the cleaners as soon as possible; tea stains are difficult to remove.'

He stood aside and added gently, 'If you go quietly Tod won't bite you.'

Tony went without a word, casting an apprehensive eye at Tod, who leered at him.

The doctor shut the door after Tony had gone and turned to look at Leonora. She was still sitting at the desk, looking at the notes on it, determined not to cry. She had been overjoyed to see the doctor but now she felt humiliated too. He seemed to be everlastingly helping her out of awkward situations; he must consider her a fool…

'Well, now that's dealt with,' said the doctor, 'we'll go back and have our lunch.'

She still wouldn't look at him. 'Thank you for coming when you did. It was lucky you did. Do you know that Mrs Crisp can't come? I'll stay here—I've nothing much to do at home this afternoon.'

'I'll take the calls on my phone; I'll drive you home when we've eaten. I'm famished.'

'I'd rather not, if you don't mind.'

'I do mind. Where is your British phlegm, Leonora?'

'My phlegm? Oh…' She smiled then and looked at him. 'Why do you always say the right thing, Dr Galbraith?' She got up and picked up the mug from the floor. 'I didn't know he was coming.' She gave the doctor a questioning look. 'Did you?'

He smiled at her. 'Not until Cricket told me. Cricket always has his ear to the ground; he never misses a whisper of gossip or news and this is a small village. And Beamish passed me in his car as I drove back.' He saw her look. 'No, I didn't intend to interfere, Leonora. I supposed that you would be home and he would have to deal with your parents as well as you, and it is hardly any of my business. But Cricket's information rather changed my plans.'

'Well, thank you very much. I expect he would have gone but I—I was glad when you came in with Tod.'

'Oh, Tod can put the fear of God into anyone,' said the doctor easily.

'I think you can too,' said Leonora.

She went with him then, back through the village and into Buntings, to find Cricket waiting, his sombre countenance breaking into a wintry smile at the sight of her. While they had been gone he had whisked up a feather-light cheese omelette, made a jug of lemonade, since he had decided that Miss Crosby wasn't a young lady to drink the doctor's beer, and prepared a little dish of chocolates to go with the coffee.

All of which Leonora enjoyed, almost her normal, matter-of-fact self once more. Only as they drank their coffee did she ask, 'You don't think he'll come back again?'

'No, I'm quite sure he won't.' The doctor handed her the dish. 'Have another of these chocolates. I don't know where Cricket gets them but they are quite good.'

Presently he drove her home. 'I'll have a word with your father if I may,' he told her as they got out of the car.

'Yes, of course. Don't leave Tod there; he likes Wilkins; they can go into the garden.'

As Tod joined them she said, 'We could go in through the garden door. I dare say Wilkins is somewhere in the garden at the back.'

He came to meet them and after a moment's wariness he lumbered off with Tod.

The garden door needed a coat of paint and its framework was by no means solid, and inside the house, going down the stone-floored passage towards the kitchen, the doctor saw the woeful state of the walls. He said nothing, of course, but Leonora said over her shoulder, 'We don't use this part of the house very much. It will be a great deal drier once we've had the roof repaired.'

'Old houses are difficult to maintain,' observed the doctor mildly, 'but it is surprising how well they last. Well built in the first place, of course.'

'Great-Great-Grandfather had it built,' said Leonora, and opened the door into the kitchen.

Nanny was sitting in her own particular chair by the Aga, knitting, and made to get up.

'No, don't move, Nanny,' said Leonora. 'We came in this way because of the dogs. I'm just taking Dr Galbraith to see Father.'

'You'll stay for tea?' said Nanny.

He refused with regret. 'I must go back and do some work—letters and so on. They do pile up. Another time if I may.'

'You're always welcome in this house,' said Nanny, 'and I speak for everyone in it.'

Leonora took the doctor to her father's study and then left them and went in search of her mother.

'Darling—you're late home. Have you been busy? The Dowlings phoned; Mrs Dowling wants you to go over when you can spare a minute—something to do with the jumble stall. I didn't hear you come in.'

'I brought Dr Galbraith through the garden door; he wanted to see Father.'

'I wonder why?' Lady Crosby put down the book she was reading and looked at Leonora. 'Is your father ill? No one told me.'

'No, no, nothing like that. Tony Beamish came to the surgery earlier; I think Dr Galbraith thought it better if he talked to Father about him.'

'Oh, dear. Was he horrid? But you weren't alone with him?'

'Only for a short while before Dr Galbraith came back to the surgery.'

'And…?' said Lady Crosby. 'Did he send Tony packing?'

'Yes,' said Leonora. She would have liked to tell her mother all about it but, much as she loved her parent, she was aware that anything unpleasant or worrying was ignored by her. She would tell Nanny presently and they would have a good laugh over it.

The two men came into the room a little later and her father said, 'I'm sorry that you have been bothered by young Beamish, my dear. I understand from Dr Galbraith that we are unlikely to see or hear from him again.' Sir William blew out his moustache and looked fierce. 'The scoundrel, wanting to turn us out of our home, pretending to be in love with Leonora. It must have been pretence; no man would behave in such a manner towards the girl he intended to marry.'

The doctor, watching Leonora, saw her blush and reflected that she should do that more often; it turned her pretty face into a thing of beauty. Even in her rather dull country clothes she was lovely. He had a sudden wish to see her decked out in haute couture and jewels—sapphires and pearls, he thought, long, dangling earrings and rings on her fingers. She had pretty hands...

'You must come to dinner one evening.' Lady Crosby's voice cut into his thoughts. 'We don't entertain much these days, but we are always glad to see our friends and neighbours.' She smiled up at him. 'Is Leonora proving satisfactory at the surgery?'

'Indeed she is, Lady Crosby. I'm thinking of asking her to stay on permanently—part-time, perhaps, sharing with Mrs Crisp when she returns.'

'Really? Well, why not? It is quite proper for us to help in the village in any way we can.'

The doctor didn't bat an eyelid. 'You are quite right, Lady Crosby; I am glad you agree with me.' He shook hands then, said a few words to Sir William, and added casually to Leonora, 'I'll see you around five o'clock,' and followed her out into the hall. At the door he whistled for Tod and got into his car, aware that Leonora was glowering at him from the steps.

He didn't drive away but opened his door and got out, leaning on the car roof, watching her come towards him.

'What's all this, then?' she wanted to know. 'Have I been asked if I want to go on working for you?' She added coldly, 'It's usual to be asked before it's talked about.'

He considered this muddled speech. 'I apologise; I

was attacking you from the rear, wasn't I? But when you've cooled down, Leonora, consider the offer, will you? And let me know when you've made up your mind.'

He got back into the car and she stuck her head through the window.

'Of course I'll come permanently,' she told him. She sniffed. 'Since I've been asked…'

'Splendid.' He raised a hand and drove away. 'Now what possessed me to do that?' he enquired of Tod sitting beside him.

Tod didn't answer. Eyes half-shut, he was comfortably drowsy after a good romp in the garden with Wilkins.

Leonora went back into the house and found her father in his study.

'You like the idea of working for Dr Galbraith?' he asked her as she went in. 'It curtails your freedom…'

'Father, if I had all day with nothing to do—' and that's a joke, she reflected, thinking of the bed-making and hoovering and cooking, about which he was apparently unaware '—I would have to fill it with doing the flowers and helping Mrs Dowling with her bazaars and visiting. I really enjoy it.'

She hesitated. 'And Father, I get well paid and I don't need the money.' A fib, that! 'Could we have the roof over the kitchen mended? If I lent you the money? I really have no use for it, and if I put it in the bank it's just there doing nothing, whereas the tiles are falling off all the time.' She saw his frown. 'Please, Father…'

'The money is yours, my dear; you must wish to spend it on some new clothes—something for your mother, perhaps.'

'There's enough for that as well. It's too soon to buy clothes for the summer anyway, but I'll take Mother up to town later on and we'll shop. The roof first, though!' She smiled at him. 'Just between us two.'

'I do not care to take money from my daughter,' said Sir William.

'You're not; I'm lending it. It makes sense, you know, for if one or two repairs aren't made the house will fall apart and won't be of much use to me when I eventually get it.'

'There's that, of course. Very well, my dear, provided that you promise to spend your money on yourself once the roof is seen to. I'll get Sims to come round and inspect it. He might deal with it while this weather holds.'

She went to him then and kissed the top of his head. 'Don't tell Mother.'

Sir William allowed himself to smile. 'No, no, I won't. In any case your mother has very little idea about repairs and so forth.'

Leonora went to the door. 'I'm going to make scones for tea…'

'Yes, yes, of course, Leonora. I'm sorry about Tony Beamish. Your whole future.'

Leonora said matter-of-factly, 'Father, it would have been a disastrous one. I much prefer the future Dr Galbraith has offered me and living here in the village. I would have been unhappy in London and I'm sure that is where Tony and I would have lived for most of the time.'

Nanny, told of Leonora's job probably turning out to be a permanent one, was pleased. 'You'll see a bit of life even if it's only the folk living around here. And you'll have a bit of money to call your own.' She glanced at

Leonora. 'You like working for the doctor? You like him as a person?'

'Yes, I do. I didn't think I was going to at first but he kind of grows on one, Nanny, and he was rather splendid when Tony turned up.'

'So you'll go every morning and evening?'

'Yes, but for the moment I'll go all day; Mrs Crisp isn't coming back for a couple of days. She had a bad migraine so she's taking a few days off, but when she starts she'll relieve me at half past twelve and stay until I go back at half past four. Of course, I'll be free on Saturday afternoons and Sunday.'

'Well, that's nice,' said Nanny cosily, and thought how well the pair of them were suited. Perhaps if they saw more of each other... 'I'll make the tea if those scones are ready; it's almost time for you to go to the surgery.'

Dr Galbraith had nothing to say about Tony when she saw him that evening. There weren't many patients and when he had seen the last one he bade her goodnight, reminded her to lock up carefully and drove away. She watched him go, feeling vaguely disgruntled, although she reminded herself that she had no reason to be.

The doctor would be away for the weekend; she had been given a phone number to contact his stand-in at Wells and the phone had been switched through to him. 'I'll be taking over again early on Monday morning. Enjoy your weekend.' He had gone before she could reply.

Well, she would enjoy her weekend, she supposed. A long-delayed visit to the Dowlings to discuss the bazaar, her turn to do the flowers in church, and her mother had some friends coming to tea in the afternoon. Leonora felt restless. She wondered where the doctor was going—to see whoever it was who had called his dog Tod? He had made no secret of his affection for her, had he? I hope she's nice, reflected Leonora; he deserves a good wife.

She thought about him a good deal during the weekend, imagining him in a variety of situations—at the theatre, dining out with the unknown girl, meeting friends. In fact she thought about him so much that she quite forgot to think about Tony. He had disappeared out of mind as well as out of sight.

Leonora's imaginings were very wide of the mark. The doctor spent his weekend with his sister, who lived with her farmer husband and three children in a lovely old house on the outskirts of Napton on the Hill, a small village in Warwickshire. Far from the theatre-going and dining out that Leonora had envisaged, he walked and rode and pottered around in old tweeds, ate huge meals in the vast old-fashioned kitchen and kicked a football around with his two small nephews. When he was tired he sat down and his small niece climbed onto his lap and demanded stories. She wanted to know about Tod too.

'He's very well,' her uncle assured her. 'Though that's a funny sort of name you gave him. A young lady I know doesn't much like it.'

'What young lady?' his sister, who had just joined them, wanted to know.

'A quite beautiful young lady with a great deal of dark hair and a sharp tongue. Very sensible too.'

'Lives in the village?'

'Yes. I imagine her ancestors owned it at one time. She lives in a lovely house that's mouldering away for lack of money, with her mother and father.'

'And does good works?'

'Oh, yes.'

'Well, go on,' said his sister. 'Is she married, engaged, and do you like her?'

'She was going to be married but luckily no longer, neither is she engaged—not at the moment. Yes, I like her. A series of—er—happenings made it possible for me to ask her to be my receptionist at the surgery. She's quite good—needs the money to have the roof repaired.'

'But if she's the daughter of the manor…' began his sister.

'I used cunning; I implied that she would be undertaking vital charitable work.'

'You've been to a lot of trouble.'

The doctor sat back with his eyes closed. 'Funnily enough, until now I was unable to understand why.' He opened one eye. 'Is it time for tea?'

He was about to get into his car on Sunday evening when his brother-in-law said, 'Molly would like to come over and see you. Would that be all right?'

The doctor smiled. 'Jeffrey, Molly wants to get a look at my new receptionist. Of course you must all come—make it a Saturday if you can; on Sunday she is much taken up with church and Sunday lunch.'

He got into his car and Tod got in beside him. 'I'll do my best to arrange a meeting but it's quite likely that she will refuse to come. She isn't sure if she likes me. You see, I have been witness to some of her more delicate situations.' He laughed. 'Why, when we met for the first time she tripped up in the lane and sat down hard a few yards from the car. Very tart she was too, and then disarmed me completely by apologising for being rude. You'll like her.'

He thought about her as he drove back to Pont Magna. 'She is beginning to take up too many of my thoughts,' he told Tod, 'probably because I haven't met a girl like her before—and I'm not sure if I want that.'

He pulled one of Tod's silky ears gently. 'Ah, well, back to work in the morning and that will give me plenty to think about.'

So when Leonora arrived on Monday and poked her head round the surgery door to say good morning she was taken aback by his cool rejoinder and impersonal blandness.

He's quarrelled with her, she reflected, finding notes and marshalling the patients into seats. A full house too—nasty coughs, a black eye, a toddler with suspicious spots and the snuffles, and the verger, who had fallen down the last few steps of the narrow, winding stairs to the church tower and had got some nasty bruises as a result.

The doctor didn't wait for his coffee after surgery. 'You've got the phone number,' he reminded her. 'I'll call in when I get back. You had better come back to my place for lunch.'

'I've brought sandwiches, thank you.' She spoke in a cool voice; if he wanted to be frosty she would be too. 'There are a lot of patients for the evening clinic. If any more phone…?'

He took a quick look at the appointments book. 'I'll see two more—anyone else, unless it's urgent, must come in the morning. That's pretty full too—and young Beamish told me it was an easy job!'

He watched the colour creep into Leonora's cheeks. Did she still love the man? Surely not… His frown was so ferocious that she looked at him in astonishment but he had gone before she could say anything.

She spent the next hour or so tidying the place—cleaning bowls and the simple instruments he had used, cleaning up the magazines and toys—and finally put on the kettle for a cup of coffee to go with her sandwiches. There had been several phone calls for appointments and she had got out the notes for the evening surgery.

She made the coffee and bit into the first of Nanny's cheese sandwiches. The phone rang and she swallowed hastily and said, 'Hello, Dr Galbraith's surgery,' in a rather thick voice.

It was a call from Willis Farm. 'It's the baby—'e don't look well; the doctor must come 'fore 'e gets any worse.'

Leonora picked up the pen. 'It's Janice, isn't it? Which baby is it? You had a boy and a girl, didn't you?'

'Never you mind; just send the doctor.'

'He isn't here, but I can get him for you, only I must know what to tell him. Now, which baby?'

'The boy—we calls 'im Billy. Looks kind of poorly and keeps screaming.'

'The little girl's all right?'

'Yes, far as I can see. Where is 'e, then?'

'I can phone him at once. Isn't your mother there?'

'Ain't no one 'ere. Ma's gone ter Radstock Market and the men are down the ten-acre field.'

'Go back to the babies, Janice,' said Leonora. 'I'm going to phone the doctor now; he'll come just as soon as he can.'

She was putting the phone down when he walked in.

'That was Janice,' said Leonora. 'She says one of the

twins is ill and she's alone—the men are at the other end of the farm, and her mother's in Radstock.'

'Did she tell you what was wrong?'

'Only that Billy looked poorly and screamed a lot.'

He went to his locked cupboard in the surgery and selected the items he wanted, put them in his bag and said, 'Right, then, we'd better go.'

We? She couldn't help casting a look at the sandwiches, but since he didn't respond she followed him out of the door, which he locked before opening the car door and urging her in.

He didn't appear to be hurrying but he hadn't wasted a moment. As they left the village street she asked, 'Why must I come with you? I don't know anything much about babies.'

He turned to look at her. 'No, no—you are coming as my chaperon.'

'Chap...' For a moment she was speechless. 'Whatever for?'

'Have you seen Janice since she came back from London?' he asked.

'No. She was a quiet girl—not very friendly with anyone else here, quite pretty, though—she had nice mousy hair...'

She gave him an enquiring look which he ignored, and he didn't speak again until he'd driven into the farmyard, got out, opened her door and fetched his bag from the back seat. A girl was standing at the open door watching them. If this was Janice, where was the mousy hair, the pretty face? This girl had shorn locks of a vibrant chestnut colour and so much make-up that it was hard to tell what she really looked like. She had a stud in one nostril, long, dangling earrings and the shortest skirt Leonora had ever seen.

'Where's this baby?' asked the doctor in a voice nicely compounded of professional reserve and kindness. 'Tell me exactly when he became ill. Is he feverish? Being sick?'

He went past her into the house, saying over his shoulder, 'Leonora, come with me, please.'

Janice led the way upstairs to where the babies were lying in their cots. The baby girl was sleeping but Billy was roaring his head off, red in the face, waving minute fists in rage. The doctor picked him up.

'He's sopping wet,' he observed mildly. 'Get some dry clothes for him—he needs changing for a start.'

Janice went to a chest of drawers and started rummaging in it and he handed the baby to Leonora, who rightly deduced that she was meant to undress the infant. She laid him gently in his cot again and took off his old-fashioned gown and the wringing wet nappy and exposed a small sore bottom.

'He needs a bath,' she said, and added, 'Sorry...'

'You haven't bathed the babies today,' stated the doctor. 'And when were they last changed? Billy isn't ill; he's wet and very sore. Get a bath ready for them; let's get both of them washed and then I'll examine them and make sure there is nothing wrong. When did the district nurse come?'

'Yesterday. Don't want 'er, old Nosy Parker; told 'er she didn't need ter come any more.'

'Your mother knows this?'

'Ma don't know nothing.' She shrugged her shoulders and went out and presently came back with a small bath and then warm water.

The baby girl—Daisy—was awake now; Leonora, without being asked, stripped the cots while the babies were being bathed, made them up again with clean sheets and then sat down with a towel on her lap so that Billy could lie on it while his poor sore bottom was examined by the doctor.

Leonora held him gently, stroking the fair hair on his small head, telling him what a good boy he was, all the while aware of the doctor's face within inches of her own as he bent down, and aware too of a peculiar feeling somewhere under her ribs which resolved itself into a flood of happiness. Not that she had the leisure to think about it. Billy was wriggling like a very small eel and crying again.

'When did they have their last feed?' asked the doctor.

'Oh, I dunno—this morning. Ma went early; she fed 'em.'

'Go and get their feed now. There is nothing wrong with either of your babies. They were hungry, dirty and wet. Tell me, would you like them to go to the children's hospital for a few weeks while you decide what you intend to do?'

'Yeah, that's a good idea. What am I supposed to do with two kids anyway? Didn't want 'em, did I?'

'They could be adopted.'

'That suits me fine.' She flounced away to fetch the babies' bottles and the doctor got out his phone while Leonora tucked Daisy in her cot once more. Billy began to bawl again, so she picked him up and cuddled him, listening vaguely to the doctor's voice. He was on the phone for a long time.

She accepted a bottle from Janice and began to feed

Billy; he gulped and choked in his haste and she wondered if he had been getting as much as he needed. The doctor must have had the same idea for he phoned again and then said, 'The district nurse is coming this afternoon; she will make up the babies' feeds for the rest of the day and make sure that they are all right. You will do exactly what she says, and as soon as it can be arranged Billy and Daisy will be taken to the hospital. I'll come and see your parents this evening.'

He glanced at Leonora. 'Ready to go? Nurse will be here within the next hour; she knows what to do.'

On the way back Leonora burst out, 'How could she? Such little babies and no one to love them—and that's all they want—food and warmth and love, isn't it?' She hadn't meant to weep but two tears escaped and ran down her cheeks.

The doctor, looking straight ahead, none the less saw them. He dropped a large hand on her arm for a moment. 'They will be adopted by people who will love them and care for them. I'll have to speak to her parents, of course, but I suspect that once she is free of the twins she will leave home again. In the meantime the district nurse will keep an eye on them and with luck we should get them transferred to hospital tomorrow or the next day.'

'It must be so satisfying to get things done,' said Leonora fiercely, 'to know what to do and to be able to get on with it.'

His reassuring grunt was comforting.

He glanced at his watch. 'It's three o'clock; at least no one has called on the phone. We'll get something to eat before we do anything else.'

'My sandwiches…' began Leonora.

'They'll be curling at the edges by now. Cricket will find us something.'

This was getting to be a habit, reflected Leonora—something which for some reason she found unsettling. 'If you don't mind I'll go straight to the surgery, Doctor.'

'I do mind—and call me James.' He didn't look at her but went on with casual friendliness, 'We are colleagues, are we not?'

'Well, yes, I suppose so,' she said doubtfully. 'You don't mind?'

His mouth twitched. 'Not at all. I should prefer it since we are to see a good deal of each other for the time being.'

Did that mean, she wondered worriedly, that he was already looking for another receptionist—a trained one who knew the difference between indigestion and a heart attack and who knew how to fend off those who came to the surgery apparently for the fun of it?

She said soberly, 'Very well, James.' After which it hardly seemed appropriate to mention the surgery again. Besides, she was hungry.

CHAPTER EIGHT

Mrs Crisp came back in a day or two—and perhaps that was as well, thought Leonora. Working for the doctor in the surgery was one thing, but somehow lunching with him in his lovely house with Cricket beaming at her—and feeling so happy while she was there—was unsettling.

She was careful to work the hours he had suggested and made no effort to talk to him unless it was about a patient or phone call. He didn't seem to mind, she reflected forlornly. True, he had stopped one morning to tell her that Billy and Daisy were in hospital and thriving and their mother had packed her bag and left home again.

'How can you possibly leave two little babies?' Leonora had wanted to know.

He had smiled thinly and shaken his head and gone away again to see to his patients.

She was handing over to Mrs Crisp on her first afternoon back when he came into the surgery, wished Mrs Crisp a good day and then said, 'Leonora, my sister is coming down on Saturday for the weekend. I'd like you to come to tea.'

If they had been alone she would have made some excuse—not that she didn't want to accept, but she had decided, hadn't she, that she would take care not to get too friendly. She wasn't very clear why this was necessary but that was beside the point. Mrs Crisp, standing there smiling and nodding, made it difficult to refuse. Besides, he didn't give her a chance to do so.

'Around three o'clock,' he said easily. 'We look forward to seeing you.'

When he'd gone Mrs Crisp observed chattily, 'I wonder who else will be there?'

Leonora felt a pang of relief and then disappointment; there would be half the village there, no doubt. She reminded herself that that was exactly what she wanted.

Lady Crosby puckered her brows when Leonora told her that she would be going to Buntings for tea. 'Strange that Dr Galbraith didn't include your father and me. Will there be many there, I wonder?'

'I've no idea. He mentioned his sister staying with him—she has three small children, Mrs Crisp tells me.'

'In that case I would have refused. With children there can be no conversation. I dare say there will be another dinner party shortly. You haven't met any of his friends?'

'Mother, I'm at the surgery; even if he had friends staying they wouldn't come there.' Was now the time to mention the lunches she had had at Buntings? she wondered, and decided against saying anything. Her mother would jump to the conclusion that Dr Galbraith—she must remember to call him James—was interested in her. Which he wasn't. Even when he had invited her to tea he had sounded exactly like the family doctor talking to a patient.

On Saturday, uncertain as to who might be there, she got into her jersey dress and a long cardigan, both in a pleasant shade of turquoise-blue and both in a style guaranteed to be wearable five years hence, arranged her hair in a chignon, made up nicely, thanking heaven that it was a dry, quite warm day so that she could wear light shoes. She had considered biking there but then she might arrive a bit tousled. She bade her parents good-bye, told Nanny she would be back around six o'clock, perhaps earlier, and walked to Buntings.

Walking up the drive to the house, she gave a small sigh of envy. It looked charming; the flowerbeds were full of spring flowers now, and the shrubbery was newly green. The door was open and as she reached it two small boys darted out.

They came to a halt by her and offered grubby hands. 'You are Leonora,' said the taller of the two. 'I'm Paul; he's George.'

Leonora shook hands. 'Hello, Paul; hello, George. How did you know who I was?'

'Uncle James told us. Come inside.'

The doctor came to meet them as they entered the hall. His greeting was casual and friendly. 'The house is in an uproar; I hope you don't mind. Come and meet Molly and my brother-in-law. There's another child somewhere—my niece.'

They all went into the drawing room and she shook hands with Molly and Jeffrey and then stooped to take the little girl's hand. 'I'm two,' she whispered, and buried her face in her mother's skirt. Presently she peeped up at Leonora. 'Uncle James and me share Tod.'

'Now, that's nice,' said Leonora, bending down. 'I've got a dog too. His name's Wilkins.'

A small hand was slipped into hers. 'I'll show you Tod.'

They all went into the garden then, and the talk was easy and pleasant and made her feel perfectly at home. Tod was admired, stroked and offered a ball while they strolled around, the children darting to and fro, the grown-ups stopping to discuss some plant or other. Molly tucked an arm into Leonora's, not asking questions, mentioning only casually Leonora's work at the surgery, but telling her about the children and her life on the farm.

'I don't do any farm work—I wouldn't know how to and Jeffrey has an agent—but it's a nice old house and there's heaps of room for the children. We ride too—do you?'

'I used to.' Something in Leonora's voice caused Molly to start an animated conversation about her children. 'They're a handful even with Nanny's help. Of course, they're as good as gold when they come down here. They adore James; he makes a marvellous uncle and, heaven knows, he has enough practice—we have four sisters, did you know? Two of them are married with children. They live a good way away, though— Scotland and the depths of Cornwall. The other two are in Canada with our father and mother—twins, waiting to go to university; they're the youngest.'

'It must be lovely to have a brother and sisters...'

'Oh, it is. We all like each other too. Here's Cricket to tell us tea is ready.'

It was a hilarious meal, sitting round the dining-room table with the children, and Cricket had done them proud. Tiny sandwiches, a plate of bread and butter cut paper-thin, fairy cakes, gingerbread men and a magnificent chocolate cake.

There was even a high chair for the little girl and

when Molly saw Leonora looking at it she said, 'James keeps one here; there's always a baby or a toddler; as fast as one is big enough to sit on a chair there's another one ready for the high chair!' She laughed. 'Mother and Father say they lose count of their grandchildren.'

It wasn't quite what Leonora had expected but she found herself wishing that she had a large family like the doctor's; their warmth and pleasure in each other's company was something she had never experienced and wasn't likely to. She didn't waste time repining, though. She ate a splendid tea, unaware of the doctor's eyes upon her, wholly taken up with the small boys sitting on either side of her.

After tea they played hide-and-seek round the house. As she raced round the passages, up and down the staircase, in and out of the rooms, Leonora's cheeks got flushed and her hair escaped in little curls; she was happy and a little excited, so that she looked prettier than ever.

Creeping up the back stairs, looking for a likely hiding place, she came face to face with the doctor.

They were at the end of a narrow passage leading to the back of the house, with doors on one side and a row of small windows overlooking the garden.

They stood looking at each other for a moment. 'Enjoying yourself, Leonora?' he asked, and smiled.

'Oh, yes—yes, I am. I'd forgotten what fun it was. We must hide…'

'We aren't really built for it, are we?' he observed. 'Rather on the big side.'

'Well, really!' began Leonora, suddenly aware of her magnificent proportions compared with Molly, who was a slender size eight. Her childish pleasure was pricked like a balloon. 'You're very rude,' she said tartly, and edged past him.

He put out a hand and stopped her very gently. 'I'm so sorry; would it make things better if I told you that I like my women big?'

He bent and kissed her quickly. 'Run along and hide. There's a large cupboard at the end of this passage.'

She wanted to run out of his house, get away from him, but she couldn't do that; she got into the cupboard and presently was discovered by a small boy shouting in triumph.

It was the children's bedtime then. Leonora was embraced in turn, shook hands with Molly and Jeffrey, thanked the doctor in a chilly voice for a pleasant afternoon, took her cardigan from Cricket and went to the door.

She found the doctor beside her. 'I'll walk with you,' he told her affably. 'The house will be bedlam until the children are in bed.'

Short of turning and running for it there was nothing she could do about it, not with Cricket watching. She said nothing at all in a rather marked manner, told Cricket what a delightful tea he had given them, and walked out of the door, stiff with dignity.

'Why are you cross?' asked the doctor blandly, strolling along beside her. 'Is it because I called you a big girl or because I kissed you?'

'Both,' snapped Leonora. 'And I would much prefer to walk home alone.'

He ignored this. 'But you are a big girl,' he pointed out in a reasonable voice. 'But, I must add, most splendidly shaped; to say otherwise would be an outrage.'

'You shouldn't talk to me like this,' said Leonora, marching along, very red in the face.

'Should I not have kissed you either? I enjoyed it.'

So did I, thought Leonora, although she wasn't going to say so. She kept a haughty silence and saw Mrs Pike peering at them from the closed door of her shop, which prompted her to say in a peevish voice, 'There is absolutely no need to walk home with me.'

He stopped and turned her round to face him. 'I do not know what has made you so contrary. We are colleagues, are we not? And I thought we were friends.' He grinned down at her. 'And I wonder what Mrs Pike thinks we are?'

'Is she still peeping? Oh, please, Dr Galbraith, may we walk on?'

'Call me James...'

'James,' she went on, 'you're impossible...'

She stopped. He wasn't impossible; he was James, who laughed at her because she was a big girl and was silly about being kissed, and she wished she had never met him. She wished too that she didn't love him. Why would she discover that in the middle of the village's main street with curtains twitching right and left of them?

They were walking on, side by side, not touching. She felt quite dizzy with the sudden discovery of her love. This was love, she realised; whatever she had felt for Tony hadn't been that—more of an infatuation, she supposed. She wanted to tell James, which was absurd; instead, anxious to break the silence between them, she started to talk about the children.

He answered her with casual good nature and it

amazed her that he couldn't know how she felt. But why should he?

At the house, he stayed for a short time, talking to her mother and father, then he bade her a brisk goodbye and strode off home, turning to wave at the open gate.

'Who else was there?' her mother wanted to know. 'He has many friends, I'm sure.'

'Well, there was his sister and brother-in-law and their three children.'

'No one else? How extraordinary. Was it boring, darling?'

'No. We played hide-and-seek all over the house—the children are charming.' Leonora smiled to herself. 'We had tea round the table in the dining room—with the children...'

'Surely there was a nanny?'

'Oh, yes. She was having the afternoon off.'

Lady Crosby picked up her book. 'Well, as long as you weren't bored, Leonora. It sounds to me like the waste of an afternoon—you would have enjoyed yourself more if you had gone to the Dowlings'. Their niece is staying—such a pretty girl; plenty of money, I hear; I'm surprised Dr Galbraith wasn't invited.'

Leonora felt an instant hatred for the niece. She said abruptly, 'I'll go and see if Nanny needs any help with dinner,' and took herself off to the kitchen, where she got in Nanny's way until she was told to take Wilkins for a walk. 'For I don't know what's got into you, Miss Leonora,' said Nanny. 'Proper crotchety you are and no mistake.'

So she took Wilkins out into the garden and then into the park, and since there was no one else to tell she told him all about James.

'I can quite see,' she told him, 'that it's being an only child. I mean I can't talk to Mother and Father, if you see what I mean—talk to them like they were all talking together at James's house, saying what they really meant and knowing that the others were listening...'

Wilkins pressed up against her, staring up into her face with soft brown eyes; he was her friend and offering sympathy, and Leonora, who almost never cried, cried a little now and felt better. 'I'll see him on Monday,' she said, and blew her pretty nose and went back indoors and laid the table for Nanny.

She woke several times during the night, thinking about James, longing to see him and at the same time dreading their meeting. She would have to behave as though nothing had changed and she wasn't sure if she would be able to manage that. To give up her job at the surgery would be the easiest way out of her dilemma; on the other hand, if she did that she wouldn't see him. Besides, Sims was going to start on the roof on Monday morning and would expect to be paid. She slept at length and woke with a heavy head.

Monday wasn't as bad as she had expected. For one thing the surgery was full and when the doctor came in there was no time for more than a brief good morning, and, for another, when he had dealt with his patients he went away at once, not waiting for his usual cup of coffee. He wasn't back when Mrs Crisp arrived and Leonora took herself off home.

If I can get through one day like that, I can get through the rest of them—until he finds a receptionist to suit him, she thought. She had calculated that Mr Sims would take three weeks to patch the roof; once that was done, if she didn't want to go on working for

James she could think up some excuse and leave. After all, she had only gone to fill a gap, hadn't she? She refused to think further than that; a future without the doctor wasn't to be contemplated...

She managed very nicely during the next two weeks, offering him chilly good mornings and good evenings, making sure that there was never a chance for them to be alone. It took all her ingenuity at times, and the doctor, puzzled and a little amused, wondered what she was up to.

He played along with her; he was kind and friendly and impassive. He knew by now that he loved her and intended to marry her but he was content to await events. Something was worrying his Leonora and, being a man without conceit, he was quite unaware of the truth.

The roof repaired, Mr Sims took away his ladders and Leonora's cheque, and since there was no further excuse to make as to why she had to continue working Leonora sought for a way of ending a situation which from her point of view was becoming increasingly awkward. Only the day before, James had suggested that she might like to have lunch with him at Buntings so that she could admire the garden. Her refusal had been so instant that he had lifted an eyebrow, watching her red face and listening to her trying to soften her sharp reply.

'That is, thank you very much, but I said I'd be home as soon as possible; I've several things to see to.'

He had smiled then and said placidly, 'Of course—another time.' Then he'd begun to talk about one of his patients who wanted to alter his appointment.

It wouldn't do—she would have to think of something.

As it turned out, she had no need to do that.

It was the following day, when she got home in time for lunch, that she found Nanny sitting in the kitchen looking flushed, and coughing a nasty little dry cough.

'You've caught cold,' said Leonora, and bustled her off to bed with a hot-water bottle and a hot drink and some aspirin. 'You stay there, Nanny—I'll see to the lunch and tea, and get supper when I get back this evening. Don't you dare get out of bed.'

'I'll feel better presently,' said Nanny, and fell into an uneasy doze.

Lady Crosby, informed of Nanny's poorly state, made a little face.

'Oh, dear, poor Nanny. Do you suppose it's flu? I'd better not go near her; you know how easily I catch things. I expect you can manage, darling. We can have an easy meal this evening—something you can deal with when you get back from the surgery. I don't suppose we need to send for Dr Galbraith.'

'Well, if Nanny's not better tomorrow I think you had better, Mother.'

'Of course if Nanny's ill she must be looked after. You'll see him this evening, won't you? Or tomorrow morning? I dare say it's just a feverish cold. Nanny is never ill.'

Leonora got the lunch, tidied up, took a look at Nanny and found her sleeping, and went to get the tea-tray ready and then examine the contents of the fridge. It would have to be a corned beef pie, disguised in a handsome dish. There were vegetables enough and some prawns in the freezer—prawn cocktails, she decided, the pie with a variety of vegetables and an egg custard.

She could make a sauce from strawberry jam when she got home that evening.

She made Nanny a jug of lemonade before she left, turned her pillows and bathed her hot face and asked her mother to take a look from time to time. 'You don't need to go into Nanny's room—if you'd just take a look to make sure she's all right.'

'Very well, dear, since there is no one else. Supposing Nanny wants something or feels worse?'

'I'm sure you can cope, Mother, and I'll be back in a couple of hours.'

Lady Crosby looked vexed. 'To think that you should have been marrying Tony and looking forward to a settled future…'

Leonora thought of several answers to that but none of them seemed suitable.

There was only a handful of patients at the surgery and Leonora glanced with relief at the clock as she started tidying up.

The doctor saw that. 'Going out this evening?' he asked casually.

'No. Oh, no. Nanny's got a bad cold so I said I'd get dinner this evening. She's keeping warm in bed.'

He was at his desk, locking the drawers, putting papers in his case.

'Not often ill, is she? A vigorous little lady.'

'She's a darling,' said Leonora warmly. 'I don't know how we would manage without her.'

'No—well, don't hang around. I'll lock up and see you in the morning. Let me know if you are worried about her and I'll take a look.'

'Yes, thank you, I will.'

She hurried home and found her mother playing patience in the drawing room while her father read.

'How's Nanny?' she asked.

Her mother looked up. 'Hello, darling. I peeped in once or twice; she seemed quite comfortable—coughing a bit, but what does one expect with a heavy cold?' She turned over a card. 'Are you going to be a clever girl and cook our dinner?' She smiled sweetly at Leonora. 'Something nice?' she added coaxingly.

'I'll surprise you,' said Leonora, and sped away, not to the kitchen but to Nanny's room.

Nanny was awake, hot and restless and thirsty. 'Your ma popped in but I didn't like to bother her,' she said when Leonora frowned at the empty jug.

'I'm going to wash your hands and face and put you into a fresh nightie and make your bed,' said Leonora. 'Then I'll bring you some soup and after that a cup of tea and some more aspirin.' She picked up the jug. 'Give me five minutes, Nanny.'

She whisked herself into the kitchen, popped the prepared pie in the oven, put the vegetables on the slow burner and set the soup to warm. There was still a lemon; she made a jug of lemonade, lavishly iced, and bore it back to Nanny's room before gently washing her, sitting her in a chair while she made the bed and fetched more pillows. Then she settled her against them, a shawl around her shoulders.

'That's better,' said Nanny. 'I do believe I'd like some of that soup.'

The dinner was cooking itself, thank heaven. Leonora took the soup upstairs and before Nanny started on it took her temperature. It was up—not frighteningly so, but none the less higher than it should be.

In the morning, she decided, she would ask James to come and see Nanny—perhaps an antibiotic…? At the moment Nanny seemed easier and when Leonora slipped up to look at her just before she dished up she was asleep.

She reassured her mother at dinner. 'Nanny's asleep at present; if she has a quiet night I dare say her temperature will be down in the morning.'

'We can't have Nanny ill,' observed her father. 'Perhaps we should get Dr Galbraith to look in tomorrow some-time.' He glanced at Leonora. 'You can manage, my dear. I dare say we can get extra help…'

He looked around vaguely as if to conjure domestic help out of the walls and Leonora said quickly, 'No need, Father, I can manage.'

And her mother said, 'Of course you can, darling, and I'll help.'

Leonora thanked her gravely, both she and her father aware that Lady Crosby had no intention of altering her gentle day's routine. She had always had a sheltered life, first as a girl with doting parents and then as a wife cherished by a husband who shrugged off her inability to cope with domestic problems.

At first that hadn't mattered, for there had been money enough to employ a housekeeper and help in the house, and now, since he had lost most of his money, it was too late to change her ways. Leonora knew that too and accepted it. All the same, if Nanny were to be ill for more than a day or two it would be difficult to manage even with the help she had from the village.

She was a sensible girl; she decided to worry about that if and when it happened, and after a last peep at Nanny went to bed.

It was just after three o'clock when she woke, and a vague feeling of uneasiness got her out of bed, to creep out of her room and along the wide corridor leading to the passage where Nanny had her room.

Nanny was muttering and mumbling to herself, half choking on a nasty little cough, and she felt hotter than ever.

'Nanny,' said Leonora, 'how do you feel? Shall I get you a drink and bathe your face—cool you down a bit?'

Nanny didn't seem to hear, looking past her at the empty room, whispering to someone she couldn't see. Leonora turned the bedside lamp so that the light shone on Nanny. Her face was grey and somehow grown small and her breathing was harsh and quick.

Leonora flew through the house and down the staircase and picked up the phone. At the sound of the doctor's quiet voice she let out a great sigh of thankfulness.

'James, it's Nanny. She's ill—hot and restless and her breathing's funny—and she doesn't know me.'

'Unlock the front door and go back to her.' His matter-of-fact manner steadied her. 'I'll be with you in ten minutes.'

It was less than that when he came quietly into the room. He was wearing a thick sweater and trousers, his hair stood on end and there was a faint stubble on his chin, but his manner was as cool and self-assured as though he were in his surgery.

He took one look at Leonora. 'Go and put on a dressing gown before you catch cold; we may be here for a little while.'

His tone was impersonal but she flushed a little, until that moment forgetful of the fact that she had rushed to Nanny in a cotton nightie and bare feet. She nodded and disappeared silently, to reappear moments later, her dressing gown fastened tightly around her, slippers on her feet.

The doctor was bending over Nanny, going over her chest with his stethoscope. Presently he stood up. 'Pneumonia. I'll give her an injection—an antibiotic—and see if I can find her a bed. She needs hospital treatment.'

Leonora's eyes looked enormous in her pale face. 'She'll hate that…'

His voice was very gentle. 'At the moment she isn't very aware of where she is—she'll only need to stay for a few days until the antibiotics do their work, then we can have her back.'

He took his phone from his pocket and dialled and Leonora stood as quiet as a mouse, holding Nanny's hand, listening to his calm voice.

'There's a bed at Bath; I'll get an ambulance; the sooner she gets there the better.' He glanced at her. 'Get a bag and pack a few things, will you?'

'Yes. May I go with her? Please…'

'I'll take you in the car; I'll see her safely in bed and bring you back here—hopefully in time for morning surgery.'

She nodded. 'I'll go and dress and get Nanny's things together. Will you be all right here?'

He checked a smile and assured her gravely that he would be.

She tore into the first clothes she laid hands on, washed her face, dragged a comb through her hair and tied it back with a bit of ribbon, before going back to pack a bag for Nanny. An easy task. Nanny's drawers were immaculate, garments folded exactly, beautifully ironed, smelling of lavender bags. Leonora packed her old-fashioned nighties, her dressing gown and slippers and brush and comb and bag of toiletries, added her spectacles and the Bible she kept on her bedside table and closed the case.

The doctor was sitting on the edge of the bed, watching Nanny, completely relaxed. 'Shall I make a cup of tea?' she asked. 'I got you out of bed very early…'

'A splendid idea, and bring a pencil and paper with you. You must leave a note for your mother and father. You don't want to wake them?'

'They would worry. Perhaps I could phone them from the hospital.'

'A good idea. The ambulance should be here in fifteen minutes or so.'

She crept down to the kitchen and made tea. Wilkins, from his basket by the Aga, was pleased to see her, accepted a biscuit and went back to sleep, and she went back upstairs with two mugs and more biscuits on a tray.

While they ate and drank she composed a note and showed it to the doctor. 'Would that do? I don't want to upset them.'

He gave her a thoughtful look, read the note and handed it back. 'That's fine. If you've finished your tea, we'll get Nanny wrapped up ready for the ambulancemen. They may wake your parents…'

'Probably not; their room is at the back of the house and there's a door to the passage leading to it. Shall I creep in and leave the note? And then if they're awake I can tell them.'

He nodded without speaking and began to wrap Nanny carefully in a blanket. She was quieter now, unaware that she was coughing.

Leonora whispered, 'Is she very ill?' She added sharply, 'Tell me the truth.'

'Yes, but I hope that we have caught it in time. She's a tough little lady.' He listened. 'There's the ambulance. Go and let them in; tell them to be quiet.'

When they came into the room, he told her to go to her parents' room with the note and then go down to the hall. 'And bring a jacket.'

Her parents didn't stir as she opened their door, put the note on a bedside table and crept out again, closing the door after her. The men were loading the stretcher into the ambulance as she reached the hall and as they shut its doors the doctor went to his car. 'Jump in—I'll close your front door.'

She got in and sat silently while he drove, keeping the ambulance in sight. It was beginning to get light now and she felt a strong urge to go to sleep but it was a comparatively short journey and she told herself that she wasn't really tired.

'Do you often do this—get up in the night?'

'Quite frequently. I don't need much sleep.' He didn't tell her that he had only been in bed for a couple of hours when she had phoned. 'How will you manage at home?'

'Oh, I'll manage,' she assured him. 'We've got help from the village now I'm at the surgery, and there's not much to do.'

Which, considering the size of her home and her mother's helplessness, wasn't true.

'You'll be able to manage the surgery as well as household chores? I dare say your mother will help out.'

Leonora's reply to that sounded so doubtful that he didn't say any more.

Trotting behind the trolley bearing Nanny to her ward, Leonora was wide awake again; the doctor was talking to a solemn-looking man in a long white coat and appeared to have forgotten her; it seemed best to keep close to Nanny.

Waiting by the bed, she saw him coming towards her, still with the same man and this time with a nurse, who told her to wait outside the ward. 'There's a rest room, dear. We'll talk to you presently.'

It seemed a long time before James came looking for her.

'Come and see Nanny and then we'll go back,' he told her briskly. 'She's in good hands and there is an excellent chance of her recovery. She won't know you but don't let that worry you. We'll come and see her this evening.'

Nanny looked comfortable propped up on pillows, very small against them. She was dozing and although she didn't respond to Leonora's kiss it seemed as though she was better.

The doctor's hand on her arm roused her to say good-bye to the nurse and go with him back to the car, and he popped her in, got in beside her and drove away.

'I'll take you home,' he told her presently. 'You can do your hair and so on and I'll collect you in half an hour. You'll breakfast with me and we'll open the surgery at the usual time.'

'Oh, but I can't—I mean, there's breakfast to get for Mother and Father.'

'I dare say your mother will manage that for once,' he observed. 'You've a day's work ahead of you, remember.'

'So have you.'

'Ah, but I have Cricket to cosset me. And he will enjoy cosseting you too.'

'Yes, that would be nice, but...'

'Dear girl, will you do as I say?' He sounded so kind that she could have wept—just because she was tired and chilly and hungry.

She said, 'Yes, James,' in such a meek voice that he glanced at her in surprise.

At the house he went in with her, but there was no sound. He left her in the hall, reminding her that he would return in half an hour, and she went to her room, showered and dressed again, did her hair in its usual chignon and made up her tired face. There was just time to go to the kitchen, put the kettle on and lay a tray for early-morning tea. Wilkins, roused from sleep, went out into the garden, and she went upstairs to wake her parents.

There wasn't time to do more than give a quick explanation.

'I'll be back at lunchtime,' she told them. 'Wilkins has been out and you'll only have breakfast to get.'

Lady Crosby sat up in bed. 'My dear child, I'll do my best. You know I always do, however poorly I feel.'

'I dare say I can boil an egg,' said her father gruffly. 'Pity about Nanny.' He sipped his tea. 'I'll ring the hospital later. Is she very ill?'

'Yes, Father. I must go; I'll come home as soon as I can.'

She reached the door at the same time as the Rolls came to a silent halt before it. James got out and opened her door for her.

'You look as fresh as a daisy,' he observed. 'Parents awake?'

'Yes. Father said he'd phone the hospital later on.'

'I shall be going to see her this evening. Want to come with me?'

'Oh, yes.' He watched her tell-tale thoughts racing across her face. 'What time? I mean, I'll have to get a meal.'

'Put something in the oven. We shan't be away long. We'll go directly after surgery.'

Cricket had the door open as they reached it and she was marched straight into the dining room, her nose twitching at the delicious smells coming from the open kitchen door. She was sat down, given a cup of coffee and then, urged by her host, fell to on bacon, eggs, mushrooms and fried bread, and then, again gently persuaded by the doctor, toast and marmalade and more coffee.

She could have curled up in a chair and slept then but she was whisked out into the garden and walked briskly round while Tod circled about them. It was a cool, bright morning and by the time they had to leave for the surgery she was wide awake again. Cricket, handing her her jacket with a fatherly air, actually smiled widely.

'That was the most delicious breakfast,' she told him, and gave him a smile to melt his elderly heart.

She thanked James too with an even sweeter smile and he, a man who prided himself on his self-control, nodded casually, so that her heart, which had been thumping happily in his company, plunged into her shoes. But what do I expect? she thought, getting into the car once again.

CHAPTER NINE

THERE WEREN'T MANY patients at the surgery; by eleven o'clock the place was empty and Leonora put the kettle on and got out two mugs and the coffee. Dr Galbraith's round was smaller than usual too—she had looked in the book to check that—so it was disappointing when he declined a drink and went away with a brisk, 'I'll see you at this evening's surgery.'

After he had gone, she had her coffee, got the patients' notes out ready for the evening, took a few phone calls and tidied the place, then sat down to wait for Mrs Crisp. She arrived punctually and Leonora explained hurriedly about Nanny.

'The poor dear,' said Mrs Crisp warmly. 'But there, she's not all that young, is she? And that great house to manage—just the two of you. I don't know how you do it; let me know if I can be of any help, Miss Leonora.'

Leonora thanked her and made for the door, to be stopped by Mrs Crisp's voice. 'I almost forgot—you've not had time to see the local paper, of course. The doctor's advertising for a receptionist—part-time, like you. I dare say you want to get back to your usual...' She paused and added awkwardly, 'What I mean is, I dare say Sir William isn't too keen on your working here in the village. The doctor did tell me you were just helping out until he could get someone to suit him. He asked me if I'd like the job full-time but of course I haven't the time for that, so he says, "Well, Mrs Crisp, you stay on part-time, and I'll find someone as soon as possible."' She smiled. 'He's a real gentlemen, isn't he?'

Leonora said brightly, 'I hope he finds someone— we're a bit out of the way, aren't we?' She smiled too. 'I must go; I'll be back on time.'

Perhaps it was a good thing she had no time to think once she got home. Her mother was in the kitchen, opening and shutting drawers and cupboards in an aimless way. 'Darling, here you are. I can't find anything, silly little me. Will you make a salad for lunch, and perhaps a cheese soufflé…?'

'Has Father phoned the hospital?' asked Leonora, dismissing the soufflé.'

'He thought it would be better to wait for an hour or so, darling. By then Nanny may be feeling better.'

Leonora went back into the hall and picked up the phone. Nanny was about the same, holding her own, she was told, and she could ring again that evening if she wished.

She went back to the kitchen. 'Where's Father, Mother?' she asked, and began opening drawers and cupboards, assembling lunch.

'In his study, dear. What shall we do about dinner this evening?' Lady Crosby sat down. 'Oh, dear, I am so upset…'

They had their lunch in the kitchen, which, Lady Crosby observed, took away every vestige of her appetite. 'I think I'd better go and lie down for a while; I've got one of my headaches coming on.'

Sir William helped to clear the table and Leonora said, 'I'm going to the hospital this evening with Dr Galbraith, Father. I'll get everything ready for supper and I'm sure Mother could manage if I'm not back. We're going directly after surgery.'

'Yes, yes, of course. I'll drive over in a day or so when Nanny feels more the thing!' He added uneasily, 'You're sure you can manage? I'm afraid your mother isn't up to doing much.'

'It isn't for long, Father, and I can manage.' She hoped she could; if and when Nanny came home, she would have her hands full. Perhaps the district nurse would help out. Time to worry about that later. There certainly wasn't time to worry now: beds to make, rooms to tidy, a tea-tray to set ready, a meal to prepare for the evening.

She arrived back at the surgery feeling tired and not looking her best.

The doctor, seeing this and saying nothing, wondered how best to help her; the wish to carry her off to Buntings and keep her there was hardly practical. Besides, he had had no indication that she would agree to that. It was a problem he had no time to solve at the moment.

Later, as he drove past her home, she cast a guilty look at the lighted windows. Her mother and father would be coping as best they could; she ought to be there looking after them.

James had seen her glance. 'They'll cope,' he told her easily. 'It will be only for a short time and both your mother and father are very fit for their age—and they are by no means old.'

'Old?' She sounded shocked. 'Mother's in her early fifties; she married very young.'

'There you are, then.' He began to talk about something else and when they reached the hospital took her straight to Nanny.

Nanny looked as though a puff of wind would blow her away, but at least she recognised them.

'Such a botheration,' she wheezed, 'me feeling poorly; your ma will never manage.' She peered up at Leonora's face. 'And you'll be worked to death.'

'No, no, Nanny, we're managing beautifully. You aren't to worry. It's only for a little while anyhow. You'll be back home in no time.'

The doctor, standing beside her, made no effort to contradict this statement. Presently he wandered away to speak to the house physician.

'He's a good man,' said Nanny between coughs. 'Tell your ma and pa not to come visiting me; there's no need. Getting the best of treatment—such nice girls the nurses are; nothing's too much trouble.' She glanced at the flowers Leonora had brought with her. 'They'll look a treat on my locker. Now don't you waste your time coming here, Miss Leonora; you've enough on your plate.'

'If Dr Galbraith gives me a lift, it's the easiest thing in the world,' said Leonora. 'Is there anything you want, Nanny—books or magazines?'

'Bless you, no.' Nanny stopped to cough; she was tired now and Leonora said quickly, 'I'm going now, but I'll be back. Take care!'

She bent to kiss her old friend and left the ward to stand about outside its doors wondering where the doctor had gone. He joined her presently.

'I've had a talk with the man in charge of Nanny. She's doing well, even after twelve hours. Not quite out of the woods yet... She was pleased to see you!'

Leonora nodded. 'Yes, she was bothered about looking after Mother and Father.' She added, 'She looks very ill…'

'She is ill but the tests which have been done are all satisfactory; give the antibiotics a chance and she'll be as good as new.'

He spoke in a manner which she couldn't help but believe; she went with him to the car feeling cheerful, ready to cope with the evening ahead.

At the house he got out of the car and helped her out, but when she asked him to go in with her he refused. 'I'm dining out,' he explained. 'I'll see you in the morning. Don't worry about Nanny; she will be all right.'

She went indoors then, after thanking him politely for the lift and saying that she hoped he would have a pleasant evening—something which she hardly expected to have herself. And nor did she; there was too much to do.

Back from his dinner party later that evening, the doctor went in search of Cricket.

'I need your help,' he told him. 'This is what I want you to do…'

So the following morning Cricket made his stately way to the Dowlings' residence and remained closeted with Jenks, their butler, for some time.

'On no account must Miss Crosby be told that these come from Dr Galbraith; tell Sir William that Mr Dowling sent them as a gift. They're quite ready to be put into the oven…'

Jenks nodded a bald head. 'I'll see that's done, but why the secrecy, or may I not ask?'

'I'm not at liberty to say more, but shall we just say that there may be wedding bells in the offing? Strictly between us, of course. Nothing said, I fancy—the doctor isn't a man to hurry and Miss Crosby needs a delicate hand. A charming young lady, I must add, but touchy about money matters; I gather there's not much of it up at the house. Any whiff of charity and she would retreat.'

When Leonora got home at lunchtime she was met by her mother.

'Darling, such luck—the Dowlings have sent over a brace of pheasants they can't use. Ready to pop into the oven too. Isn't that marvellous? Now you'll have almost no cooking to do this evening.'

Leonora, who had been cudgelling her brains as to how to present sausages disguised as something else, was relieved at the news.

Evening surgery wasn't busy, which was a good thing, for the doctor was called away as his last patient was preparing to leave—Mrs Squires, complaining of aches and pains, demanding a bottle of tonic. There was nothing like it, she assured the doctor. 'And I dare say you may be a very clever man, but there's a lot you could learn about tonics.'

He agreed placidly, wrote out a prescription and left her in Leonora's hands, bidding them goodbye as he went.

A mean trick, thought Leonora, longing to get home to deal with the pheasants and delayed by Mrs Squires, eager for a nice long chat. By the time she did get home she was tired and cross; the pheasants still had to be dealt with...but first of all she phoned the hospital. Nanny was doing well, responding to the antibiotics, eating a little, sleeping well. She told her father and he agreed to drive over to the hospital on the following day.

'In the afternoon, Father,' urged Leonora. 'If we go directly after lunch we can be back in time for surgery.'

At morning surgery the doctor told her that he had talked to the house physician at the hospital. 'Nanny's doing well; they'll be sending her home in five or six days; can you manage?'

'Oh, easily,' said Leonora instantly, and added mendaciously, 'I've help from the village, you know.'

'Splendid. I shall be driving to the hospital this evening; do you want a lift?'

'Father's going this afternoon and I said I'd go with him. Thank you for the offer.'

Determined to preserve a cool front, she succeeded in sounding frosty instead.

Later, sitting in his study with Tod sprawled over his feet, James pushed aside the work he was doing and applied his powerful brain to the subject of Leonora's sudden coolness. What had he done or not done? he wondered. Surely she hadn't found out about the pheasants? If she had he was sure that she would have taxed him with that in no uncertain terms. She was avoiding him and although she was tired and worried her distance was caused by even more than that—something was making her unhappy.

Surely she wasn't still in love with Beamish? With five sisters he was only too well aware of the vagaries to be encountered in the female. He wished very much to tell her of his love for her but if he spoke now he might ruin his chances...

As the days went by it was so obvious that Leonora was avoiding his company that he took care that they spent as little time together as possible. An outbreak of chickenpox kept him busy both in and out of the surgery, and though he drove her to see Nanny one evening he was careful to behave with detached friendliness. From Cricket he heard that the help from the village was quite inadequate, that Lady Crosby seemed unable to lift a finger round the house, that Sir William didn't seem to notice any shortcomings as long as he had his meals, and that there were lights showing at the house long after sensible people were in bed.

Nanny was to be sent home in two days' time; the pneumonia had been banished but she was still in need of rest, good food and attention. At the hospital Leonora greeted the news with a cheerful face, casting aside Nanny's anxious worries as to how they were to manage; indeed, to hear her, one would have thought that she had boundless help! The doctor said nothing until they were in the car going home.

'I will arrange for the nurse to come each day and get Nanny up and dressed, and again in the evening to settle her back in bed.'

'There's no need...'

He said levelly, 'I must remind you that I am Nanny's doctor, Leonora.'

'Oh, well, yes. Thank you.' She added in a stilted manner, 'We do appreciate your care and kindness. How long will it take Nanny to get quite well?'

'Ten days, two weeks. If she wishes to potter before then there is no reason why she shouldn't, but it would be best if she takes things very easily for another week.'

'I'll make sure of that.'

'I'll fetch her home on Sunday morning; perhaps you will come with me?'

'Yes, please.' She thanked him again as he dropped her off at the house.

She watched him drive away and then walked round the house to the garden door with Wilkins beside her. 'It's no good, Wilkins,' she observed. 'Everything's gone wrong, hasn't it? He's just the family doctor!'

He lived up to that for the next two days—always kind and friendly and at the same time aloof.

On Sunday she got into the car, delighted to be with James even if he was keeping her at a distance. But she need not have worried; he kept up a steady flow of cheerful talk and at the hospital went with her to the ward to fetch Nanny, who was dressed and ready and pale with the excitement of going back home again.

Leonora sat in the back of the car with her, exchanging places with Tod, who sat motionless beside his master, and listened to Nanny's observations about the nurses and doctors, the food and the treatments. 'They were all very kind,' said Nanny, 'but, of course, it's not like home, is it?'

The doctor carried her indoors and up the staircase to her room, taking no notice of her protests. 'I shall come to see you in a day or two; mind and do exactly what Leonora says—a week doing nothing much, Nanny. After that you can resume your reign in the kitchen.'

He spent a short time with Sir William and Lady Crosby while Leonora got Nanny back into her bed for a rest. 'Nurse will come morning and evening for the next week,' he told them. 'Leonora will need some help until Nanny is on her feet again; she has been quite ill and must do nothing much for a while.'

'Of course not,' agreed Lady Crosby. 'You may be sure we'll take good care of her. You'll stay for coffee? I'm sure Leonora will make some.'

'Thank you, I won't stop, but if I may I'll take a look at Nanny before I go.'

Nanny was sitting up in bed telling Leonora where to put her clothes. She turned a shrewd eye on him as he went in. 'This child will be worn out looking after me and this blessed great place; it's time I was on my feet.'

He sat down on the side of the bed. 'Just stay quiet for a little longer, Nanny. I won't allow Leonora to get worn out. Nurse is coming to help you each day and you may get up and sit here and walk about the room, but no more.'

He glanced about him. It was a cosy room and quite well furnished; someone had put flowers in a vase on the little table near the bed and the place was warm. He supposed that there was some kind of central heating, although keeping a house this size even comfortably warm must be a problem. Fortunately the weather was mild. He bade her goodbye, told Leonora not to see him out, and went away.

'Now that's the man for you,' said Nanny, twitching her elderly nose. She hadn't been blind, watching the pair of them behaving as though they'd only just met. She closed her eyes, ready for a nap. She need not worry; the doctor was a man to sort out his own problems, Leonora's with them too, of course.

The week went slowly by; Leonora went to and from the surgery, presenting a smiling face when anyone looked at her. After only four days she was tired already, but things would get easier, she told herself, and the nurse was a great help. Besides, Nanny was getting better each day; the doctor had been to see her that morning and pronounced himself more than satisfied. As he'd left he had asked Leonora if she was managing.

'Oh, yes. Thank you,' she had told him brightly, her eyes daring him to ask any more questions.

The next evening, dining at Colonel Howes' house, he was surprised to see Sir William and Lady Crosby among the guests. He went to speak to them as soon as he could. 'Is Leonora not with you?' he wanted to know.

'Well, Nanny can't be left and Leonora said she was tired anyway; a nice quiet evening will do her good,' Lady Crosby told him.

Dinner was barely finished when he told his host that he had a night call to make. 'I'll slip away quietly,' he said. 'Otherwise it might break up the evening.'

He went to his home first and found Cricket in the kitchen.

'Food, Cricket,' said the doctor. 'Something nice and quick to eat. I'll get a bottle from the cellar. What have we got?'

'Cold chicken, Parma ham, some of my pâté if you can make the toast. Egg custard. A salad, if I can have five minutes.'

Ten minutes later the doctor, with Tod beside him, was driving through the village. Turning into the gates, he saw that most of the downstairs lights were on and, bidding Tod be quiet, he got out of his car and walked round the house to the garden door. It wasn't locked and he went in, restraining Tod as Wilkins began to bark. The old dog came running down the passage but stopped barking when he saw who it was and the three of them went on to the kitchen.

Leonora had her back to them. 'What's up, Wilkins?' she asked, and turned round. The look on her face when she saw James brought a gleam to his eyes although he remained unsmiling.

His expression showed nothing of his thoughts. That she offered no beautiful picture bothered him not at all. She was lovely—the most beautiful girl in the world—even dressed as she was in a worthy dressing gown and a pinny tied around her waist. Her hair hung in an untidy plait and her make-up had long ago passed its best. She was mopping the kitchen floor and the mop dripped unheeded as she stood looking at him.

He said in a soothing voice, 'Hello—I hope I didn't scare you. I thought we might have supper together.'

'Supper?' She stared at him and then smiled. 'Mother and Father have gone out to dinner…'

'Yes, I know; I was there.'

'You've had dinner—'

'I wasn't hungry but I am now.' He put his basket down on the kitchen table, took the mop from her, swabbed up the puddle it had made, and took it and the bucket over to the sink.

Leonora looked down at her person. 'I got ready for bed but it was a chance to get the housework done. I'll go and dress.'

'No need. Take off that pinny and wash your hands. I'm going to lock the garden door.'

When he came back he unpacked the basket, took the champagne from its cooler and poured two glasses.

'Champagne,' said Leonora faintly, and took a reviving sip. Somehow everything was all right; she looked a fright but James didn't seem to mind. They were friends again; if only they could stay like that. Only she would have to be careful not to betray her feelings. He found knives and forks and plates, and set out the food, refilling her glass.

Champagne on a very empty stomach did wonders

for her ego; with a sigh of delight she demolished the delicacies Cricket had provided and had another glass of champagne.

'Stay there; I'll make coffee if you tell me which cupboard to get it from.'

They had their coffee, and she, in a delightful haze, had no idea what they talked about; all she knew was that she was happy.

James was happy too but to propose to his Leonora when she was so delightfully bemused with champagne wouldn't do at all. He cleared the supper things away, washed the dishes and put everything away tidily, and Leonora, watching him, said on a slightly boozy giggle, 'You'll make a good husband, James.'

He had his back to her. 'I value your opinion, Leonora,' he told her. Then in a quite different voice he added, 'I'm going to see Nanny; then when I am gone you are to go straight to bed—I want your promise about that.'

She gave the tiniest of hiccups and he smiled a little. 'I promise.'

He went away, going quietly through the house, and presently returned.

'Nanny is awake and perfectly all right. Come with me to the door and lock it after me.'

At the door she stooped to caress Tod. 'Thank you for a lovely supper, and please thank Cricket too.' She smiled up at him and he bent his head and kissed her—a hard, quick kiss which took her breath—and then walked swiftly away.

She locked the door then and went back to the kitchen to settle Wilkins and put out the lights, all the while in a glow of happiness.

Upstairs she wandered into Nanny's room to say goodnight.

Nanny gave her a thoughtful stare. 'Didn't I say that's the man for you?' she wanted to know. 'Go to bed, and sweet dreams, my pet.'

So Leonora did just that.

She went to work still in a glow of happiness the next morning, and the doctor gave a sigh of relief at the sight of her face as she wished him a good morning. His Leonora had at last allowed her feelings to show...

There were a lot of patients but none of them were seriously ill; they finished a little early and Leonora went to put the kettle on, turning to smile at James as he came into the waiting room.

'An easy morning,' he observed. 'Nanny is going on well?'

'Yes. She is longing to get into the kitchen; I do wonder what she is doing when I am not there.'

She had spoken jokingly but he answered seriously, 'Well, that's soon remedied. I have a receptionist coming on Monday so you will not need to come to the surgery any more.'

Leonora went pale. 'Not come? You mean you are giving me the sack?'

'Yes.'

'You don't want me here any more?'

'No. Oh, you have been entirely satisfactory—I'm not sure what I would have done without your help—but you did know that it was a temporary arrangement.' He smiled and her unhappy heart did a somersault. He went on, 'I hadn't meant to say anything—not here—but perhaps you'll come to Buntings and have lunch with me—there will be time to talk.'

'What about?' she asked, and before he could answer she said, 'No, I'm afraid I can't; I have to go home. Besides, there is nothing to talk about.' She went on rather wildly, 'And even if there was I wouldn't want to hear it.'

He turned off the gas under the kettle. 'Then you will have to hear it now...' He took the phone up as it rang and stood listening.

'Lacock's Farm? I'll be with you as quickly as possible. Get an ambulance and the fire brigade.'

He put the phone down. 'Where is Lacock's Farm exactly? Somewhere close to Norrington Common? How far?'

'Four miles. Off the road; there's a cart track to the farm.'

He was in the surgery, putting things into his bag. 'A barn roof has collapsed; there were a number of children inside. They've got three out, injured; there are several more inside.'

He came back into the waiting room, sweeping her along with him. 'You'll have to show me the way.'

He locked the surgery door, urged her into the car and drove off.

'Take the first turn on the left about half a mile away,' said Leonora, and moments later she added, 'Here, the road narrows. The track's about a mile on the right.'

The Rolls ate up the mile at a speed which boded ill for anything coming the other way; she let out a breath as James turned into the track. The pace was slower now. 'The farm is only a few hundred yards ahead,' she told him. 'You can't see it for the trees. It's on the left.'

The farmyard was large, with the farmhouse on its farther side and outbuildings on two sides, and beyond the house was the barn, its collapsed roof in a vast, sprawling pile, thatch and bricks and cob-walls still crumbling slowly.

The doctor drove up to the house, got out and opened Leonora's door, picked up his bag and strode to the barn. There were several people there: a woman standing in tears with a little girl in her arms, two men and a young boy climbing over the rubble searching.

The woman saw them first. 'Miss Crosby—Doctor. Tracey's hurt—her arm—and little Tim and Jilly are over there; there's no one to look after them.'

'See what you can do,' said the doctor to Leonora, and went over to the men.

'Into the house, I think,' said Leonora, hoping she would remember at least some of her first-aid lessons. 'I'll get the other two.'

She went to where they sat huddled on the ground, thanking heaven to find that they were more frightened than hurt. They had bumps and scratches but once in the house, where she could see them properly, she could find no bad injury. She sat them side by side on the old-fashioned sofa in the living room and turned her attention to Tracey.

The little girl was weeping copiously, which Leonora hoped was a good sign, but one small arm hung awkwardly, swollen and already showing bruises. Leonora opened drawers and cupboards, found a dinner napkin and made a sling. A warm drink, she remembered—sweet tea.

She sat a shocked Mrs Lacock beside the two children, settled Tracey on her lap and went in search of the teapot. She was in luck; the pot stood keeping warm beside the stove and if the tea was stewed she didn't think it would matter. She found mugs, milk and sugar and hurried back to the living room.

'Can you help the children to drink this and have some yourself? I'm going to see if I can do anything...'

The yard was slippery; they had been muck-spreading and she had to scramble carefully to where the men were clearing away rubble from the far end of the barn. As she reached them she saw the doctor stoop, draw a child out of the ruins and bend over her for a moment. She fetched up beside him and he handed the child to her. 'Take her indoors, lie her flat and cover her—a broken leg and concussion, I think; I'll come as soon as I can.'

The child was unconscious; Leonora laid her on a rug at Mrs Lacock's feet. 'Keep an eye on her,' she begged, and made her way back to the barn.

They were carefully edging a boy out of the medley of beams and thatch and stone and this time the doctor carried him back to the house and laid him down carefully beside the girl. 'Stay with him,' he told Leonora. 'There's still another child.'

She did what she could, thankful in a way that the two children were unconscious, keeping them covered warmly, wiping their small, dirty faces, gently cleaning the cuts she could reach without moving them. The sound of the ambulances, followed by the deeper note of the fire engine, didn't come a moment too soon, for the children needed expert care and despite her first aid there was little she could do.

There was activity now, men coming and going, taking over from the men and boy and James, who came into the house and began to examine the children. The paramedics came with him and Leonora, sitting with one of the children on her lap, watched him. For the moment she had forgotten that he had no interest in her, had made it clear that they were no more than acquaintances, living in the same village; he was the man she loved and always would love, unflappable in disaster, knowing what to do, never raising his voice, kind...

She watched for what seemed a very long time while he worked on the unconscious little boy and girl, who were taken away in the ambulance just as a shout heralded the rescue of the last child. Another boy. In a still worse state, she guessed, covered in dust and bits of thatch and blood. It was a long time before James was satisfied that he was well enough to be taken to the hospital. She could only guess at the emergency treatment he had been given.

It was the turn of the three children with Mrs Lacock, who between them were suffering from shock, a small broken arm and bruises and who after careful examination were got into the third ambulance and sent after the others.

The police were there now and James went away to talk to them, and a policewoman came into the house, asked Leonora if she was all right and went to make tea for everyone. Presently James came back, rolling down his shirtsleeves and putting on his jacket.

'You're all right?' he wanted to know. He spoke very gently. She looked like a scarecrow, covered in dust and earth and blood, her hair with half the pins missing. He thought she had never looked so beautiful.

'We'll go home,' he told her, 'and get clean and have a meal.'

Leonora got to her feet and followed him out to the car and sat quietly while he phoned Cricket. 'Let Lady

Crosby know that Leonora is coming back with me, will you? We need to clean up and eat.'

'No,' said Leonora. 'I wish to go home.' Everything came rushing back then. 'And I do not wish to go to the surgery or to your house ever again!' She added as an afterthought, 'Thank you.'

James started the car. 'Ah, yes, I was interrupted, wasn't I? You will at least hear me out before you blight our lives for ever. Don't expect me to say any more at the moment; this infernal track takes all my patience.'

As he swept into the village she said once more, 'I want to go home.'

For answer he turned into his own gates. 'This is your home—or will be very shortly.'

She sat very still, not looking at him. 'You sacked me this morning...'

'Well, of course I did, you silly goose.'

He got out and ushered her into the house and Cricket came to meet them, tut-tutting at the sight of them.

'Show Miss Crosby to a room and a bathroom, Cricket, will you? And see if you can find a dressing gown or something similar while someone fetches some fresh clothes for her from the house.'

She was led away up the stairs to a pretty room with an adjoining bathroom. 'Just you have a nice hot bath, miss,' said Cricket, sounding very like Nanny. 'I'll arrange for someone to fetch your things and put a gown in the bedroom for you. And there's a tasty lunch ready when you are.'

Leonora stood in the middle of the room and looked at him. If only he knew how delightful it was to be taken care of. She blinked away tears and smiled. 'Thank you, Cricket; I won't be long.'

There were bath salts, bottles of fragrant oil, the very best of soaps, vast sponges and a shelf of lotions. There wasn't time to wash her dusty hair but she gave it a good brushing and got into a towelling bathrobe. It trailed on the ground and she had to roll up the sleeves and it shrouded her from neck to ankles. She went downstairs and found the doctor, very correctly dressed, in dark grey worsted and a dignified tie.

'We will eat first, then we will talk,' he said, resisting a strong desire to take her in his arms there and then; she was still wary of him and still cross...

Tod pranced to meet her and she bent to pat him before sitting down in the chair James was holding for her, surprised to find that she was hungry. Certainly the lunch Cricket served them would have tempted her even if she had had no appetite at all, and despite her unease the doctor's calm voice, rambling on in a soothing manner about nothing much, did a great deal to restore her usual good sense.

So she had got the sack, she reflected, spooning up a nice old-fashioned junket with clotted cream, but that was to be expected; she'd had no reason to expect otherwise, had she? And she had been warned: Mrs Crisp had told her about the advertisement. She wondered what the receptionist would be like. Young and clever, never keeping James waiting, highly efficient and pretty...

'You aren't listening,' said James. 'We will go into the drawing room, where you will clear your sadly muddled thoughts and listen to me.'

'I must go home,' said Leonora, striving for common sense.

'Have you forgotten what I told you just now?'

They had crossed into the drawing room and were standing by the door into the garden while Tod dashed in and out.

'No, no, of course not.' She looked up at him. 'Only I'm not sure what you meant.'

He took her in his arms. 'Then I will tell you, and I will repeat what I am about to say as often as necessary for the rest of our lives. I've fallen in love with you, my darling; I think I did that when we first met even if you weren't at your dignified best.' He smiled down at her. 'I love you, my dearest Leonora, and I want to marry you.'

She looked up at him with shining eyes. 'Oh, James—and I want to marry you too, only I thought that you didn't love me, or even like me very much, so I tried to stop loving you, only I couldn't...'

He kissed her then, gently. 'My dearest love. So you will marry me—and soon?'

'As soon as we can.' She paused to think. 'Well, I must have some clothes and Mother will want to arrange things, I expect. I wish we could just creep away and get married now.'

He kissed her again, this time in a manner to leave her breathless.

'Mother and Father and Nanny,' said Leonora presently. 'Who will look after them? And Mother will want me to have a big wedding and Father can't afford that... Oh, dear!'

James gathered her closer. He said with calm assurance, 'Will you leave everything to me, my darling?'

Leonora, looking up into his face and seeing the love

in it and hearing his calm, assured voice, said at once,
'Yes, of course I will, James.'

She smiled at him, wanting him to kiss her again.

Which James duly did, to her entire satisfaction.

* * * * *

Enjoy this sneak preview of
THE RETURNING HERO,
the first in Soraya Lane's
THE SOLDIERS' HOMECOMING *duet!*

"LET ME STAY for a few days, let you catch up on some sleep while I'm here."

His voice was lower than usual, an octave deeper. She shook her head. "You don't have to do that. I'll be fine."

She might have been telling him no, but inside she was screaming out for him to stay. Having Brett here would make her feel safe, let her relax and just sleep solidly for a few nights at least, but she didn't expect him to do that.

And her intentions weren't pure, either. Because ever since she'd starting thinking about Brett in a certain way last night, remembering how soft his lips had been, how sensual it had been pressed against his body, she'd thought of nothing other than having him here. Keeping him close. Wondering if something could happen between them, and whether he wanted it as much as she did, even if she did know it was wrong.

"If I'm honest, Brett, having you here for a few days sounds idyllic." She wanted to stay strong, but she also wanted a man in her house again. Wanted the company of someone she could actually talk to, who wasn't afraid of the truth. Of what had happened to her husband. Because she had no one else to talk to, and no one else to turn to. She'd lost her dad and then her husband to war, and she was tired of being alone. "But only if you're sure."

She listened to Brett's big intake of breath, watched the way his body stiffened, then softened back to normal again.

"Then I'll stay. As long as you need me here, I'll stay."

She dropped her head to his shoulder. "He would have liked you being here. You know that, right?"

Brett shrugged, but she could tell he was finding this as awkward as she was. "You know, he made me promise to look out for you if anything ever happened to him. I just never figured that we'd actually be in that position."

Jamie smiled. "I'll never forget what you've done for me, Brett."

Brett was her friend. Nothing more. She just had to keep reminding herself of that, because falling in love with her husband's best buddy? Not something that could happen. Not now, not ever.

Brett could have been the man of her dreams—*once*. But now wasn't the time to look back. Now was about the future. The one she had to build without her husband by her side. No matter how much she was thinking about *that* kiss.

Don't miss THE RETURNING HERO by Soraya Lane, available March 2014. And look out for the second in this heartwarming duet, HER SOLDIER PROTECTOR, available April 2014.

HARLEQUIN® Romance

Road Trip With The Eligible Bachelor
Michelle Douglas

The beginning of a very long journey...together?

Quinn Laverty and her young sons are planning to start a new life on the other side of the country! With her family abandoning her, and her ex choosing wealth and privilege over fatherhood, her boys are all she's got.

But when an airline strike interferes with her plans, Quinn finds herself taking the car and up-and-coming politician (who is seriously gorgeous!) Aidan Fairhall to Sydney. Quinn and Aidan are trapped together on a weeklong road trip and sparks soon fly as they begin the most unexpected journey of their lives....

Available next month from Harlequin Romance, wherever books and ebooks are sold.

HR74281

HARLEQUIN® Romance

Safe In The Tycoon's Arms
Jennifer Faye

The man behind the headlines...

When billionaire Lucas Carrington returns
to his neglected New York mansion, he never
expects to find beautiful stranger Kate Whitley.
Invited by his aunt to stay, he discovers she's
a woman in need. She's trying to raise funds
for her sick daughter, so he agrees to let her
stay—temporarily!

Kate may not belong in Lucas's world, but
behind closed doors, she sees there is more to
this tycoon than the headlines realize. Yet with
so much at stake, Kate must decide whether
to trust herself and her heart with New York's
most eligible bachelor!

***Available next month from Harlequin Romance,
wherever books and ebooks are sold.***

HR74282

HARLEQUIN® Romance

Rescued by the Millionaire
by Cara Colter

Wanted: A second pair of hands!

Daniel Riverton is handsome, eligible…and a
confirmed bachelor. The only thing he finds more
frightening than commitment? Children!

So when his neighbor Trixie Marsh appeals for
his help with her twin nieces, his instinct is to
steer clear. But there's something about Trixie
that makes her hard to say no to….

Only problem is, the more time Daniel spends
with this little family, the less he likes the idea
of his empty apartment. There is one way to
solve his dilemma…but is he up to
the challenge?

*Available February 4, 2014 from
Harlequin Romance wherever
books and ebooks are sold.*

HARLEQUIN®
Romance

Heiress on the Run
by Sophie Pembroke

Once a Lady…

Having barely survived the scandal of a public
betrayal, Lord Dominic Beresford needs his luck to
change. But with his business on the rocks, it's not
looking good….

Three years ago Lady Faith Fowlmere left her painful
past *and* identity behind, but life on the run has left
her jobless, penniless and alone.

When fate throws the two together, it seems they're
the answer to each other's prayers. But Faith is
finding it harder to keep her identity secret, and as
she gets closer to Dominic she realizes that this time,
if she runs, she might leave her heart behind.

Available February 4, 2014 from
Harlequin Romance wherever
books and ebooks are sold.